An Old Story of My Farming Days
Vol. III

by

Fritz Reuter

An Old Story of My Farming Days
Vol. III
by Fritz Reuter

Copyright © 2024

All Rights reserved.

No part of this publication may be reproduced, stored in a retrieval system, or transmitted in any form or by any means, electronic, mechanical, photocopying or Otherwise, without the written permission of the publisher.
The author/editor asserts the moral right to be identified as the author/editor of this work.

ISBN: 978-93-64284-40-0

Published by
DOUBLE 9 BOOKS
2/13-B, Ansari Road
Daryaganj, New Delhi – 110002
info@double9books.com
www.double9books.com
Tel. 011-40042856

This book is under public domain

ABOUT THE AUTHOR

Fritz Reuter (1810-1874) was a renowned German novelist and a pivotal figure in 19th-century German literature. He is especially noted for his writings in Low German (Plattdeutsch), which vividly portray the rural life and culture of Northern Germany, particularly Mecklenburg. Early Works: After his release, Reuter began his literary career. Major Works: Reuter's major contributions to literature include a series of novels and stories that depict rural Mecklenburg life with a blend of realism and humor. Notable works include: "Ut de Franzosentid" (During the French Period): A collection of stories set during the Napoleonic Wars. "Ut mine Festungstid" (During My Time in Prison): An autobiographical account of his imprisonment. "Ut mine Stromtid" (During My Apprenticeship): A semi-autobiographical novel regarded as one of his masterpieces. "In the Year '13: A Tale of Mecklenburg Life": A historical novel set during the Napoleonic Wars, exploring their impact on rural Mecklenburg. Reuter's use of Low German in his writing was significant in preserving and popularizing the dialect. It added authenticity to his portrayal of rural life and connected deeply with his audience. His works are characterized by their realistic depiction of rural life, combined with humor and a deep understanding of human nature. Reuter's stories often address social issues, reflecting the struggles and resilience of rural communities. Fritz Reuter is celebrated for his contributions to German literature and for promoting Low German. His works continue to be appreciated for their cultural and historical significance. Reuter is honored through numerous schools, streets, and institutions named after him, particularly in Northern Germany. Fritz Reuter remains a significant literary figure, known for his contributions to preserving Low German culture and for his engaging, realistic depictions of rural German life.

CONTENTS

CHAPTER I 7
CHAPTER II 21
CHAPTER III 31
CHAPTER IV 41
CHAPTER V 52
CHAPTER VI 66
CHAPTER VII 76
CHAPTER VIII 80
CHAPTER IX 93
CHAPTER X 107
CHAPTER XI 120
CHAPTER XII 134
CHAPTER XIII 146
CHAPTER XIV 154
CHAPTER XV 163
CHAPTER XVI 175
CHAPTER XVII 187
FOOTNOTES 196

CHAPTER I

The day after Christmas was passed very busily in Mrs. Behrens' house in Rahnstädt. Louisa was continually to be seen running up and down stairs, for she was finishing the arrangement of her father's room. Whenever she thought it was quite ready, and looked really nice, she was sure to find something to improve, some alteration that must be made to ensure perfection. Dinner-time came, but her father had not arrived, though she had prepared some little dainties especially for him. She laid a place for him, however, as perhaps he might come before they had finished dinner.--"I don't know why it is," she said to little Mrs. Behrens, "but I feel as if some misfortune were going to happen."--"What?" cried Mrs. Behrens, "you've only lived in town for three months, and you have presentiments already like a tea-drinking town-lady! What has become of my light-hearted country-girl?" and as she said this, she stroked her foster-child's cheek with a tender touch and loving smile.--"No," answered Louisa, taking the kind hand, and holding it tight between her own, "such indefinite presentiments never trouble me. Unfortunately it is a very definite fear lest my father should weary of the inactivity of a town-life, after what he has been accustomed to in the country."--"Why, child, you talk as if Rahnstädt were a great city; no--thank God!--the geese go about bare-foot here just the same as at Pümpelhagen, and if your father likes to see farming-operations going on around him, he has only to watch the two manure-carts belonging to our neighbour on the right, and the three belonging to our neighbour on the left. If he wants to talk about farming he need only go to our landlord Mr. Kurz, who will be too happy to harangue him about grazing fields and town-jails till he's as sick of these subjects as we are."--Louisa laughed, and when the dinner-things were cleared away, she said: "Now, mother, suppose you lie down and have a little nap, while I go down the Gürlitz road, and see if I can't meet my father."

She put on her cloak, and a warm hood, and set off down the road, which had always been her favourite walk since she came to Rahnstädt, for it was the one that led to the place where she had been so happy. When she had time she used to go to the hill from which she could see Gürlitz village, the church, the parsonage, and the church-yard, and when she had a little more time she used to run down to the parsonage to see Lina and Godfrey, and have a talk about the old days and the new. She walked on and on; her father was not in sight; the east-wind blew in her face, and made her cheeks bright and rosy, so that her lovely face, framed in her dark cloth hood, looked for all the world like a sunny springday which gives the promise of hope and joy to man. But her eyes were full of tears. Was it because of the rude east-wind? Was it because she was looking so keenly down the road in search of her father? Was it because of her thoughts? It could not be the east-wind, for she was now standing still, and gazing out into the west with her eyes full of tears. It could not have been the keenness of her search for her father, for she was now looking straight over at the place where the sun was setting behind the black pines on the horizon like a red ball of fire. It must have been her thoughts that made her weep. Such thoughts as come to the young making their joy and sorrow, which sometimes crown their brows with gladness unspeakable, and at others make them weep in agony, when they suddenly feel the thorns in what they had thought was only a garland of roses. Why was she gazing towards the west? She knew that he whom she loved was there, and her heart repeated the words of the poet:

"Haste westward, ever westward ho
Thou boat at my behest!
E'en dying, I should long to go
Where all my hope doth rest!"

She blushed, when she found what she was saying to herself, and how she was dreaming of happy days to come.

She reached the place where her father had stood a couple of hours before, and had drunk his cup of sorrow to the very dregs. She stood still, and looked down upon Pümpelhagen and Gürlitz, and let the thought of all the love she had been blessed with overflow her heart. Where the poor old father had stood and cursed those who had so cruelly injured him, the daughter now stood and prayed, weeping tears of love and gratitude, and her prayers and tears washed away the curse from the tablet on which all human events are noted down.

The distance from Rahnstädt to Gürlitz is five miles, and as the winter-sun was setting, Louisa could linger no more, she had to go home at once. But she saw a man coming towards her from Gürlitz, perhaps it was her father. She waited a few minutes. No, it was not her father, so she walked on a short way, and then looked round again. This time she saw it was uncle Bräsig, who was trying to overtake her.--"Bless me, Louisa! What are you doing here? Do you find it a pleasant amusement standing on the public road in a wind like this? Aren't you coming down to the parsonage?"--

"No, uncle Bräsig, not to-day. I only came to meet my father."--"He passed long ago. Preserve us all! Where can he be?"--Bräsig suddenly remembered Hawermann's strange manner, but when he saw how anxious Louisa looked, he said to comfort her: "We farmers have often to change our plans; we have to go here, there and everywhere. Perhaps he turned to the right here and went to Gülzow, and perhaps he has got to Rahnstädt by this time and is seeing about some business. But I," he added, "am going with you, childie, I have something to do in Rahnstädt, where I am going to spend the night. You see I want to win the nine shillings back from that overwise man, Kurz, the shopkeeper, which he got out of me at that confounded game Boston. This is club-night."

When they had gone a little further they met a dog-cart coming towards them from Rahnstädt. It was Christian Degel with Dr. Strump. The doctor ordered Christian to stop: "Have you heard the news?" he asked. "Mr. von Rambow has met with an accident with his fowling-piece; he has shot himself in the arm. But I hav'n't time to wait, the coachman is late enough as it is, for I was out when he came for me. Drive on."--"What is the meaning of this?" cried Louisa. "My father leave Pümpelhagen when the family are in distress! He could never have done that."--"But it may have happened after he left," said Bräsig, though when he remembered how Hawermann had looked in the morning, he did not believe that it could have been the case. Louisa was more uneasy than before and walked on quickly. She could not understand why her father was so late, nor could she understand how he could have left Pümpelhagen at all, after such an accident, and yet she felt that the two strange facts were somehow connected.

Meanwhile Hawermann had arrived at Mrs. Behrens' house in Rahnstädt. He had left the high road and had gone round by a field-path, that he might have time to regain his composure before meeting his daughter. When he reached Mrs. Behrens' house he had regained his self-command, but the struggle had fatigued him so much that he looked ten years older than usual when Mrs. Behrens saw him. She was making the coffee when he entered the room, and was so startled by the change in his appearance that she allowed the coffee to boil over, and sprang to meet him, exclaiming: "Good God! Hawermann, what's the matter? Are you ill?"--"No--Yes, I think so. Where's Louisa?"--"She went to meet you, didn't you see her? But sit down, do. How very tired you look!"--Hawermann seated himself and looked round the room as if to make sure that he and Mrs. Behrens were alone.--"Hawermann, please tell me what is the matter," she said, taking his nerveless hands between her own.--"It is all over with me now. I must go through the world as a useless, dishonoured man."--"Oh, don't! Don't! Don't say that!"--"I had grown accustomed to the thought that my work was done, though it was hard to bear at first. But the misery of losing my honest name is more than I can endure; it crushes me."--"But who wants to deprive you of that?" asked Mrs. Behrens looking at him affectionately.--"The people who can do it most thoroughly, Mr. von Rambow and his wife," said the old man, and then he began to tell her all that had happened in a weak, broken voice; but when he got to the part when Mrs. von Rambow had also deserted him, had turned her back upon him, and had let him be ordered out of the room as a thief and a cheat, his anger broke out again; he sprang to his feet and began to pace the room with flashing eyes and clenched fists, as though he wanted to fight against the world. "Oh," he cried, "that is not all. They have hit me harder than they knew. They have wrecked my child's life as well as mine. There, read that, Mrs. Behrens," and he gave her Frank's letter.--She read it, the paper trembling in her hands from nervous excitement, and while she read it, he stood before her, his eyes fixed on her face the better to read her thoughts. "Hawermann," she said, taking his hand, when she had finished, "don't you see the finger of God in this. One cousin has sinned against you, and the other makes it right."--"No, Mrs. Behrens," he replied sternly, "I should be the scoundrel the world will call me from henceforth, if I were to let a good and trustful man take a wife with a stained name into his house. Poor and honest, let me be that; but dishonourable, never."--"Oh me!" cried Mrs. Behrens, "why isn't my pastor here? If my pastor were only here, he could have told us what to do."--"Indeed he could," said Hawermann sadly. "I *cannot* do it," he exclaimed, "Louisa must decide for herself, and you must help her. You have been able to teach her to distinguish right from wrong as I never had the chance of teaching her. If she thinks it right and honourable to enter into this engagement in spite of what has happened, and you agree with her, I will give my consent. I will not influence her in any way, and will not even see her until she has decided. Here is Frank's letter to her. Give it to her after you have told her what has happened. It was all exactly as I told you. I'm going to my room now; I'll have nothing to do with her decision." He left the room, but came back again to say: "If you think it is for her happiness, never mind me! Forget what I said about it's being impossible. I will do what I can to hide my dishonoured name." He left the room once more, and as he went upstairs, he said to himself: "I can't do otherwise, I can't do otherwise." When he threw himself upon the sofa in his little room, and saw how his daughter had arranged everything for his pleasure and comfort, he covered his eyes with his hand and murmured: "And I must do without all this perhaps." Then with a deep sigh: "And why not? Why not? If it is for her happiness," he exclaimed aloud, "I'll never see her again." The doorbell rang, he heard Bräsig's voice, and then his daughter's; then all was still; he listened intently for any sound, Mrs. Behrens was telling about it, and

Louisa was suffering the pain of hearing the story. At last footsteps were to be heard coming slowly and heavily upstairs. Bräsig came in, he looked as calm and solemn as if he had seen the dead rise from their graves and come to meet him; his eyebrows, which were usually raised as high as his hair when he heard of anything extraordinary, now hung low down over his eyes. He seated himself beside his friend on the sofa, and merely said: "I know it, Charles. I know all."

They sat for a long time silent in the half-darkness. At last Bräsig took Hawermann's hand in his, and said: "Charles, we have known each other for fifty years. You remember at old Knirkstädt's? What a happy life we had when we were young, always contented with our lot and merry hearted. And except for a few silly tricks I played with you, we have nothing to reproach ourselves with. Charles, it is a pleasant thing in one's old age, when one's conscience only reproaches one with follies, and not with wickedness." Hawermann shivered and drew away his hand. "Charles," said Bräsig, "a good conscience is a great blessing in one's old age, and it's a remarkable thing, a very remarkable thing, that these good consciences always cling to each other in their old age, and that nothing can divide them from each other. Charles, my dear old boy!" and he fell upon his friend's neck and wept bitterly.--"Bräsig," entreated Hawermann, "don't make me more miserable than I am, my heart's heavy enough as it is."--"And why, Charles? What makes it heavy? Your heart is as pure as Job's, and should be as light as a lark which soars up to heaven, for the story about the confounded.... No, I don't mean that; I was going to say.... Pshaw! what was it we were talking about? Oh, to be sure, it was about the conscience. The conscience is a very strange thing, Charles. For instance, take Kurz's, for he has one as well as you or I, and I believe that it will enable him to appear in the presence of God at the Last Day, and that it will justify him, but still it doesn't justify him in my eyes, for he peeps at the cards, when he's playing at Boston; he has what may be called a penny-conscience, for in great things he's most scrup'lous; for example; with Mrs. Behrens' house rent, but if he can take a hair's breadth off a yard, or give just the least atom short weight, he's not ashamed to do it, that's to say when he can manage it, which isn't always. I wanted to say, Charles, that you'll have to see a good deal of him, while you're here. You'll find the pleasure of his acquaintance quite as so, so, as his conscience, for he will try to discuss farming matters with you, and that's as unpleasant as driving in a cart without springs. I'm afraid you'll find it a little dull, so I think that as soon as I've got the young parson's spring sowing done, and everything is in order, I'll come here to you, and then we'll be able to cheer each other up. I can go out to Gürlitz again when the harvest begins, that that poor boy, the parson, mayn't get into any difficulty. Indeed I'm sure there's no danger of that, for, George, is a thoughtful sort of fellow, and takes a good deal of the management upon himself--thank God for that--and also that Lina backs him up when it's necessary. When the first year is over you'll see that Godfrey will pitch all his Methodistical trash overboard, but we must give him time to learn that there are certain worldly matters which are better suited to man than hymn-books are. And then I'll come to you, Charles, and we'll enjoy life as much as if we were in Paris, and you'll see that the last quarter of our lifetime will be the best part of the whole ox."--Here he threw his arm round his friend's shoulder and went on talking to him, mixing up the past and the future, and making them into a regular medley just as a mother does, when she tries to change the current of her child's thoughts.

The moon shone in at the window, and what can better soothe a wounded spirit than the soft light of the moon, and the love of an old friend who clings to us through good and evil report. I have always thought that the clear bright sunshine is most suited to lovers, while the calm moonlight is best for friendship.

While they were sitting together the door opened, and a slender figure came softly into the room and remained standing in the full light of the moon. The girl's arms were crossed upon her breast, and her pale face looked like that of a white marble statue against the dark wall: What can have happened to thee, thou poor child?

Bräsig went out of the room silently, and Hawermann covered his eyes with his hand as if they pained him, pained him to the heart. The girl threw herself down by his side, clasped him in her arms, and laid her pale face against his. Not a word was said by either of them for a long, long time, but at last the old man heard a low whisper at his ear: "I know what you think it right to do; I am your child--am I not?--your dear child?" Hawermann put his arm round his dear child and drew her closer to him. "Father, father!" she cried, "we can never part! My foster-father, who is now with God, told me how you wanted to keep me with you when you were in such sorrow, although that good woman, the labourer's wife, offered to take charge of me. Now that you are again in sorrow do you really wish to part from me? Do you think that I could let you go?" and pressing him in her arms, she said: "Your name is my name, your honour is my honour, your life is my life."

They talked a long time together in the sweet moonlight, but what they said no one else has a right to know, for when a father and child speak to each other heart to heart and soul to soul, God is with them, and what they say is between themselves, the world has no part in it.

Down stairs in the parlour it was very different. Mrs. Behrens was sitting in her arm-chair weeping bitterly. The dear good woman was torn in two by conflicting opinions, and her heart was sore for Hawermann and his sorrows; but when she foresaw the terrible struggle she was obliged to cause in the heart of her adopted daughter, and when she saw it awake, and saw faith and courage get the victory in spite of misery, she felt as if she herself had brought all these misfortunes on the head of her darling--remorse and compassion filled her heart, and she burst into bitter tears as soon as she was left alone.--Bräsig on the other hand had left all his compassion upstairs, he had expended all that he had upon Hawermann, and now his wrath, which he had before restrained with infinite difficulty, burst forth, and as he entered the dark room, he exclaimed: "The infamous Jesuitical packages! What do they mean by blotting the fair fame of such a man as Charles Hawermann? It's a Satanic deed! It's just like one man holding the cat, while the other impales it! Curse the ...."--"Bräsig, Bräsig, *please* don't!" cried little Mrs. Behrens. "Don't let us have any of your unchristian ways here."--"Do you call that unchristian? It sounds to me like a song of the holy angels in paradise, when I say that sort of thing about the infernal plots of these Jesuits."--"But, Bräsig, we are not their judges."--"I know quite well, Mrs. Behrens, that I am not a judge, and that you hav'n't a seat on the municipal board; but still you can't expect me to look at vermin with the same pleasure as at beautiful canary-birds! No, Mrs. Behrens, toads are toads, and Pomuchelskopp is the chief toad that has squirted its venom over us. What do you say to the trick he has been trying to play me lately? You see, he has put up a fence across the foot-path that leads to the glebe, and which has been in existence for a thousand years for anything I know, and has sent me a message that if ever I cross that fence he'll have my boots pulled off and let me hop away home through the snow in my stockings like a crow. Do you call that a Christian sentiment? But I'll go to law with him. The fellow daring to even me to a crow! And parson Godfrey must go to law with him also, for trying to deprivate him of the use of the foot-path. And young Joseph must go to law with him, for he has said, several times, and publicly too, that young Joseph was an old fool, and young Joseph is not obliged to take that quietly. You must also go to law with him for not having built you a dowager-house, as he was obliged to do by law, at least one or two old people have told me so. Then Charles Hawermann must go to law with Mr. von Rambow. We must all get up a rev'lution against those Jesuits, and if everyone will agree with me, we might all drive to Güstrow to-morrow to see the Chancellor, and summons the whole lot of them on a bit of parchment. We can engage five barristers, that'll be one for each of us, and then, 'Hurrah for the lawsuit!'" If Bräsig had had any idea that Louisa had to suffer more than anyone else from "the Jesuits," he would have insisted on engaging a barrister to plead her cause also, but he had not the remotest notion of her misery.--Mrs. Behrens tried to calm him down, but she found it a very difficult task, for the misfortunes of his old friend had caused him much mingled anger and sorrow, and all the small rages proper for a farmer, and the irritability brought on by gout and losing at cards combined to augment his rage.--"I came here," he said, "to amuse myself because it was club-day, and because I wanted to win back the nine shillings from that old sharper Kurz, that he fleeced me of with his confounded trickery, and now the devil is holding his d--d telespope before my eyes that I may the better see some utterly vile human actions! And that's to be my amusement! Now, Mrs. Behrens, if you don't mind I'd like to spend the night here, for I shouldn't make much of that stupid game, Boston, this evening, and it might be as well for me to sleep in Charles' room so as to be able to cheer him up whenever he gets low."--Mrs. Behrens replied that she would be much obliged to him if he would do so, and she spent the rest of the evening trying to calm down the irascible old man. Neither Hawermann nor Louisa came back to the parlour, and when Bräsig went upstairs he found that Louisa had gone to her own room.

When Bräsig took leave of his old friend on the next morning, he said: "You may leave it all in my hands, Charles, I'll drive over to Pümpelhagen, and get your things. You shall have all your belongings though it makes me ill to cross the threshold of the house where you were so badly treated."

On the same morning Hawermann sat down to write to Frank; he told him honestly and clearly what had happened at Pümpelhagen, even to the terrible ending of his stay there, and the accusation which had been made against him, and said that he and his daughter were of one mind in declining the offer Frank had made. He wanted to tell the young man of his warm friendship for him, but somehow the words would not come as easily as usual, and when written seemed rather forced. He ended by entreating Frank to leave him and his daughter to go their way alone, to forget them, and allow them to live out the rest of their lives by themselves.

Louisa also wrote, and when she had sent Mrs. Behrens' maid out in the evening to post her letter, she went to the window, and watched the servant as if she were taking a last long leave of what was very dear to her, and then looking at the setting sun, she murmured:

> "E'en dying, I should long to go
> Where all my hope doth rest!"

She did not blush to-day when she said these words, as she had done only yesterday; her face was pale, and when the last rays of the setting sun were hidden behind the houses, she sighed heavily, and slow tears gathered in her eyes and rolled down her white cheeks. She did not weep for her own sorrow, but for his.

As soon as Bräsig reached the parsonage, Lina ran out to meet him, exclaiming: "Oh, uncle Bräsig, I'm so glad that you've come. Such dreadful things have happened here, I don't mean *here*, but at Pümpelhagen. Dr. Strump has been here--George was taken ill suddenly last night--so I had the doctor's gig stopped in the village as he was coming back from Pümpelhagen, and he told us such a frightful story--I don't mean the doctor, for one could hardly get a word out of him on the subject--but his coachman said that--oh *do* come in, there's such a draught here," and she drew the old bailiff into the parlour. When there, she told him that the people said her dear uncle Hawermann had shot Alick, and had then gone away no one knew where, but most probably to take his own life. Bräsig comforted her by assuring her that Hawermann was alive, and after having convinced her of that, he asked how Mr. von Rambow was getting on. Lina told him that Dr. Strump did not think him dangerously wounded, and then Bräsig went to see George who was apparently suffering from congestion of the lungs. After that it was time for him to go to Pümpelhagen for Hawermann's things as it was about twelve o'clock, so he set out in search of a man who could act as coachman instead of George.

He asked several of the villagers to go with him, and help him to bring away the things, but they all refused on one pretext or another, and he soon found that he would have to go alone. But at the last moment old Rührdanz, the weaver, came forward, and said: "I don't care what he says; if he chooses to make a scene he can do so, it's nothing to me, I'll go with you, Mr. Bräsig."--"What do you mean by making a scene, Rührdanz?" asked Bräsig.--"You see, sir, he has forbidden us to do any kind of work for the parsonage people, we ar'n't even allowed to go a single step in their service."--"Who forbade you to do so?"--"Why *he* did. Our master Pomuchelskopp."--"The infamous Jesuit!" muttered Bräsig below his breath.--"He told us that if we disobeyed him we might feed our cattle on saw-dust, for he would give us neither hay nor straw, and we might burn stones to warm ourselves, for he would give us neither wood nor peats."--Bräsig grew more and more furious every moment, and the old weaver, having got into the full swing of talk, went on: "And then you see we've to be ready night and day when he wants us. I myself have been from home all the Christmas holydays, and only got back at ten o'clock last night."--"Where were you?"--"At the old station in Ludwigslust."--"What were you doing there?"--"I wasn't doing any thing there."--"Why you must have been sent on business?"--"Yes, I was sent on business, but nothing came of it, as there were no papers."--"What *do* you mean?"--"You see, I was sent to the station with a ram, and I got there all right. I found a fellow waiting for me, so I said to him: 'Good-morning,' I said, 'here he is.'--'Who?' he asked.--'The ram,' I said.--'What has he come for?' he asked.--'I don't know,' I said.--'Are there any papers?" he asked.--'No,' I said, 'there are no papers about him.'--'You fool,' he said, 'are you sure that there are no papers?"--'Yes,' I said, 'the ram has no papers.'--'Confound you!' he said. 'Hav'n't *you* brought me some papers yourself?'--'What?' I said. 'I? What's the good of *my* having papers? I'm not to be sold to you here.' Then the fellow grew very rude and had me turned out and the ram after me, and so there we were both left standing before the station. 'Ugh! Ugh!' coughed the old ram. We were turned out into the road because he had no papers, and I had none either. What was to be done? I drove him home again, and when I got back last night, there was a frightful scene. I thought our master would have eaten me up he fell upon me so viciously. But it wasn't my fault. If the man ought to have had papers they should have sent him some. But of this I'm sure, that if our master wasn't such a great man and didn't happen to be so much too strong for us, and if we only stuck to each other properly we'd manage to take him down a peg. As for his hop-pole of a wife, she's a thousand time worse than he is. It was only last spring that she nearly beat my neighbour Kapphingst's girl to death. She beat the girl three times with her broom-stick, and then locked her up in the shed without food. And why? Because a hawk had carried off one of her chickens. It wasn't the girl's fault that the hawk carried off the chicken, nor was it my fault that I wasn't given any papers."--Bräsig listened to the weaver's story, and although only yesterday he had wanted to bring about a revolution against Pomuchelskopp, he was now silent, for he would never have forgiven himself, if he had thoughtlessly helped to excite the labourers against their master.

They got to Pümpelhagen at last, and stopped at the farm-house door. Fred Triddelfitz sprang out, and ran up to Bräsig: "Oh, Sir, Sir," he cried, "it wasn't my fault that Mary Möller packed the book by mistake amongst my things, and I knew nothing about it till I was changing my clothes at Demmin."--"What book?" asked Bräsig quickly.--"Why, Hawermann's book, about which there has been such a row."--"And that book," cried Bräsig, seizing Fred by the collar and shaking him till his teeth chattered, "you took to Demmin with you, you infamous grey-hound that you are." Then pushing him towards the house: "Come in, and show me the book."--Fred brought it tremblingly, and Bräsig snatched it out of his hands: "Do you know what you have done, you infamous grey-hound? You have brought the man, who tried in all kindness and gentleness, to make a responsible human being of you, and who always covered your follies with a silken mantle, to misery and shameful suspicion."--"Oh, *don't* Mr. Bräsig," entreated Fred turning deadly pale, "indeed it wasn't my doing; Mary Möller packed the book with my things, and I galloped home with it from Demmin this morning as hard as I could."--"Mary Möller," cried Bräsig, "what have you got to do with Mary Möller? Oh, if I were your father or your mother, or even your aunt, I'd thrash you till you ran round the wall like a squirrel. What have you got to do with that stupid old woman Mary Möller? Do you think that galloping on the public road is the way to make good your folly? Is your innocent horse to suffer for your sins? But now come away, come away. You must appear in Mrs. von Rambow's Court of Justice. You must tell all about it there, and then you can explain the mystery about Mary Möller." When he had said this he set off to the manor house, and Fred followed him slowly, like hard times when they come into the land, and his heart was full of grief and pain.

"Will you let your mistress know that this young man and I want to speak to her," said Bräsig to Daniel Sadenwater, pointing at the same time to Fred. Daniel made a half bow, and went. Fred waited, and amused himself by making a face, in the same way as he used to do at Parchen, when he was called before the headmaster of his school to answer for some piece of mischief. Bräsig meanwhile was pulling up his boots in the corner, the better to show their yellow tops, and at the same time holding the book tightly under his arm. When Mrs. von Rambow crossed the hall on her way to the drawing-room, Bräsig followed her, his face quite red with inward excitement, and with stooping. Fred came slowly after, looking pale and anxious.--"You have something to say to me, Mr. Bräsig," said the lady turning from one to the other of her visitors.--"Yes, Madam, but under the circumstances, I'd be much obliged by your first listening to what this apothecary's son, this ...."--"infamous grey-hound" he was about to have said, but stopped himself in time--"has to say; he has a nice little story to tell you."--Mrs. von Rambow looked enquiringly at Fred, who began to stammer out something very like what had really happened, turning red and pale as he spoke. The only thing he left out was Mary Möller's name, and he concluded his story thus: "So the book got into my portmanteau by accident."--"Out with it about Mary Möller," interrupted Bräsig, "the truth must be made known."--"Yes," said Fred, "Mary Möller packed my things for me as I had so much to do that day."--Mrs. von Rambow had grown very uneasy: "Then," she said, "it was all owing to a wretched mistake?"-- "Yes, Madam," answered Bräsig, "and here's the book. Look, Hawermann's account is balanced in the last page, and besides his sal'ry, you see that he has to be paid sixty pounds. You may be sure that it's all right, for Charles Hawermann never added up wrong in his life; he was always better at accounts from a boy than I was."--Mrs. von Rambow took the book with a trembling hand, and as she looked at the column of figures on the last page, the thought flashed into her mind, that as Hawermann was proved innocent in this particular, he might be equally innocent of the other charge brought against him, and in which she herself had never believed. Fred's story bore truth on the face of it, and so she saw that she had done the old bailiff a grievous wrong. But he had shot her husband! She had an excuse for her conduct in that. She said: "What made him shoot at Alick?"--"Madam," said Bräsig, raising his eyebrows and putting on his gravest expression, "allow me to say that that is a false accusation. It was your husband who got the gun, and when Hawermann tried to take it from him, it went off. That's the whole truth, for Hawermann himself told me, and he never lies."--She knew that well, and she also knew that she could not say the same of her husband. In the first excitement he had certainly declared: "He is not a murderer;" but ever since then, he had said that Hawermann had shot him. She sat down and covered her eyes with her hand. She tried to regain her self-control, but it was only with a great effort that she roused herself to say: "You have come, I suppose, to receive the money for the bailiff, but my husband is ill, and I cannot disturb him by asking for it just now. I will send it."--"No, Madam, I hav'n't come for that," answered Bräsig, drawing himself up to his full height, "I came here to tell the truth, I came here to defend my friend, my old school-fellow of sixty years ago."--"That was unnecessary if your friend has a good conscience, which I believe he has."--"I see, Madam, that you don't understand human nature. Every man has two consciences, one of which is within him and of that no devil can deprive him; but the other is external, and is known as his good name, and that can be stolen from him by any rascal who has power and cleverness enough to do it. When his good name is taken from him, the man dies morally, for no one lives for himself alone, but also for the world. Evil reports are like the thistle-down which the devil and his accomplices sow in our fields. The better the ground, the more the weeds flourish, and when they are in seed the wind comes--no one knows whence it cometh, or whither it goeth--and carries the thistledown with it, scattering it over the land, and next year the field is full of thistles. Then people come and abuse the land, but no one will lend a hand to pull up the weeds, for each man is afraid of hurting his fingers. And you, lady, have also feared the pricks. That was what pained my friend Charles Hawermann most of all, when he was turned out of the house as a cheat and a thief. That is what I came to tell you--and now farewell--I will say no more." He then left the room, and Fred slunk after him.

And Frida? Where was the high spirited young woman with the wise eyes and clear judgment, who could see what ought to be done so calmly and decidedly? She was changed now, her calm judgment was gone, and uneasiness had taken its place, and a veil of sorrow had fallen over her eyes, which hindered them seeing as clearly as before. "Oh," she exclaimed aloud. "Another untruth! All these suspicions were only born of lies, self-deception and unmanly weakness! My anxiety about him and my love for him, have made me participate in his guilt; have made me wound the noblest heart that ever beat for me. But I will tell him all," and she sprang to her feet, "I will tear the net in which I am entangled." Then falling back in her chair again, she went on sadly: "No, not now; I can't yet; he is too ill." Ah me! She was right: self-deception and lies had gained ever more power and strength, and her true heart would find it very difficult to keep itself uninfluenced by its surroundings, and to distinguish between what was real and what merely seemed to be real.

When Bräsig got back to his carriage, he found that Rührdanz had collected nearly all of Hawermann's possessions with the help of Christian Däsel, and the rest of the things were very soon got together. As Bräsig was getting into the carriage beside Rührdanz, Fred Triddelfitz pulled him back, and said: "Mr. Bräsig, please tell Mr. Hawermann that I am innocent; that it wasn't my fault."--Bräsig was not going to have answered him at first, but catching sight of his miserable face, was sorry for him, and said: "Yes, I'll tell him that; but see that you improve." And then he drove away.

After they had gone a short distance Rührdanz said: "It's nothing to me, Sir, and that's why I speak of it, but who ever would have thought it! I mean about Mr. Hawermann."--"What are you talking about?"--"Oh, nothing! I mean that he should have gone away so suddenly, and then the shooting!"--"That's all nonsense," said Bräsig angrily.--"I said so too, Sir, but Christian, the groom who helped me to pack told me it was true. He said the quarrel was all about some confounded papers, for Hawermann's papers wer'n't right. Yes, that was it, the confounded papers!"--"Hawermann's papers were all right."--"That's just what I said, Sir, but then there's the shooting. Our young master Gustavus was telling the story all over the village this morning."--"Gustavus," cried Bräsig furiously, "is a young rascal, a puppy! A puppy whose ears ar'n't shorn yet!"--"That's just what I said, and I hope you won't be angry with me, Sir; but still he's the best of the lot up at the manor. You see, my father's sister's son came here from the Prussian district near Anklam last week, and he told us what sort of a man our squire is. He always had some human skin sticking to the end of his cane, he was so fond of thrashing folk, but the Prussians would stand it no longer. The people had him up before the county-court or the country-court--I forget what the thing's called--and the Landgrave punished him severely. I only wish that we had a Landgrave like that close at hand, for the Chancellor's office is too far away."--"Yes," cried Bräsig crossly, "if you had a Landgrave like that, you'd have rare doings."--"That's just what I say, Sir; but Mr. Pomuchelskopp once went too far, he beat a woman who was in the family way very brutally, and--don't be angry with me. Sir--I think that was a horrible thing to do. The king happened to hear of it, and commanded that he should be imprisoned for life at Stettin with hard labour. Then his wife went to the king and fell at his feet, and his majesty granted her request on condition that he wore an iron ring round his neck for the rest of his life, and that he did convict's work at Stettin jail for a month every autumn. He was there this autumn. He was also banished from Prussia, and so he came here. Now tell me, Sir, where do you think he will go if he is chased away from here?"--"Where the pepper grows, for all I care," cried Bräsig.--"That's just what I say, Sir; but--don't be angry with me--I don't believe that they'll take him there even, for you see he has money to buy himself off, though indeed there are his papers against him. If the king sees from his papers that he has to wear an iron ring round his neck, and that that's the reason he wears such a large handkerchief round his throat, he won't let him buy himself off."--"Ah, then you see you'll have to keep him," said Bräsig.--"Yes, of course that'll be the way of it; we'd have to keep him because he'd be given into our charge. Tche!" he said to the horse and then they drove on at a slow trot through the village of Gürlitz, Bräsig thinking deeply.--What a strange world it is! he thought. A fellow who is well known to be a rascal has the power to take the good name from an honourable man, and the world believes the evil speaking of the bad man, while it turns a deaf ear to the asseverations of him whom he calumniated. Bräsig believed, from what he had heard of the stories Gustavus had been telling that Pomuchelskopp was doing his utmost to spread evil reports of Hawermann.--"It's scand'lous," he said to himself as he got out of the carriage at Mrs. Behrens' door in Rahnstädt, "but wait Samuel! I've got the better of you once in preventing you having the glebe, and I'll get the better of you again. But first of all I'll have the law of you for likening me to a 'crow'."

CHAPTER II

New year's day 1846 had come with all its pleasures. The Rahnstädt people congratulated themselves on the cold weather outside, and on their warm rooms. There was a great deal of sledging in the morning, and many salt herrings were eaten because of Sylvester, Eve. Amongst the young people there was much talking of this and that thing they had noticed at the ball on the previous evening, and the fathers and mothers talked, not of what had happened at the ball, but of what was going on in the world. The story of the quarrel between Hawermann and Mr. von Rambow was one of the chief subjects of conversation at all the dinner tables in the town. As every house has its own style of cookery, every house spices its gossip to suit its own palate, and Slus'uhr and David added the one pepper and the other garlic to make the Pümpelhagen dish of scandal more appetising. So it came to pass that in Rahnstädt and its neighbourhood the story was now so highly seasoned that it satisfied all who partook of it, more especially as each individual had thrown into it some of his favourite spice. It was said that Hawermann had been cheating the young squire and his late father for years, and had amassed such a large fortune that he had impoverished Mr. von Rambow; that he had got possession of half of the money stolen by the labourer Regel, for which reason he had assisted the thief to escape, and had at the same time provided the man with an estate pass to help him on his way. No one had quite made up his mind as to what part Joseph Nüssler had taken in the business. At last Mr. Frederic Triddelfitz, son of the apothecary, a very clever young man, had discovered the roguery on one occasion when he was privately looking through the farm book. He had told the housekeeper, Mary Möller, what he had found out, and they had both agreed that Triddelfitz must take possession of the book until Hawermann was gone. The young man had therefore taken the book to Demmin with him, intending to hand it over to Mr. von Rambow on the first opportunity. Hawermann had missed the book next day, and had taken it into his head that Mr. von Rambow had seized it, so he had gone to him and told him he was a thief and that he must give him back his book. The squire had refused to admit that he had it, and so he had rushed at him with a gun. The squire had then tried to get the gun away from him, but it had gone off and Mr. von Rambow was now lying wounded to death. Hawermann was hidden away somewhere in the town. The story current in the town was much the same as this, and everyone wondered why the mayor did not put such a dangerous man in irons instead of letting him go at large.

Fortunately there were two wise men in the town who would not believe the story, and one of these was Moses, who when his son told him his version of what had happened, only said: "What a fool you are, David!" and then went back to his work. The other was the mayor himself, who only shook his head when the story was told him and then went on with his work.--Rector Baldrian did not go back to his work, for it was holiday time. He said that there must be something in the story as the whole town was full of it; but of this he was so certain that he would take the Holy Sacrament on it, that his son Godfrey's father-in-law, Joseph Nüssler, was *not* in the plot.--Kurz said: It might be true, though he would never have thought it of old Hawermann, but no one could see into the heart of another. At the same time, he must confess that the affair seemed to be improbable, for he could not imagine Fred Triddelfitz acting with so much precaution, and he therefore thought the story must be much exaggerated.--The apothecary of course believed it, because it redounded to his son's honour, and so he went about spreading the news in the town.

Strangely enough while the whole of Rahnstädt united in praising Fred, he looked upon himself as a great criminal, and humbling himself before Hawermann entreated his forgiveness with piteous earnestness, assuring him that he had wronged him unintentionally. Hawermann stroked the lad's red hair gently, and said: "Never mind, Triddelfitz! Remember this. Many a good action has evil consequences in this life, and many a bad action good consequences; but we have nothing to do with the consequences of our actions, they are in other hands than ours, and the consequences of our deeds do not make them good or evil. If you hadn't done wrong in trying to deceive me about the corn account your conscience wouldn't prick you, and you wouldn't have had to come to me to-day. But I forgive you heartily, and here's your receipt for the money. Try to be good, won't you? And now good-bye." He gave Fred the receipt for the money Mr. von Rambow had sent him for his wages, and for what he had expended for Alick.

Fred went to the inn where he had left his horse. A crowd had collected, and several people came up to him, and said: "Well, how is it? You behaved very well!"--"Is Mr. von Rambow dangerously wounded? And is he still alive?"--"Bless my soul! can't you be quiet and let Mr. Triddelfitz tell us about it."--"Tell me ....."--"Have you got Hawermann's place?"--Fred was not at all in the mood for talking, and besides that, he had no wish to publish the tale of his own folly. He forced his way through the crowd with a few "pishes" and "pshaws", and mounting his horse rode away, so all the Rahnstädters said with one voice that he was a very modest young man, who did not wish to sing his own praises.

The Rahnstädters had surrounded Fred, and had tried to get at his news, as if they had been a swarm of flies and he a bottle of syrup, but they had made nothing by the move. Still New-year's-day was not to pass without news. Scarcely was Fred, outwardly proud and haughty and inwardly sad and humble, gone away, when a carriage drove up to the inn--the gentleman was driving himself and the servant was on the back seat-- the Rahnstädters flattened their noses on the window panes and wondered who it was. "I'm sure I know his face," said one.--"Yes, and I've seen him before too," said another.--"Isn't it ....?" began a third.--"My patience!" said Bank, the shoemaker. "You mean that it isn't him."--"I know who it is," said Wimmersdorf, the tailor, "I've made many a coat for him. It's the Mr. von Rambow who lives at Hohen-Selchow on the other side of Schwerin, and he's a cousin of the squire of Pümpelhagen."--"The tailor's right, it's just him."--"It's just him."--"It's just him."--"Of course he has come because of the quarrel."--"Most likely, for the squire of Pümpelhagen's too ill to attend to business. You'll see that matters will soon be put to rights now."--When Frank went into the coffee-room to take off his furs, the worthy town's folk present turned their backs to the window, the stove, and the wall, and looked with all their eyes into the middle of the room where he was standing. They resembled hungry spiders enclosing Frank like a helpless fly in the web of their curiosity.

Frank went out, and after saying a few words to the hall-porter set off in the direction of the marketplace.

"John," asked one of the Rahnstädters, putting his head out of the window, "what did he say to you?"--"Oh," said John, "he only asked whether I thought that the mayor would be at home."--"Did you hear? He has asked for the mayor. Something's going to be done in real earnest now."--"John," enquired another, "was that all that he said?"--"He asked whether the clergyman's wife, who has come to live here, didn't live in the house next to Kurz the shopkeeper."--"Aha! Did you notice? The bailiff is probably hidden in Mrs. Behrens' house. Good-bye now."--"Why, Wimmersdorf, where are you going?"--"I'm going to Kurz the shopkeeper's."--"Wait a moment. I'll go with you."--"Of course," said another, "Kurz's house is the best place to see from."--"Yes, let's all go there."--And before long Kurz's shop was fuller of customers than it had been for a very long time. Everyone had a glass of something, several people even indulged in two glasses, and Kurz said to himself: "Thank heaven, the new year is beginning well."

After a short time Frank came back from the market place and passing by Kurz's shop, made his way straight to Mrs. Behrens' door.--"Faith, he hasn't brought a policeman with him," said one.--"Höppner isn't at home to-day. He has gone to Prebberow's to fetch his pig."--"Oh, to be sure!"--"I wonder how the old bailiff feels, now that he knows he's in a regular scrape," remarked Wimmersdorf.--"My feet are growing cold, lads, so I'm going home," said Bank the shoemaker.--"Won't you wait and see the end of it?" asked Thiel, the cabinet-maker.--"D'ye know," said Bank, "it has just occurred to me that the whole story's a lie from beginning to end."--"What?" cried Thiel, the cabinet-maker, "and yet it was you who told me all about it this morning."--"Yes, that's true, but morning talk and evening talk are different. I've had time for consideration since then."--"That's to say you've got cold feet," said Wimmersdorf the tailor.--Everyone laughed.--"That's a pack o' rubbish," said the shoemaker, "and the whole story's a pack o' rubbish. The old bailiff has had his boots made by me for many a long year, and he always paid his bill to the day, and you're not going to make me believe that he has taken to stealing and shooting in his old age."--"It's all very well to say that, but the whole town is full of it."--"The whole town! Here's Mr. Kurz, ask him if the bailiff didn't always pay him honestly for everything he got. Ask him what he says to that."--"What I say to that? I say nothing," said Kurz, "but still I don't believe the story, and I have my reasons for not believing it."--"D'ye hear that?"--"Yes, it's very possible."--"And I always said it seemed improbable."--"Well," answered Wimmersdorf, "he never employed me, and so I don't see why I shouldn't believe it."--"Quite right, tailor, don't let yourself be laughed out of your opinion."--"Come, lads, let's laugh the tailor out of the idea."--"I'll tell you something," said Bank thumping the counter with his fist, "come here all of you--Mr. Kurz give us another glass all round--let's drink to the health of the honest old bailiff."--After that they separated, and all went home with entire faith in Hawermann's innocence. Excepting Wimmersdorf, the tailor, they one and all restored his good name. And why? Because Bank, the shoemaker, had cold feet.

The good and evil opinion of men often depends on causes as slight as that. These men had just declared that they did not believe the tales circulated about Hawermann, but what chance has the good opinion of a few poor operatives of conquering that secret invisible power, which in small towns governs the fate of men, and awards them friendship or hostility according to their supposed actions. I mean the secret bed of justice held by the women when they gather round a tea-pot with their knitting in the dusk of evening. At these meetings every sinner has judgment pronounced on him untempered with mercy. He is pricked with knitting needles, pinched with the sugar-tongs, burnt with the flame under the urn, and every bit of biscuit or Muschüken[1] eaten by the members of the council is looked upon as an effigy of the culprit. What effect had Jack Bank's good opinion or cold feet on the Rahnstädt council of women? or even the knowledge that Hawermann had paid all his bills? These judges set to work more seriously than the men, they took, what lawyers call, the circumstantial evidence into consideration, and came to the conclusion that things looked badly for Hawermann, Louisa, Mrs. Behrens, and even for Bräsig. Mally and Sally Pomuchelskopp had--as diplomatists say--prepared the ground, by dropping a word here, and another there. Slus'uhr had collected all of these costly pearls of speech, and had arranged them in what learned men call, one point of view, and then David had added a few more items, so that the council had a very good idea of Frank's love for Louisa, of Hawermann's and Mrs. Behrens' matchmaking powers, and of Bräsig's shocking conduct in carrying letters between the lovers.

Just as all the first questions were answered, the town clerk's wife, and Mrs. Krummhorn, the merchant's wife, came in, and were greeted with a scolding from their hostess for having arrived so late. The two ladies excused themselves in a few unmeaning phrases, and then seated themselves with an important rustle. When they took out their knitting, they set to work vehemently and waggled their heads in what would have been a supremely ridiculous manner, if it had not shown that they knew something that was worth telling. The ladies then only did their duty when they began to feel their way carefully and by degrees to the mystery, but the town-clerk's wife and Mrs. Krummhorn were prepared for the veiled attack, and pursed up their lips as tight as oyster shells, and although the council were determined to get at the news, they could not persuade the oysters to open their shells by force or diplomacy. The ladies all sighed, and dipped some muschüken in their tea, and the two oysters soon found to their terror that their news had a good chance of becoming stale and losing its freshness, they therefore unclosed their shells, and the town-clerk's wife asked the mayor's wife whether a young gentleman had not called on the mayor that afternoon.-- Yes, said the mayor's wife, Mr. von Rambow's cousin had been with her husband, they had just been talking about it.--"What did he want?" asked the town-clerk's wife.--"He came to ask why the search for the stolen money had been given up, and he also asked what had taken place at Pümpelhagen- -you know--about the shooting--and what was done about it."--"And what else?" asked the town-clerk's wife, without raising her eyes from her knitting.--"My husband told me that that was all," answered the mayor's wife.--"And you believe that," asked the town-clerk's wife. Now it is an insult to any court of justice, and a much greater insult to the women's council, to ask the members of either of these bodies to believe a simple natural action. The mayor's wife felt the sneer that was hidden in the question, and said sharply: "If you know better, my dear, perhaps you'll put us right."--The one oyster looked at the other, and then they both burst out laughing. Now when a comfortable looking oyster--the town-clerk's wife was stout and comely and Mrs. Krummhorn was not far behind her-- indulges in a hearty laugh, it always makes a great impression on the auditors. The members of the council let their knitting fall upon their laps and gazed at the oysters.--"Good gracious!" exclaimed the hostess, "what do you know?"--"Mrs. Krummhorn may tell you," answered the town-clerk's wife, "she saw as well as I did."--Now Mrs. Krummhorn was a most excellent woman, and could tell a story well and truly, but her tongue had the same fault as old Schäfer's legs, it would not go straight, and she might have said to her neighbours: "put me straight," and "turn me round," as he did to his. She began: "Yes, he went right across the market-place ....."-- "Who?" interrupted a stupid little girl, who did not quite understand,-- "Hush!" cried they all.--"Well, as I was saying, he went right across the market-place, and I recognised him at once, for he had bought a new suit of clothes from my husband some time before, it was a black surtout and blue trousers--bother! what was I saying--I meant a blue surtout and black trousers; I see him now as distinctly as I did then, he always used to wear yellow leather breeches and top-boots--or was it Fred Triddelfitz who did so? I really can't quite remember. What *was* I going to say?"--"He went right across the market-place," cried three voices at once.--"To be sure! He went right across the market-place and turned into the street where the town-clerk lives, I was calling on the town-clerk's wife at the time, for she wanted to show me the new curtains she had bought from the Jew Hirsch--oh, I remember now, it was from the Jew Bär, who was declared bankrupt the other day, that she got them. It's a very odd thing, but my husband tells me that all our Jews become bankrupt now and then, after which they are richer than ever, so that a Christian merchant has no chance against those rascally Jews. But where was I?"--"He turned into the street where the town-clerk lives."--"Oh of course! The town-clerk's wife and I were standing at the window and so we could see right into Mrs. Behrens' parlour, and my friend was just telling me that her husband had told her that if Mrs. Behrens would only go to law--no, not Mrs. Behrens--the church, or the consistory or something, Mr. Pomuchelskopp would be obliged to build a new parsonage at Gürlitz, and my friend ....." But the town-clerk's wife was dying to tell the story herself, and in asking Mrs. Krummhorn to do it, she had laid a nice little rod in pickle for her own back, she could stand it no longer and said: "He went straight into Mrs. Behrens' house, and without waiting in the hall, ran right upstairs into the parlour. The old lady started up from the sofa when she saw him, and made violent signs to him to keep away from her. She looked as miserable as if some great evil had come upon her, as perhaps it may. Then she set a chair for him and signed to him to sit down, but he wouldn't do it, and when Mrs. Behrens left the room, he began to walk up and down just like--like ....."--"Why," interrupted Mrs. Krummhorn, "you said such a pretty verse about it this afternoon."--"Ah well, 'The lion is the king of the desert when he goeth through his domain.' He walked up and down like a king of the desert, and when the old bailiff came into the room with his daughter, he went up to him and reproached him bitterly."--"But," interrupted the same stupid little member of the council as before, "you don't mean to say that you heard all that was said?"--"No, my love," replied the town-clerk's wife, laughing at the member's stupidity, "we didn't *hear* what was said, but Mrs. Krummhorn and I *saw* all that happened, we saw it with our *own* eyes. The old bailiff stood before the young man like a miserable sinner with his eyes fixed on the ground, and without defending himself, while his daughter threw her arms round his neck as if to protect him."--"Yes," interrupted Mrs. Krummhorn, "it reminded me of the scene when Stahl, the old cooper was arrested for stealing the hoops. Mary Stahl sprang between her father and Höppner, the policeman, saying that she wouldn't let him be taken up because of his white hair, and yet he had stolen the hoops, and I *know* that he had, because he put three new hoops round my milk pail, and my husband said it was all the same to us whether they were stolen or not, and it didn't matter for the milk either, for he said the hoops having been stolen wouldn't make the milk turn sour, but all the same I noticed ....."--"Yes indeed, Mrs. Krummhorn," said the town-clerk's wife, stopping her friend, "you noticed how very pale the girl looked, and how she trembled when the young man turned to her and broke off his engagement."--"No," replied Mrs. Krummhorn, "I saw that she was deadly pale, but I didn't see her trembling."--"Then I did," said the town-clerk's wife, "she trembled like this," and so saying the lady began to shake in her chair as if it were a summer's day and the flies were always settling on her face; "and he stood before her like this," here she rose, "'The bond is broken,' as my son, the student, sings, and then he looked at her this way," and she stared so angrily at the little member, that the poor girl got quite red, "then Mrs. Behrens forced her way between them, and tried to make matters up, and patted him and talked so much that she must have made some impression on him, for he shook hands with them both when he went away; but still when his back was turned to them you could see in his face how glad he was to be done with the whole thing. Now wasn't it so, Mrs. Krummhorn?"--"I didn't notice that," answered the merchant's wife, "I was too much taken up watching the girl. She stood there with her arms folded across her chest looking, oh so pale. I've seen a good many pale girls, and my brother's daughter amongst the number, it comes from poverty of blood, and the doctor always says: 'Iron, iron;' but she has enough iron as her father is a blacksmith. He might have been something else if he had liked, for our late father ....."--"Poor girl!" cried the stupid little member, "and she's so pretty. The poor old man too! I can't believe that he with his venerable white hair has done anything to be ashamed of."--"My love," said the town-clerk's wife, with a look that might have been literally translated into, "you donkey," "my love, beware of showing compassion in the wrong place, and beware of making acquaintance with people who are accused of crime."--"Of course he did it," passed from mouth to mouth, from stocking to stocking, and from cup to cup.--The little member was quashed, but suddenly two old and experienced advocates rose to take her part. People who on former occasions had brought accused parties before that same tribunal, and who had seemed to agree with most of the speeches of the town-clerk's wife; but that lady had now gone too far, she had forgotten the relationship of Mrs. Kurz and Mrs. Baldrian to Hawermann, and it was time that she should be put down.--"How do you know, dear, that Hawermann is a criminal?"--"Don't you know, dear, that Hawermann is my brother's brother-in-law?"--"My dear, you should really keep your sharp tongue in better order."--"You know, my dear, that it has often got you into scrapes before now."

A war of "dear," and "my dear" now began across the table. The teaspoons clattered in the saucers, cap ribbons waved up and down under the ladies' chins, and the knitting was rolled up into hard balls and put away in the work-bags. The mayor's wife joined the party of the two advocates of Hawermann's cause, for she had not forgotten the sharp words of the town-clerk's wife. The hostess went from one to the other and besought them, by God, and all His saints not to disgrace her by quarrelling at her tea-table, and the little member began to weep bitterly, for she thought herself the cause of the dispute. But it was over and done with, half of the guests rose and went away, and the other half remained; so Rahnstädt was divided into two parties.

Meanwhile the people who had been the subject of the dispute were sitting quietly in their parlour thinking no evil, and never dreaming of the pains and trouble their fellow townsfolk were taking, in settling their affairs for them. They did not imagine that the sharp eyes looking out of the red face of the town-clerk's wife could harm them, and little Mrs. Behrens said more than once, that the town-clerk's wife, who lived over the way, must be a person of very decided, strong character, and one who would be well able to rule her household. And Louisa had no idea that the pretty young girl who so often passed the house and glanced up at her window was full of loving pity for her, or that she was the stupid little member of the women's council who had taken her part at the tea-party. No, they had all too much to do to have time to think of such things. Louisa had to teach her sad heart to suffer and be still, that her father might never guess how hard it had been for her to give up Frank, Hawermann had been even more silent and thoughtful since then, and had no eyes for anything but his child. When he saw her looking paler and more dreamy than usual he used to go out into the little back garden and walk up and down in search of peace. What became of his hatred when he saw his daughter's love? What became of his anger against the world, where he found so much kindness and affection in the little world with which he himself had most to do? Hatred and anger had passed away from his heart, and their place was filled by sadness and a deep compassion for his only child. Little Mrs. Behrens thought no longer of her duster, she had something else to do now, and she applied herself heart and soul to the work of comforting her companions, but as far as Hawermann was concerned, her labour was in vain.

The old man's strength was leaving him. His courage and love of life were gone, and the unwonted inactivity of his existence at Rahnstädt helped to depress him. His condition would have given his friends cause for uneasiness had it not been that his daughter's sweet voice was always able to banish the evil spirit of melancholy from him, in like manner as the songs of David chased away the evil spirit from King Saul. He refused to act differently from what he had done until he was proved innocent of the charge of theft which had been brought against him, and although Frank had tried to prove to him that the principal charge had been that of falsifying the accounts, and that that had fallen to the ground as soon as the farm-book had been restored, he said that as long as the other accusation remained, he was a marked man and he could not consent to Frank marrying his daughter. In vain Frank implored him to remember what a weak, thoughtless man his cousin Alick was, and that he was different and did not believe the charge. Hawermann remained firm.

That was a great mistake on his part. Many people would say, why didn't he, being strong in the knowledge of his own innocence, stand up and throw the lie back in the teeth of the world? And I say to anyone who asks me that question, you are right. He ought to have done so, and he would have done so--if he had been the old Hawermann of former days. But he was that no more. He was broken-spirited through being pained, offended and constantly thwarted; then came the public accusation, the horrors of his parting interview with the squire, and lastly Mrs. von Rambow, for whom he would have given his life, had deserted him. The climax came at a moment when his heart had opened to a dream of happiness. In winter frost does no harm, for spring is coming to make all right again; but it is very different when the frost comes and shrivels the green leaves and flowers; when snow falls on the tender shoots of hope and kills them, it is sad, very sad; and it is sad when the little singing-birds which have put faith in the spring are frozen to death in their nests, and the wood is silent as the grave. The old man had allowed the spring of hope to blossom in his heart, and now it was gone and dark gloomy forms had taken its place. He had received a blow from which he could not recover. Take from the miser the treasure that he has scraped together during the last sixty years, and you kill him; and yet that is only a 'treasure that the rust doth eat;' what is it in comparison with a man's good name.

Mrs. Behrens' only comfort was in Frank's last words; he had said, he could wait, he would come again.

CHAPTER III

Hawermann kept very much alone, and when visitors came to see Mrs. Behrens, he either remained in his room or went out into the garden. There were a great many visitors, for the one half of Rahnstädt thought they could not better show their contempt for the other half, which had put Mrs. Behrens' house under the bann, than by going there as often as possible. So it came to pass that rector Baldrian and Kurz the shopkeeper came to see Mrs. Behrens nearly every day, for their women-kind had preached Hawermann's innocence to them so vehemently at home, that they found it impossible to retain their doubts any longer. Young Joseph, his wife and Mina, and parson Godfrey and Lina often came in from the country and dined with them. Bräsig made Mrs. Behrens' house his headquarters, and was always coming in and out like the dove to the ark bringing any news from Rexow, Pümpelhagen and Gürlitz he could pick up for his old friend. He told him that the ground was dry and fit for ploughing; and sometimes when he spoke of what Pomuchelskopp or Alick were about, he forgot his character of dove, and dropping the olive branch, would show himself to be neither more nor less than a raven. He would not be denied when he came, but told Hawermann to his face that he had come to cheer him up, and if he did not succeed on that occasion, he was not at all put out, and returned to the charge next day as if nothing had happened, telling his friend all about the weather and the crops.

In the spring of 1846 there was a great deal to be said about both the weather and the crops. The winter had been warm and wet, so the spring was early, and everything was green before anyone looked for it. The grass and autumn sown corn were green in February, even the clover was sprouting, the fields were as dry as one could wish, and the weather was like harvest time. "Charles," said Bräsig, "you'll see that harm will come of it, the spring is too fine, and when a bird sings too early in the morning, a cat eats him before night; you'll see, we'll all be groaning by autumn. The devil take every early spring!"--On Palm-sunday he brought a rape-flower in full bloom and laying it on the table before Hawermann, he said: "Look there! Look there! That's from your rape-field at Pümpelhagen. You'll see, Charles, the Louis d'ors will be in flower in a week's time; but it's all vinegar, it's covered with beetles."--"Oh, Zacariah, we've often had that before and yet we've had good rape all the same."--"Yes, Charles, *black* beetles, not *grey* ones--I've brought the proof of your convarsion with me--," he felt in his pocket and pulled out a small paper-parcel, but when he opened it, it was empty. "What did I tell you, Charles! These grey beetles are cunning dogs and are not to be counted on for anything even to the harm they do. You'll see, Charles, that this year'll be neither more nor less than a cake made of nest eggs, everything's going contrary to nature. Why? The rye is seldom tall enough before May-day to hide a crow, this year a good sized turkey-cock could easily hide itself in it. No, Charles, the world has gone quite round. The parsons have been preaching about it from the pulpit, they say that the moon's going slap in among the stars, and then the sun 'ill be too near the earth, and everything 'ill catch fire. They say that 'ill be the beginning of the Day of Judgment, and that everyone ought to repent of his sins at once."--"Bless me, Zachariah! That's all nonsense."--"I say so too, Charles. It's a mistaken kind of repentance that has been shown too, for the labourers at Klein-Bibow have given up work, have sold all their possessions to the Jews, and are spending their time drinking and devouring their goods. Parson Godfrey wanted to preach the same kind of sermon in his church, but I hid myself behind Lina, and she talked him out of it. But things are looking ill, Charles."--"I think perhaps we may have a bad harvest; but Kurz was here yesterday and he told me that the winter corn was looking beautiful."--"Well, Charles, I thought you had been a wiser man. Kurz, if you please, Kurz! He understands all about salt herrings, for he's a good tradesman; but he must get up earlier in the morning if he wants to express an opinion about corn, for it needs a farmer, and a good farmer, to understand *that*. You see, it's just as I say, Charles, everyone puts his finger in our pie, and these town's people are about as wise as bees. If any man takes to farming *poor passer le tongs*, because he likes the amusement, *à la bonhour!* I have nothing against it, but when he tries to derive advantage from it--pshaw!--Kurz! He may peep into a sugar barrel or into another man's hand at cards; but when he tries to peep into a field of rye, the meaning of what he sees, is hidden from him. But what I was going to say, Charles, is this; I'm here, bag and baggage, next week."--"No, Bräsig, no, if this is going to be a bad year the young people will need you, and Godfrey understands too little about farming to be able to do without your help."--"Yes, Charles, you're right, and if you think I ought--for I have given myself entirely to you--I will stay with him. But now good-bye! I don't know why, but I feel rather stomach-achy, I must go and ask Mrs. Behrens if she can give me a little kümmel." With that he left the room, but next moment he put his head in at the door again, and said: "I had almost forgotten to tell you about Pümpelhagen. There's such an infernally queer kind of farming going on there just now that you might almost warm your hands and feet at it. I met Triddelfitz yesterday near the shed, and although he's an infamous grey-hound, he was nearly crying about it: 'Mr. Bräsig,' he said, 'I lie awake at night bothering over the farming, and tire myself out thinking, till I can't fall asleep at all. When I've got it all beautifully arranged in my head, and have told the people in the morning what they are to do, the squire comes out with his arm in a sling and undoes all my arrangements. He sends the labourers off to the fields in twos and threes, this way and that, so that they are all running about like chickens with their heads cut off, and I have to chase them and gather them all together again. Then when they're all collected and working in the afternoon, he comes out, and scatters them once more.' It must be a great satisfaction to you to hear this, Charles, for it shows that they can't get on without you." After that he went away, but soon put his head in again to say: "What I wanted to say, Charles, was this--half of the horses at Pümpelhagen are done up; a few days ago I saw them standing while the carts were being filled with marl, the poor things were hanging their heads and ears down devotion'ly as the labourers do in church, and it isn't over work that makes them do it, but want of food. The squire hasn't too much fodder in his barns, for he sold three loads of oats, and two of peas, to the Jews this spring, and his granary floor is now as empty as if the bull had licked it. He has to buy oats, but the poor farm horses get none, for the oats are all given to the thoroughbred mares who do nothing for their living, and so steal the days when they should be at work from God. There is great injustice in the world! Now good-bye, Charles." He went away really this time.

It was a sad picture that Bräsig had drawn of the condition of affairs at Pümpelhagen, but matters were even worse there than he suspected. He had said nothing of the influence want of money was having on Alick's character, and that was the worst part of the whole business. Pressure of that kind does not only make people irritable, it also makes them hard to their dependents, and poor Alick, like other men in his position fell into the mistaken idea that the reason he was so hard up was because his labourers were too well treated. It was Pomuchelskopp who first taught him that this might be the case. So he took a little here and a little there from his people, and then when his natural good-nature got the better of him he gave them back a little here and a little there, in both cases without method and just as the fancy seized him. At first the labourers had all laughed at the new mode of farming their young master had introduced, but very soon their laughter was changed to murmuring, and then their murmurs became complaints. Under Hawermann's rule the labourers had always received their corn and money punctually, so they did not like waiting till there was some to give them. When they complained to their master, they only got sharp words in answer to their grumblings, and that they thought even worse. Discontent was spreading.

Alick comforted himself with looking forward to the new harvest, and the money he would get for it; but unfortunately Bräsig's predictions came true. The crops looked thin as they stood in the fields, and when they were cut down, and carried in, the barns were only half full. Experienced old farmers said to the young beginners: "Take care! Save what you can, for hard times are coming. That corn won't be worth much." It was good advice, but what was the use of it to Alick? He must have money, so he had the corn thrashed out at once for seed and for sale. It brought a fine price when it was sold, for the corn-Jews saw from the first what was surely coming, and bought up all the corn they could on speculation, and so the natural dearth was succeeded by an artificial dearth. The old labourers at Pümpelhagen shook their heads when they saw the waggons driving out of the yard: "What's to become of us! What's to become of us! We'll have no corn to make our bread." And the women stood at their cottage doors wringing their hands: "Look Daddy, that little heap of potatoes is all I have remaining, and they're all diseased. What are we to do this winter?"--So dearth had come into the rich land of Mecklenburg like a thief in the night. No one had expected it, and no one had made preparations to defend himself against it. What was to be done?--It fell most heavily on the small towns, and on the artisans in those towns. The labourers always had work, and the children could beg from door to door, and then soup kitchens were organised for them. But the poor artisan had nothing to do, for no one got anything made; he did not know how to beg, indeed he was too proud to do so. I once went to see the wife of an honest hard-working tradesman during that time. The dinner was on the table and the hungry children were standing round it ready to begin. When I went in, the woman threw a cloth over the dish, and while she was out of the room calling her husband I lifted the cloth, and what did I find under it? Boiled potato skins! That was all they had for dinner.

At such a time God sits in heaven and picks out the good men from amongst the evil ones, that all may see clearly which is which; He supports the good, and rejoices to see them bear fruit; but the wicked fall under the flail and the scourge, that is to say, under the power of their own evil wishes, unrighteous actions, and unjust thoughts, so that when they grow up and the time comes for them to bear fruit they are choked by weeds which are sometimes so fair to the eye that the world looks at them with admiration, but when the harvest comes, and the sickle is put to their roots, the crop of grain is found to be very small, then the Lord of the harvest turns away from the field, for it is written: "By their fruits ye shall know them."

Many people, during these hard times, gave to the poor with large hearted charity in spite of the pressure of their own difficulties, and the sheriff, Mr. von Ö .., the chamberlain, Mr. von E .., farmer H .., our old friend Moses, and many other people were of those who bore good fruit in the sight of God in those hard times. But Pomuchelskopp was not one of that good company, nor were Slus'uhr nor David, for these three sat together in Gürlitz manor and laid their plans for completing Alick's ruin. David and Slus'uhr felt no qualms of conscience in doing their work, but they had not enough money to go on with it, for they wanted to use all they had of their own for lending to those who were in desperate need of it, at the highest possible rate of interest. They had used up all their own capital and so they now applied to Mr. Pomuchelskopp for money, promising that he should go shares with them in their gains. But they found their friend too wide-awake to do anything of the sort; he feared lest it should become known that he had done so, and lest he should be blamed. He therefore said that he had no money, but what he required to keep his cattle and his people alive during the famine.--"I agree with you about the cattle," answered Slus'uhr, "but it's great nonsense about the people. Don't deceive yourself on that point, pray! Your people are going everywhere begging. As we drove past the parsonage just now I saw all the wives and children of your labourers collected in the yard, where your old friend Bräsig was standing with two large pails full of porridge which young Mrs. Baldrian was distributing."--"Let her go on! Let her go on!" said Pomuchelskopp. "I never interfere with anyone's good works. These people may be able to afford it, I cannot, and I have no money."--"But you have the Pümpelhagen bills," said David.--"They're of no use just now. Mr. von Rambow's harvest was worse than anyone else's, and he has threshed out and sold all the grain he had."--"That's the very reason you should do something," replied Slus'uhr. "Now's the time to act. You won't have such a good opportunity again in a hurry, and he can't take it ill of you, for you are in such desperate need of money that you have had to sell some of his bills to David and me. You must wait no longer. Shake the tree, for the plums are ripe."--"What is the sum total?" asked David.--"H'm!" said Pomuchelskopp, going to his desk and scratching his ear thoughtfully. "I have bills for sixteen hundred and fifty pounds."--"Is that all?" asked Slus'uhr, "I wish it had been more."--"Yes, that's all, except a mortgage for twelve hundred pounds that I've had for the last year and a half."--"Then you've acted very foolishly. You have always to give proper notice before you can foreclose. However, it do'sn't matter so much after all. Give me the bills for the sixteen hundred and fifty pounds, and I'll see that they give him trouble enough for the present."--Muchel would not at first consent, but Henny, who had joined them, was so determined that he had to give way and hand the bills over to Slus'uhr and David.

The old game was once more played at Pümpelhagen. Slus'uhr and David came and made Alick suffer the torments of purgatory. They would not hear of the bills being renewed. He must and should pay, although he had not a penny and could think of no plan for raising the money. The blow came upon him as suddenly as Nicodemus came by night, and for the first time the thought flashed into his mind that it might be a plot to ruin him, that his kind neighbour at Gürlitz perhaps had his finger in the pie, and had set these two rogues to badger him; but how it could be so remained hidden from him. What was the use of thinking and troubling about that. He must have money and from whom could he borrow it? He knew of no one who could lend it to him. Then in spite of his misgivings of a few minutes before his thoughts turned to his neighbour Pomuchelskopp once more. He must help him; who else could do it? He got on his horse and rode over to Gürlitz.

Muchel received him very kindly and heartily as if to show that he considered it to be the duty of neighbours to cling to one another, and uphold one another in these bad times. He groaned over his wretched harvest, and complained loudly of the difficulties he was in for want of ready money, so that Alick found it impossible to urge his request and felt much ashamed of troubling a man, who was himself straightened, with the tale of his difficulties. But necessity is a hard master, and so he at last asked Pomuchelskopp why he had parted with his bills to those two usurers. Whereupon Muchel folded his hands across his stomach and looking compassionately at the young man, said: "Ah, Mr. von Rambow, I couldn't help it.--Look" and opening his desk he pointed to a drawer in which there were perhaps thirty pounds, "look that's all the money I have, and I must buy provisions for my cattle and labourers, and I thought you might perhaps have money by you."-- Alick then asked him why he had not come to him himself.--"I couldn't do that," answered Muchel, "you know the proverb, 'Money binds strangers to each other, but it separates friends,' and you and I are friends." That was all very true, Alick replied, but the usurers had pressed him hard and he did not know where to turn for help. "Did they really?" cried Pomuchelskopp. "They oughtn't to have done that. I expressly stipulated that they shouldn't dun you. Of course you will renew the bills--it'll cost you a trifle, but that can't be helped under the circumstances." Alick knew that as well as he did, but he would not allow himself to be talked over this time, and passionately entreated Pomuchelskopp to help him with his credit if he could lend him no money. "Willingly," said Muchel, "but how? Who has money just now?" Alick asked whether Moses would not help. "I don't know him," was the answer, "I've never done any business with him. Your father found him useful, and you know him yourself, so I advise you to turn to him."

That was the only comfort Alick could get; Pomuchelskopp slipped through his fingers like an eel, and when he rode home his thoughts were as gloomy and disagreeable as the evening itself.

David and Slus'uhr came back. They dunned him in the most shameless manner, and when he told them that Pomuchelskopp was too hard up to help him, they refused to listen, and only demanded their money the more fiercely.

Alick rode from one place to another, knocking at this door and at that, but all in vain, he could not raise the money. And when at last he came home worn out and despairing, he read in his wife's quiet eyes that she knew all, though she kept silence, her lips firmly closed, reminding him of a beautiful book containing words of comfort which was now closed to him for ever, for he had lost the key which would have unlocked it. Since the time she had learnt the great wrong she had done Hawermann on the day he had been turned off with ignominy, a wrong she had done him from love to her husband, she had never again spoken to Alick of his money difficulties. She could not help him, and she would not tempt him to tell her what was false either about himself or others. His restless manner and anxious expression showed that he was even more unhappy than usual, and when she went to bed that night and saw her sleeping child, her heart softened and she remembered that he was her baby's father, so bursting into tears, she determined to speak to him gently on the next morning about his difficulties, and to show herself ready and willing to bear her share of his burden.

But next morning Alick ran down-stairs whistling and singing, called Triddelfitz and gave him his orders, and then calling Christian Degel told him to get the carriage ready and to put up clothes enough to last him for several days. When he met his wife in the door-way he looked so bright and happy that the words she had been prepared to speak died unuttered. "Are you going anywhere?" she asked.--"Yes, I have to go away on business. I shall probably go to Schwerin also, have you any message for my sisters?" She told him to give them her love, and soon afterwards Alick bade her farewell, and getting into the carriage, drove off towards Schwerin. He had again told his wife but half the truth, his only business was in Schwerin, at his sisters' house. He had suddenly remembered during the night that his sisters had money. His father had left them a small house and garden and rather more than two thousand pounds. The money was put out at 4½ per cent interest, and on this income, small as it was, they managed to live.

Their father had not been able to do more for them, and had trusted that the married sisters, and especially Alick, would help them now and then. It was this money Alick had thought of in the middle of the night; it was just what he wanted; it would tide him over his difficulties, and he could pay his sisters a reasonable percentage on it as well as strangers. He determined to give them five per cent instead of the 4½ they had had before, and he would himself be free from those rapacious money lenders, and at small cost to himself considering the greatness of the benefit to be obtained. It was this thought that had cheered him.

When, on reaching Schwerin, the young squire had explained his necessities to his sisters, and had told them of his grievous losses that year, the poor women were filled with pity for him and comforted him to the best of their ability. When Albertine who was much the wisest of the three sisters and who had the charge of their money affairs, began to speak hesitatingly about good security, the other two, especially Fidelia, fell upon her and accused her of hardheartedness; their brother required the money, and in that he was only like very many other farmers; their brother was their pride and their only support, their father had himself said so when he was dying, and when Alick promised that the estate should be security for the money, Albertine gave way and rejoiced with her sisters that they were able to be of use to their brother. Alick was fortunate in being able to draw the money at once, although, of course, he met with a considerable loss on the transaction. However he had made up his mind that such must be the case, and had determined that he would take the loss upon his own shoulders and that his sisters should not suffer, indeed they would gain by lending him their money, for was he not going to give them five per cent for it.

He came home punctually in the second week of January 1847, and a few days later, when David and Slus'uhr returned to press him for the money, he paid it down, took possession of his bills and bowed them out of the room.

"What's the meaning of all this?" asked Slus'uhr when they were seated in the carriage. "Why, hang it!" said David. "He has got money after all. Did you notice that he had a lot more bank notes than what he gave us?"--"Yes, who the devil did he get them from?"--"I say, let's ask Zebedee." Now Zebedee was a poor relation of David, who always used to take him with him as coachman, but his real occupation was spying upon the owner of any estate in which his master was interested. "Zebedee, have you seen or heard where he went lately?"--"The coachman told me he had been to Schwerin."--"To Schwerin? What was he doing in Schwerin?"--"He got the money there," replied Zebedee. "In Schwerin? Didn't I always tell my father that these aristocrats uphold each other through thick and thin? He must have got it from his rich cousin."--"Ah," muttered Slus'uhr taking the packet of bank notes out of his pocket and thrusting it under David's nose: "just smell that," he said. "These notes wer'n't got from a nobleman! They smell of garlic, so he must have got them from one of you d--d Jews. But, it's all the same where they were got. We must go and tell Pomuchelskopp. Ha, ha, ha! How the little rascal will dance with rage!"

And he was right enough there! Pomuchelskopp was neither to hold nor to bind when he heard that his plot had failed: "I told you so, I told you so. I knew that the right time hadn't come yet. Oh, Henny, Henny, it's all your fault, you made me do it."--"You're a fool!" said Henny leaving the room.--"Come now, don't be angry!" said Slus'uhr. "It'll do you no good you know. Tell him that you expect him to pay up the twelve hundred pound mortgage at midsummer."--"No, no," Pomuchelskopp whimpered, "that's the only foot-hold I've got on the estate, and if he pays it, I shall have lost the game. You're sure that he has more money," he continued, addressing David.--"Yes, a large roll of notes, and a small one also."--"Well," said Slus'uhr, "you may have your will, like the dog in the pond, but this much I'll maintain, he must be a greater fool than I take him for if he doesn't smell a fox now; if he doesn't see that you're trying to ruin him, and if he has got an inkling of that, it doesn't matter whether you dun him for the money now or a couple of years hence."--"But, but," exclaimed the honest old law-giver, stamping and puffing about the room like a steam-engine, "even though he may have guessed something of what is going on, it doesn't si'nify much, for he can't do without me. I am the only friend who can help him."--"Well then, don't help him. Midsummer is the best time to make him pay up, for he has no money coming in at that time."--"Hasn't he though? He'll have the price of the wool and the rape."--"Hang it, man, you forget that he has to pay off the interest of a lot of money, and besides that, you may be sure that he always spends his income before he gets it."--"I can't do it, I tell you, I can't do it. I can't draw back the foot I've planted on his land for anything," repeated Pomuchelskopp, and he was not to be persuaded to change his mind.

"It's a great pity," said the attorney as he was driving home, "when a man hasn't courage to carry out his intentions and so stops short in the middle. Mark my words, our work at Pümpelhagen is finished. I wish I had to do business with the old woman, she'd have gone through with it."--"She's a fearfully clever woman," said David.--"It's no good talking," grumbled Slus'uhr, "our milch cow at Pümpelhagen has gone dry. We'd have got on all right if you hadn't been such an idiot, David. Why couldn't you have made your father foreclose his mortgage? If you had done that, we'd both have made a pot of money."--"Good heavens!" cried David. "He won't do it, I tell you. He goes to see old Hawermann, and they sit for hours together talking. When I say to him 'foreclose', he tells me to attend to my own business and he'll attend to his."--"Then he must be in his second childhood, and a man who knows so little how to act for his own advantage ought to be put under guardians, who will act for him."--"Well, d'ye know--I've thought of that several times; but you see--it's so--so--and then you see; my father's far too sharp for that to be tried."

CHAPTER IV

By the help of the remainder of his sisters' money, Alick got through the spring and half of the summer of 1847 pretty well, and when that supply was at an end, he sold off his wool rather than apply to his friendly old neighbour for help. He was sure that Pomuchelskopp had a great deal to do with his troubles somehow or other, and the suspicion grew stronger within him, that he had been shorn like a sheep for the benefit of the man who had pretended to be a true friend and neighbour to him, but how or why it was done was a mystery to him. His manner to Pomuchelskopp grew much colder than before, whenever they chanced to meet. He visited him no longer, and he slipped out into the fields through the garden when he happened to see his former friend coming to call upon him. Frida silently rejoiced in the change. We should also have rejoiced in it if he had only acted wisely and thoughtfully, and if he had striven with quiet courage to set himself free from his entanglements, but instead of that he acted foolishly. Persuading himself that he could not bear the presence of the man he now hated and despised, he went so far as to refuse to shake hands with him, when Pomuchelskopp greeted him warmly at a patriotic meeting in Rahnstädt, and not contented with that, spoke of him in such insulting terms that everyone present soon knew pretty well how Pomuchelskopp had been employing his money. Though Alick's conduct on this occasion was honest, it was very foolish. He owed Pomuchelskopp twelve hundred pounds, and had not the wherewithal to pay him. If he knew the squire of Gürlitz as well as he said he did, he must have been aware of the danger of such conduct. Pomuchelskopp could stand a few hard words as well as anybody, but the scene at the meeting was a little bit too much for him, and means of revenge lay too close at hand for him not to make use of it. He made no reply, but rising, went to attorney Slus'uhr and said: "Let Mr. von Rambow know that if he does not pay me my twelve hundred pounds by S. Antony's day I shall foreclose. I know now where I am. I shan't have another chance, and so I'll do the best I can now."--"If Moses would only foreclose too!" cried Slus'uhr; and this pious wish was to be fulfilled also, but later.

There was a great change in young Joseph, which no one but Mrs. Nüssler had noticed. She had always had a suspicion that Joseph would some time or other take to new and evil ways, that he would at last refuse to be guided by any one. This time was now come. From the very beginning of his married life Joseph had been accustomed to lay by some money every year. At first it was only ten pounds, but at last these ten pounds had increased to hundreds, and he was very happy when his wife told him on New-year's-morning that she had made up the farm-books for the year, for she always kept the accounts, and that they had so much to lay by. His soul rejoiced in his savings, why, he hardly knew; but in all these long years of his married life he had grown accustomed to having a larger or smaller sum of money to put in the bank or to invest, and custom was Joseph Nüssler's life. When the bad year came, Mrs. Nüssler had said to her husband during the harvest: "This'll be a bad year, and I'm afraid that we'll have to take up some of our capital."--"Mother," Joseph had answered, staring at her in blank amazement, "surely you'd never do that." But on this New-year's-morning his wife came to him and said, she had drawn four hundred and fifty pounds, and that she only hoped and trusted that that would be enough. "We can't let our people and our cattle starve," she said in conclusion.--Joseph sprang to his feet, a thing he had never done before; he trod on Bolster's toes, another thing he had never done before; stared at his wife gloomily and said nothing, a thing that he often did, and then walked out of the room with Bolster limping at his heels. Dinner-time came, but Joseph did not return. A beautiful bit of sirloin was put on the table, but Joseph did not return. His wife called him, he did not hear. She sought him, but could not find him, for he had taken refuge in the cow-house and was busily engaged with a tar-pot in one hand and a brush in the other, in making little crosses on his cattle, and Bolster was standing at his side. After a long search his wife found him thus employed: "Goodness gracious me, Joseph," she asked, "why ar'n't you coming to dinner."--"I hav'n't time, mother."--"What are you doing here with the tarpot?"--"I'm marking the cows that we ought to sell."--"Preserve us all!" cried Mrs. Nüssler, snatching the tar-brush out of his hand, "what do you mean? My best milkers!"--"Why, mother," answered Joseph calmly, "we must get rid of some of our people and of our cattle or they'll eat up our very noses and ears."--It was indeed a fortunate circumstance that he had fallen upon the cows first and not upon the people, otherwise the farm-lads and lasses might have borne tarry crosses on their backs on that New-year's-morning.--Mrs. Nüssler got him to leave off his work with great difficulty, and then took him back to the parlour. When once more seated there, he announced that he would not farm any more, and said that Rudolph must come and marry Mina, and take the farm into his own hands. Mrs. Nüssler could make nothing of him, so she sent for Bräsig. Mina, who had heard enough, rushed upstairs to her garret-room and clasping both hands upon her heart, said to herself, that it was wrong to harass her father, why could he not be allowed to rest when he wanted, and why should Rudolph not manage the farm, Hilgendorf had written to say that he could do it. If uncle Bräsig took part against her in this she would tell him plainly that she wouldn't be his god-child any longer.

When Bräsig came and had heard the whole story, he took his stand in front of young Joseph, and said: "What's the meaning of all this, young Joseph? Why did you spend the holy New-year's-morning in painting tarry crosses on your cows? Why do you want to sell your wife's best milkers? And do you really mean to say that you're going to give up farming?"--"Bräsig, Rudolph can attend to the farm, and why can't Mina marry him at once? Lina is married, and Mina is as good as her sister."--As he said this he glanced at Bolster out of the corner of his eye, and Bolster shook his head in grave agreement with his master's sentiments.--"Joseph," said Bräsig, "justice is a great virtue, and I must confess that your folly has for once driven you to speak the words of wisdom"--Joseph raised his head--"no, Joseph, I'm not going to praise you, it is only that you have for once in your life said something I can agree with. I also think that Rudolph should be sent for, and that he should manage the farm. Hush, Mrs. Nüssler!" he added, "come here for one moment please." He drew Mrs. Nüssler into the next room, and explained to her that he intended to remain with parson Godfrey until Easter. He could look after matters at Rexow till then, but after that Rudolph must come, "and it's better for you that it should be so," he continued, "for he'll never paint crosses on your cows, and it will be equally good for him, for in that way he will gradually learn to manage a farm on his own responsibility. Then the marriage must be in the Easter holidays of next year."--"Goodness gracious me, Bräsig, that'll never do, how can Mina and Rudolph live in the same house? What would people say?"--"Ah, Mrs. Nüssler, I know how hard the world is in its judgment of engaged couples. I know it well, for when I was engaged to the three--toots, what was it I was going to say? Oh, it was this, that Mina might go to parson Godfrey's. My room at the parsonage will be empty after Easter, for I'm going to Hawermann in Rahnstädt then."--"Yes, that'll do very well," said Mrs. Nüssler. And so it was all settled.--Rudolph came to Rexow at Easter, but Mina had to go away then, and when she and all her luggage were packed into the carriage, she wiped the tears from her eyes and thought herself the most miserable creature on the face of the earth, for was not her mother sending her out of her own father's house to live amongst strangers--by which she meant her sister Lina--and without any good reason that she could see. She doubled up her fist when she thought of

Bräsig, for her mother had said that Bräsig thought the arrangement a good one. "Pah!" she cried aloud, "and I am to have his room at the parsonage; I'm sure it'll smell of stale tobacco, and that the walls will be so well smoked that one might write one's name upon them with one's finger!" But when she entered the room at last, she opened her eyes wide with astonishment. There was a table in the middle of the room, and it was covered with a white cloth, while right in the centre of it was a glass vase full of the most beautiful flowers that could be got at that time of year, blue hepaticas, yellow acacias, and wild hyacinths. Beside the flower glass lay a letter directed to Mina Nüssler in uncle Bräsig's hand-writing, and when she opened it, she was more surprised than ever, for it was written in poetry, and this was the first time she had ever had verses addressed to her. Uncle Bräsig had learnt an old proverb, used in house building from Schulz the carpenter, and had adapted it to a room. He had then added a few lines of comfort entirely out of his own head. This was the letter.

To my darling god-child.

This room is mine,
And yet not mine.
Thou who hadst it
Didst think it thine.

When thou didst go
I did come in,
When I am gone,
Some one comes in.

Sad are both parting and absence,
But a year soon vanishes hence,
So find comfort in this, my dear.
That with next spring the wedding's here.

Mina blushed when she read the bit about the marriage, and throwing her arms round her sister Lina's neck, began laughingly to abuse Bräsig for his stupidity; but in her heart of hearts she blessed him. Thus Mina went to Gürlitz, Rudolph to Rexow, and Bräsig to Mrs. Behrens and Hawermann at Rahnstädt.

With Hawermann everything was going on in much the same way as before. He led a very retired life in spite of the efforts of his friends. The rector often gave him a little lecture; Kurz inveigled him into many a farming talk, and even Moses now and then made his way upstairs, spoke to him about old times, and asked his advice on various business affairs;

but the old man kept on the even tenour of his way uninfluenced by any of them. He thought night and day of his daughter's fate and nourished a faint hope that the labourer Regel would return sooner or later, and by telling the truth would wash away the stain of dishonesty which had been fastened upon him. The labourer had written home several times lately, and had sent his wife and children some money; but had always kept his whereabouts a secret. Little Mrs. Behrens was much afraid that his sorrows were preying on her old friend so heavily as to make him more or less morbid, and she feared that he might in time become a monomaniac, so she thanked God heartily when Bräsig came to live with them. Bräsig would do him good, he was the man to do it, if any could. His restless nature and kind heart made him try to rouse his friend; he would oblige him to do this or that, would persuade him to go out for a walk with him, would make him listen to all sorts of silly novels which he got from the Rahnstädt lending library, and when nothing else had any effect, he would give utterance to the maddest theories in order to induce his friend to contradict him. Hawermann grew better under this mode of treatment, but if ever the words Pümpelhagen or Frank were mentioned in the course of conversation, all the good was undone for the time being, and the evil spirit of melancholy once more possessed him.

Louisa got on much better than her father, she was not one of those women who think that when they have been disappointed in love they ought to go about the world sadly, and show every one by their woe-begone faces and languid movements how much their poor hearts have suffered, saying by their manner, that they are only waiting for death to release them from a world, in which they have now neither part nor portion. No, Louisa was not that kind of woman. She had strength and courage to bear her great sorrow by herself, she did not need the world's pity. Her love was hidden deep down in her heart like pure gold. She spoke of her feelings to nobody, and only took from her treasure what was required for the needs of the day, for the loving-kindness she lavished on all who came near her. When God sees a child of man striving valiantly for victory over a crushing sorrow, and in spite of his own misery, doing what he can to make the lives of others easier and pleasanter to them. He gives him help and strength to go on with his battle, and sends him many little accidental circumstances that assist him on his way, but which pass unnoticed by outsiders. What is called chance is, when regarded from a truer point of view, only the effect of some cause which is hidden from our eyes.

Such a chance help, as I have mentioned, came to Louisa in the spring after the meeting of the stormy council of women, which divided Rahnstädt into two parties.

One day when Louisa was returning home from visiting Lina at Gürlitz, as she was walking along a foot path at the back of some of the gardens at Rahnstädt, one of the garden doors suddenly opened, and a pretty little girl came up to her with a bunch of elder-flowers, tulips and acacias. "Please take these flowers," said the little member, blushing deeply, for it was she who had come to speak to Louisa. When Louisa looked at her in surprise, wondering what it all meant, tears began to roll down the girl's cheeks, and covering her eyes with her hand, she murmured: "I w-wanted to give you a little pleasure." Louisa touched by the kindness of the girl, threw her arms round her neck and gave her a kiss. They then went into the garden together and seated themselves in the arbour made of the interlaced branches of elder. There Louisa and the warm-hearted little member began an acquaintance which soon ripened into a firm friendship, for a heart full of love is easily opened to friendship, so it came to pass that the little member became a daily visitor at Mrs. Behrens' house, and whenever she appeared all the faces in the household brightened at her approach. As soon as Hawermann heard the first notes struck on Mrs. Behrens' old piano, he used to come down stairs, and seating himself in a corner, would listen to the beautiful music the little member played for his entertainment. When that was over Mrs. Behrens would come in for her share of amusement, for the little member was a doctor's daughter, and doctors and doctors' children always know the last piece of news that is going; not that Mrs. Behrens was curious, she only liked to know what was going on, and since she had come to live in a country-town she had been infected with the desire, all inhabitants of such towns feel, to know what their neighbours are doing. She once said to Louisa: "you see, my dear, one likes to hear what's going on around one, but still when my sister Mrs. Triddelfitz begins to tell me any news I don't like it, her judgments of people's actions are so sharp and sarcastic; it's quite different with little Anna, she tells such funny innocent stories that one can laugh over them quite happily; she is a dear good child."

This new friendship gained strength and significance when the bad harvest brought its consequences of famine, want and misery into the town. Anna's father was a doctor, although he had not the title of Practising Physician, but he had something that was better than any such title, he had a kind heart, and when he came home and told of the poverty and wretchedness he had seen, Anna used to go to Mrs. Behrens and Louisa and repeat to them what her father had said. Mrs. Behrens used then to go to her larder and fill a basket with food and wine, which the two girls carried out to the homes of the starving people in the dusk of the evening, and when they came home they gave each other a kiss, and then they kissed Mrs. Behrens and Hawermann, that was all, not a word was said about it.

When arrangements were to be made about the soup kitchens, all the ladies in Rahnstädt held a great 'talkee-talkee,' as Bräsig called it, to settle how the distress in the town could best be alleviated. The town-clerk's wife said that if there were to be soup-kitchens at all, "they must be on a *grand* scale." And when she was asked what she meant, she answered that it was all the same to her, but if any good was to be done it must be on "a grand scale." Then the elder members of the council agreed that a difference must be made between the converted and unconverted poor, for a little starvation would do the latter no harm. After that a young and newly married woman proposed that some man should be appointed manager of the charity, but her motion was quashed at once, as all the other ladies voted against her, and the town-clerk's wife remarked that as long as she had lived--"and that's a good many years now," interrupted Mrs. Krummhorn--all cooking and charitable societies had been managed by women, for men didn't understand such things, but she would once more impress upon them that the charity must be done on a grand scale. The Conventicle then separated, every member as wise as she had been at the beginning. When the soup kitchens were opened, two pretty girls of our acquaintance became active workers in them. They flitted about the great fire in their neat gowns and long white linen aprons, and ladled out the soup from the large pots into the tins the poor women brought with them. They sat on the same bench as the converted and unconverted, and helped them to peel the potatoes and cut the turnips for the next day's use. That was the way that Louisa expended what she took from the treasure of love hidden away in her heart, and Anna also added her mite.

Bräsig took a good deal of the distant visiting of the poor off the little member's hands, saying that running messages was just what he was made for, and when he had not got gout he trotted about the town wherever he was wanted. He said to Hawermann one day: "Charles, Dr. Strump says there's nothing like polchicum and exercise for gout, and the water-doctor says, it ought to be cold water and exercise. They both agree in advising exercise, and I feel that it does me good. But what I wanted to say was this,--Moses sends you his compliments and desires me to say that he intends to come and see you this afternoon."--"Why, has he returned from Dobberan already? I thought that he didn't want to come home till August."--"But Charles, this is S. James' day, and harvest has begun. But what I wanted to say was this,--the old Jew has quite renewed his youth. He looks almost handsome, and ran up and down the room several times to show me how active he was. I must be off now to see old widow Klähnen, she's waiting for me in her garden, and is very impatient, for I've promised her some turnip seed. And then I must go to Mrs. Krummhorn's and look at her kittens, she has promised to give us one of them, for, Charles, we require a good mouser; after that I have to go and speak to Rischen the blacksmith about the shoes for Kurz's old riding horse. The poor old beast has as many windgalls as Moses' son David has corns on his feet, I'm not joking, Charles. I suppose you hav'n't heard yet that Mr. von Rambow has already invested in a horse with windgalls, otherwise he might have bought Kurz's horse to complete the infirmary at Pümpelhagen. I have to go and see the mayor's wife later in the afternoon, for she has got some newly mown rye, and wants me to to make her some beer as we have it in our farms. She is going to make quite a festival on the occasion of the beer making. Now good-bye, Charles, I'm going to read aloud to you this afternoon, and I've got a book that I'm sure will amuse us both." Then he went away, and ran up one street and down another, visiting this house and that, and doing all in his power to help his neighbours. As the inhabitants of a small Mecklenburg town are more or less interested in agricultural matters, Bräsig was continually appealed to for advice and assistance, and finally became the oracle and slave of the whole town.

In the afternoon Bräsig seated himself beside his friend Charles, and opening his book prepared to read aloud. If we were to look over his shoulder we should read on the title page: "The Frogs by Aristophanes, translated from Greek." We open our eyes wide with astonishment, but only think how much wider the old Greek humourist would have opened his, had he seen to what heights education had advanced in Rahnstädt, had he known that his frogs had taken their place, two thousand years after his death, in the same shelf of the Rahnstädt circulating library as "Blossoms," "Pearls," "Forget-me-nots," "Roses," and other annuals. How the old rascal would have laughed! Uncle Bräsig did not laugh, but sat there gravely and seriously. He had put on his horn spectacles, that looked for all the world like a pair of carriage lamps, and was holding the book as far away from him as the length of his arm would allow. When he began: "'The Frogs'-- he means what we call 'puddocks,' Charles--'by Aristop-Hannes'--I read it 'Hannes,' Charles as I look upon 'Hanes' as a misprint, for there's a book called 'Schinder-Hannes'[2] that I once read, and if this is only half as horrible, we may be well satisfied, Charles." He now began to read after school-master Strull's, fashion, only stopping for breath, and Hawermann sat still seeming to listen attentively, but before the first page was finished he was buried in his own thoughts again, and when Bräsig wet his finger to turn the fourth page, he discovered to his righteous indignation that his old friend's eyes were closed. Bräsig rose, placed himself in front of him and stared at him. Now it is a well known fact that the miller wakes when the mill stops working, and that the hearers wake when the sermon is done. So it was with Hawermann, he opened his eyes, pulled at his pipe, and said: "Beautiful, Zachariah, most beautiful."--"What? you say 'beautiful' and yet you were asleep!"--"Don't be angry with me," said Hawermann, who was now thoroughly awake, "but I couldn't understand a single word of it. Put the book away, or do you understand it?"--"Not so well as usual, Charles, but I paid a penny for the hire of it, and when I pay a penny I like to have my money's worth."--"But if you can't understand it?"--"People don't read in order to understand, Charles, they read *poor passer lour temps*. Look," and he tried to explain what he had read, but was interrupted by a knock at the door, which was followed by the entrance of Moses.

Hawermann went forward to meet him and said: "I'm very glad to see you Moses. How well you're looking!"--"Flora says so too, but it's an old story with her, she told me so fifty years ago."--"Well, how did you like the watering-place?"--"I'll tell you some news, Hawermann. One is very glad of two things at a watering-place. The first is that one can go there, and the other is that one's going away again. It's just the same as with a horse, a garden, and a house one rejoices to have them, and rejoices to get rid of them."--"Yes, I see that you wer'n't able to stand the full course of it; perhaps however it was business that brought you home."--"How I hate business. I am an old man. My business now is not to enter into new transactions, and gradually to withdraw my money from old ones. That's what has brought me here today I want to have the ten hundred and fifty pounds I lent on Pümpelhagen."--"Oh, Moses, don't! You would plunge Mr. von Rambow into great difficulties."--"I don't know that. He must have money; he must have a great deal of money. David, the attorney and Pomuffelskopp tried to ruin him at the new year, but he paid them up sixteen hundred pounds at once. I know all that David has been about; I questioned Zebedee. 'Where were you yesterday?' I asked. 'At the Court's,' he said. 'That's a lie, Zebedee,' I answered. But he swore it was true till he was black in the face. I always said: 'You know you're telling a lie, Zebedee.' At last I said: 'I'll tell you something. The horses are mine, and the carriage is mine, and the coachman is mine. Now if you don't tell me the truth, I'll send you away, for you're a scoundrel.' Then he confessed and told me about the sixteen hundred pounds, and yesterday he said that Pomuffelskopp had given Mr. von Rambow notice to pay up the mortgage he holds on Pümpelhagen, on S. Anthony's day. Now Pomuffelskopp is a wise man, and he must know how it stands with him."--"Merciful heaven!" cried Hawermann quite forgetting his hatred to Alick, and feeling all his former loyalty to the von Rambow family revive, "and you are going to follow his example? Moses, you know that your money is safe."--"Well, I'll confess that it is safe. But I know many other places where it would also be safe." Then looking sharply at the two old bailiffs, he said very emphatically: "I have both seen him and spoken to him."--"What? Mr. von Rambow? Where was it?" asked Hawermann. "In Dobberan at the gaming-table," said Moses angrily, "and also in my hotel."--"Alas!" said Hawermann, "he never used to do that. What will become of him poor fellow?"--"I always said," exclaimed Bräsig, "that too much knowledge would be the ruin of the lieutenant."--"I assure you," interrupted Moses, "that I saw these people round the table with piles of Louis d'ors before them. They sat at one part of the table and then at another. They pushed about the money in this direction and in that, and that's what they call business, and what they call pleasure! It's enough to make one's hair stand on end. And he was always at it. 'Zebedee,' I said, for Zebedee had brought my carriage ready for me to go home on the next day, 'Zebedee, stand here and keep your eye on the Squire of Pümpelhagen. You can tell me afterwards how he gets on. It makes me quite ill to watch him.' Zebedee came to me in the evening, and told me he was cleaned out. And a little later Mr. von Rambow came and asked me for a hundred and fifty pounds. 'I'll tell you something,' I said, 'I'll act like a father to you, come away with me, Zebedee has the carriage all ready, I'll take you with me, and it shan't cost you a farthing.' He refused my offer, and was determined to remain."--"Poor fellow, poor fellow," sighed Hawermann. "That boy," cried Bräsig, "has actually a wife and child! If he belonged to me, what a wigging I should give him."--"But, Moses, Moses," entreated Hawermann, "I implore you by all you love not to demand payment. He will come to his right mind, and your money is safe."--"Hawermann," said Moses, "you also are a wise man; but listen to me; when I began business as a money lender, I said to myself: when anyone comes to borrow money from you who has carriage and horses and costly furniture, lend him what he wants, for he has goods to be security; when any merry-hearted young fellow who laughs and jokes and drinks champagne wants to borrow money from you, lend it to him, for he'll earn enough to pay you back; but if a man should come to you for help who has cards and dice in his pocket, and who frequents gambling-tables, beware what you do, for a gamester's money is never to be counted on. And besides that, Hawermann, it would never do. People would say that the Jews incited the young man to gamble, so as to ruin him the quicker, and make sure of seizing his estate," and Moses drew himself to his full height. "No," he continued, "the Jew has his own code of honour as well as the Christian, and no man shall come and point to my grave, and say: that man drove a dishonest trade.--I won't have my good name taken from me in my old age by a man whose own conduct is not immaculate. Has he not stolen your good name, and yet you are an honest man and a true-hearted man. No," he went on, as Hawermann rose and began to walk up and down the room, "sit down, I won't talk about it. Different people have different notions. You bear your fate, and you have your reasons for doing so; I should not bear it if I were in your place, and I have my reasons for saying so. Good-bye now, Hawermann; good-bye Mr. Bräsig. I shall demand my money at S. Anthony's day all the same," and so saying he went away.

It was thus that the black clouds rose on this side also of Alick's sky, and they rose when he did not expect them. The dark storm clouds hemmed him in on every side, and when once the storm burst who could tell how long it might rage, and how many of his brightest hopes might not be destroyed by it for ever. He would not let himself think that ruin was staring him in the face, he comforted himself by looking forward to a good harvest, by counting up the money he expected to get from the grain merchants and wool-staplers, and with the hope that some lucky chance would stave off the evil day of reckoning a little longer. People always think when things are going ill with them that chance will come to their rescue and make everything easy to them. They treat the future as if it were a game at blind man's buff.--So the year 1848 began.

CHAPTER V

This is not the place to decide whether the year 1848 brought most good or evil into the world. Let everyone give his verdict as he thinks best, I will not be drawn into expressing an opinion one way or the other, and will only describe how it affected the people about whom I am writing, for if I did not do that, the end of my book would be rather incomprehensible to my readers.

When the February explosion took place in Paris, the Mecklenburgers imagined that it would affect them as little as if it had taken place in Turkey, or some such distant country, and most people thought it a good joke that anything so exciting should still be possible in the world. The good folk of Rahnstädt began to take much more interest in politics than they had ever done before, and the post-master said that if matters remained as they were, the thing would have to be enquired into. He had been obliged to order eleven new newspapers, four of which were the "Hamburg Correspondent," and seven were numbers of the "Tante Voss." He regarded this preponderance in favour of the latter paper as a very bad sign, for the "Tante Voss" inculcated the necessity of overthrowing the existing order of things; perhaps the editor meant no harm by it, but he did it all the same. Thus we see that forty-four politicians were provided with the latest news, for every four of them took a paper amongst them which they each read in turn, and the olive-branches of the various subscribers might be seen running with the newspapers to the different houses at which they were due, looking as if their parents thought it well to bring up their children to be post-men. But what were eleven newspapers in a town like Rahnstädt? The artisans were still unprovided for, that had to be seen to; and it was done before long.

"Where are you going, John?" asked Jack Bank's wife.--"Well, Dora, I'm going to Grammelin's."--"You're going much too often to the public-house. I don't like it."--"Oh, Dora, I only drink *one* glass of beer. Lawyer Rein is going to read the newspaper aloud there this evening, and one likes to know what's going on in the world."--So Jack Bank and about fifty other artisans went to the ale-house.

Lawyer Rein seated himself at the head of the table, newspaper in hand, glanced down the table to see that there was a good audience, and then coughed twice. "Silence!"--"Silence!"--"Bring me another glass of beer, Grammelin."--"Hold your tongue, Charles, he's going to begin."--"Hang it! Surely I may order a glass of beer first."--"Hush! *Do* be quiet!"--The lawyer now began to read. He read about Lyons, Milan and Munich. The revolution had broken out at all of these places, the whole world seemed to be going mad. "Here's something more," he said. "Faröe islands 5th. The country is in an uproar, because the meridian, which we have had in our island for the last three hundred years, is to be removed to Greenwich, England. There is a strong feeling of hostility against the English. The people are getting under arms, and both of our hussar-regiments are ordered out for the defence of the meridian."--"Well, well; very soon all of them will be at it."--"Ah yes, lad. This isn't by any means a small matter. When one has had a thing for three hundred years, one do'n't like having to give it up."--"I say, lad, do you know what a meridian is?"--"What can it be? It seems to be something that the English like to have. Now, then, you wouldn't believe me when I told you yesterday that the English were at the bottom of all the mischief, and you see that I was right."--Lawyer Rein laid the newspaper down on the table and said: "Things are getting very bad, and one can't help feeling rather anxious when one reads the news."--"Why, what is it?"--"Has anything worse happened?"--"Just listen. North-pole, 27th February. A very dangerous and extensive revolution has broken out amongst the Eskimos. These people obstinately refuse to turn the axis of the world any longer, and give as a reason, the want of train oil for greasing the machinery, which is caused by the failure of the whale fisheries last year. The consequences of this revolt will be indescribably disastrous to the rest of the world."--"Heaven preserve us! What does all that mean? Where is the mischief to stop?"--"Surely the government will do something."--"The gentry won't allow that."--"I don't believe it," said Jack Bank.--"You don't believe it? Well, being a shoemaker you ought to know. Has the price of train-oil risen since last year?"--"Well, lads," said Wimmersdorf the tailor, "it looks very bad to me."--"I don't care," cried another. "When the sky falls the sparrows will all die. But I will say this. *We* must all work hard, and yet those cursed dogs at the North-pole are sitting with their hands folded in their laps doing nothing. Another glass of beer, Grammelin."

Three things are to be remarked from this scene at the ale-house. Firstly, that Lawyer Rein trusted as much to his invention, as to the newspaper, for the information he gave the people. Secondly that the Rahnstädt artisans were not quite well enough educated for newspapers to be properly understood by them, and thirdly, that people are apt to be rather indifferent to that which does not come home to their own stomachs.

But it was to come nearer them now. One day the post from Berlin did not arrive, so the Rahnstädters crowded round the post-office, and asked each other what it meant. The grooms who had come to fetch the letter-bags for the country places wondered whether they ought to wait or not. In fact the only man who was perfectly satisfied with the state of affairs was the post-master, who was standing at his own door, twirling his thumbs. He said that during the thirty years he had held the office of post-master he had never had such a pleasant time of leisure at that hour as he was then enjoying. Next day, instead of the little boys, the subscribers to the newspapers came themselves, and instead of the grooms, the squires rode into Rahnstädt to ask for their letters; but that did not help them much, for the post did not arrive that day either, and it began to be whispered that Berlin had also risen. One man told one story and another gave a different version, each vouching for the truth of his own. Old Düsing, the potter, said that he had heard the distant roar of cannon all morning, and everyone believed him although Berlin was nearly a hundred and twenty miles from Rahnstädt. His neighbour Hagen the carpenter was the only man who doubted, and he said: "I made the noise of cannon, for I was hacking up some wood in my yard all morning."--The post arrived on the third day, but not from Berlin; it only came from Oranienburg, and with it a man who could tell them all they wanted to know, as he had just come from Berlin. The only pity was that he had talked so hard the whole time he had been travelling that he had no voice left when he reached Rahnstädt. He was a candidate for the ministry, and was born in the neighbourhood, so the Rahnstädters plied him with egg-flip in hopes of making him speak. He drank a great deal of the flip, but all in vain, he could only touch his throat and chest, and shake his head sadly. He then tried to go away. Now that was a stupid thing of him to do, for the Rahnstädters had not come to the post-office to look about them and hear no news. They would not let him pass, and he had to make up his mind to describe the revolution in Berlin as best he could, helping himself out by means of signs. He showed them that barricades were erected in the streets, naturally only by signs, otherwise the police would have been down upon him. He shouldered his stick like a musket, and showed how the barricades were stormed. He rushed into the midst of the Rahnstädt crowd to show them how the dragoons came up at a hand-gallop, and then he imitated the roar of cannon by saying "boom," that being the only word he had uttered, and it was said with infinite difficulty.

That was how the Rahnstädters learnt what a revolution was like, and how it ought to be conducted. They sat in the public-house, and while they drank beer, they disputed about politics. The state of affairs had now become so grave that Lawyer Rein no longer dared to read despatches from the North-pole. The gentlemen who subscribed for the newspapers also began to frequent the ale-house, in order that they might make themselves known to, and liked by the artisans in case there should be a revolt here also. Such a consummation would have surprised nobody.

There were advanced thinkers in Rahnstädt as elsewhere, and if the town as a whole had no particular grievance, a great many individuals amongst its inhabitants had small wrongs which might be magnified by discontent into instances of gross injustice. One man had this, another that, and Kurz had the town-jail. So it came to pass that all were of one mind in thinking that the present state of things might be altered with advantage to the community, and that in order to improve their affairs they must needs have a revolution like their neighbours; but still they thought that in their case a small one would be sufficient.

Thus the meeting of ignorant men for reading the papers was changed into a Reform-club with a chairman and a bell, and the former irregular attendance was changed to a regular attendance. The members of the society adjourned every evening from the bar of the public-house to a private room where they deliberated, but unfortunately they always carried the fumes of the beer they had drunk with them. Everything was done decently and in order, and this was a circumstance worthy of the greater admiration that the whole company was composed of discontented people, with the sole exception of Grammelin the landlord. Speeches were made at the meeting. At first whoever had anything to say spoke from his seat, but after a time that was all changed. Thiel the cabinet-maker made a sort of pulpit, and the first speech delivered from it, was when Dreier the cooper accused Thiel of having taken the work out of his hands, for in his opinion he ought to have made the pulpit and not the cabinet-maker. He concluded by begging the meeting to uphold his rights. He gained nothing by his appeal, although it was apparent to every eye, that the pulpit was exactly like a vat belonging to a brandy-making establishment, and not like a pulpit at all. Mr. Wredow, the fat old baker, moved that the pulpit should be made over again, for it did not allow a man sufficient room to turn; but Wimmersdorf, the tailor, said that such things were made large enough for ordinary mortals, and that no one was expected to make them to suit the fancy of people who chose to smother themselves in fat. So the matter was settled much to the satisfaction of the thin members, while the fat ones were so disgusted that they ceased to attend the meeting, and this the others maintained was no great loss. But it was a mistake on their part, for they thus got rid of the "calming element"--as it was called--which would have kept the meeting in check, and instead of it, the vacant places were all filled by labourers, so the revolution might begin at any moment. The only two stout people who were still members of the Reform-club, were uncle Bräsig and Shulz the carpenter.

No one was more satisfied with the unsettled state of affairs than uncle Bräsig; he was always ready; he was like a bee, or rather--like a bumble-bee, and looked upon every house-door and every window in Rahnstädt as a flower from which he might extract news. When he had gathered enough he would make his way home and feed his friend Charles with the bees-bread he had collected.--"I say, Charles, they've chased away Louis Philippe."--"Is that in the newspaper?"--"I've just read it there myself. What a cowardly old humbug he must be, Charles. How can a king allow himself to be turned out?"--"Ah, Bräsig, such things have happened before. Don't you remember Gustavus of Sweden? When a nation unites against him, what can the king do? He stands alone."--"That's all very true, Charles, but still I'd never run away in such a case. Hang it! I'd seat myself upon my throne, put my crown on my head and hit out with arms and legs at any one who attacked me."

Another time he came, and said: "The Berlin post hasn't come to-day either, Charles, and I saw your young squire galloping through the streets to the post-office to ask why it hadn't come, but I'm sorry he did so, for some of the artisans collected in a crowd and asked each other whether they were bound to stand a nobleman galloping through their streets any longer. He rode from the post-office to Moses' house, and got the worst of it there. I also had something to say to Moses, and so I followed him. Just as I got to the door, Mr. von Rambow came out, and looked at me as he passed, but did not seem to know who I was. I didn't take it ill of him, for he appeared to be full of his own thoughts. I heard Moses say: 'What I have said, I have said: I never lend money to a gambler.' Moses is coming here this afternoon."

Moses came as he had promised: "Hawermann," he said, "it's quite true; it's quite true about Berlin."--"What? Has the revolution broken out there also?"--"Yes," he answered, "but don't repeat what I tell you. The son of Manasseh came to me this morning from Berlin. He travelled by post to get here sooner, for he wants to do business with some flints he has had since the year--15."--"What on earth does he expect to get for his flints," cried Bräsig, "everyone uses percussion-caps now."--"How can I tell?" said Moses. "I know a great deal, and I know nothing. He means that if the revolution spreads all the old muskets for which flints were used will be brought into requisition again. He tells me that the soldiers in Berlin fired upon the people with muskets, pistols and cannon, and hewed them down with their sabres. The fighting lasted for a whole long night. The soldiers fired on the populace, who returned their fire from the windows and from behind the barricades. They also made use of stones. It's horrible, very horrible, But don't speak of it on any account."--"Then there was a regular cannonade?" cried Bräsig.--"Merciful Heaven!" exclaimed Hawermann, "what times we're living in, what dreadful times!"--"What do you mean by that. The times are always bad to stupid people; the wise find all times good. These wouldn't be good times for me, if I didn't make sure of getting my money paid up here and there. I, who am an old man, find the times very good."--"But, Moses, do you never feel anxious when you see everything going topsy-turvy? You are said to be a rich man."--"No, I'm not a bit afraid. Flora came to me whimpering and David came trembling. He said: 'Father, where are we to go with our money?'--'We'll just remain where we are,' I said. 'We'll lend where we have good security and we'll make money where we can; we'll be on the side of the people if it's required of us. And David, let your beard grow,' I said, 'the times are in favour of a beard.'--'Well, and if the times change?' he asked.--'Then cut off your beard,' I said, 'the times will no longer require you to wear it.'"

They now began to discuss Alick, his difficulties, and the fact that neither money nor credit were to be had. They found much to say on that score, for when credit goes the estate must go too, and many a landowner would be unable to save his estate the times were so bad. After Moses went away the two old bailiffs went down-stairs and spent the evening with Mrs. Behrens. They talked together sadly, and Mrs. Behrens every now and then clasped her hands and exclaimed at the wickedness of the world, for the first time thanking God for having taken her pastor to himself before these evil days had come upon the land, and for having thus prevented him seeing the unchristian actions which were now ruling the world. Hawermann felt like a man who had given up some dearly loved occupation, only to see his work brought to nought by his successor. Bräsig alone took things easily, he held his head in the air, and said: that the restlessness which had come into the world was not only owing to man, but that God had helped to cause it, or at least had allowed it, and it was a well known fact that a storm cleared the air. "And, Charles," he added,--"I'm not talking about you, Mrs. Behrens-- but if I might advise you, Charles, you'd come to Grammelin's with me to-morrow evening, for we ar'n't rebels, I assure you. And do you know what it feels like to me? Just the same as a thunderstorm. It's dreadful when one looks at it from outside, but it's a very small affair, when one's in it."

That was how Bräsig came to join the Reform-club, and every evening when he returned home, he told his friends all that had happened. One evening he came back later than usual, and said: "It was a mad meeting to-night, Charles, and I have consumed a couple of glasses more beer than usual because of the greater importance of our proceedings. You must know that a number of labourers have become members of our club, and why shouldn't they, we're all brothers. And the confounded rascals have voted that all the land in the Rahnstädt district should be redistributed, so that everyone living within the district should have an equal portion of land. Then as to the town-woods, they want to give everyone the right of cutting down a fine old beech-tree every autumn for his firewood during the winter. After that the people who owned the land near Rahnstädt got up and opposed the motion; they approved of equality as much as the labourers did, but still they wanted to keep their land. Kurz got up and made a long speech about arable fields and meadows, of course ending with the town-jail, and when he was done they all called him an aristocrat and turned him out of the room. Then Wimmersdorf, the tailor, rose and preached about free-trade. No sooner had he done that than the other tailors fell upon him and thrashed him unmercifully: they all wanted equality, but still their guild must be kept up. Whereupon a young man came forward and asked sarcastically: What about the seamstresses, must the guild be maintained amongst them likewise? Then it was said that the seamstresses should be admitted into the tailor's union, but others opposed it, and there was a great row in which the old tailors got the worst of it. Meanwhile rector Baldrian was making a long, long speech in the body of the hall, in which he talked a great deal about the emancipalation--or some such long word--of women, and said that if the tailors wouldn't admit the seamstresses into their guild, the latter were quite able to set up one of their own, for they were human beings and sisters like the rest of us. So the motion was carried and the seamstresses are now admitted into the guild; and it was arranged before I left that all the seamstresses should dress themselves in white the day after to-morrow--you remember the yellow faced old maid who passes this house regularly, Charles? Well, she's one of them; they always call her 'auntie'--and go and thank the rector, and give him a woollen jersey and a pair of drawers on a cushion in token of their gratitude."--"Bräsig, Bräsig," remonstrated Hawermann, "how can you talk such nonsense. You're all acting as if there were no lawful authority remaining, and as if you could each do what is right in your own eyes."--"Why not, Charles? Who wants us to do otherwise. We pass our resolutions to the best of our knowledge, and if nothing comes of them, why nothing comes of them. As far as I can see, nothing can possibly come of them, for everyone wants to gain something, and no one will give up anything that he has."--"That's just as well, Zachariah, and I don't think for my own part that this little town will do much mischief to anyone with its speechifying, for parties are very equally divided. But just fancy if the labourers throughout the country were to take it into their heads to divide the estates of their masters amongst them! What a dreadful thing it would be!"--"Oh, they'll never do it, Charles."--"It's one of the deepest desires of human nature, Bräsig, to wish to call a bit, however small, of the earth one's own, and those ar'n't the worst men who try to gain some of it for themselves. Just look round you. When an artisan has made a little money, does he not at once lay it out on a small garden or field? and is not his pleasure in his purchase as great as his gain? The town labourer does the same, for he has the power to do so, and that's the reason that I don't think the discontent of the Rahnstädt labourers will ever rise to a dangerous height. But it's utterly different with the country people, they have no property and can never even by the greatest economy and diligence attain to any. If these new opinions should happen to take root amongst them, and if they are egged on by demagogues, there is no telling what harm may come of it. Yes," he exclaimed, "the bad masters will suffer first, but what assurance have we that the good masters will not be attacked next?"--"Well, Charles, you may be right, for Kurz said to me this evening--that's to say before he was turned out--that two Gürlitz labourers were talking very strangely in his shop last Sunday."--"Well," said Hawermann, taking up his candle to go to bed, "I don't wish anyone harm, although some people have perhaps deserved it, but the pity of it to my mind is, that the innocent will suffer as well as the guilty, and that the whole country will share the fate of the few, who by their misconduct have brought all the misery upon themselves."--He then went away and Bräsig said to himself: "Charles, may be right after all, and dreadful things may happen out in the country, so I must go and see what young Joseph and parson Godfrey are about. However young Joseph's in no danger, for he has never angered his labourers in any way, and so they'll let him alone. George at the parsonage isn't a rebel either, I'm sure of that."

Hawermann knew the nature of the people amongst whom he had worked for so many years. A feeling of uneasiness was spreading like a fever throughout the land. Reasonable complaints together with the most unreasonable and insane demands flew from mouth to mouth; what at first had been only whispered, was soon to be spoken of openly. The landowners were most to blame for that. They had lost their heads. Each of them acted as it seemed good to him, selfishly worked for his own safety regardless of others, and as long as he was at peace with his own people cared nought for his neighbour's fate. Instead of meeting their people honestly and straightforwardly, and showing them the real state of the case, some of the squires granted every demand their labourers chose to make in their folly and ignorance, while others, getting on horseback, wanted to reduce their labourers to order with swords and pistols, and I know several landowners who never went out to drive in their own grounds without taking a couple of loaded muskets in the carriage with them. And why was this? Because their conscience pricked them for their former conduct, and because there was no kindly human sympathy between them and their dependents. Of course that was not the case with all the masters.

Alick was one of those landowners who had never ill-treated his people. He was not hard on them generally speaking, but he could be hard if he thought his position was becoming insecure. During that time of political and social excitement the hidden qualities of all men were clearly revealed, and he who could look calmly on the march of events, and do what had to be done with quiet circumspection, who could distinguish good from evil, and steer his ship through the breakers which threatened to engulf it, was a wise and far-seeing man. That was not Alick's character. He was surrounded by his discontented vassals, and tried now this way, and now that way, of stemming the rising tide of insubordination, so it came to pass that he made two of the mistakes we have before alluded to; at one time he would foolishly submit to the villagers' demands, and at another, he would return to the ideas of a cavalry-officer and threaten his people with fire and sword. The peasantry also were changed, and it was his own fault that this was the case. He had taken from them little customs to which they were attached from use and wont, and at other times he had, in his good-nature, given them all kinds of injudicious liberties, that had only made them greedy of more, for he did not understand human nature as a whole, nor did he understand the peasantry at his gates. He had praised the people when they were idle, and he had scolded them when they were working hard, for he didn't know their capabilities. In short his actions were not guided by right and justice, but by his impulses, and as he had been rather low spirited of late, the discontent of the labourers was increasing, and threatened soon to break out into a blaze.

There was a hotbed of disaffection close to where Alick lived, and that was Gürlitz. It had once been as quiet and well doing a place as any in the country side, but in spite of the efforts parson Behrens had made for many years to keep it so, matters had gradually been growing worse and worse. Each of the new owners into whose hands it had passed had helped to bring about this state of things, and that old wretch Pomuchelskopp rejoiced when he saw it, for--dreadful as it is to say--there are some people who would rather see their labourers badly off than happy and comfortable, for they think that when their people are suffering from want, they will be the better able to rule them autocratically. Pomuchelskopp did not remember that when revolutions are the order of the day a half starved peasantry may be easily induced to revolt altogether, while those who are well off have not the same inducement to go so far. The neighbouring gentry who had long seen that the Gürlitz labourers were growing disaffected, never thought that the fire which Pomuchelskopp had fanned--without understanding its force--for his own ends, might spread throughout the district. The Gürlitz labourers had become accustomed to the taste of brandy, for there was a brandy-distillery up at the manor, and what they drank there was deducted from their wages. So in course of time they became beggars, and every penny they made, over and above what they spent at the still, was expended in the Rahnstädt public houses, where they soon learnt how the world was wagging. The waiters at the spirit shops told them what was going on throughout the country, and when they came home with their heads muddled with the brandy they had been drinking, they began their besotted ignorance to add their unreasonable desires to the tale of their real wrongs, and so added to the miserable complication. Their starving wives and children stood about them looking like ghosts; the only way they could get a morsel of food was by begging; thus they carried story of their wretchedness through the country-side written on their famished faces, and sparks of the revolutionary fire were kindled everywhere.

Nothing was as yet ripe for revolt, there was still too much to be made in other ways, and the people were also restrained by the well meant advice of kindly souls, who understood and felt for them. Another thing that kept them from open revolt was the old feeling of loyalty to their masters, and the remembrance of former benefits received from them, to say nothing of the eternal sense of right and law which survives wonderfully long even in men who are led astray. These things all combined to keep the fire from bursting forth, even with the Gürlitz villagers. If they had been able to read what was going on in the heart of their master, they would perhaps have risen at once, for hardness and cowardice were striving for the mastery in his soul. His conscience had died long ago, and he had no need to accuse himself of any kindly action to an inferior. At one moment he would exclaim in a rage: "Oh those wretches! If I only.... The law must be changed! What's the use of a government which possesses soldiers, and yet doesn't march them out? Why, my property's in danger; and it's the duty of my government to protect my property." Next moment he would perhaps call Gustavus to come to him out of the yard, and would say: "What a fool you are Gus, why are you running after the threshers; let them thresh what they like, I won't have a row with my people." On one such occasion he turned to his wife immediately after saying this, and seeing her sitting on her chair as stiff and unbending as a poker, looking at him contemptuously with her pointed nose and sharp eyes, he added: "I know what you're thinking, Henny. You want me to go out and show myself a man; but that would never do. It really wouldn't do, Chuck. We must temporise, we must temporise, and we may perhaps get the better of them by judicious temperamentation." Henny expressed no opinion upon this proposal of her husband's, but she looked as if she had no intention of acting in accordance with it, and Pomuchelskopp then said to Mally and Sally: "Children, let me beg you not to repeat what I have just said. Especially take care not to tell any of the servants. Be as kind to them as you can, and try to induce your dear Mama to be kind to them also. I am always in favour of kindness, for my own part." Then Mally and Sally went to their mother, and said: "You don't know what dreadful things have happened Mama. John Joseph told the servants this morning that the work-women of the X. estate have whipped squire Z. with nettles. We must give way, Mama, we must give way, there's no help for it."--"How silly you all are," cried Henny, rising to leave the room. "Do you think that I'm afraid of such people?" she asked scornfully as she closed the door. But she was alone in her unnatural heroism, and got no sympathy from anyone, for Muchel was not to be sneered out of his fear of stormy weather, and the other members of that "quiet family" for once agreed with their father. "Children," cried Pomuchelskopp, "treat everyone kindly. The confounded rascals! Who would have thought of this three months ago? Now Phil and Tony remember this. I won't have you beat the village children or paint an ass' head on the back of old Brinkmann's smock-frock. The ragamuffins! I'm sure that they're egged on by the Reform club at Rahnstädt, and by the Jews and shopmen. Just wait a bit ...!"--"Yes, father," said Sally, "did you know that Rührdanz the weaver has become a member of the Reform club and that the other villagers want to join it also? It's a bad look out, isn't it?"--"Bless me! you don't mean to say so! But wait, I must join it too. I'll get myself elected."--"*You!*" cried both his daughters in a breath, looking as much astonished as if their father had just announced his intention of setting fire to his own house. "I must, I must. It'll make the artisans like me, and will prevent them setting my people against me. I'll pay up all my bills, at once, that's the first step--it's a horrid thing to do, but it's necessary in order to check-mate my labourers."--Mally and Sally were frightened, they had never before seen their father in such a state; but they were still more startled when he added: "I've got another thing to say to you, and that is, be sure that you're polite to the parson and his wife--for mercy sake remember that--your mother won't--Oh Henny, Henny what misery you cause me! The parsonage people may be very useful to us or very hurtful as the case may be. A squire and a parson can do what they like, if they only hold together! We must invite Mr. and Mrs. Godfrey Baldrian to dine here some day, and then afterwards when times are better, we can break off the acquaintance if we find them unpleasant people."

This was done! A few days after this conversation parson Godfrey and his wife received a note of invitation from Mr. and Mrs. Pomuchelskopp,--for good old Henny had given in to her husband in this point--, they presented their compliments and hoped to have the pleasure of their company at dinner, and concluded by saying that the maid was waiting for an answer. Bräsig had just arrived at the parsonage to see how everything was going on. When Godfrey had read the note of invitation, he looked as thunderstruck as if he had just received a summons to attend a meeting of Consistory because of teaching false doctrine, or leading an immoral life. "Well!" he exclaimed. "Here's an invitation to dine at the squire's! Where's Lina? Lina," he shouted putting his head out at the parlour door. Lina came. She read the letter and stared at Godfrey, who stood before her not knowing what to do. She looked at Bräsig, who was sitting in the sofa corner grinning at her like a fox at Whitsuntide. "No," she said at last, "we wont go there."--"Dear wife," said parson Godfrey, for he always called her "dear wife" when he was going to put his clerical dignity in the scales against her opinion, at other times he contented himself by saying "Lina," "dear wife, it is wrong to thrust away the hand one of our brethren extends to us in kindness."--"But Godfrey," answered Lina, "this isn't a hand, it's a dinner, and besides that, this brother's name is Pomuchelskopp. Am I not right, Bräsig?" Bräsig made no reply except by a grin. He sat there like David the son of Moses when he was engaged in weighing a Louis d'or, for he wanted to see which would turn the scale, Godfrey's clerical dignity or Lina's sound common sense. "Dear wife," said Godfrey, "it is written: 'Let not the sun go down upon your wrath,' and 'if any man strike thee on thy right cheek ....'"--"That's got nothing to do with it, Godfrey. We are'n't angry, and as for the slap on the face, I agree with Bräsig about that. May God forgive me if it's a sin! It may have been different in those old times; but I know that if it were the fashion to do that now-a-days, there would be a great deal more fighting than there is, and all the world would be running about with swelled faces."--"But, dear wife ..."--"You know, Godfrey that I never interfere with your management of clerical affairs, but a dinner-party is a worldly matter, and when it's at the Pomuchelskopps it's even more than that. And then you forget that we have a visitor. Isn't uncle Bräsig here? And wouldn't you much rather eat pea soup and pig's ears here with uncle Bräsig, than dine at the Pomuchelskopps? Besides that they hav'n't invited Mina," she added as her sister came into the room, "and yet they know that Mina is staying with us." All this had a great effect upon Godfrey. He was very fond of pea soup, and pig's ears pickled at home were his favourite dish; then I may add that he had a real affection for uncle Bräsig, and was very grateful to him for the help he had given him; indeed one of his greatest puzzles was how a man like Bräsig, who was so honest and true in all his dealings could be so poor a Christian and churchman. He therefore excused himself and his wife from dining at the manor. But unfortunately whilst they were at dinner, Bräsig was so far left to himself as to mention that he had really become a member of the Reform club in Rahnstädt, and Godfrey, pig's ears or no pig's ears, sprang to his feet, and spoke strongly of the evil influence exercised by that society. Lina tried to pull him back into his chair by his coat tails several times, for the soup was growing cold, but Godfrey would not stop. "Yes," he cried, "the scourge of the Lord has come upon the world; but woe to the man whom God shall choose as His scourge!" As he was not in church this time, Bräsig interrupted the clergyman, and asked who was the scourge to be chosen by God. "That is in the hands of the Lord," cried Godfrey, "He may choose me, or Lina, or you."--"Neither Lina nor I will be chosen," answered Bräsig, wiping his mouth, "for Lina fed the poor in the year '47, and last week I voted for equality and fraternity at the Reform club. I am not a scourge, for I do no one any harm; but if I could only get hold of Samuel Pomuchelskopp for one moment--then ...." Godfrey was too much taken up with the importance of what he had been saying to allow Bräsig to finish his sentence: "Oh!" he said. "The devil is going about the world like a roaring lion, and every platform erected at these Reform meetings is an altar on which men offer him sacrifice. I will oppose all such altars by another. I will preach in God's house against these burnt offerings made to the Devil, against these reform meetings, against these false Gods and their altars." He then sat down and eat a couple of spoonfuls of pea soup. Bräsig watched him for some time in silence, and as soon as he saw that the reverend gentleman had got over his excitement, and was beginning to enjoy the pig's ears, he said: "You're quite right in one respect, parson, the place where the speeches are made at our Rahnstädt meeting looks just like one of the devil's altars, that's to say, it's shaped like a vat such as are used in a brandy-distillery. Still I can't say that any one sacrifices to the devil at our meetings. If any one does, it must be Wimmersdorf, the tailor, or Kurz, or perhaps your own father, for he makes the longest speeches of the whole--now hush--I only want to say that from my knowledge of the devil, and I've been acquainted with him for many a long year, I'll answer for it that he'll have nothing to do with the Rahnstädt Reform club, he isn't such a fool."--"You know Godfrey," said Lina, "that I never interfere with your management of clerical matters, but surely you will never mention such a secular thing as a Reform club in the pulpit." Godfrey answered that that was just what he intended to do. "All right then, do," said Bräsig, "but it'll only prove that people are wrong in saying that the clergy understand their own advantage better than any other class of men, for instead of preaching your church *full*, you'll preach out everyone who goes to hear you."--Uncle Bräsig was right, for after Godfrey had preached one Sunday with great zeal and fervour against the spirit of the times--which, let it be remarked in passing, he understood as little as a new born child--and, against all reform meetings, concluding by saying that he would finish what he had to say on that subject on the following Sunday, he found that Lina, Mina and the beadle were his only audience when he got into the pulpit, for he did not count a few old women who had only come to church for the soup Lina always gave them after service. So he went home with his sermon and his womankind, followed by the old women with their soup cans, and the beadle locked up the church. Godfrey felt like a soldier who, carried away by military ardour, has gone too far, and finds himself surrounded by the enemy.

Everything was going wrong throughout the land, and every man's hand was against his neighbour. The world had been turned topsy-turvy, and those men who had formerly made themselves of much account were now unheeded, while those who had nothing, thrust themselves forward. The men who used to be accounted wise, were now looked upon as foolish, and those who had been called foolish, were supposed to have grown wise in the course of a single night. The great were abased; the nobles gave up their titles, and the labourers wanted to be called Mr. so and so. But two threads ran straight through the maze of cowardice and impudent self-assertion, and served to comfort and cheer humanity. The first of these was parti-coloured, and anyone who could free himself from the general fear, and general greed of moneymaking, sufficiently to follow its course, might enjoy many a quiet laugh at the oddity of human nature. The second thread was of a rosy hue, and on it depended all that made the happiness of mankind; pity and compassion, sound judgment and reason, honest service and self-sacrifice, and the name of this thread was love, pure human love, which made its way right through the tangled web of selfishness, showing the truth of God's decree that love is to remain unimpaired by misery, so that it may in the end change even the dull grey of the web of selfishness into its own rose colour, for--God be thanked!--that thread is never cut.

CHAPTER VI

All was quiet at Rexow. That is to say amongst the labourers, Mrs. Nüssler and Rudolph; but young Joseph and young Bolster were not quite so easy in their minds. Young Bolster had gone into the cow-house one day and had there seen a little puppy under the charge of Flasskopp the cowman. Now this puppy was the very image of himself, and what was more, it was also called Bolster. He remembered his own youth perfectly and how he had succeeded Bolster "the sixth" on the throne of Rexow, and so after much gloomy thought he came to the conclusion that this small image of himself, which Joseph Flasskopp was rearing so carefully on nice sweet milk, might possibly succeed him under the name of "Bolster the eighth"; indeed that was very likely in the present state of affairs. He was miserable, but did not know what ought to be done. Should he divide his power with Bolster the eighth, or should he treat him as a pretender to the throne, drink up the sweet milk in the dish before his very eyes, pick a quarrel with him and send him off on a long journey on the other side of the Rexow territory; in short, get rid of him altogether. He looked up at young Joseph for advice, but young Joseph had enough to do attending to his own affairs. The times were so bad that even these two old friends ceased to share each other's thoughts; both of them were restless and anxious, but from opposite causes. Bolster shuddered at the thought of an heir to his throne, while nothing would serve Joseph but instant abdication of his rights. Bolster, after having tasted the pleasures of power, hated the idea of retiring into private life and getting bones without any meat on them, while Joseph regarded private life as a golden cup which Mina should fill with coffee every morning, which his wife should fill with beer at dinner and with chocolate in the evening, and which should contain punch every time that Bräsig came to stay with them. He was determined to give up the reins of government, especially at the present moment when his pipe might be put out by keeping them. He continued to read the Rostock newspaper, but would often throw it aside, and say crossly: "They've never taken any notice of the geese yet, mother." He imagined that everyone looked upon him as a hard master, because he had, by Rudolph's advice, bought up his labourers' right of keeping geese for a round sum, and as he had subscribed to the Rostock paper for forty years, he looked upon it as the duty of the paper to take his part about the geese. The Rostock paper might have done this quite easily I think, for Joseph was as innocent of doing wrong as a new born child, but perhaps the editor may have forgotten to notice the circumstance, or he may even never have heard of it at all. Joseph could not get it out of his head. If he saw two farm lasses talking together about their cap ribbons, he thought they were saying that no goose's eggs were to be set that year at Rexow; and if two labourers threshing out the oats stopped their work for a minute and talked about the oats, he thought they were complaining of having no geese to eat some of the grain they were threshing. He felt lost in these new times and could not understand the new arrangements introduced into the farm. He would not consent to rule any longer, he was determined to abdicate, and as Bolster was of a different opinion the bond uniting them burst.

As I said before, Mrs. Nüssler was herself quiet and calm, but Joseph's condition began to make her anxious, and she continually hoped that Bräsig would come. "I wonder," she said to Rudolph one day, "why Bräsig hasn't come to see us. He has nothing earthly to do, and yet he never looks near me."--"Ah, mother," answered Rudolph, "you know him; when he has nothing to do, he always makes himself work. But he's coming to-morrow all the same."--"How do you know that?" asked Mrs. Nüssler.--"Well, you see, mother," said Rudolph rather shyly, "I was over at our rye field by the Gürlitz march this morning, and as I was there at any rate, I--I just ran into the parsonage for a moment. Bräsig was there, and he told me he was coming here to-morrow."--"Now, Rudolph, I won't have it. Remember that I don't allow you to be running over there. It's quite different when I can go with you on Sundays. You go and chatter to each other, and you put all kinds of nonsense into Mina's head about marriage and such like things, and yet you know that that can't be yet awhile."--"Why, mother, if we don't marry soon we'll be growing too old and cold for such a thing."--"Rudolph," said Mrs. Nüssler, as she left the room, "what's to become of Joseph and me if you do. We are still young and have plenty of work in us. Are we to be shelved before our time?"--"Nay," answered Rudolph after she was gone, "you're not so very young now. Old people should rest. Uncle Joseph would be only too thankful to retire, but my aunt has work enough in her to kill off three young women. Well, Bräsig's coming to-morrow, and I'll prompt him a bit."

Next day Bräsig arrived. "Good morning," he said. "Sit still, Joseph. Well, have you got a small rebellion here too?"--"Ah," said Joseph smoking like a chimney, "what's to be done now--Bolster?" He pretended to be speaking to Bolster, for Bräsig had left the room before he had had time to finish his sentence, and was now calling Mrs. Nüssler in the passage.--"Good gracious, Bräsig," she said, drying her hands on her apron, for she had been washing them when she was called away, as she had been busy baking and did not wish to give her old friend a floury hand to shake. "Good gracious, Bräsig, why don't you come to see us in these bad times? How's my brother Charles?"--"'Bonus', as lawyer Rein would say, or 'Bong', as the grey-hound would put it, or 'he's in very good case', as I should say myself. The only pity is that he *will* go on thinking about the loss of his good name, and of the separation of little Louisa and Frank. These inward sorrows prevent him interesting himself in the doings of the Reform-club, of parliament, and in great political thoughts."--"Thank God!" replied Mrs. Nüssler. "I know my brother Charles too well to think that he'd even mix himself up with such folly."--"Mrs. Nüssler," returned Bräsig drawing himself up and looking his old love full in the face, "you have unintentionally said a great thing, as rector Baldrian said the other day when the potato-ground of the labourers was spoken about; but in these times one must take care what one says--They turned Kurz out the other day--and as I am a member of the Reform-club I can't allow the word 'folly' to be applied to our doings."--"Mercy me!" cried Mrs. Nüssler putting her arms akimbo, "I really believe that you'll want to turn me out of my own kitchen next."--"Did I ever say so?" asked Bräsig. "They've turned out Louis Philippe, and the Bavarian Louis, and Louis Kurz; is *your* name 'Louis'? No, I came here to see that you were all right. If the revolution should break out here I'll come to your assistance with the Rahnstädt club, and the civic guard--we've all got ourselves pikes as well as muskets: I'll protect you, never fear."--"You shan't come here with your pikes and muskets," cried Mrs. Nüssler, "tell your wretched rabble from me that they'd better provide themselves with an extra set of legs and arms before they venture into my farm-yard, for if they come here they shall lose those they have," so saying Mrs. Nüssler turned round and going into her larder, shut and locked the door.--Those were sad times when the devil sowed the seeds of dispeace between old friends. Bräsig waited as long as Bolster had often done before, expecting the larder door to open every minute, and when it did not, he returned to Joseph in the parlour with his ears hanging like Bolster's under the same circumstances. "Yes," he said to Joseph, "these are dreadful times, and yet there you sit moving neither hand nor foot, although rebellion has broken out in your own house."--"Ah, Bräsig, I know that, it's because of the geese," said young Joseph; "but what can be done? I say, Bräsig, help yourself to a little kümmel," pointing with his foot at the lowest shelf of the wine-cupboard, "you'll find the bottle there."

Bräsig thought a good deal of a little kümmel! He went to the window and looked out at the weather. The wind was driving sharp spring showers over the sky, and these as they passed away were succeeded by bursts of sunshine. In like manner one sad gloomy thought after another came into his head: "What?" he said to himself, "and *this* is to be the end of it? She thrusts me from her side when I am trying to help her!" Then the sun's rays once more penetrated his heart, but with a clear cold light which did not soften him, and he added with a scornful smile: "Ha! ha! I wish I could see her fighting against the whole of the Rahnstädt civic guard, headed of course by Wimmersdorf, the tailor, and the wise old dyer 'For my part'!"--At this moment Rudolph crossed the yard, and seeing Bräsig at the window, came in, as he wanted to speak to him. "How-d'ye-do, uncle Bräsig."--"How-d'ye-do, Rudolph. How are you getting on? I mean the labourers? Is all quiet?"--"Yes, quite. There has been no difficulty as yet."--"Ah, but you'll see that this affair of the geese ...." interrupted young Joseph.--"Never mind the geese, father," said Rudolph.--"What's all this about the confounded geese?" asked Bräsig.--"Nothing," said Rudolph. "You see I had such a deal of trouble about those geese, they destroyed the edges of the ditches, they eat up our young cabbages and did a lot of damage to the corn, so I called all the labourers together and promised them twelve shillings each at harvest time if they'd give up keeping geese. They agreed readily to my proposal, but my uncle has taken it into his head that the villagers all look upon him as a monster, and that there will be a rebellion about the geese."--"Goodness gracious me!" cried Mrs. Nüssler coming in, "the geese again!" and throwing her apron over her face, she burst into tears.--"Why, mother," exclaimed Rudolph springing to her side, "what's the matter? What has gone wrong?"--"What's to be done now?" asked Joseph rising.--Bräsig would also have spoken if he had not guessed that he knew more of what was passing in Mrs. Nüssler's heart than any of the others, so he turned away to the window and stood there gazing hard at the April weather with his eyebrows raised as high as they would go.--Mrs. Nüssler at last got up, dried her eyes, put aside both Rudolph and Joseph--rather hastily too--went up to Bräsig, and throwing her arms round his neck, exclaimed: "I know that you meant me well, Bräsig, and I won't hack off anyone's arms or legs."--"Oh, Mrs. Nüssler," said Bräsig with a very April face, for he was smiling with tears in his eyes, "you have my full permission to treat Wimmersdorf, the tailor, and the would-be wise old dyer 'For my part' as you like."--"What *is* the meaning of all this?" asked Rudolph.--"I'll tell you," said Bräsig, freeing himself gently from Mrs. Nüssler's embrace, and taking her by the hand, "and it's this. You've got a real angel for a mother-in-law. Not a so-called angel such as you meet at balls and in the promenade at Rahnstädt, but the grand old kind we read about in the Old Testament; a warlike good angel, who doesn't fear the devil in a good cause, and is worth three of you any day." With that he turned upon Rudolph as though he had done Mrs. Nüssler some great wrong.--"Preserve us!" cried Rudolph. "I've done nothing that I know of," and he looked at Joseph, who looked at

Bolster, but neither could help him, so Rudolph added: "I really don't know what ....."--"It isn't necessary," said Bräsig, then turning to Joseph: "and as for you, young Joseph, if you don't look out there'll be a revolution in the house, and all because of your stupidity about the geese. The best thing you can do is to sit there quietly. Now then, Rudolph, come away with me, I want to look over the farm and see what you have learnt from Hilgendorf."

Sitting still was what Joseph liked better than anything else, and going out with Bräsig gave Rudolph the very opportunity he wanted to egg his old friend on to arrange that his marriage should soon take place. So neither of them made any objection to Bräsig's decree.

Fred Triddelfitz came to the farm that afternoon as he was out riding at any rate. He was mounted on a horse with a very extraordinary action, for it walked like a human being with its fore feet, and never thought it incumbent on it to use more than three legs at a time, thus showing that nature sometimes puts herself to unnecessary trouble by creating a superfluous limb, for instance the tail of a Dandie Dinmont, the ears of a pug and the left hind leg of a horse that finds three legs sufficient for its wants. Fred's steed was by no means beautiful, especially when in motion; but he was a very courteous animal and kept on bowing the whole way along the public road. In this respect he suited Fred very well, for the lad had grown to have extremely good manners from his intercourse with Mr. von Rambow. When anyone made game of his horse Fred used to smile and say to himself: "You fools! I've always made by my horses. I was paid in ready money when I exchanged the sorrel-mare for the black, the black for the brown, and then the brown for this horse." The horse bowed itself politely into the farm-yard at Rexow where Fred dismounted politely, went into the house politely, and said: "How-d'ye-do" politely.--"Mother," said young Joseph, "give Mr. Triddelfitz something to drink," for they happened to be at coffee at the time.--"Bless me!" thought Bräsig. "He's called *Mr.* Triddelfitz now, is he?"--Meanwhile Fred divested himself of his waterproof coat, took something out of his pocket, and sitting down, placed a pistol to the right and left of his coffee cup.--"Sir," cried Bräsig, "the devil take you and your pistols! What makes you put these infernal implements on the coffee table amongst our cups?"--Then Mrs. Nüssler rose quietly, and taking the fire-arms in one hand, lifted the tea kettle with the other and poured hot water down the muzzles of the pistols, saying calmly: "There now, they can't go off."--"Oh, dear!" cried Fred, "that was the last shot we had ....."-- "Sir," interrupted Bräsig, "do you think that you're in a robber's cave when you come to see young Joseph?"--"The whole world is a robber's den just now," replied Fred, "Mr. von Rambow proved that clearly in his speech to the labourers yesterday, and so I went to Rahnstädt and bought these two pistols--one of them for him--we are going to defend ourselves to the death."--Mrs. Nüssler looked at Bräsig with a half ashamed smile, and Bräsig burst into a roar of laughter: "And so you and Mr. von Rambow think you'll be able to stop the labourer's mouths with a speech and a pair of pistols!"--"Yes, the squire told the people plainly that he would rule them mildly but strictly, and that they must do as they were desired."--"Ah well, it all depends upon circumstances," interposed Joseph.--"You may be right this time, young Joseph," said Bräsig, "for every man must cut his coat according to his cloth, but Mr. von Rambow is not the man to conduct a case like this properly. He'll be sure to treat impudent pretentions mildly, and timidity with sternness."--"So he has made another speech?" said young Joseph.--"A splendid one," cried Fred enthusiastically. "I don't know how he managed it."--"It doesn't matter," replied Bräsig. "But, tell me, what did the labourers say to the explanation made them?"--"The rabble," answered Fred, who had learnt something besides politeness from his master, "wasn't worth the trouble he took. When I was going about the farm-yard afterwards I heard different groups of labourers talking of 'equality' and of what they called the 'gee hup and gee wo' style of farming."--"It was you they meant, of course," said Bräsig with a grin.--"Yes," said Fred honestly, "but only think what happened. Five of them came to the squire in the afternoon; they were some of those I had always thought the most sensible of the lot. Old Flegel, the carpenter, was the spokesman, and he said he had heard that Mr. Pomuchelskopp had advanced money to all his people, had promised them more potato-land and various other things, but they would say nothing more on that head, for they were by no means so badly off as the Gürlitz villagers, indeed they were quite satisfied with what they had; but they didn't like the way in which they were treated. They were often scolded when they had done nothing wrong, were knocked about when they didn't deserve it, and were hunted from yard to field and back again without knowing what they were expected to do. They thought Mr. von Rambow would do well to get rid of me, for I was not up to the work, and was too young to have the management of so large an estate and so many labourers. There was one other request they wanted to make, and that was, that they entreated the squire to get old bailiff Hawermann back again. Just imagine! What a people!"--"Hm!" said Bräsig with a broad grin. "And what did the squire say to that?"--"Oh, he soon showed them what he thought of them. He said that if he was satisfied with me--here he pointed to me, and I made a polite bow--these gentlemen, the labourers, might be satisfied too. Then an old white-haired fellow, John Egel, came forward--you know him, he's one of the oldest of them all--and said, that they were not 'gentlemen,' no one knew that better than they did, and they had only come to speak to him, their master, out of the goodness of their hearts, and not to exchange sharp words. Mr. von Rambow was master, and could do as he liked."--"What an infernal old rascal," said Bräsig still on the broad grin.--"Ah, but listen. That wasn't nearly all. The thick end of the wedge came last. Towards evening I noticed that one of the labourers after the other went to the stable where the riding horses are kept, and as I knew that Christian Däsel, the groom, doesn't quite like me, I thought some mischief might perhaps be going on, so I went into the stable next to that where the men were, and in which there is a hole that goes through to the other, and then I heard what Christian Däsel was putting the labourers up to."--"That's to say," interrupted Bräsig, "that you listened."--"Well--yes," answered Fred.--"All right then," said Bräsig, "go on."--"I must begin by telling you that Christian Däsel announced that he had made up his mind to marry Sophie Degel with whom he has been 'keeping company' for several years, and the squire won't have a married groom on any account, for he thinks a married man will be more careful over his children than the foals, and I've no doubt he's right in that. But he won't part with Christian because he thinks him a good servant and attentive to the horses--however I can't say that I agree with him there, he isn't as particular as he might be. Now Christian Däsel went on to say that he would be allowed to marry Sophie if it were not for the paddocks, he was certain of that, so he wanted the labourers to demand that the paddocks should be given them for potato-ground."--"Of course you went straight to Mr. von Rambow and repeated what you had heard?" asked Bräsig.--"Naturally," said Fred, "it was necessary that he should know, in order that he might be prepared. At last they came and asked for the paddocks, saying that their wives and children were every bit as good as the squire's mares and foals, and yet the latter were better off than the former. Then Mr. von Rambow sent them away double quick with a flee in their ear. I need not add that Christian Däsel's wages were at once paid up and that he was turned off on the spot."--"And what does Mrs. von Rambow say to it?" asked uncle Bräsig.--"H'm," replied Fred, shrugging his shoulders, "how am I to know? She says nothing. I don't know what's the matter with her. She always used to notice me--courteously, but perhaps rather stiffly--and ever since that stupid mistake of Mary Möller about the farm-book, she has never even looked at me. Mary went long ago, I'm happy to say, for she was really growing very foolish, and Mrs. von Rambow is now her own housekeeper. I must confess that she keeps everything in splendid order, though she takes no notice of me. Caroline Kegel says she only works so hard to prevent herself thinking, that she often writes long letters and then tears them up again, lets her hands fall in her lap and sits still watching the baby sadly. Caroline says that it goes to her heart to see her. Mrs. von Rambow manages the housekeeping very quietly; she never scolds or rushes about; she only desires that a thing should be done, and she's obeyed at once. Caroline Kegel wishes she had a friend to speak to--I'm no longer to be called that--and the squire has no friend either."--"That's enough for me," cried Mrs. Nüssler, starting to her feet, "I'll go and see her tomorrow. And as for you, Joseph, I think you ought to go to that poor misguided young fellow and bring him to hear reason. In times like these neighbours should stand by one another."--"Ah, mother, what can I do? And then there's our own scrape about the geese. But Godfrey and Lina ....."--"True, true," cried Mrs. Nüssler, "the von Rambows helped to set them up in life, and we ought never to forget that."--"But," interposed Bräsig with a sly roguish look, "Mr. von Rambow has a friend! What would Mr. Samuel Pomuchelskopp say if he had heard what you said a minute ago?"--"Pomuchelskopp?" asked Fred. "We have nothing more to do with him," he added contemptuously; then bending towards Bräsig, he whispered: "He has demanded his money, principal and interest. I heard it from Zebedee, Moses' coachman Zebedee. So you see that there's no longer any friendship between the two. Slus'uhr either comes or writes daily, but we have also engaged a lawyer to help us, Mr. Rein. Do you know him?"--"Yes," whispered Bräsig, "I know him through the North-pole and the Faroe islands."--"Isn't he a very clever fellow?"--"Certainly. He can lead most people by the nose. But," he said aloud, "what is your master going to do about the labourers?"--"I'll tell you," answered Fred, "we've both determined to defend ourselves to the death, and so I had to go to Rahnstädt and buy these pistols."--"And if the labourers come back?"--"Then we'll shoot," said Fred.--"Right," said Bräsig taking up one of the pistols and playing with it carelessly, "but, Mrs. Nüssler," he went on, "you've made it quite wet and perhaps it'll rust." Then he proceeded to rub it up on the outside with the skirt of his coat, and while Fred explained the use and management of the other to Joseph Nüssler, he took it to the window as if to examine it better. "Where's your tool-box, Joseph?" he asked. Mr. Nüssler pointed to a cupboard with his foot. Fred heard a great knocking and hammering going on behind him and then a sharp sound as if something had cracked. When he turned round to look what it was, Bräsig held the pistol out to him, but without its dog head which he had just succeeded in twisting off with a pair of pincers. "There!"--"Confound it," cried Fred, jumping up. "Now," said Bräsig, "there's no fear of your shooting in the people's faces."--"How dared you destroy my pistols. Sir?"--"Because you're a foolish boy, and children oughtn't to play with fire-arms."--"You're an old ...."--"'Ass.' I suppose that was what you were going to say, and perhaps I am an ass for interfering with you; but, Sir, I am here in your aunt's stead, and I did what I did for her sake."--"My master told me to buy the pistols and I always do as he desires me."--"That's right. Here's the one for your master. Let him shoot with it if he likes. He has shot before now--

but you ...." and suddenly thinking of Hawermann, he continued: "Wretched boy, hav'n't you done mischief enough already?"--Mrs. Nüssler exclaimed: "Hush, Bräsig. Not a word on *that* subject. But, Triddelfitz, you ought to be ashamed of yourself for talking so lightly of taking human life."--"What?" cried Joseph, springing to his feet, "he wasn't going to have shot at the people? Was he, mother?" Bolster was also affected by the excitement, and expressed his horror by giving utterance to one or two sharp barks, and Fred was so much confused by what he heard, that, forgetting all his former courtesy, he snatched up his waterproof, thrust the remaining pistol into his pocket and rushed away, only turning when he had reached the door to say with great emphasis that ten horses should never drag him over that threshold again. "It isn't at all necessary," replied Bräsig calmly. But if he had heard what Fred was muttering as he went along the road towards Pümpelhagen gazing blankly at his broken pistol, he might not have taken things so quietly. For Fred bestowed so many titles of honour on him that those of the emperor of Austria were few in comparison.

Fortunately he did not hear, and he thought and cared little that Fred should have put the Nüssler's house under the ban. That very morning he had seen how easily even old friendships are dissolved in troublous times, and he had promised solemnly, that under no circumstances whatsoever should he lead the Rahnstädt civic guard to Rexow. His quick temper often carried him further than he intended, but his good heart always conquered in the end. He wanted joy and peace to be everywhere, although his way of trying to bring them about often caused noise and strife instead.

In the dusk of evening when Joseph and Bolster were sleeping by the fire-side, uncle Bräsig thought there could not be a better time for him to say a few words about Rudolph and Mina, so he began: "Mrs. Nüssler, do you remember the saying: Long love, makes old love, and long ...."--"Have done with your stupid old proverbs, Bräsig. They don't suit either you or me. I know what you're going to say, and I agree with you that things can't go on much longer as they are, but what's to become of him and me?"--"Mrs. Nüssler, you mean young Joseph ...."--"Hush, Bräsig. Name no names I beg of you. If it were only him," pointing to Joseph, "you might do so as much as you liked, but he," pointing to Bolster, "is sharper than all of us put together, so take care what you say before him. Just look how he's pricking his ears."--"H'm!" said Bräsig, peering under Joseph's arm chair, "so he is, but that doesn't matter. Well, Mrs. Nüssler, this business must come to a happy end."--"Yes, Bräsig, that's just what I tell myself every day. But tell me, what's to become of me, and what's to become of him?" here she pointed at Joseph once more. "If Mina and Rudolph are to have the management of everything, what am I to do? and what is he to do?"--"Why,

Mrs. Nüssler, you will have rest and quiet, and can rejoice in the happy life of your posterity."--"That's all very well, Bräsig, and I know that people can get used to anything, can even get used to idleness. But look at me. You see how stout I am in spite of my active life, and you know that if I were to sit still and do nothing, I'd grow so fat and unwieldy that I'd become a perfect monster."--"No, no, Mrs. Nüssler," replied uncle Bräsig, rising and standing before her, his heart full of the memory of their youth, "you have always been beautiful, and you will be beautiful as long as you live," and he bent over her and seized her hand. "Don't be silly," said Mrs. Nüssler, drawing away her hand, "just look at the old dog, he understands all that's going on. But it do'sn't so much matter about me, as about *him*. What's to become of him? I can always find something to do, but he--what sort of life will he have when he has no work?"--"He'll smoke and sleep," answered Bräsig. "Ah," she said, "he can do so now. But he is changed, very much changed lately. I won't speak of the silly affair of the geese, for I'll be able to talk him out of that, I know,--but he has grown so contradictious, and opposes everything that's done; when he has nothing to do I'm sure he'll get into some frightful scrape."--"*Joseph?*" cried Bräsig in amazement. "Yes, but it's no use going on now. Look!" On turning round, Bräsig saw Bolster get up and rub his tail twice under Joseph's nose, whereupon Mr. Nüssler stretched himself and asked in a very wakeful voice: "What o'clock is it, mother?" Then he stretched himself again, and becoming aware of Bräsig's presence, said: "What a clever fellow Mr. von Rambow is to have made another speech."

Rudolph came in, lights were brought, and Bräsig made a grimace at Rudolph across the table. He did not mean the young man any harm, he only intended to say: "Hold your tongue and trust in me. Your affair is progressing favourably." The evening passed very slowly, for each of the party was busied with his own thoughts, and when they all went to bed, Bräsig was the only one who fell asleep at once. Rudolph was thinking of Mina, and his marriage; Mrs. Nüssler, of the terribly idle life that lay before her; and Joseph, of the geese and Mr. von Rambow's speech. This last thought kept him from sleeping all night, and when Mrs. Nüssler turned on the other side towards morning in hopes of getting a little nap, she saw Joseph leaving the room fully dressed with Bolster at his heels. She could not make it out. The devil might know what he was about, she did not.

CHAPTER VII

Young Joseph walked up and down the yard followed by Bolster. He often stood still during his walk and rubbed his forehead as if he did not know what to do next. Whenever he did so, Bolster also stood still, wagged his tail, and then immediately lost himself in sad consideration of the divided sovereignty that lay before him, Rudolph came out: "Why father," he said, "up already!"--"Yes, Rudolph, and it's all because of the geese;" he was going to have said something more, but the words did not come to him, and Rudolph exclaimed: "Don't bother your head about that, father, it's an old story now; but I'm very glad you're up, for you can give the overseer his orders, and I'll go and see how the field's getting on that I was at yesterday on the Pümpelhagen march. We must do the same as yesterday, cart manure to the potato land."--"Yes, Rudolph but ...."-"That's all you've to do, father; now I must be off," and he hastened away. Joseph resumed his walk up and down the yard till at last Kalsow, the overseer came to him: "Kalsow," said Joseph, "send all the workpeople here to me," and having given this order he went into the house accompanied by Bolster. The labourers, labourer's wives, and work-people crowded into the court and asked each other: "What are we to do?"--"I don't know," answered Kalsow, the overseer. "Ah then, just go and ask him, will you?"--Kalsow went into the parlour where he found young Joseph pacing up and down, followed by Bolster, for as Joseph had not taken off his cap. Bolster thought his company was required. "The villagers are all here, sir," said Kalsow.--"Good," replied young Joseph. "What are we to do now?" asked Kalsow.--"Wait," said Joseph.--Kalsow then went out and told the people, so they waited. In a short time he returned to his master: "They're waiting, sir," he said.--"Good," answered Joseph, "tell them to wait a little longer, for I'm going to make them a speech." Kalsow went out again and desired the people to wait, adding that Mr. Nüssler was going to make them a speech. They waited for a long time, but nothing came of it, and at last Christian the coachman, said: "I know him Kalsow. Go back and wake him up." So Kalsow went in again and asked: "Well, sir, how about the speech?"--"Confound you!" stormed Joseph, "do you think that my thoughts are growing on my back ready to be plucked when I want them." The overseer retired and said to the people: "It was of no use, it only made the master angry, so we must wait."--"Goodness gracious me!" cried Mrs. Nüssler, when she had finished tidying up the larder, "what's the meaning of this? Why are the people all standing in front of the house doing nothing?" and opening the window, she called out: "What are you doing there?"--"We're only waiting, mistress."--"What are you waiting for?"--"We don't know mistress, but the master's going to make us a speech."--"*Who?*" asked Mrs. Nüssler. "The master," said Kalsow. "What did you say he was going to make?"--"A speech," said Kalsow.--"A nice state of affairs this!" muttered Mrs. Nüssler as she slammed down the window. Then hastening to her husband, she seized him by the arm, and shook him as if she wanted to bring him back to his senses: "What are you going to do? You're going to make a speech? What sort of a speech are you going to make? Is it to be about me? or about Rudolph and Mina?"--"Mother," said Joseph firmly, "it's to be about the geese."--"May God have mercy upon you," said Mrs. Nüssler angrily, "if you ever dare to speak to me about the geese again."--"What?" cried Joseph, rising in open rebellion against his wife for the first time. "Mayn't I make a speech? Everyone does it; Mr. von Rambow does it; Bräsig speaks in the Reform-club, and you don't think me good enough to follow their example." Then striking the table with his fist: "I am *master* here, woman, and will speak about my own geese if I choose!" Mrs. Nüssler turned very pale, and stared at Joseph silently. After waiting a minute, she pressed one hand over her heart, and groped for the door handle, which having found she turned slowly, and then left the room backwards, her eyes still fixed on Joseph--in like manner as a lion tamer treats a wild beast which has defied his authority. As soon as she was safely out in the passage, she threw herself down on a bench and began to cry. Ah yes, the year 1848 was a terrible time. Lawful government was no longer held of any account, and open rebellion was the order of the day.

Bräsig came down stairs whistling merrily, but stopped short when he caught sight of his old sweetheart weeping bitterly. "As sure as your nose is in the middle of your face, tell me what's the matter? What makes you cry at *this* time of day, Mrs. Nüssler? it's only half past six." So saying he threw himself on the bench beside her, and tried to pull the apron away from her face, but she signed to him to let her alone. "Mrs. Nüssler," he exclaimed, "for God's sake tell me what has happened." After a long time she managed to ejaculate: "Joseph."--"Good God!" cried Bräsig. "He was quite well yesterday. Is he dead?"--"Dead? not he!" she exclaimed, throwing down her apron and showing her red eyes, "but he has gone quite mad!"--"God have mercy upon me!" cried Bräsig, springing to his feet, "what's he about?"--"He's going to make a speech."--"What? Young Joseph? A speech? that's a very bad sign!"--"Oh me, me!" groaned Mrs. Nüssler. "The labourers are all waiting for him to begin, and he almost turned me out of the room, indeed I hardly know how I got out."--"Well, I never thought of such a thing in my wildest conjecturation!" exclaimed Bräsig. "But keep your mind easy, Mrs. Nüssler, I'm not afraid, I'll venture into the parlour." And he immediately went away.

Joseph was walking up and down the room, and rubbing his forehead every now and then. Bräsig seated himself on a chair near the door and followed his every movement with his eyes, but did not say a word, and Bolster sat at the opposite side of the room silently watching his master. It was an anxious moment, at least to Joseph and Bräsig; Bolster took the state of affairs pretty quietly upon the whole. At last Bräsig asked very gently: "How are you, Joseph?"--"I don't know," answered Joseph, "I have rather a buzzing in my head, and my thoughts are jumping about as if some one had poured a bushel of wild oats into my brain."--"I believe you, Joseph, I believe you," said Bräsig, still watching him as he went up and down the room. At length Joseph suddenly stopped and exclaimed indignantly: "Who the devil can make up a speech when you two are staring like that?"--"Oh you're going to make a speech, are you? What's it to be about?"--"Am I worse than any other man Bräsig? Are my labourers worse than other people's labourers? In these bad times they must be pleased like the workmen on other estates, but I'm not good at it, it's too hard a task for me; you are quicker-witted than I, so please make the speech for me."--"Why not?" said Bräsig, "if it will really be a relief to you. But now don't disturb me." And Bräsig in his turn began to pace the room while Joseph sat down and watched him. Suddenly the bailiff opened the window and shouted: "Come here, all of you!" and the labourers did as they were desired. "Fellow citizens!" began Bräsig; but--bang--he shut the window, exclaiming: "Hang it! That won't do at all, these people are labourers, so one can't call them 'fellow-citizens.' Now you see Joseph what a difficult thing it is to make a speech, and yet you wanted to meddle with a thing that even I cannot manage."--"Ah, Bräsig, but ...."--"Hold your tongue, Joseph, I know what you're going to say." He then went to the window, opened it, and said: "You can all go back to your work now, there won't be any speech to day."--"All right," said Kalsow, "but the master ...."--"Has thought better of it," interrupted Bräsig, "he thinks that spring is rather too early in the year for such a thing, but he hopes to make you a stunning good speech in autumn after the harvest is secured."--"Very well," answered Kalsow, "perhaps that'll be the best time for it. Come away then," and so he and the labourers all went back to their work.

Now that the coast was clear, Bräsig turned to Joseph, addressed him with all the dignity he could command, and used all the influence he had gained over him in the course of many years: "How? You were said to be mad! You are no more mad than either Bolster or I; you are only *stupid*. What ever induced your dear--I mean to say--late--I mean to say--confounded parents to bring you into the world? Was it that you might make speeches and distress your good wife who has tended you for five and twenty years as anxiously and carefully as if you had been a little new born child? Come away at once, and beg her pardon, and promise that you'll never do it again." Joseph was quite willing to do as he was bid, but he was saved going out in search of his wife by Mrs. Nüssler coming into the parlour: "Josy, Josy," she said, "how very miserable you have made me!"--"Ah mother ...."--"Josy you'll bring me with sorrow to the grave!"--"And that with confoundedly imposing language," interposed Bräsig.--"Mother, I won't ...."--"Ah Joseph, I don't believe you'll ever give it up now that you've once begun." But Joseph assured her that he had had enough of it. "God grant that it maybe so," said Mrs. Nüssler, "and that you may see that I also can give way, Rudolph may marry to-morrow if you like."--"Ah," said Bräsig, "that's good, there's peace in the house again, and you'd better seal it with a kiss--now another, Joseph, that the left side of your mouth mayn't have short measure."

As soon as that was settled, uncle Bräsig made the best of his way to Gürlitz to visit his little god-child, and tell her of her happy prospects. He went by the short cut, by the very foot-path in which Muchel had put up the fence alleging that it belonged to him, but Godfrey had been egged on by Bräsig to go to law about it, and having won his suit, the fence was now cleared away and the road was once more open to the public.

When Bräsig was going along this path who should meet him but the squire of Gürlitz, who on seeing him put on a friendly smile, and said, as soon as he got near enough to speak: "Good morning my dear ...." He could not finish his sentence, for Bräsig thus accosted him, without vouchsafing to look at him: "A certain person, who shall be nameless, threatened to pull off my boots here, and to leave me to hop home with bare feet like a crow," having said this he walked on without once looking back.

After he had told Mina what had brought him to Gürlitz and had rejoiced at the sight of her happiness, Lina asked him to remain with them, though as it was Saturday, Godfrey must write his sermon instead of enjoying his society. He answered: "No, no, Mrs. Lina, everyone has his work to do in the world, and if parson Godfrey has to write a sermon, why shouldn't I have one to preach also? I must go to the Reform-club to-night." And having said good-bye, he returned to Rahnstädt.

CHAPTER VIII

When Bräsig had told Hawermann and Mrs. Behrens all the news he had picked up at Rexow and Gürlitz, and had answered all their questions, he rose to go away again: "Don't be angry with me, Mrs. Behrens, or you either, Charles, but you see I must go to the club as soon as I have put on another pair of boots. You should come with me, Charles. We're going to choose a new president this evening, for the old one, as he himself confesses, is quite lost amongst us, I'm going to vote for lawyer Rein.--Do you know him? He's a nice fellow, and a man of the world; besides that I must say he's a bit of a wag. Then we have to decide a very important question--rector Baldrian says that it has a strong connection with the spirit of the times--I mean that we want to discover the cause of the large amount of poverty there is in the world. You should come with me, Charles." But Hawermann was not to be persuaded, so Bräsig went alone.

The first person Bräsig recognised on entering the hall of meeting was--Samuel Pomuchelskopp, who hurried forward to greet him, saying: "How d'ye do, brother! How are you, Zachariah?" Only a few people saw the expression of Bräsig's face when the squire of Gürlitz thus addressed him, and of those who saw, hardly anyone understood the meaning of what he had seen; but Bank the shoemaker told me about it: "Fritz," he said, "his face looked for all the world as if it had been reflected in a shoemaker's-ball. His mouth was as large again as it is by nature, his nose was twice as thick as usual and his face was glowing like a furnace. Can't you imagine what he looked like when he answered: 'Mr. Samuel Pomuchelskopp we are not on sufficiently intimate terms for you to address me so familiarly.' Well, he looked exactly like the picture of old Hofer, landlord of the Sands in the Tyrol, which is hanging on the coffee room wall of Fuchs' inn at Ivenack, except that he hadn't a musket in his hand. Then he turned his back upon Mr. Pomuchelskopp, and what a back! went to the election table and gave his vote in a loud clear voice that could be heard all over the hall, saying: 'I vote for Mr. Rein (pure) for our cause and actions must be pure, and if a scoundrel should chance to come in amongst us, he must be turned out' No one understood what he referred to, but there was a dead silence, for everyone knew that something had happened. When he went back to his seat everyone made way for him, because he looked like a bull ready to toss whoever opposed him, but he sat down quietly in his place, and every member of the club knows all that went on afterwards."--That was what Jack Bank told me, and I believe that he told the truth, for he was a great friend of mine and an honourable man although he was only a shoemaker. He was murdered by a ruffian while still a comparatively young man when he was standing up for the right. I mention this fact although it has nothing to do with my story, because he was my friend, and because I don't wish his virtues to be known only from the epitaph on his grave stone.

So Zachariah Bräsig seated himself in an out of the way corner of the hall looking like a thunder storm that might burst at any moment. Mr. Rein was elected president, so he rang the bell, crept into the vat or pulpit, thanked the members of the club for having done him the honour of electing him as their president and then added: "Gentlemen, before we enter on the question of the evening regarding the origin of poverty, allow me to mention that Mr. Pomuchelskopp of Gürlitz has applied for admission as member of this Reform club. I believe that no one has any reason to oppose his being admitted as one of us."--"Ah," cried a voice behind him sharply, "are you so sure of that? I beg to be allowed to speak," and when the new president turned round he saw uncle Bräsig standing beside the pulpit. "Let Mr. Bailiff Bräsig say what he has to say," answered the president, so uncle Bräsig clambered into the pulpit and began: "Fellow-citizens, how long is it since we swore to maintain liberty, equality, and fraternity in this hall, which used to be Grammelin's dancing saloon? I will say nothing just now about liberty, although I have no room to move in this confounded barrel; of equality I will also say nothing, for our new president shows us a good example in that respect by always wearing a grey coat, instead of going about in a blue surtout with brass buttons like some people; but it is of fraternity that I am going to speak. Fellow-citizens, let me ask if it is brotherly conduct for a man to threaten to have his neighbour's boots pulled off, and to leave his fellow man to hop home barefoot through the snow, and if there should be no snow, through the mud? Is it brotherly to be proud of saying such things? and of making a fool of another? I ask you if that is brotherly conduct? and I tell you that Mr. Samuel Pomuchelskopp is a brother after that fashion. I will say no more." He descended the pulpit and blew a long trumpet blast of defiance upon his nose. Wimmersdorf the tailor was the next to speak, he said that it was a great honour to the Rahnstädt Reform club that it was now to number a large landowner amongst its members; as far as he knew Mr. Pomuchelskopp was the only squire in their ranks, for Mr. von Zanzel was not to be counted although he had an estate and was a member of the club, as he neither bought anything in Rahnstädt nor had anything made there. He therefore voted for Mr. Pomuchelskopp's admission. "Bravo!"

was shouted by many voices. "Wimmersdorf is right. You're right lad. How can we expect to live if we don't uphold such people?"--"I don't agree with you," said Schulz the carpenter letting his head appear above the edge of the pulpit by slow degrees, like that of a fat old snail out of a shell which has become rather a tight fit. "That's all nonsense, Wimmersdorf, great nonsense. If the Gürlitz potentate had ever troubled himself about us before, if he had paid his bills at once it would have been all very well, but he needs us now. If he were outvoted, would he go out modestly? I tell you no! And why? Because he is a great Mogul. Away with him, I say, away with him!" Then the snail crept back into its shell, but its speech had had a great effect. "Out with him! Out with him!" cried several voices, while others shouted: "Go on! Begin again from the beginning!" and a mischievous journeyman shoemaker sang in a loud clear voice:

"Little snail, pray don't be shy
Point your four-fold horns on high!"

But Schulz was much too wise to show himself again, he knew that he might only weaken the decided effect his speech had made if he said any more, so he took his stand by Bräsig at the back of the pulpit and joined him in shouting: "Out, out!" They would certainly have gained the day if the devil had not sent David and Slus'uhr to take their places in the speaker's pulpit, where they now made their appearance their upper lips adorned with moustachios to show their liberal principles. These two then proceeded to sing Pomuchelskopp's praises as though to the music of a psaltery and fiddle. Slus'uhr called the squire of Gürlitz: "An angel of charity."--"Yes, a fine solid angel!" cried the witty journeyman shoemaker--he had helped many a poor man in Rahnstädt (Slus'uhr did not think it necessary to mention that his friend had charged ten per cent interest for these little loans) and he was willing to do even more than that for the town. David sang a song to the same tune, but perhaps his eulogies were even more highly coloured and spiced than those of the attorney: "Gentlemen!" he began, making at the same time a peculiarly low bow to the witty shoemaker as if to ask him to be silent and let him go on: "Gentlemen, consider, only consider the weal of the whole town. Look here, per primo, there's Mr. Pomuchelskopp in person, and then there's Mrs. Pomuchelskopp--a horribly clever woman she is too!--then there are Miss Sally and Miss Mally, Mr. Gustavus, Mr. Anthony and Mr. Philip; then come Miss Mary, Miss Sophie and Miss Milly and the little Masters Christian and Josy, and last of all there's the baby. Wait a bit, I hav'n't done yet--then there are the housemaids, cooks and nursery maids, and the wenches who attend to the pigs--now who else is there?--then come the coachman, the grooms and the cowherd--there's something else he needs? Why shouldn't he need something? Every one does! You all require coats and trousers, shoes and boots, stockings, shirts and night shirts. In cold weather you must have warm coats, and in warm weather, light coats. Then on Palm Sunday when you are confirmed you must have good coats, and at Christmas likewise. Ah yes, have I not always said that this Christ you worship must have been a great man? How busy everyone is at Christmas time! We fill our shops and keep all sorts of beautiful things. Who buys them from us? Mr. Pomuchelskopp to be sure! I'll say no more." And indeed it was not necessary for him to say more, for no sooner had he finished his speech than all the shoemakers and tailors began in thought to make shoes and boots for the little Pomuchelskopps, and to sew trousers and coats for them, while the shopkeepers imagined themselves doing a large business with Muchel, and Kurz went so far as to sell him half the contents of his shop--in thought.

But in spite of all this Bräsig and Schulz cried out the more: "Out! out!"--To which others replied: "No, remain!"--"Out! out!"--"Remain!"--At last there was a frightful uproar. The material interests of Rahnstädt in the shape of Pomuchelskopp's boots, trousers, &c. opposed the ideal of fraternity; it was a hard battle.--At last the president's bell produced a lull, and Mr. Rein began: "Gentlemen!" he said--"Out! out!"--"No, stay!"--"Gentlemen," he said once more, "God be thanked!"--"Out! out!"--"Stay!"--"Thank God, the opinion of this assembly has already been so clearly expressed that we may at once proceed to voting. So: Let all who wish to admit Mr. Pomuchelskopp into our club go to the musician's platform, and let the rest go to the other side."--The members of the Rahnstädt Reform-club were now all in motion. They stamped their feet as hard as they could on the floor as they walked, in order to show how firmly their minds were made up. It sounded in the distance as if Grammelin had set a fuller's mill to work on his premises, the consequences of which act would soon be seen, for Grammelin rushed in and exclaimed: "Mr. President, my lads, I entreat you to choose another way, a quieter way of voting!"--"What!" cried Thiel, the cabinetmaker. "We *must* vote or this wouldn't be a Reform-club."--"That's quite true, Thiel, but your voting is bringing down the plaster of my ceiling."--They all saw that it was true and so they agreed to Grammelin's request to vote with their hands instead of their feet.

The votes were counted and Pomuchelskopp was admitted to be a member of the Rahnstädt Reform-club,--Schulz, the carpenter, turned to Bräsig: "Ah, Mr. Bräsig," he said, "if things go on like this, what's to become of Germany?"--"I don't care," said Bräsig, "but don't let anyone talk to me of fraternity."

Then the question of the origin of poverty was brought forward. The president put the subject clearly before the meeting thus: "When did poverty first show itself in the world, and why does it still exist?"--Rector Baldrian was the first speaker. He mounted the pulpit from behind like everyone else, and as soon as he had taken his place, he leant forward and took a large bundle of books from his head pupil that he might the better prove the truth of his statements. When he had arranged before him on the ledge, the Bible, Xenophon, Plato, Aristotle, Livy, Tacitus, and as many volumes of Cicero as he happened to possess, he made a bow, and said that these books were an army of authorities he had brought to help him.--"Ah, lad," said John Bank to Deichert, the shoemaker, "it'll be slow work now, I know the man, let's each send for another glass of beer before he begins."--The rector now showed from the testimony of the Bible that poverty was known to the Jews of old.--"That isn't true!" cried a hoarse voice from amongst the crowd behind the speaker, "these cursed Jews have all the money. *They* know what a poor fellow feels?"--The rector paid no attention to this interruption, he showed all that could be learnt from the Bible on the subject, then taking up Xenophon he explained the condition of the Spartan Helots, but his audience did not seem to understand a word of what he was saying. After that he took up Plato, opened it at the part about the Republic, and added in all good faith that if the Rahnstädters had what Plato had imagined for the Athenians on these evenings, then every Rahnstädt labourer would have roast-beef and potatoes every day for dinner, and would be able to drive in a carriage every Sunday afternoon, and the children would have gold chains instead of ribbons to tie round their necks.--"He ought to tell us more plainly how we can have all that?" said some. "Hurrah for Plato, hurrah!" cried a number of voices.--"I say, lad, does he mean the old Jew Platow who can only see out of one eye?"--"Ah, lad, I used to know him well, he has often cut up a bit of beef in my shop," said Krüger, the butcher.--The president's bell rang and produced silence, then that rascal Mr. Rein turned to the rector, and begged him in the name of the assembly to be so kind as to give the Rahnstädt Reform-club a clear description of Plato's Republic. That was a terrible request! The perspiration stood in large drops on the poor rector's forehead as he three times began to explain the nature of that ideal Republic, and as often broke down, because his own ideas regarding it were not of the clearest. At last he said that Plato's Republic was a republic, and that he was sure all of his politically educated hearers knew what a republic was. As everyone was agreed on that point, the rector went on to speak about the Romans, and told his audience as a very curious fact that the Romans had now and then suffered from starvation, and had then shouted at the tops of their voices for "panem et circenses." "Now, my dear hearers," he continued, "you must know that 'panem' signifies 'bread,' and 'circenses' 'public games'."--At this moment Deichert, the shoemaker, sprang upon his bench, in spite of the efforts Jack Bank made to drag him back by the coat tails, and exclaimed: "The old Romans weren't such fools after all, and what they did we Rahnstädters can do any day. Why as things are now if I and Bökel, Jürendten and others were to play a game at vang-toon when we are sitting together at Pfeifer's, the mayor would have our cards taken away from us, and we should have to appear in the town hall with Daddy Pfeifer and pay a fine and costs! Why, I say again like the old Romans: Let's have free public games."--"You're right there, lad," cried Jürendt, "three cheers for the old Romans and Mr. Baldrian."--"Hurrah! hurrah!" and once more "Hurrah!" was shouted.--The rector bowed his thanks both for himself and the Romans, and as he saw how often the president glanced at the clock, he soon brought his speech to a conclusion. "My honoured hearers," he said, "when we consider the poverty at present amongst ourselves, we find that it is only the children of poor people and of journeymen who are obliged to go about our town begging." He then came down from the pulpit with his army of authorities under his arm.

He was succeeded by John "For my part".--"Gentlemen," he said, "for my part, I am a dyer," here he stretched both hands out over the edges of the "vat" to show how blue they were dyed by his work, "I was in Mr. Baldrian's school when I was a boy, and I say that he's right, we must have a republic. You may choose Plato's if you like, for my part, or any other; but what the rector says of the journeymen is a sin and a shame; I mean the journeymen, for my part, and not the rector. Gentlemen, I, for my part, have travelled to other lands in my calling as a journeyman dyer."--"You sat quietly at home with your mother," cried a voice.--"What's that you say? I went as far as Birnbaum in Poland, and even further; for my part, onward was my motto, as far as the blue sky extends and an honest dyer in blue can get work," here he beat upon his breast. "And gentlemen," he went on, "I could, for my part, have two men under me; but I can't manage it, for indigo is too dear."--"Ah, you rogue!" cried Deichert, the shoemaker, "you use logwood."--"I think, for my part, that you're talking nonsense," replied John.--"What indigo?" exclaimed a number of voices, "he dyes with logwood!"--"Yes," cried the wit, "anyone can tell the women who get their things dyed by him in a moment, they all have a washed out look, for that wretched logwood comes off so dreadfully."--"Young man," asked John with a grand air, "have you ever examined my tubs?"--"You should hold your tongue when people speak of poverty. You're a rich man," cried another.--"For my part, gentlemen, I think that's all bosh. It's true that I've built myself a new house ...."--"Of logwood," cried the shoemaker.--"Of logwood," shouted a dozen voices.--"No," cried the dyer, "of pine, with oaken posts."--"Of logwood!" was shouted again by the assembly.--"For my part, gentlemen," exclaimed the dyer beating his breast with his blue hand and drawing himself up to his full height, "I'm a Rahnstädt citizen and that's all that I've got to say."--"And it's quite enough," cried a number of voices.--"Then you're a very good thing," said some of the labourers, "down with the slow coach, we know all that he has to say." So John "For my part" had to come down from the speaker's desk.

Kurz was the next to address the meeting: "Fellow citizens," he said, "we came here to talk of poverty and the honourable gentleman who spoke last told us about indigo instead. It's enough to bring down a judgment upon him! How can we tradesmen be expected to pay our taxes when every dyer imports his own indigo. Now the honourable gentleman who spoke last does this in order that no one may guess how much logwood he adds to the tub of indigo! He takes care to keep his trumps out of sight."--"You always peep at the cards," cried some one behind him; he stared Bräsig full in the face, and then went on as if nothing had been said to interrupt him: "If he chose he might buy his indigo from me at a much lower price than he can get it in Rostock. But, gentlemen, our subject is poverty. If matters remain as they are we shall soon all be poor."--"He's right there, lad," said Deichert to Jack Bank.--"Fellow citizens," continued Kurz, "I bought myself a carriage and horses to send about the country side with my wares, for I must neglect no possible mode of turning an honest penny in these hard times."--"These small profits don't seem likely to come any more," said Fred Sievert, the driver.--"But," Kurz went on, "they took possession of my carriage last year at Tetterow."--"Because you didn't pay the tax," interrupted Fred Sievert.--Kurz cared nothing for such a small matter as an interruption, for he had once been turned out of the meeting and had come back again at another time, so he went on: "The mayor sent for me and asked me, what van I employed to carry my wares.--'My own van,' I answered.--'Then you do it per se,' he said.--'No,' I said, 'not per sea; Rahnstädt isn't a sea port town; per van.'--'Oh, I was talking Latin,' he said with a laugh."--"Fellow citizens, what is the world coming to when our judges begin to talk Latin? When our horses and carriages are put under arrest? That's the way to become poor! How are we trades-people to carry on business when we make such very small profits on coffee, sugar, tobacco and snuff as we now do?"--"You'd better hold your tongue about your confounded snuff," interposed Deichert, "it gave me such a swelled nose," and he covered his nose with his hand, but did not make much by that action, for everyone laughed when they saw that it stretched out beyond his hand both to the right and left.--"Fellow citizens," said Kurz, "I know very well that poverty must exist, but I think it ought to be kept within reasonable bounds. I mean, it should never be more than each man can deal with by himself without becoming a burden on his neighbours. But is that possible in the present sad condition of our town? Fellow citizens, I have been struggling for many years past to put an end to certain unjust privileges in the possession of which some people are revelling through the favouritism of the authorities."--"I say, lad," said Thiel, the cabinetmaker, to Jürendt, "you'll see that he's going to speak about the town jail, and if he does, he'd better get out of that, for Wredow, the baker, is my brother-in-law."--And sure enough he was right!--"Fellow citizens," cried Kurz, "I mean the town jail; that un ....."--"Down with him!" shouted Thiel, the cabinet-maker.--"Yes, down with him!" was echoed throughout the hall.--"We won't listen to anything about jails or pails," cried a number of voices.--"He won't allow anyone to make a small profit except himself," said Fred Sievert.--"He wants to have everything for himself, and the town jail into the bargain."--The president rang the bell in the most inhuman manner, while Kurz gesticulated wildly, and shouted: "Fellow citizens ...."--"What's all this row 'fellow citizen'?" said Thiel and Deichert while dragging the unfortunate shopkeeper out of the pulpit by the tails of his coat. He soon disappeared into the hollow of the "vat", but his two hands were long to be seen grasping the sides of it convulsively, reminding one of a pot of soup boiling on the kitchen fire, in which the fat bubbles up with a sound like "town jail--jail--jail," then all was silent and Kurz fell almost fainting into Bräsig's arms. Bräsig and Schulz took him out of the room between them.--"Hold your foolish tongue," said uncle Bräsig shoving Kurz into the room next to that in which the meeting was held, "do you want to be turned out in good earnest?"--Then the two old fellows placed themselves on guard, one on each side of Kurz, like the two men in the "willen Manns-Gulden" who watch a rampant lion lest he should suddenly spring upon the people. The only difference was that Bräsig and Schulz acted more wisely than the wild men in having each a long pipe instead of a whip in their hands.

Meanwhile Fred Sievert had shown that the poverty they were suffering from was caused by their having to pay so much for keeping up the roads, and had proposed that the road tax should be done away with. Wimmersdorf the tailor had then given it as his opinion that something must be done for the poor, and had thought that, at that moment, the only feasible plan was to write on the door of the Grand Duke's castle it Rahnstädt that it was "national property." If the castle were sold and the money that it brought were distributed amongst the poor, he considered that there would be no more pauperism in Rahnstädt. This motion was carried unanimously, and seven men were sent to the castle armed with Grammelin's stable lantern and a bit of chalk to see about putting the plan into execution.

"Christian," said a voice behind Mr. Pomuchelskopp, "I like this sort of thing very much. You can write too, so you must write that on our squire's front door to-morrow evening." Pomuchelskopp looked round; he thought he recognised the voice, and found himself--face to face with one of his own labourers, who had joined the Reform club before him, and who had the assurance to nod to him on catching his eye. He was very much taken aback, and did not in the least know what to do. He asked himself what card he should play, whether being 'master' was still a trump card, or whether 'fraternity' had taken its place. Something had to be done at once. He must at least bring the opinion of the meeting round to his side. So just as Bräsig and Schulz came back into the hall after having seen Kurz safe home, the president said: "Mr. Pomuchelskopp is going to make us an address." Pomuchelskopp forced his way slowly through the crowd, and as he passed them, he seized the opportunity of shaking hands with Thiel the carpenter, of giving Wimmersdorf the tailor a friendly slap on the back, and of speaking to the witty journeyman shoemaker. When he had got into the tribune, he said: "Gentlemen." Now it always makes a great impression when a man dressed in a blue surtout with brass buttons addresses a crowd of smock-frocked labourers and poorly dressed mechanics as "gentlemen," so a murmur went through the hall: "He's right!"--"He knows how to treat us!"--"Gentlemen," repeated Pomuchelskopp as soon as the murmurs had ceased, "I am not an orator, but a simple farmer. I have heard better speakers," here he bowed to rector Baldrian, John 'For my part' and Wimmersdorf, and even Fred Sievert's services were recognised by Mr. Pomuchelskopp on account of his speech about the road money, "and I have also heard worse," here he glanced towards the door out of which Kurz had been led but a short time before, "than myself, but gentlemen, I didn't come here because of your eloquent speeches, but because of the *principles* that actuate you."--"Bravo, bravo!"-- "Gentlemen I am heart and soul for liberty, heart and soul for equality, and heart and soul for fraternity. I am very grateful to you for having admitted me into your noble association." He now pulled a white handkerchief out of his pocket and placed it on the ledge by his side. "Gentlemen, you were talking about poverty. I have spent many a silent hour in thinking over that question, and have passed many a sleepless night in considering how the evil may best be remedied." He wiped the perspiration from his forehead with the handkerchief as if to impress his auditors with the deep anxiety this subject caused him. "Of course, Gentlemen," he went on, "I allude to the poverty that exists in small towns, for there is no such thing as poverty in the country."--"Oh! oh!" cried a voice behind him, "It's time for you to speak, Christian."--"Our labourers," pursued Muchel, paying no attention to the displeasure to which his last remark had given rise, although he knew who had spoken quite well, "our labourers have each a free house and garden, grazing for a cow, as well as hay and straw for its winter fodder; they have fire wood and peat; as much potato and flax land as they require, and every week they are given a measure of barley and the same quantity of rye or three shillings in money. Then there's all the thresher's corn, and the labourer's wives can make six pence a day besides if they like. Now, I ask you gentlemen, if the labourers in town are as well off as that? What can a labourer want more?"--"Nothing! nothing!" cried all the town labourers. "Gentlemen," said a journeyman carpenter named Stephen Rutschow, "I am a journeyman carpenter, and my wages in summer are ten pence a day, one penny of which I have to give back to my master. I'd much rather be one of Mr. Pomuchelskopp's labourers than what I am."--"You donkey!" cried Schulz. "You might have had plenty of work all spring, but you're too fond of lounging about."--"Silence! silence!"--"Gentlemen," continued Pomuchelskopp, "I have told you what the position of my labourers is, and will now tell you how they're treated. Any labourer may give warning at any time and go to another place. Isn't my conduct worthy of all honour? Isn't that enough?"--"Christian speak, the time has come," cried the same voice as before. "Gentlemen," said Pomuchelskopp in conclusion, "I have been induced to become a member of your noble association because of your high principles, and because of the great poverty existing in all small towns such as this. You shall see that--although I am not a rich man--I will do all that lies in my power to help you. And now, gentlemen, I ask you to help me in return, for if town and country are only true to each other, order will be maintained, and everything will be conducted to a peaceful end by this most admirable assembly. Long live the Rahnstädt Reform club!"--"Hurrah!--Hurrah!--Hurrah!" was shouted from every corner of the hall, interspersed here and there with: "Three cheers for Mr. Pomuchelskopp!" Muchel then returned to his seat bowing and smiling.

The very moment he left it, the pulpit was again filled, and Zachariah Bräsig's red face showed itself above the book board. His face did not shine down on the assembly with the peaceful radiance of the sun or moon, no, it more nearly resembled the thunderbolt that God sometimes sends down upon the world as a punishment for its sins. "Fellow citizens," he cried, looking at his fellow citizens with an expression that seemed to say that he had devoured two of them for breakfast that morning, and intended to pick out the fattest of them for supper, "Fellow citizens, if Mr. Samuel Pomuchelskopp had remained quietly in his own farm-yard at Gürlitz, I should have said nothing; if he had not spoken too familiarly to me here tonight; if he had not told a whole string of most unblushing lies in this sublime corner of our fatherland," here he thumped the "vat" to show that it was it he alluded to, "I should have said nothing."--"That's got nothing to do with it," interrupted Wimmersdorf, "that's only abuse."--"Silence! He can speak as well as anybody."--"Mr. Wimmersdorf," said Bräsig, "if you don't like my speech you may shut your ears for all *I* care, as I think you're a foolish fellow. Now you may go and have me taken up for libel if you like, I am bailiff Bräsig."--"Quite right--go on," was the cry. "Fellow citizens, I repeat that I should have said nothing, for I hold it to be very wrong of any farmer, or of any man, to speak against a master in the presence of his labourers. But when a man,"--"a great Mogul!" shouted Schulz--"places himself on the altar of fraternity in order to throw dust in the eyes of this assembly, and knowingly give them a false idea of the condition of his labourers, I *will* speak. Fellow citizens, my name is bailiff Zachariah Bräsig."--"Hear, hear."--"Mr. Samuel Pomuchelskopp has told you that there's no poverty in the country, because he has arranged everything that affects the labourers so perfectly. 'Bonus,' as our honoured president says--but, fellow citizens, these things sound very well, in like manner as with the roast beef and plums of life--they are uncommonly good to eat--but very few of us can get them. For example, take the houses. To the right of Gürlitz farm is a kind of pig sty, that is called a cottage, in which Willgans lives--is Willgans here?" Willgans was not there. "It doesn't matter. The thatch has never been mended during the last three years, so that the rain comes in in streams, and when there is a storm whilst he and his wife are out harvesting, the children may be seen paddling about in the kitchen like frogs in a pond. When he asked his master to have it mended, Mr. Pomuchelskopp said his name was Willgans (wild goose) and water was always pleasant for geese to swim in."--"Faugh! He oughtn't to have said that."--"And now with regard to the grazing and hay for a cow. Where is the field for the cow to graze in? About two miles and a half from the village, at the very edge of the estate, is a large meadow on which nothing but twitch and fir trees will grow, and the women have to go all that distance three times a day to milk the cows. That's to say, three of them have to do so, for eighteen labourers out of the whole one and twenty have lost their cattle from disease, and the three cows that remain are just like dancing masters, their figures are so slight and elegant!"--"What a great Mogul the fellow is!" cried Schulz from behind. "Out with him, out with him!"--"Silence! Let Mr. Bräsig go on."--"Yes, fellow citizens, I will go on. As for the fire wood and peat: The peat is bad, it crumbles away without giving any heat, and the fire wood is nothing but any branches and cones the children can find in the woods and bring home on their backs. And the potato and flax land? Where is it? A poor bit of ground at the outside of the estate. And who manures it? The birds manure it, and when one sees the few handfuls of potatoes that are dug in autumn, one clasps one's hands above one's head and exclaims: 'Great God! And that's what's to feed the people and the pigs all winter!' But they can't live on it, they steal what more they require. They don't steal from Mr. Pomuchelskopp; they know better than to do that; but they steal from the neighbours, and a friend of mine, Mrs. Nüssler, has given orders that if any of the Gürlitz labourers are caught stealing from her potato-stores, they are to be let off, for they're starving."--"Hurrah for Mrs. Nüssler!" cried John Bank. "Hurrah!" was shouted throughout the hall, and again, "hurrah!"--"And the flax," pursued Bräsig, "is only so long," showing about a foot's length on his arm, "indeed Attorney Slus'uhr, who is a particular friend of Mr. Pomuchelskopp, said jestingly in my presence, that the Gürlitz women all wear short chemises because the staple of the flax is too short to make long cloth."--"What a wretch the fellow is, to make a joke about other folk's misery," cried Schulz, "Out with him, out with him!"--"Fellow citizens," continued Bräsig, "I tell you that the houses, cow's grass, fire wood and peat, potato and flax land are the roast beef and plums of the labourers in the country; they are pleasant things, but are not to be had, that's the reason of the poverty in country districts. What is the cause of poverty in towns? I will tell you, fellow-citizens, for I have lived in Rahnstädt long enough to have observed the human nature to be seen here; *the great poverty in towns arises from the extreme pauverté to be found there?*" Having said this he descended the pulpit, and "Bravo!" was shouted throughout the hall. "He's right!" said some. "Long live Mr. bailiff Bräsig!" cried others. The president then closed the meeting, for he said that no one would care to speak after that last address. Everyone surrounded Bräsig, congratulated him, and shook him warmly by the hand. The only exceptions to the general rule were Pomuchelskopp and David Berger, leader of the town band; for the one had slipped away quietly, and the other had run home to collect his fellow musicians. When Bräsig got out at the inn door he found himself in the presence of seven performers on brass instruments, who stood round him in a half circle, and played: "See the conquering hero comes!" in his honour, while David Berger, who had put on his spectacles, beat time with one of Grammelin's billiard cues. The Gürlitz labourers then came up to uncle Bräsig, and Rührdanz the weaver said: "Don't be afraid, Sir; you've stood by us, and we'll stand by you." And so when Bräsig was solemnly conducted through the marketplace and through all the principal streets in Rahnstädt, this small band of oppressed and saddened men followed him faithfully, for it was the first time that any one had spoken as though he understood and felt for them in their dire necessity, and the knowledge that one is not quite forsaken does more to develop and keep alive the good that is in the human heart than any admonitions however well intended.

Bräsig said a few words of farewell to his guard of honour when they all reached Mrs. Behrens' house. He said he could not ask them in, as it was a sort of parsonage, but added that he invited all present to drink a bowl of punch at Grammelin's on the following evening. The invitation was accepted with a 'hurrah,' and when Bräsig was comfortably in bed and was telling his friend Charles all the events of the evening, the musicians struck up: "High stand the laurels o'er the bed where the warrior sleeps." Meanwhile the Gürlitz labourers were walking home talking gravely and seriously as they went. "We must rebel, lads," said Rührdanz the weaver "there's no help for it, but let us act quietly and firmly, not violently; for what would the Grand Duke and Mr. Bräsig say if we were to be so ungrateful for his speech as to act like brutes instead of honest men?"

CHAPTER IX

On the afternoon of the next day, when service was over, for it was Sunday, Kurz came to see Hawermann and Bräsig. "How-d'ye-do, how-d'ye-do," he said, "I'm very much put out, for one thing after another has happened to trouble me to-day. I never knew such a set of people! They won't let one finish what one has to say. It's much pleasanter work herding swine than being a democrat! These people cheer the stupidest speeches, and give serenades during the night when everyone ought to be asleep, while they always try to silence any one who endeavours to make an important matter clear to them. And yet they call themselves a *Reform* club!"--"Listen, Mr. Kurz," said Bräsig, walking straight up to him, and making himself appear at least two inches taller than usual, "it is very unseemly of you to make any slighting remarks about the serenade which was played in my honour, and let me tell you that you would have received some very hard knocks if Mr. Schulz and I had not good-naturedly taken you under the shadow of our wings. Why? Have you never heard the good old proverb: 'You may ride your hobby to town when fashion allows it;' but as you know already, you can't career through the Reform club on your hobby the town-jail, and if you attempt to do it, you must expect that both you and it will be kicked out, for the Reform club was never meant for such doings."--"I don't care; it's nothing to me!" cried Kurz. "But other people ride on donkeys there, and yet they are made much of."--"You're a rude barbarian!" exclaimed uncle Bräsig, "you're an impenetrable fellow, and if this were not Charles Hawermann's room, I'd fling you down stairs till you had to carry your bones home in a bag."--"Hush, Bräsig, hush!" said Hawermann, getting between them, "and as for you, Kurz, you ought to be ashamed of beginning a quarrel about such nonsense."--"There was nothing but noise and quarrelling last night, and it has just been as bad today. No sooner was I awake this morning than my wife began to lecture me. She says that I'm not to go to the Reform-club any more."--"She's quite right," said Hawermann angrily, "you ought never to have gone, for your hasty temper and thoughtless words have done nothing but mischief." Then leaving Kurz, he went up to Bräsig, who was running up and down the room puffing like a grampus, and said: "He didn't mean what he said, Bräsig."--"It's all the same to me, Charles, what such a cross-grained, dunder-headed, addle-pated idiot thinks of me. Ride on a donkey forsooth! Pooh! it's nothing but small-minded jealousy."--"I never meant you," cried Kurz, beginning to walk up and down the other side of the room, "I was alluding to my brother-in-law, Baldrian, and to the dyer, and one or two other fools of the same kind. It's enough to drive one mad! First of all I had words with my wife about the Reform-club; then I had to scold the shopman for not getting up till nine, in consequence of having gone singing through the streets last night, and of having remained at an ale-house till four this morning; then I had words with the groom and the vet about my riding horse which has got influenza, and after that I had another quarrel with my wife, who says that I mustn't set up a farm of my own."--"She's quite right," interrupted Hawermann, "you'd never make anything by farming, because you know nothing about it."--"I know nothing about it, do you say? I'm thwarted everywhere. Again at dinner the stupid table-maid gave us such a long table-cloth that it reached to the floor on every side. Whilst we were at dinner a customer came, and as the shopman didn't get up quickly enough to please me, I jumped up myself, got my feet entangled in the table-cloth and so pulled the soup tureen and all the plates clattering on to the floor. Then my wife caught me by the arm and said: 'Go to bed, Kurz, you're unlucky to-day,' whenever she sees that I'm in a bad humour she tells me to go to bed! It's enough to drive anyone mad."--"Then again your wife was right, for if you had gone to bed as she told you, you wouldn't have brought your quarrelling here," said Hawermann.--"Ah," said Kurz, "have you ever spent a whole day in bed when there was nothing the matter with you, and only because it was an unlucky day for you? I'll never do it again, however my wife may entreat me to do it. It just makes one in a worse humour than before. Whenever she gets me to go to bed like that, she takes away my boots and trousers, and so I have to lie still and fret over not being able to get up when I want."--Here uncle Bräsig burst into a loud fit of laughter, and Hawermann asked: "So you came here to have it out with some one, did you?"--"Oh no," said Kurz, "I didn't mean him, I only came to ask you both to come and look at my land and tell me whether it's time for me to begin to plough."

Through Hawermann's good offices peace was soon restored and the three friends set out together to visit the field belonging to Kurz, who amused himself and his companions by his constant use of the most abstruse agricultural terms he could remember, so that Bräsig could not help asking himself, "who was riding the donkey now?"--"My field," said Kurz, "is 150 square poles, and I bought ten waggon loads of manure for it from Krüger, the butcher, most capital stuff; I intend to plant beetroot there; the manure was spread yesterday; don't you think there's enough? Just look!" and turning off the high road he led the way to a field.--"It's very badly spread," said Bräsig, "properly manured land should be as smooth as a piece of velvet," and when he had said this he began to break up a larger lump with the end of his walking stick.--"Oh, that doesn't matter," said Kurz, "something's sure to grow there all the same, for the manure is good, it cost me thirty shillings."--Next moment he came to a sudden standstill, beat the air with his hands, and gazed confusedly around him.--"Preserve the man!" cried Bräsig, "what's the matter?"--"This is some of the devil's own work!" exclaimed Kurz. "It isn't my field. The one next it is mine, and yet the confounded fellow carted the manure I had bought on to another man's land, and I was foolish enough to tell him to spread it. Thirty shillings for the manure; then the carter's wages, and the spreader's wages! It's enough to drive one mad!"--"Don't take the accident so much to heart, Kurz," said Hawermann, "your neighbour will understand how it happened, and will of course pay you for what you have expended on his land."--"Why that's the worst of it," cried Kurz, "the field belongs to Wredow, the baker, the man I've tried to turn out of his office at the jail, and he's certain to revenge himself now."--"You think yourself fit to be a farmer," said Bräsig very quietly, "and yet you lay down manure on another man's land instead of on your own."--"Isn't it enough to drive anyone mad!" cried Kurz, "but what talking can do shall be done," and having said this he hastened to the edge of the field, speared a lump of manure with the point of his stick, and flung it over on to his own ground. He knocked about the manure so vehemently that he soon lost his breath with rage and hard work, then stopping short and looking pale and exhausted, he flung away his stick and panted out: "I wash my hands of it all. Why didn't I go to bed? If I can only lay hands on that rascally carter when I go home--Oh, friends, help me--if you don't take care something dreadful will happen."--"Trust me," said Bräsig, seizing him by the collar, "I'll keep you out of mischief."--"There's no use leaving the stick there," said Hawermann going on and picking it up.

Something was hanging to the end of the stick. Kurz in his vehemence had thrust the point through something that had remained on the stick when he threw it away. Hawermann was about to knock it off, when on looking more closely at it he remained motionless with surprise. Bräsig meanwhile was too much occupied with Kurz to be able to attend to what his old friend was doing, so he now called out: "Come along, Charles. We can do nothing more here." Not getting an answer, he turned round to see what was the matter, and perceived Hawermann standing still, turning something black round and round in his hand and staring at it blankly. "Bless me, Charles, what's the matter?" asked Bräsig going towards him.--At length with a mighty effort and in a low tremulous voice, he said: "The pocket-book! The pocket-book! This is the pocket-book!" and he held out to Bräsig a piece of black waxcloth.--"Why? What pocket-book do you mean?"--"I had it in my hand once before. I've seen it for years in my sleeping and waking dreams! Look, there are the Rambow arms. And there's where the clasp was! It was folded so, and was as large as that. That's how it was folded when the three hundred pounds were in it. This is the pocket-book that Regel was to have taken to Rostock." The words fell from him interruptedly and with infinite difficulty as though he were speaking in a trance, and he looked so overcome by his surprise and excitement, that Bräsig sprang to him, and supported him in his arms. The old man clung to the bit of waxcloth as though it were his dearest possession, and would hardly allow Bräsig to look at it closely.--Kurz now came up to them. He had been too much engrossed with his own wrongs to pay any attention to what his companions were doing, and he now exclaimed: "Isn't this enough to drive one mad? My thirty shillings worth of manure is lying on Wredow the baker's field instead of on my own."--"Hang it!" cried Bräsig. "Do have done with your moans about the manure. When once you begin to talk, it's a never ceasing stream. There now, take your stick and let's go home. Come, Charles, don't take on so!"--After Hawermann had gone a few steps the colour returned to his face, and he suddenly became possessed of a restless uneasy longing to get on quickly, and a desire to ask questions. He asked Kurz from whom he had bought the manure; where the carts were loaded; what sort of man Krüger, the butcher, was; and then he again stood still, folded the pocket-book and examined the tear in the waxcloth and the seal, till Kurz forgetting his anger stared at him, lost in wonder that he should feel so little sympathy with him in his unlucky farming transaction. At last Bräsig had to explain what had happened to Kurz, at the same time adjuring him by all he held sacred to keep his knowledge of the matter to himself, "for," he said in conclusion, "you are one of those people whose tongue runs away with them."--The three then stood together on the high road and wondered how the cover of the parcel of money had got into the butcher's yard. Kurz and Bräsig agreed that it was impossible for the butcher to have had anything to do with the affair, for he was a very respectable man.--"Yes," said Hawermann, and as he spoke all the old activity, decision and quick-witedness that had marked his character, and which he had apparently lost during the time of his sorrow and suffering, seemed to have come back to him, "yes, but one of his neighbours may have thrown it over the wall, and can you tell me whether anyone besides Krüger and his family live in that house?"--"He has let the small house at the back of his own," said Kurz, "but he doesn't know what sort of people his tenants are."--"I must go and speak to the mayor," said Hawermann, and as soon as they reached the town, he went to his house. Kurz wanted to go with him, but Bräsig held him back, saying: "Neither of us has lost anything." When they parted at Kurz's door Bräsig added:

"You insulted me terribly to-day, but I forgave you your speech about the donkey. Remember this, however, if you ever say a word to anyone about Charles Hawermann's affairs, I'll twist your neck while you're alive. You old humbugging sugar-prince, you!"

Hawermann found the mayor at home, and told him of his discovery; he folded the waxcloth by the tear, and the mayor became more and more interested every moment. At last he said: "True, true! I had the pocket-book in my hand once also, when I wrote out the pass for the messenger, and the examination I had to make soon afterwards impressed the whole circumstance more clearly on my memory. If I were required to bear witness as to this pocket-book I should be obliged to confess that it is either the same that the labourer had, or else it is exactly like it. But you see, Mr. Hawermann, the evidence is very slight. Krüger certainly could have had nothing to do with the affair; he is one of the most respectable citizens in our town, and it is impossible that he could have had a hand in any roguery."--"But, I'm told that he has tenants in the house at the back of his yard."--"That's true! H'm! Wait a moment, who is it that lives there? We'll soon find out." He rang the bell, and a parlour maid came in: "Sophie," he asked, "who lives in the small house in Krüger the butcher's yard?"--"Oh, Sir, that's where widow Kählert and Schmidt, the weaver, are living," answered Sophie.--"Schmidt? Schmidt? Is that the same weaver Schmidt who is divorced from his wife?"--"Yes, Sir, and it is said that he's going to marry widow Kählert."--"Oh, ah! People say that, do they? Well, you can go now, Sophie."--When she had left the room the mayor began to walk up and down in deep thought; at last he stopped in front of Hawermann, and said: "It is certainly a very strange concatenation of circumstances; this weaver Schmidt was the husband of the woman I had up before me for examination about this very thing. You remember the woman who said she had found the Danish Double Louis d'or which she was suspected of having stolen."--Hawermann made no reply; fear and hope were contending for mastery in his breast.--The mayor rang the bell once more and Sophie came back: "Sophie," he said, "go and ask Krüger, the butcher, if he will be so good as to come and speak to me here in about a quarter of an hour."--Sophie went, and then the mayor turned to the old bailiff, and said: "Don't forget, Mr. Hawermann, that we have very little evidence to go upon as yet; but it is quite possible that by following this clue we may discover something that may lead to the truth, it is only fair to warn you, however, that I hav'n't much hope. Even though we don't arrive at any absolute certainty, it doesn't much matter, for no sensible man can suspect you. I have been very sorry to see how much you have taken the baseless suspicion against you to heart. But now I must ask you to go away, the people look upon you as being personally interested in this case. Say nothing about what you know, and try to persuade Kurz and Bräsig to be silent also. Yes--let me see--send Mr. Bräsig to me at nine o'clock to-morrow morning."

Hawermann went away, and Krüger arrived almost immediately afterwards. "Well, Mr. Krüger," said the mayor, "I have sent for you to ask you some questions. Widow Kählert and Schmidt the weaver are living in the small house in your yard, are they not?"--"Yes, Mr. Mayor."--"I hear that Schmidt is going to marry Mrs. Kählert? Does the woman know that there are legal hindrances to Schmidt's marrying again?"--"Well, Sir, as to your last question, I don't know; I never trouble my head about such people; but you know that whenever there's the prospect of a wedding women folk are just like bees, they bring so much news into the house. Don't take it ill of me, Mr. Mayor, my wife isn't a whit better in that respect than her neighbours, and she told me the other day that the matter was now settled so far, that Mrs. Kählert was determined to marry the weaver, who hadn't yet consented to do as she wished. Widow Kählert had said to Mrs. Borchert that as she had cooked and washed for Schmidt for a full year, it was high time for him to propose to her, and she was sure that he would have done so long before, if it hadn't been for his divorced wife, who came in and out of the house, and tried to persuade the weaver to marry her again. If the woman ever came back, Mrs. Kählert had added, she would give her a beating and would then leave Schmidt to cook and wash for himself as best he could."--"What a foolish woman the widow must be," interrupted the mayor, "to want to marry that man. She has money of her own on which she can live, while he has nothing but his loom. That all came out at the time of the divorce you know."--"Yes, I daresay that was the case then. But you see, sir, I don't trouble my head about such things. If my tenant pays his rent punctually that's all I require of him, and Schmidt has always done so hitherto to the very day. A year ago, I think it was, he rented another small room from me, that adjoined his own, and my wife, who went into it one day with Mrs. Kählert, told me that it was beautifully furnished with a sofa and chairs and pictures on the wall."--"Then I suppose that he has a great deal of work, and gets well paid for it?" asked the mayor. "Oh, sir, he's a weaver you know! Weaving's a horrid trade for telling tales, the whole neighbourhood hears when the loom's silent, and I can bear witness that I often don't hear its music for many days together. No, no, he must have money of his own."--"I suppose that he lives on the fat of the land?"--"That he does! He has meat for dinner every day, and I say to my wife that dame Kählert wants to marry him because of his good beef and mutton."--"Now, Mr. Krüger, tell me frankly--I ask you this in confidence--do you consider Schmidt to be an honest man?"--"Yes, sir, I'm sure he is. I'm a good judge of such things. I've had tenants who would sometimes be seen standing in my yard with a splinter in their hands, but when once they were safe in their own kitchen it turned out to be a good lump of my fire wood, or perhaps when they were in the privacy of their own houses they would pull out of their pockets a pound of my beef, or some apples from my apple-tree. But he isn't one of that sort, I assure you; not a bit of him!" The mayor was a kindhearted man, and an honourable man, but on this occasion it must be confessed that he was sorry to hear the good character given to the weaver, he would much rather have heard that every one looked upon Schmidt as a rogue. It is difficult to explain why such a thing should be, but in truth there is many a dark spot in human nature, and a dark spot such as this, showing itself in an unscrupulous judge has doomed many an innocent man to unjust punishment. "Let him that judgeth take heed that he judge uprightly! God is thy Lord and thou art His servant!" That is a fine old saying, and I well remember how often my father used to repeat it to me when I was quite a little boy; but the pitiful weakness of human nature does not always attain to that, to say nothing of open wickedness which seeks its own advantage.

After the butcher had gone, the mayor paced the room considering how he could best discover the way in which the pocket-book had got into Krüger's yard. He had two weighty reasons for desiring that the matter should be completely cleared up; one of these was his deep compassion for Hawermann, and the other was the firm conviction that the bit of wax cloth that had been discovered that day was the self same piece that had been wrapped round the roll of notes. Still he could find no clue to the mystery; the only thing he had found out was that the weaver's divorced wife kept up an acquaintance with her former husband.

Meanwhile Hawermann was also walking up and down in his room hastily and restlessly. What prevented him telling his daughter and Mrs. Behrens all his hopes and expectations? It was because he feared to make them hope lest they should afterwards be disappointed. His own anxiety was enough for him to bear. Bräsig sat still in an arm-chair, and turned his head with every change of movement made by his friend. He watched Hawermann with much the same intensity as Bolster had watched young Joseph when he had put on his cap in the house. "Charles," he said at last, "I am very glad of this for your sake. You've grown quite active again and I'm sure that that activity will do you good. But you ought to engage a lawyer. I advise you to choose Mr. Rein, he's a clever fellow, and knows how to turn and twist about in spite of his height. You'll never be able to manage the affair alone Charles; but he'll help you, and if you like I'll bring the matter before the Reform club, and then your fellow-citizens will be able to help you to our rights."--"For heaven's sake, Bräsig, do nothing of the kind! How can you think of publishing such thing? I am only afraid lest Kurz should speak of it."--"Kurz? No, Charles, don't trouble your head about him, he'll not talk about it to-day at least, for I've been to see him and have lectured him until he can neither hear nor see, and to-morrow he's in for a sore throat, and so won't be able to speak."--"What do you mean, Bräsig? Kurz in for a sore throat?" cried Hawermann laughing in spite of his anxiety. "What are you talking about?"--"Don't laugh, Charles. You must know that his riding horse has inflorenza, and the vet has ordered that the old beast was to be separated from the others for fear of infecting them. Kurz is amusing himself just now by purring over the sick horse in his wadded dressing gown and then going to see how the other horses are getting on. So he's certain to infect the whole stable, for nothing carries infection so well as cotton wool--indeed wadding is looked upon as the best known absorbant of infection--you'll see that he'll catch the disease himself and will have a sore throat to-morrow. The Glanders is infectious, so why not inflorenza?"

Hawermann spent a very restless night; but though he had not slept he felt strong and capable of exertion next morning, for a ray of hope had pierced through the night of his sorrow and had gilded the future with its brightness. He could not remain in the house; the four walls seemed to impede his breathing; he must have more room for his restlessness to expend itself, and long before Bräsig went to the town hall at nine o'clock in pursuance of the orders he had received from the mayor, Hawermann was walking along the quiet path-way through the green spring fields. And what a beautiful spring it was! It seemed as though the heavens were saying to the earth: "Hope on!" and as though the earth repeated the message to man: "Hope on!" The old bailiff hearing the good tidings told him by the fresh green leaves and the joyous songs of the birds, cried aloud: "Hope on!"

The Heavens did not always keep their word to the earth, for the last year had been a year of scarcity; nor did the earth always keep her promise to man, for the last year had been one of misery; would she be as good as her word to the old man now? He could not tell; but he put faith in the message he had received. He walked on and on, right through Gürlitz. He was now going along the very footpath down which he and Frank had walked together on that Palm Sunday when his daughter was confirmed. He knew that it was on that day that Frank's heart had first wakened to thoughts of love--the young man had written to him lately, he often wrote to him--and now a bitter feeling rose in his heart that so much innocent happiness should have been destroyed by the ignorance and unrighteousness of others. He turned into another path to the right that led to Rexow, that he might not be obliged to go through the Pümpelhagen garden. He saw a girl coming towards him with a child in her arms, who, when she came close to him, stopped short, and exclaimed: "Good gracious, Mr. Hawermann, is it really you. I hav'n't seen you for such a long time."--"How d'ye do, Sophia," said Hawermann, looking at the child, "how are you getting on?"--"Oh, Sir, very badly. Christian Däsel did something that angered the squire. You see he was determined to marry me whether Mr. von Rambow allowed it or not, and so he was turned away and I was to have gone too, but my mistress wouldn't part with me. Well do you want to get down? Run then," she said to the child who was kicking and struggling to get out of her arms. "I have always to take the little one out at this hour," Sophia went on, "because my mistress is busy with the housekeeping, and the child used to get restless." Hawermann watched the little girl. She was plucking flowers by the side of the path, at last she came up to him, and said: "There--man," at the same time giving him a daisy. And immediately he remembered that other daisy which a child--his own child--had given him long years ago. He took the little girl in his arms and kissed her, and she stroked his white hair murmuring "ah--ah." Then he put her down again, and said as he turned to go: "You'd better go straight home, Sophie Degel, it's going to rain." As he walked on a spring shower began to fall in slow drops upon the earth, and his heart rejoiced in it, as much as the tender shoots of grass. What had become of his feeling of hatred?

When Hawermann reached his sister's house, Mrs. Nüssler hastened to meet him as fast as her stoutness would allow: "Charles," she exclaimed. "Bless me, Charles! Here you are at last! How much more cheerful you look, and so well too! What has happened, brother Charles? Anything good?"--"Yes, dear, yes, but I'll tell you afterwards. Where's Joseph?"--"Joseph? Good gracious, that's a difficult question to answer. No one knows where he is. Now-a-days he comes and goes like a bird upon a branch. Ever since it was settled that Rudolph and Mina are to be married next week, on Friday--of course you'll come to the wedding?--he has had no rest either day or night. He sometimes goes out to see how the farm's getting on, sometimes he goes to find out that the spring sowing's all right, or perhaps he walks about the fields and comes in late in the evening quite worn out. It really seems as if he were trying to get through all the work in the last eight days before the marriage, that he had neglected to do during the whole five and twenty years in which he has idled away his time."--"Ah, well, leave him alone, there's no harm in that."--"That's just what I say, but Rudolph is angry with him for poking his nose into everything."--"Things will soon right themselves, never fear. Are all your people quiet?"--"Oh yes, and if Joseph hadn't wanted to make a speech about the geese, we should hardly have known that there was such a thing as disaffection in the neighbourhood, but from what I hear matters look badly at Gürlitz and Pümpelhagen."--"At

Pümpelhagen too?"--"Yes, indeed. Neither of them confesses it; he doesn't say so, nor does she; but everyone knows that there may be an explosion there any day. He is terribly in debt, and the labourers want their wages, which he has allowed to mount up I suppose. The wisest thing he could do would be to get you to go back to him as bailiff."--"Pshaw! That last is nonsense."--"I said so too. I told Mrs. von Rambow that you could never go back there."--"What?" asked Hawermann quickly, "have you been to see her lately?"--"Yes, didn't Bräsig tell you that we intended to go?"--"He said that you spoke of going, but I didn't know that you had really gone."--"You see, Charles, this was the way of it. Triddelfitz brought all kinds of firearms here, which he told us he was going to use against the people, so I said to Joseph that we ought to go and see Mr. and Mrs. von Rambow. They had rather held aloof from us before, and so we needn't have gone; but, Charles, these are hard times. I wouldn't give much for neighbours who won't do each other a kindness in such times as these. Well we drove over to Pümpelhagen. Joseph saw the squire, and what passed between them will of course never be known to any human being.--'Joseph,' I asked, 'what did he say to you?'--'Nothing,' he answered.--'What did you say to each other?' I asked again.--'What was the good of talking much?' he said.--'What was the last thing he said to you?' I asked.--'He said good-bye,' he answered, 'but, mother,' he added, 'I'll never go there again. One either grows mad or foolish there.'"--"And how did she receive you?" asked Hawermann.--"Ah me, Charles, I believe that if she had shown what she felt, she would have thrown her arms round my neck, and would have wept tears of blood. She made me go into her morning-room and looked so kind and friendly, that I told her, that as her neighbour I felt drawn to come and see her, and ask if I could be of any use to her in the present state of affairs. She looked up in my face quietly and trustfully, and asked: 'What is your brother doing just now?' When I told her as, thank God, I could, that you were getting on pretty well, she asked after Louisa, and as I could also give a good account of her, I did so, and she looked pleased. She then told me how she managed her household, but she didn't dwell upon it as a woman in my position would have done; still I could see that she understood how to practise economy. Poor thing, necessity may have taught that. Then, Charles, I called up all my courage, rose and taking her hand in both of mine, said: She must not repulse me; no one could tell what might happen in these days; she might be in need of help some time or other--of course she had many friends, but they might be too far away to be appealed to--and I only wanted to assure her, that if ever she wanted me, I was ready to go to her, and that as I was her neighbour, I was, as Mrs. Behrens would say, 'the nearest' to her, I would do anything I could for her. Well, Charles, her eyes filled with tears. She turned her face from me to wipe them away, and when she looked at me again it was with an affectionate smile, and taking my hand she said she would thank me in the best way she knew. She then took me into another room, and lifting her little child in her arms, she held it towards me, telling it to give me a kiss. What a little darling it is, to be sure!"--"Yes," said Hawermann, "I saw the child this morning. But didn't she complain to you of anything?"--"No, Charles, not a word. She said nothing about him, or her position, and when we came home we were no wiser than when we set out; at least, I can only speak for myself, for Joseph told me nothing of what had passed between him and Mr. von Rambow, if indeed they *did* say anything to each other."--"Well, that doesn't matter, dear. All the world knows that Mr. von Rambow is in great want of money: Pomuchelskopp sent him notice to pay up the mortgage he holds on the estate on S. Anthony's day, and as the squire failed to do so, he has now entered into arrangements for going to law with him. Moses wants his money at midsummer, and he won't get it either, for it would be impossible for Mr. von Rambow to raise the money by that time, the country is in such a state. I fear the place will have to be sold to pay the creditors and that Pomuchelskopp will buy it. But if the times should change for the better, and the estate were only well managed, it might be made to weather the storm in spite of all that's come and gone. You will do what you can to help Mrs. von Rambow, and so will I. If the squire will only consent to have the farming matters put into good hands, I'll give him all my savings willingly. Still that's not enough. You might do something too, and I would speak seriously to Moses. Matters will indeed have come to a pretty pass if honest men can't beat a rogue in the long run. Pomuchelskopp thinks he has muddied the water sufficiently to enable him to land his fish."--"Ah, Charles, if he'd only take to farming properly and get you to go back there as bailiff, then ....."--"No, dear," said Hawermann decidedly, "I'll never go back there. But that doesn't matter. Thank God there's no lack of good farmers in the country, and he can easily get another bailiff. It's only possible to help him on the express condition that he puts the entire management of his property into the hands of a responsible person."--"That's all very well. We have now to provide Mina's outfit. Kurz might do more than he does for his only son, but he always croaks about poverty--and we want to settle matters out and out with Rudolph. Besides that we have to make arrangements for our own old age, and our money is mostly laid out in mortgages."--"Moses will help you to arrange that. Look here, Sis, you told the poor lady that you would help her, and I know that you really meant what you said--the time has come for you to keep your promise."--"Yes, Charles, but Joseph--what will Joseph say?"--"Oh, Joseph has obeyed you for five and twenty years, and he won't refuse to do your bidding now."--"You're right, Charles, he *must* do this.--I've always acted for the best, and now he's beginning to set himself up against me. He makes so many difficulties about everything that I can hardly manage him," and as she spoke, Mrs. Nüssler sprang from her chair, and struck the table vehemently with her clenched hand in front of her brother as if he were Joseph.--"You've succeeded in doing many a kind good action in the years that are past, Dorothea, and I'm sure that you won't fail now. God keep you, dear, and now, good-bye." He then kissed his sister and went away.

How he enjoyed that walk! The anxiety that had oppressed him the day before and early that morning had quite left him now, and his heart was full of hope. The blue sky and the green earth seemed to participate in the rest and peace that had taken up their abode in his soul, and when he reached home he smiled so cheerfully in answer to his daughter's scolding, and to Mrs. Behrens loudly expressed astonishment at his not having come in to dinner, that Zachariah Bräsig stared at him blankly, and thought: "Charles must have discovered some new piece of evidence," for he had learnt a good deal that was new to him of the nature of evidence that morning. So he began to make frightful grimaces at his friend, which Hawermann at last interpreted as signs that he should go upstairs and have a talk with him.

When they were safely in Hawermann's room, the old bailiff exclaimed excitedly: "Is there anything new Bräsig? Have they found out anything more?"--"Charles," said Bräsig, sticking a long pipe in his mouth and beginning to put on a pair of leggings, which he perhaps found rather uncomfortable, for he never wore them except on this one occasion: "do you see nothing different from usual in my appearance?"--"Yes," answered Hawermann, "these new leggings, and also that you seem to be pleased about something or other."--"Oh that's nothing. Higher up if you please!"--"Nay, then I can't tell."--"Charles," said Bräsig, standing upright before his friend, "as sure as you see me here, I've been appointed assessor in the criminal court, and shall have four pence an hour whenever I have to appear in my place there."--"Ah never mind that just now; tell me how my case is getting on." Bräsig looked his friend full in the face, winked at him solemnly and said: "I mustn't tell you, Charles, and I won't. His worship the mayor expressly forbad me to speak of what I knew to anyone in our town, or even to you, for he says it would only trouble you needlessly. We must have better evidence, he told me, before we can make out a case. The greatest secrecy is necessary the mayor says, in order to unravel this cursed mystery, and if the whole town were to know what we were about, the band of plotters would be warned to hide any remaining traces of their villainy. This much I can tell you; they've been telling no end of lies, and they're sure to go on lying, till they get themselves into such a fix, that they can't get out of it again."

There was a knock at the door. A postman came in and gave Hawermann a letter; "from Paris," he said as he went away. "Bless me, Charles, what grand acquaintances you've got," said Bräsig, "from Paris, indeed!"--"It's from Frank," answered Hawermann opening the letter hastily, and his hand trembled as he did so. He often heard from Frank, and yet a vague uneasiness always came over him when he got the letters, for he never could make up his mind whether he should tell Louisa about them. He read. The letter was full of the old friendliness and affection. Every word recalled the remembrance of earlier days, but there was not a single allusion to his love for Louisa. Frank concluded by saying that he intended to remain in Paris until midsummer, when he would go home. Hawermann told Bräsig the last bit of news, and then put the letter in his pocket. Meanwhile Bräsig had been walking up and down the room thoughtfully, and Hawermann might have heard what he was muttering to himself: "Marvellous! It's really like a sign of God's favour! The mayor can have nothing to say against this plan. Paris has nothing to do with the evidence for or against, and this is quite a private matter--Charles," he at last asked aloud, going up to Hawermann, and looking at him as he had that morning seen the mayor look at the weaver: "Tell me the truth, and the whole truth. Does your young Mr. von Rambow, I mean your old pupil, know that I know what you and Mrs. Behrens know of what passed between him and Louisa, and which no one is to know?"--"I can't tell, Bräsig...."--"All right, Charles, I see that I hav'n't expressed myself clearly. I mean, does he think like you and Mrs. Behrens that I wish him success in his love for Louisa. That's what I wanted to say, so tell me your opinion."--"Yes, Bräsig, he knows that you know about it, and that you wish him well; but what's the good of talking of it?"--"All right, Charles, I understand. But I must go now; I have invited David Berger, his trumpetting angels and all the male members of the choir to drink punch with me at Grammelin's this evening, and so I must have everything ready. Good-bye," and then he went away, but returned immediately to say: "Charles, will you tell Mrs. Behrens that I shan't come home to supper this evening. If I were to tell her about the punch she would make some spiritual remarks about the wickedness of my conduct. Don't be alarmed if I am rather late, I've got a latch key." A few minutes afterwards he once more came back to say: "What can be done, Charles, shall be done."--"I believe you," said Hawermann, for he thought of the punch, "you'll do your best." Bräsig nodded to him as much as to say that he might trust to him, and then went away.

Hawermann sat still, and taking his letter out of his pocket read it again. Who can blame him if he allowed all kinds of hopeful fancies to blossom in his heart? The warm affection that showed itself in every line of Frank's letter cheered him in the same way as the bright spring weather had done that morning, and sounded as pleasant to his ear as the happy songs the birds had sung to him during his walk. Was his hope to be again destroyed? Time would show! Ah Time, and Hope! They are often as much opposed to each other as light and darkness. What man, who after watching through a long night, ventures to admit a ray of hope into his trembling heart, and sees the first glimmer of light showing itself on the dark sky, does not long for time to pass quickly and let the sun shine out in all its glory.

CHAPTER X

Next morning when Zachariah Bräsig got up, he put both hands up to his head, and said: "You may be glad, Charles, that my headache isn't worse than it is, for otherwise who could act as assessor to-day? If I had allowed Grammelin to make the punch after his confounded receipt I should have had neither more nor less than a frightful buzzing in my head. As it was, I made the punch myself."--"I suppose," said Hawermann, "that you never missed your turn."--"Well certainly the younger ones didn't. I kept rather back. I sat beside David Berger, and--oh Charles--what that fellow can get through! I suppose it's because of his business, but he drank one glass after another without a pause! It was only quite at the end that he grew what is called sentimental, and, seizing my arm, said with tears in his eyes, that his earnings were so small in these times of political agitation, that both I and Mr. Süssmann--Kurz's shopman--would be sorry for him if we knew it. Mr. Süssmann then proposed that a fraternity ball should be got up for David Berger's benefit, that's to say, a political ball at which all classes; nobles, squires, tenant-farmers, and towns-folk should meet, shake hands and dance together, indeed they might even kiss each other if they liked for all that I care. The motion was at once carried, and next Sunday week is the day chosen for the ball. Mr. Süssmann has prepared a list, and I have secured tickets for you and me, Mrs. Behrens and Louisa."--"Bräsig! What could you have been thinking of? How can Mrs. Behrens or Louisa go to a ball, or I either, for that matter."--"You must go. It's for a noble purpose."--"You won't be able to go either Bräsig, for Mina is to be married on Friday week, and on the following Sunday, she's to go to church in state. What would my sister say if you were not to be at Rexow because of a stupid ball?"--"Of course that's a good reason for changing my mind about the ball, so good-bye for the present, Charles, I must go and see Mr. Süssmann at once about this alteration, and then I have to be at the town hall--you understand? Four pence an hour."

On leaving home Bräsig went straight to Kurz's shop, but Mr. Süssmann was not there. Kurz was fussing about, opening drawers and shutting them again with a bang. "Good morning, Kurz, where's your young gentleman?"--"I have no young gentleman. I'm master here."--"Take care, Kurz, remember that we are living in a democratic age, and that...."--"What do you mean? Take care, do you say? I think very little of democracy when it makes my shopman lie in bed till this hour of the morning and spend the night in drinking punch. Old people should be ashamed ...."--"Stop, Kurz, don't begin to make me flattering speeches again like those of last Sunday, I won't allow it because of my position in the law courts. Now good-bye, Kurz, I'm sorry for you. You've got inflorenza and ought to go to bed, you have pains in all your bones, and if you were to feel your glands you would find that you were in for a regular sore throat." He then went away, leaving Kurz in a worse humour than that in which he had found him. The latter knocked about the things in the shop, abusing everything and everybody, till at last when the shopman appeared, Mrs. Kurz came to the rescue, and carrying off her worthy husband made him go to bed, and so kept him quiet for the time being.

After this little scene Bräsig went to the town-hall, where he earned one and eight pence without any trouble to himself, for the sitting of the justices lasted five hours. When he came home dinner was over, and so he had to content himself with something that had been kept hot for him, and Mrs. Behrens grumbled about irregular hours, saying that Bräsig had not come in until two o'clock that morning, and now he wanted to have dinner at two in the afternoon. The old bailiff listened to her scolding with a broad self-satisfied grin on his face, as much as to say: if you only knew what hard work I've been doing, and how useful I've been, you would pat me and stroke me, kiss me and pet me as you've never done before. When he had finished dinner, he rose and said solemnly: "It'll all come to light, Mrs. Behrens, as his worship, the mayor, would say," and winking at Hawermann, he continued: "Bonus! as Mr. Rein says." Then going to Louisa, he took her in his arms and kissed her, saying: "Louie, dear, will you give me a sheet of your best writing paper? I want to send a small--piece of evidence let me call it--so that it may carry well, it has a long way to go." As he left the room with the sheet of paper he turned round again, and said: "As I told you before, Charles, what can be done shall be done." He came back once more to say: "I shall be at home in good time for supper, Mrs. Behrens."

He went to the post-office. The post-master was at home, but he was always at home. He had allowed himself to be confined in a regular bird-cage of a room, which he dignified by the name of an office, for the salary of twenty two pounds ten a year. When he was not occupied with any postal business, he amused himself by whistling and singing like a canary-bird. He was thus employed when Bräsig came in, and said: "Good morning, post-master. You are a man of honour, so I do not hesitate to speak to you about an affair of great delicacy. You needn't be told what it is exactly, for it is a secret, and you must promise not to breathe a word of what I am at liberty to tell you. I am going to write to Paris."--"To Paris? Confound you, what have you got to do writing to Paris?"--"To Paris," repeated Bräsig, drawing himself up.--"What the devil's the matter now! One bailiff gets a letter from Paris, and another wants to send one there. Well, I'll look and see how much the postage will cost." He looked it up in his book, and said at last: "I can't find it here. But it'll cost a pretty penny, it can't be less than sixteen pence."--"That doesn't matter. I earned one and eight pence this morning at the town-hall."--"Who are you going to write to?"--"To young Mr. Frank von Rambow."--"Do you know his address, the place where he lives?"--"Why, Paris!"--"But Paris is a large place. You must know the name of the street and the number of his house."--"God bless my soul!" cried Bräsig. "What a fuss to make about such a small matter! I don't know either."--"Can't you ask Hawermann?"--"But you see that's impossible. I don't want him to know anything about it."--"Then the only thing I can think of, is to send the letter to Dr. Ürtlingen at the Mecklenburg Embassy, perhaps he may find out where he lives."--"Of course he *must*," said Bräsig, "for the letter is one of great importance, and he's paid for doing such things. But I was going to ask, if I might write here in your house, as I don't want Hawermann to know anything about the letter?"--"Oh, certainly," replied the post-master, "come in here that my wife mayn't see you, for though properly speaking this is only a waiting room, she won't allow anyone under the rank of a count to enter it. I'm afraid that I must lock you in."--Bräsig consented, so there he sat from three in the afternoon till dusk of evening writing his letter. In the office in front of him was the post-master whistling merrily. The post-mistress tried to get into her best parlour, but all in vain did she rattle at the door, her husband had the key in his pocket, and went on whistling and singing as if he had nothing to do with it. Bräsig wrote and wrote. At last the letter was finished. He read it over and we may now see what he had written, it was as follows:

"Honoured Sir,

"A very strange thing has happened here. Kurz, the shopkeeper had the manure he bought for his own field carted to, and spread over that of Wredow, the baker, who is his rival in respect to the town jail. Hawermann found a bit of black waxcloth with the Rambow arms upon it amongst the manure, and this has been a great comfort to him, because of the suspicion resting on him of having taken part in the theft of the Louis d'ors in the year '45, especially as the mayor says that it is a piece of evidence. The mayor has just appointed me assessor, in which post I can make a little money, but at great inconvenience to myself, for I have always been accustomed to lead a very active life as farm-bailiff, and indeed I ought still to take a great deal of exercise because of my gout. I havn't to work hard, but sitting still so long makes me horribly sleepy. However there's one good thing in it, and that is, that I get to know what the mayor won't let me tell Hawermann. But as you are in Paris, and not in Rahnstädt, I can tell you as a friend, all that is going on. The thing is this. The weaver told a lie when he said he had never had any communication with his divorced wife, and that, the mayor says, is another piece of evidence. Indeed we have so many of these links in the chain of evidence, that it's enough to make even a dog howl to think that more can't be made out of them. The central point of the story is widow Kählert. Now widow Kählert is determined to marry the weaver, and has discovered that he won't have her, because his divorced wife has made up her mind to marry him again. This discovery has given rise to an evil feeling in dame Kählert's breast, which may be characterised as jealousy, and so she has let fall some new bits of evidence that the mayor tells me are both important and relevant, or as I should say, to the point. The mayor says, however, that one has to be very cautious about believing the woman, for she is so enraged that she wouldn't stick at a lie if she thought it would serve her cause. I don't know about the lies, but I'm sure that she told the truth when she said that the weaver showed her a number of Danish double Louis d'ors which he has in his possession, for Krüger, the butcher, has twice borne witness to his having them. And this morning while the weaver was giving us new evidence of his powers lying, Höppner and some other detectives were busy searching his house, where they found *nine* Danish double Louis d'ors in the secret drawer of his desk. He tried to deny all knowledge of them at first, but did not succeed in convincing any one. The former Mrs. Schmidt is also arrested as a principal actor in this affair, for the police have found in her possession a snuff box which belonged to the late Mr. Behrens, and which had always been kept under a glass case as a sort of heir loom. This theft has gained her free quarters in the jail. Dame Kählert is there too, but merely for puncto cichuriarum,[3] for in her passion she managed to insult all the members of the town-council including his worship the mayor, and myself the assessor. They all tell lies till they are black in the face, but what good does that do them? The mayor says he is morally certain that these people committed the theft, and that it will be proved that they did so some time or other. What a triumph it will be for my friend Charles Hawermann, when he is proved in his old age to be as innocent as an angel, and can go about among the people in his white hair and white robes of innocence. They will all be as much ashamed of themselves for ever having suspected him, as a poodle is, when a can of water is poured over him. I allude--respectfully of course--to Pomuchelskopp and the squire of Pümpelhagen; by the way I must tell you that these two are no longer friends, because Samuel has gone to law with the other; but I will say no more about that, for I have already given Pomuchelskopp a bit of my mind at our Reform-club, and your cousin of Pümpelhagen can't abide me. Things are going badly with him just now, as besides what I have told you, Moses has given him notice to pay up his mortgage at midsummer. He has no money and no fodder, so how is he to live? He is very ignorant. Remember, you must never let Hawermann know that I have written to you, for it is a secret. I thought you would like to know who the real rogues were, and that Charles Hawermann--God be thanked!--is not one of them. He has grown much more cheerful since the beginning of these discoveries, and can kick out now like a colt when its saddle is taken off. I look upon this as a good sign for the future. The only news I can give you of your old friends here is, that Mina and Rudolph are to be united in marriage on the Friday of next week. Mrs. Nüssler, whom you no doubt recollect as an extremely handsome young woman, is very well indeed, but has perhaps grown a little fatter than she used to be. Joseph also enjoys very good health, and is bringing up a new heir to the throne in preparation for his retiring on a pension. Your old fellow pupil, Triddelfitz, is now factotum at Pümpelhagen. Hawermann declares that he will turn out well in the end, but I say that he is a greyhound, for he went about shooting at the people, and has put Mrs. Nüssler and me under the ban because we have put a stop to that little amusement. We have got up a Reform-club at Rahnstädt. Young parson Godfrey preaches against it, but Lina knows how to calm him down. Rector Baldrian has carried the cause of the seamstresses and a man called Plato, Platow or Patow through the Reform-club; but Kurz has been turned out of it repeatedly; his four horses have all got inflorenza; the first to take the illness was his old saddle horse, and he himself will be the last, for he has begun to show symptoms of having taken the disease. Old Mrs. Behrens is still the honoured head of our house, and provides us with meat and drink and lodging, for Hawermann and I live in her house and have our daily bread there. She, as well as Hawermann, would beg to be remembered to you, but she can't send you any message as she doesn't know that I am writing. We often talk of you, for you are an ever present picture before our eyes. I think that I have nothing more to tell you--oh, I forgot--Pomuchelskopp has got himself elected member of the Reform-club; Schulz, the carpenter, is a very good fellow, he stood by me bravely on that occasion; Christian Däsel has been turned off by your cousin; and no traces of Regel have as yet been found; but Louisa Hawermann is, thank God, quite well.

"Hoping that my having written will neither trouble you nor cause you any discomfort, I have the honour to take leave of you with the greatest respect, and to give you my good wishes for your happiness as an old friend. I am,

"Your very obedient

"Zachariah Bräsig,

"formerly bailiff, now Assessor."

"Rahnstädt. May 13th, 1848."

"P.S. I think it is as well to mention that I am writing this letter in the post-mistress' sanctum, into which the post-master has locked me for the express purpose, and he has promised to tell no one of my letter. The reason for my keeping it such a secret is that I don't want Hawermann or Mrs. Behrens or Louisa to know anything about it. Louisa gave me this sheet of paper, and I think you will like to know that it was from her I got it, for I remember the days of my own youth when I had three sweethearts all at once. Louisa goes about her father, doing little things for him with all love and humility, to everyone else she is a costly pearl of humanity. When I hear from you that you would like to have another letter from me, I will write from time to time and let you know the latest news of these thievish wretches. If you happen to be in our part of the world on Sunday week, I will give you an invitation to our fraternity ball, all the seamstresses are to be asked to it.

"Z. B."

As soon as Bräsig had finished his labours, he knocked and battered at the door, and when the postmaster unlocked it and let him out, great drops of perspiration were standing on his forehead.--"Bless me!" cried the post-master, "how ghastly you look! Work that one's unused to is the hardest of all, isn't it?"--He then took the letter and put it in an envelope which he addressed to Mr. von Rambow, and after that he enclosed it in a second envelope addressed to the Mecklenburg Embassy at Paris. Bräsig paid down his sixteen pence, which turned out to be the exact price of the postage, so the letter might now go on its journey at once in the mail cart which was waiting at the door. Whilst he was putting up the letter the post-master sang: "A student of Leipzig, &c. &c.", but when Bräsig was going away he changed his song to: "A weighty despatch old Custine sendeth, to Paris quick his messenger wendeth. The Saxons and Prussians are marching fast, to bombard Mayence and I must at last, capitulate if help comes not, &c. &c."--"You may capitulate as much as you like," said Bräsig, "it's nothing to me; but mind you hold your tongue about what I told you, remember your promise." Our old friend then went home, and besides the happy feeling of having done a good action, he had the pleasant consciousness of having surmounted a great difficulty with no little skill, for he felt not a little triumphant that he had been able to bring Louisa's name into the transaction.

Now when any one goes home after having accomplished a good deed of this kind and desires to sun himself in the remembrance of it, he thinks it very hard when instead of meeting with a kind reception, he comes in for a perfect storm of reproaches and scolding. It was so with Bräsig when he entered the parlour where Mrs. Behrens and the little member were sitting. Louisa was not there. Mrs. Behrens was busy lighting the lamp, but the matches would not strike, partly because those Kurz sold were not of the best, and partly because Mrs. Behrens--perhaps from a desire to be economical--was in the habit of putting any broken or headless match back into the box, thus giving a useless match twenty times the amount of enjoyment during its short life that a good one could have. But although it may have been a very pleasant life for the match, it generally succeeded in putting the human being who was trying to strike it into a rage. "There you are at last," cried Mrs. Behrens angrily as she endeavoured to strike a match. "So you've really come home, have you?" trying a second. "You do nothing but gad about the town," another match, "but you always take care to go with your eyes shut"--two matches at once this time--"and your ears too"--another match--"and still you think you know all that's going on"--another match--"but when it comes to the point you know nothing"--three matches at once. Bräsig always treated Mrs. Behrens courteously and showed himself willing to do anything in her service, so he now took the box from her, saying: "Allow me!" a match. "How do you mean?"--a second match--"Have I offended you in any way?"--a third--"Kurz may cover himself with these things without being in danger of catching fire!"--two matches at once. "Things that ought to catch with him, don't, and what oughtn't to catch, does,"--three matches--"These beastly things must have got inflorenza too!" So saying he flung the match box on the table and taking his own box of vesuvians out of his pocket, lighted the lamp. "Bräsig," said Mrs. Behrens, as she carefully replaced all the matches that had been tried in the match-box, "I have a right to be annoyed with you. I am not curious, but when anything happens that concerns Hawermann and Louisa, I consider that as I am the nearest to them, I ought to be told. Why do you leave it to our little Anna to tell me what you ought to have told me long ago, for you knew all about it, I see in your face that you did."--"Why, what do you mean?" asked Bräsig, pretending to look unconscious; but Mrs. Behrens was too indignant to listen to him, for she thought herself badly used, so she continued: "Now don't pretend, it's of no use. I know that you know all about it, and that you've been keeping me in the dark." Then she began to cross-question the old man, and Anna helped her to the best of her ability. So the two women cast their nets round Bräsig and never let him alone, until they had got all he knew out of him, for keeping a secret was not one of his strong points. At last he exclaimed in despair: "I know no more, I assure you," but little roundabout Mrs. Behrens went up to him, and said: "I know you Bräsig. I see it in your face. I see that you *do* know something more. Out with it! What is it?"--"Why, Mrs. Behrens, it's a private matter altogether."--"That doesn't signify. Out with it!" Bräsig sidled about on his chair, looked to the right and left for help; but all in vain; he had to confess what he had done, so he said: "I wrote to Paris to tell Mr. Frank von Rambow what is going on; but Charles Hawermann must never know what I've done."--"You wrote to Paris," cried Mrs. Behrens, putting her arms akimbo, "to young Mr. von Rambow! And pray what did you write to him about? You've been writing about Louisa, I see that you have! You've told him what *I* should have been afraid even to whisper to myself, that's what you've done," and hastening to the bell, she rang violently. "Sophie," she said to the servant, "run to the post-office and ask the post-master to be so good as to give you the letter that Mr. Bräsig has just written to Paris."--"Tooteritoo!" was that instant heard under the window, and the mail cart dashed down the street, bearing Bräsig's letter straight to Paris, and Mrs. Behrens, throwing herself back in the sofa corner, ordered Sophie to return to the kitchen. I am sorry to say that as soon as the maid had left the room, Mrs. Behrens began to murmur against Providence for having allowed the Rahnstädt mail to start--for the first time she had ever known it do so--at the right hour, on that day of all others, thus insuring the safe arrival of Bräsig's nonsense in Paris. Bräsig swore that he had conducted the affair with the greatest delicacy, and that no possible harm could come of the letter. "Did you write that she wished to be remembered to him?" asked Mrs. Behrens. "No," answered Bräsig, "I only told him that she was well."--"Did you say nothing more than that about her?"--"I only said that she had given me the sheet of paper on which I had written, and that she was a costly pearl of humanity."--"That she is," interrupted Mrs. Behrens. "And then I finished the letter in a very friendly way by asking Mr. Frank to come to our fraternity ball."--"That was very stupid of you," cried Mrs. Behrens, "he'll think you mean to try and arrange a meeting between him and Louisa."--"Mrs. Behrens," said Bräsig drawing himself up, "your sentiments do you honour, but tell me, is it either stupid or wicked to try to bring two people together who have only been separated by the malice and evil-doing of others? I confess that such was my intention, and that that was the reason I wrote the letter. Hawermann couldn't do it, for he is Louisa's father and it would be unfitting for him to stir in the matter. You couldn't do it because the good people of Rahnstädt would call you all manner of pretty names if you did; indeed they have done so already. But as for me, I don't care a pin if they dub me letter carrier. I never trouble my head about such things. I've just sent off a letter to Paris, and if he, to whom I sent it, looks upon me as a man of honour and a true friend to Charles Hawermann and Louisa, I don't care whether the Rahnstädters nickname me 'go between' or not."--"Yes, Mrs. Behrens, yes," cried Anna throwing her arms round the old lady's neck, "Mr. Bräsig is right. What does Rahnstädt gossip matter? Who cares for the silly prejudices of the world as long as one can make two people happy? Frank must come, and Louisa must be happy," and then running up to Bräsig, she put her arms round his neck and kissed him in order to show how she rejoiced in what he had done, saying: "You're a dear old uncle Bräsig, that's what you are." Bräsig returned her kiss, and answered: "And you're a dear little musical girl, a sweet little lark. You must also be happy in the same way as Louisa. But stop. We mustn't count our chickens before they're hatched. We can't see our way clearly yet. The scoundrels hav'n't confessed their crime, and I know Charles Hawermann well enough to be sure that he must be quite free from suspicion before he will give his consent. That's the reason I wanted to keep the whole affair secret from him and Louisa for fear of making them uneasy. It's by God's providence that Kurz is laid up with inflorenza, otherwise he would never have held his tongue."--"Well, Bräsig," said Mrs. Behrens, "Taking it all in all, I believe that you've done right."--"Yes, hav'n't I, Mrs. Behrens, and wer'n't you only displeased with me because you wished that you had done it yourself? I'm sure that that's it, and so you shall have the honour of writing to Mr. Frank when everything is known."

Three days after this conversation when Bräsig came home he met Mrs. Behrens in the front hall. Her right hand was in a sling for she had sprained her wrist the day before by falling on the stairs leading to the cellar. He said with great seriousness and very impressively: "I'm coming down stairs again immediately, Mrs. Behrens; I've got something particular to say to you." After which, he went up to Hawermann. When he entered his friend's room he neither said: "Good day," nor anything else, but went in with a solemnity that was unusual to him, and walking right through the sitting room, went into the bed-room beyond. He got a glass of cold water and giving it to Hawermann, said: "There, Charles, drink that."--"But, why?"--"Because it'll do you good. You'll find it necessary afterwards, so it can do you no harm now."--"What's the matter, Bräsig," cried Hawermann, pushing away the water. He saw that something had happened which was of interest to him. "Well, Charles, if you won't, you won't; but prepare yourself to hear what will surprise you, prepare." He then began to walk up and down the room, and Hawermann, who had turned very pale, watched him anxiously, for he felt from Bräsig's manner that his fate was now to be decided. "Charles," asked Bräsig, standing before him, "are you ready?" Yes, he was quite ready; he rose and said entreatingly: "Tell me at once, Bräsig; I can go on bearing what I've borne so long already."--"I don't mean that," answered Bräsig, "The murder's out! The rogues have confessed, and we've got the money, part of it at least." The old man had prepared himself to hear the bad news he feared was coming bravely, the destruction of the hope he had allowed to grow in his heart during the last few days, but when a new day of joy and certainty broke for him thus suddenly, his eyes were blinded by the unaccustomed brightness, and he fell back in his chair: "Bräsig, Bräsig," he gasped, "my honest name! My Louisa's happiness!" His friend offered him the glass of water, and when he had drunk some of it, he felt better, and clasping Bräsig, who was standing before him, round the knees, asked: "Zachariah, you have not deceived me?"--"No, Charles, it's the truth, and you'll find it in the indictment. The mayor says that the wretches are to be sent to Dreibergen, but they'll have to go to Bützow for their trial."--"Bräsig," said Hawermann, rising and going to his bedroom, "leave me alone for a little, and say nothing to Louisa.--Oh, please, tell her to come to me."--"Yes, Charles," said Bräsig going to the window, and staring out as he wiped the tears from his eyes. When he went out of the room, he could see Charles on his knees beside his bed.

Louisa went upstairs to her father; Bräsig told her nothing more.

But in Mrs. Behrens' parlour the matter did not go off so silently.-- "Good gracious!" cried the good little woman, "there's Louisa gone now, and Hawermann hasn't come down yet, and as for you, Bräsig, you're never in time. The dinner will be spoilt and we have such a nice bit of fish. What was it you wanted to say to me, Bräsig?"--"Oh nothing," he answered, looking as mischievous as if the rogues he had seen that morning had infected him with their evil ways, "only Hawermann and Louisa aren't coming to dinner. So we'd better begin."--"But, Bräsig, why ar'n't they coming?"--"Because of the apron."--"The apron?"--"Yes, because it was wet."--"What apron was wet?"--"Dame Kählert's. But we must begin, Mrs. Behrens, the fish will be cold."--"Not a bit of it!" cried Mrs. Behrens, putting a couple of plates over it, and then a table napkin, and lastly her own two round little hands. She looked at Bräsig with such round frightened eyes that he could not bear to tease her any longer, and said: "It has all come out, Mrs. Behrens. They have confessed, and we've got back the greater part of the money."--"And you never told me before," she exclaimed, trotting off in search of Hawermann.--Bräsig stopped her, and bribed her to sit down quietly on the sofa, by promising to tell her the whole story from beginning to end. "Well, Mrs. Behrens," he said, "you must know that widow Kählert's evidence was the most damaging of the lot, and that it was all through her wicked jealousy that we got anything out of her at all. Jealousy is a terribly common failing in women, and it often leads to the most dreadful consequences. I'm not alluding to you remember, only to Mrs. Kählert. You see the woman had made up her mind to marry the weaver, and he wouldn't hear of it. She then came to the correct conclusion, that the reason he wouldn't marry her after all, was because of the influence of his divorced wife, and so she watched everything her rival did, and that was how when her apron--I mean widow Kählert's--was wet one day, she took it out to the hedge in the garden to dry. While she was spreading it out to dry, she saw from her hiding-place the weaver and his former wife holding a *randy-voo*--you know what that is, Mrs. Behrens."--"Now, Bräsig, I tell you that ...."--"Don't be afraid, Mrs. Behrens. They were not sitting in a ditch, but were standing up behind a row of scarlet-runners. The woman must have climbed over the hedge from the other side in order to get into the garden without going through the house. The widow was so malicious in her jealousy, that she called Mrs. Krüger, the butcher's wife, to come and see what was going on. They watched the two vanish behind the bean stalks, and then saw the woman get over the hedge, and the weaver going up the garden path, whereupon they both left their hiding-place. Mrs. Krüger swore to the truth of this. The mayor told me that if we could only get widow Kählert to begin to talk we'd soon get to know more. So I said: 'Female jealousy, your worship.'--'But how can we make use of that?' he asked.--Then I said: 'Mr. Mayor,' I said, 'I understand that sort of thing from my old experience when I had three sweethearts at once. Jealousy is a frightful thing, it knows neither mercy nor compassion. Let me see what I can do.' When dame Kählert came in again I said quietly: 'Well, if it's illegal for Schmidt to marry any other woman, there's nothing to prevent his remarrying his former wife.'--The mayor understood my lead, and answered: 'Yes, he may do that if he likes; the Consistory cannot make any objection.' The widow immediately got into a state of desperation, and shrieked out: If that was the case she would tell everything. The weaver had got some money out in the garden, for although he hadn't had a farthing in his desk that morning, yet when she looked there afterwards she found a number of double Louis d'ors. You see she had done for herself by this confession, for she had acknowledged that she had a false key to open other people's desks. So the mayor sent her off to prison. We had the three canaries safe in our hands now. When the weaver was brought before us again he lied about the way he got the money, and he lied in Mrs. Krüger's face by declaring that his wife had not been with him in the garden. Mrs. Krüger grew very angry and said, she had not only seen the creature in the garden, but she had also seen her legs as she got over the hedge--pardon me, Mrs. Behrens--that was just what she said. The weaver was ordered ten stripes on the jacket, for--God be thanked--a man can still be given a thrashing for lying in our courts of justice. The mayor put heaven and hell plainly before him, and threatened him with the disgrace of being turned out of the weavers' guild; but he wouldn't be persuaded. No sooner had he felt the first three blows, than he fell upon his knees, the sight of which horrified me so much that I had to turn away. Then he said, he would confess all, and that it wasn't he who had stolen the money, but his wife. The woman had taken the black packet out of the labourer Regel's waistcoat pocket while he was drunk, and had hidden it under some bushes in the wood, where she had left it for two years, for she was always able to help herself to a few gold pieces whenever she went to gather sticks, and these Louis d'ors she had changed by the help of some old Jewish women--and one, as you know, she tried to pass in Kurz's shop. About a year and a half ago she met the weaver, and asked him if he would marry her again, now that she was no longer poor. To prove that she was speaking the truth she made him a present of a double Louis d'or, but he would not do as she asked him, for he had meanwhile fallen in love with widow Kählert. With widow Kählert, if you please. You might give *me* widow Kählert on a salver and *I* should never think of falling in love with her. However he took the Louis d'or, and that only made him wish for another, so she kept him supplied at intervals, and thus succeeded in arousing a faint liking for her on his part, and making him give up caring for the other woman. Then she showed him her whole treasure, and they tried to hide it in different places; at last this spring they shut it up in a box and throwing the waxcloth into the butcher's yard, proceeded to bury the money in the garden. We went there with the weaver, and found two hundred and ten pounds worth of Louis d'ors amongst the potatoes. The rest they had spent on furniture, &c."--"Good gracious!" cried Mrs. Behrens, "both you and the mayor must be frightfully clever to have found out so much!"--"Of course we are, Mrs. Behrens," said uncle Bräsig calmly.--"But the woman?" asked the old lady, "she is the nearest to him, you know."--"Yes, Mrs. Behrens, that was a sublime moment when the mayor, with the small box and the money hidden away in his every day hat, confronted the woman with her former husband and called upon her to tell the truth. She lied again. The mayor then took up his hat and said: 'It doesn't matter. We've got the money.' The moment she caught sight of the box, she fell upon the weaver like a fury, and in one second, before you could look round, had torn his face with her nails, exclaiming: 'The wretch! I wanted to make him happy and now he has made me miserable!' Ah, Mrs. Behrens, love is even madder than jealousy. Mrs. Kählert would never have done that! But, Mrs. Behrens, I think that our fish must be growing cold."--"Oh, Bräsig, how can you think of such a thing just now! But I must go to Hawermann and tell him ...."--"How glad you are that he's cleared at last," said Bräsig, drawing Mrs. Behrens gently back to the sofa, "and so you shall, but not quite yet. You see I think that Hawermann wants to have a little quiet time to tell God all about it, and that Louisa is helping him, which is quite right. It's enough for her to be there, for as you know being a clergyman's wife, that our God is a jealous God, and doesn't suffer people to meddle when he is speaking to a soul that is filled with gratitude to Him. He draws back all such as would interfere, and now leads the way with human compassion as He once did with the Shining Light."--Little Mrs. Behrens gazed at him in speechless amazement. At last she murmured: "Oh, Bräsig, I've always looked upon you as a heathen, and now I see that you're a Christian."--"I know nothing about that, Mrs. Behrens. I'm sure of this, however, that what little I've been able to do in this matter has been done as an assessor and not as a Christian. But, Mrs. Behrens, our fish dinner is quite spoilt, and besides that, I'm not at all hungry. I feel as if I hadn't enough room to breathe here, so good-bye for the present, I'm going out to get a little fresh air."

CHAPTER XI

Friday, the marriage day of Rudolph and Mina, had come, and the weather was as beautiful as it ought always to be at Whitsuntide. Beside the modest farm house at Rexow Schulz the carpenter had erected a peculiar looking building by Joseph Nüssler's orders. From the outside, the building was not much of an ornament to the place, for it was made of rough planks nailed together, and was very like a common shed. But the inside of this "work of art" was very different. The walls were hung with sky-blue and yellow carpets, that is to say, one half of the room was hung with blue and the other half with yellow, and the reason of there being two colours was that there was not enough of the one to hang so large a hall, to be got in all Rahnstädt, especially when it was wanted in a hurry. There were six great beams put across to support the roof, for Schulz refused to undertake the business unless he was allowed to have the beams; indeed he declared that there ought by rights to be nine supports, the span of the roof was so great. Now the truth was that the building was much too large, and the expense of it too great for such an occasion, but Joseph knew nothing of carpentry, and Mrs. Nüssler was too busy seeing that there was sufficient for her guests to eat and drink to be able to attend to anything else; while Bräsig was far too grateful to Schulz for his support at the Reform club to overlook and curtail his plans, so that Mr. Schulz had his own way in everything, and put up the six beams without anyone saying him nay. To each of these beams Bräsig fastened Chinese lanterns, after which Christian, the coachman, bestrode the beams in buckskin breeches every day for a week while festooning them with garlands of oak leaves; he succeeded in making them look beautiful, but at the expense of his breeches which the rough wood tore to tatters. Joseph seeing this took the price of a new pair out of his red purse, for he wanted everyone to be happy on his daughter Mina's wedding day, and he knew what would please Christian. "Mother," he called to his wife, "Come and look. What else can be done now?"--"It looks very nice," she said, "but, good gracious, we must put candles in those lanterns." She was going away when a voice addressed her from the clouds, that is to say, from the clouds of oak leaves, and at the same moment a man's head showed itself amongst the foliage, and the voice went on solemnly: "That's attended to already, Mrs. Nüssler." When she looked up, she saw the jolly red face of her old lover Bräsig peering down at her through the oak leaves and tallow candles, for he had tied the candles round his neck to keep his hands free for climbing. As soon as he had finished he came down, and the three stood side by side looking at the effect of the decorations. "Really Joseph," said Bräsig, "its just like one of the fairy palaces in the thousand and one nights that I read about last winter in one of the books I got from the lending library." And Joseph answered: "Yes, Bräsig, it all depends upon circumstances. This is only to last for one night though; I'll have it taken down the day after the wedding."--"It's very strong," said the carpenter, "these six beams will last for an age, and any number of fairies can come in here as soon as they're baked and born."

Next day the fairies came, but not quite as Mr. Schulz had imagined them. They all came dressed in crinolines, that is to say in petticoats made of horse hair; not in the bells, barrels, and bee-hives, or clad in the armour of steel hoops that they delight in at the present day. Still they liked their petticoats to stick out even then, and old aunt Klein from Rostock had run a good large hoop of strong oak into her under petticoat, which had knocked against her sister's shins during the whole drive, hurting her so much that she had to hop about on one leg at the marriage. The fairies wore wreaths of real flowers in their hair, not artificial flowers bought from a milliner. Now that was a great pity, for at the end of the evening when the dancers were tired, and their eyes began to close from weariness, and their hair was somewhat dishevelled as if it had been blown about by the wind, the poor tired flowers hung their heavy heads towards the earth seeming to whisper faintly in each other's ears: "I wish it were over; nothing has ever made me long for the sweet calm night so much as this burning glare."--Now-a-days people manage better. However tired they may be, the artificial flowers they wear in their hair are as fresh and neat as at the beginning of the ball. These flowers might say: "Here we are as good as ever. The wire and thread on which we rest have kept us firm and strong, and when we have been put away in a box for a time, we shall be quite ready to begin again."--Some people say: How much prettier girls are now than they used to be! Ah well, as long as they keep their youth, health, and innocence, they may dress in oaken or steel hoops and artificial flowers for all that I care!

Joseph and Mrs. Nüssler had allowed Bräsig to invite anyone he liked, so he had asked a number of nice and pretty girls in Rahnstädt and the neighbourhood to the festivities at Rexow, and also some men. If one or two of these last had rather bowed legs, he thought it did not matter, for the shape of their legs was clearly seen, and so no one need be deluded into dancing with them. Besides the Rahnstädters, Joseph had made Rudolph invite all their mutual relations to the marriage, and they were many in number. There were cousins scattered throughout all Mecklenburg and western Pomerania. There were uncle Lewis, uncle Christian, uncle John, and cousin Bill of whom Joseph said: "He's my second cousin, and is a very amusing fellow, especially when eating and drinking are going on."--Then there were aunt Dina, aunt Stina, aunt Mina, aunt Lina, aunt Rina--and lastly there was aunt Sophie, who as Joseph said: "had been a very choice specimen of womanhood in her youth."--"That must have been a long time ago," remarked Bräsig.--One grand carriage after another drove up to the door at Rexow, and all the different members of the Nüssler clan crowded round Joseph, greeted each other heartily, and asked after each other's well-doing during the last fifteen or twenty years, for they had each lived almost entirely at home for that time, and had heard nothing of their relations, as those of them who could write, had never taken the trouble to do so.--On seeing this Bräsig whispered sarcastically to Mrs. Nüssler: "They're a very faithful and strong race, these Nüsslers! Genial and hearty too, Joseph is of another stamp from the rest in being so very thin and silent." He then went to the "temple of art" as the carpenter called it, and found Schulz sitting in wrapt contemplation of his work over a bottle of Bavarian beer: "Schulz," he said, "you've done your part, and I've done mine, but you'll see that Joseph has spoilt the whole evening with bringing such hosts of his foolish relations here, by the end of the evening they'll take themselves off like a large dish of curds."--"I've got nothing to do with it," said Mr. Schulz, "for I myself am only one of the guests; but if they're what you describe, then all I can say is: Out! out!"--Bräsig now went out into the garden and wandered up and down like a tree frog; I do not use this simile because he was wearing a green coat, for he had on his best brown coat and a yellow waistcoat; no, the reason he was like a tree frog was that he prophesied bad weather at night. Suddenly he looked over the garden hedge and saw Joseph's own "phantom" coming towards the house, driven by a labourer instead of by Christian. On closer inspection he perceived two women seated in the carriage, and on closer inspection still, he discovered that it was his own sister, Mrs. Korthals, widow of a dairy farmer, and her only daughter. They lived in a distant village in western Pomerania and were in very straitened circumstances.--"God bless me!" he exclaimed. "My sister! And that must be her daughter Lotta. This is her doing!" he cried as he rushed through the kitchen and out into the hall where he met Mrs. Nüssler, and said to her: "This is your doing, I know. Oh, you are ....."--At this moment the two women came into the entrance hall in very very simple dress, but they were both beautiful, *most* beautiful! The elder with tears of joy and gratitude rolling down her kind, honest old face; and the younger with her bright unaffected manner, her large blue eyes and golden hair. The latter came forward at once and asked: "Where is my dear good uncle Zachariah?" she had only seen him once long ago when she was a little child.--"Here, here!" he cried, drawing his sister and niece forward to where Mrs. Nüssler was standing, and adding: "There she is. Thank her for this."--When the two women had told Mrs. Nüssler how happy she had made them by bringing them to Rexow, they looked round for Bräsig, but he was gone. He had forced his way through the heavy sack-like Nüsslers like a miller who had set his mill properly to work, and then had taken refuge in the arbour in the garden, where he employed himself in blowing such loud trumpet blasts on his nose, that Schulz, the carpenter, came out of the temple of art to see whether it was the musicians who were coming.

But they did not appear until later. First of all Kurz and the rector came, each of them accompanied by his good old wife. When they had been in the parlour for some little time and had been introduced to the Nüssler family, uncle Lewis Nüssler, a thick-set, over-bearing sort of man, went up to Kurz, and said: "You may count yourself fortunate in having succeeded in arranging a marriage between your son and one of this family, for we are rich and well-to-do. Look," pointing at uncle Christian, who had just thrown himself on the sofa, "he's worth fifteen thousand pounds."--"I've got nothing to do with this," remarked uncle Christian. Kurz felt very cross, but he restrained all expression of his feelings for the time. Uncle Lewis went on to ask: "Did you ever see so many rich people in one room before?" and Kurz, who had now quite lost his temper, answered: "No, nor so many fools either!" He then turned away, and his wife, who had overheard what he had said came up to him, and whispered: "Pray, take care, Kurz. You're beginning your democratic ways here, and you'd much better go to bed." He would not do that, however, and he was shunned by all the Nüsslers for the rest of the evening.

At last parson Godfrey and Lina arrived. They were received with all honour by their parents because they were to perform the marriage ceremony. Don't let any one misunderstand me--Lina was not to take any actual open part in the ceremony, that would never have done, but she had interfered with Godfrey this once, so far as to read over and alter the address her husband was to make to the newly married couple, and she assured Godfrey that she had a perfect right to do so, as it was more a family matter than a clerical one. She maintained her right as Mina's twin sister, who cared for her so much more than any other sister could do, to know what was going to be said to her, and so Godfrey was obliged to give her her own way.

Hawermann came next, in a glass coach, accompanied by Mrs. Behrens, Louisa and Anna. Mrs. Behrens would consent to go in no other conveyance. She had once been obliged to decline an invitation to a marriage at Rexow, for she happened to be in great sorrow at the time, so she wanted to go to this wedding in greater state than she would otherwise have done. She wanted to show by their manner of going how happy they all were: "For we are all very happy to-day, ar'n't we?" she said pressing, Hawermann's, Louisa's and Anna's hands alternately. Soon after they got to Rexow, Hawermann caught sight of Bräsig's sister, whom he had known long years before, and sitting down beside her, began to talk over old times with her. Every third word they said was, "Zachariah," and Louisa and Anna took Lotta between them and told her about "uncle Bräsig."

A great harvest waggon covered with flowers and garlands of leaves now drove up to the door, driven by Christian the coachman, who on that day acted as postillion. Christian had on his new buckskin breeches, his whip had a knot of red and blue ribbons on the handle, and he himself had a wreath of roses round his hat, making it appear as if his old hat were seizing this opportunity of celebrating its golden marriage day. On the first cushion in front of the waggon was David Berger, the town musician who was playing on a clarionette: "Three jolly post boys, drinking at the Dragon" &c. &c.,[4] and behind him were the rest of the band, playing the same air but not in the same time, because sitting on the second, third and fourth cushions they were naturally somewhat behind Mr. David Berger, who was in possession of the first. Besides that Mr. Berger himself got wrong when he turned his head quickly, or when Christian wanted to hasten the horses by using his whip, for at such times he always felt something tug his back hair; and no wonder; one of the members of his band had tied the lash of Christian's whip to his hair, so that whenever the coachman twitched the whip, or when he himself moved, his hair got a good pull.

Behind this waggon, came another as large, filled with girls dressed in white, with wreaths of roses and pinks, which peeped shyly out from amongst their thick curls, as much as to show how ashamed they were of themselves for appearing to show themselves in rivalry beside the blooming faces of the young girls. These were the little fairies. And amongst the fairies sat the post-master in his new uniform, which was the only one that Rahnstädt had to boast of, and to the honour of wearing which he had only lately attained. There he sat like a chaffinch in his bright new plumage, singing his merriest songs amid a garden of flowers. This waggon was followed by a third, full of partners for the fairies, chosen from amongst the best dancers in Rahnstädt. Foremost amongst these was Kurz's assistant, Mr. Süssmann, who was amusing himself by dancing along by the side of the waggon followed by the rector's youngest pupil, a schoolboy, who footed it lightly and airily behind him.

The guests all looked supremely happy, but Mrs. Nüssler felt not a little uncomfortable, for she did not know any of the new arrivals, Bräsig has chosen them more because they could dance well, than for any other reason. She called Bräsig, but before he could come to her rescue, Christian, the coachman, had smoothed away all difficulties and had made himself master of ceremonies. He opened the kitchen door and the dining-room door, and invited all whom he had brought with him from Rahnstädt to enter: "Go in, go in," he said, "sit down quietly, and rest a bit, the other man will soon come." His advice was good, for one of the groom's men had not yet arrived, and so the marriage could not take place at once. It was Fred Triddelfitz for whom they were waiting; he had been induced by Rudolph's entreaties to take off the ban from the Nüssler's house, and to undertake the office of groom's man.

At last he came riding into the court, and then dismounting, came into the room amongst the other guests with such a stately air, bowing gracefully to the right and left as he entered, that the stupid little schoolboy whispered to Mr. Süssmann, next whom he happened to be standing: "What a pity it is that it's all settled, that fellow would have done capitally." Whereupon Mr. Süssmann looked at the boy compassionately, and then turning to Bräsig who was standing on his other side asked: "Do you know, sir, that they've chosen me to be leader of the dance at our fraternity ball, which is to be the day after to-morrow?" Bräsig was on the point of telling him that he would be a fool if he accepted the position, for Kurz would discharge him at once if he did, but at that very moment the bride and bridegroom came in.

Rudolph was a very handsome bridegroom. His usually merry smile had given place to an expression of serious gravity, and you could see in his brown eyes a firm determination to fight his wife's battles gallantly as became a good husband. Yes, he was a handsome bridegroom, and when does a man ever look better than when he enters the battle of life full of courage and hope. Who could blame his mother for going up to him and kissing him, stroking his brown curls, and secretly pulling his cuffs a little further down over his hands, that they might be better seen?

And Mina! Mina looked for all the world like a rosy apple lying on a silver plate surrounded by its green leaves as she stood there in her white satin gown and myrtle wreath. Outwardly she was calm and still, but inwardly her heart beat faster than usual, and was filled with hope and deep happiness at the thought that before Godfrey gave his address, she and Rudolph would have been married. Mrs. Nüssler wept silently and whispered to Bräsig: "I can't help it, for she is my last, my youngest." Bräsig looked at her affectionately, and said: "Courage Mrs. Nüssler, it'll soon be over." Then going to Louisa Hawermann, he made her a bow, and said: "If you are ready, Miss Hawermann, we had better take our places." On all other occasions he called her "Louie," but he was groomsman to-day and must address the bridesmaid with whom he had to stand more distantly than the girl he had known from her babyhood. Fred Triddelfitz and Anna made the other groomsman and bridesmaid. Then Kurz and the rector placed themselves one on each side of Rudolph, and young Joseph was pushed and shoved with great difficulty up to Mina, while Hawermann had already taken his place at her other side. When this was done the procession moved off to Schulz's temple of art, where they found Godfrey standing behind a white and green altar ready to begin Lina's address.

I know that people have begun to think that a marriage in a house is hardly a marriage at all, and that a church is the proper place for such things. I have nothing to say against these notions, because I myself was married in church even then; my wife being a clergyman's daughter, nothing else would have been suitable; but in one respect at least the marriage ceremony was better then, than it is now. We had nothing in our service that could make anyone feel uncomfortable. I think that it is unnecessary to read such passages as I allude to simply because they are in the Bible. If that argument were to hold good, the parsons might just as well read the Song of Solomon, for it is also in the Bible. I believe that if Christ were to come into the world again. He would have mercy on innocent children and would drive many things that are now tolerated, out of His temple. If such teaching would be most pernicious from the lips of a mother or even from those of a saintly priest, what can it be when it proceeds from a young man who has just preached his first sermon, and entered on the duties of the living to which he has been appointed, immediately after passing from the gay life of a student at one of the great universities.

Well, as I said before, the ecclesiastical court had not then appointed a certain form of address to be used at weddings, so that the old fashion still prevailed, and young people were married in the same way as their parents had been before them. Christian Schult says that the new mode had come in even then, but certainly Godfrey did not know of it, and even if he had, Lina would never have allowed him to use it. Lina was a married woman, and she would not have consented to let her husband make a laughing stock of himself in the eyes of the rich, fat, drowsy Nüssler-faction, or in those of the Rahnstädt tradesmen and school-boys. She would not have allowed her twin-sister's wedding-day to be spoilt by the orders of any consistory, although she was the most zealous parson's wife in the world, that is to say, after Mrs. Behrens, who was still 'the nearest' in all such matters.

As soon as the marriage ceremony was concluded, the twins threw themselves into each other's arms, and Rudolph embraced them both at once, while Mrs. Nüssler, who was standing a little apart, looked at them over the edge of her pocket handkerchief, and leant her head on one side, as though she were listening to something above her--perhaps it may have been to an angel's song. Then the fat, rich, drowsy Nüsslers trooped up to offer their congratulations, and young Joseph took up his stand amongst them and bowed and bowed as if he were the principal person concerned, and were being married over again: "Uncle Lewis," he said, "this is my Mina. Cousin Bill, this is our little governess! What is to be done now, aunt Sophie?" After that, the men of the Nüssler clan pressed forward in their bright coloured waistcoats, with heavy gold chains attached to their watches, and after them came the women with regular flower-pot caps, and tears dropping slowly from their eyes, thus making it appear as if the flowers had been too much watered, and so the extra amount of moisture was running out. Then the men and women of Joseph's clan kissed and embraced Rudolph and Mina as if to show them that they were ready to receive them into their rich, fat, drowsy family, thereby making Kurz furious, for they barred his way so effectually that he could not get near his new daughter-in-law, and on this occasion his wife quite agreed with him, for she could not get at her own son. The guests from Rahnstädt forced their way as near the bride and bridegroom as they could, and made their curtsies to them from behind the Nüsslers, for they could do no more. Amongst these Fred Triddelfitz and little Anna were to be seen, Fred, who had been appointed commander of the dancing forces reared his tall slight figure high above the rest, and behind him stood the rector's youngest pupil ready to carry out as well as he could with his short body and black cotton stockings, what Fred succeeded in doing with his long body and black silk stockings. He was Fred's shadow, that is to say, his noon-day shadow, which is always a short one.

Quite apart from these, four people were standing together without making any attempt to join the throng round the bride and bridegroom, for they had enough to do with themselves. These were Hawermann and his daughter, uncle Bräsig and Mrs. Behrens.--Louisa was leaning her head upon her father's shoulder and looking up in his face. She looked as if she had been long ill, and had now for the first time got out of her sick-room into the fresh clear air, and as if the blue sky were telling her to get better, get better; her father's face was so calm and happy that it might easily be likened to the sky, from which sun, moon and stars, rain and dew came to quicken and refresh her heart.--Right in front of these stood Zachariah Bräsig with his arms round little Mrs. Behrens' round waist. His eyebrows were raised as high as they would go, and he blew his nose energetically as he said: "My little Mina! My little god-child! How happy she looks!" and every time one of the fat old Nüsslers gave Mina a kiss, he bent down and kissed Mrs. Behrens, as much as to imply, that he thought this would prevent any contamination of his god-daughter by the foolish old Nüsslers with their wretched worldly notions.--"You see I did it from such and such a motive," is the excuse my servant, Lisette, whom I engaged when I came to live at Eisenach, always makes when she is found fault with about anything, and does not know what else to say. So Bräsig kissed Mrs. Behrens, and she let him do it and thought no harm, but when she saw aunt Sophie, who used to be considered a sort of Venus amongst the Nüsslers, kiss Rudolph two or three times, she was very much shocked, and when Bräsig was about to salute her again, she said: "You ought to be ashamed of yourself, Bräsig. What have I to do with you?"--Then Bräsig drew back rather crestfallen, and said: "Don't take it ill of me, Mrs. Behrens, my feelings ran away with me." After that he led Mrs. Behrens to Hawermann, and said: "Now, Charles, you ought to look after this lady. Louisa is my bridesmaid, for I'm a bachelor, and as both you and Mrs. Behrens have been married already, you'll go very well together."

Mina was holding Rudolph's hand, and as soon as she saw her oldest and dearest friends standing aside, unable to speak to her, she tried to force her way through the crowd of closely packed rich, fat, drowsy Nüssler sandbags, and through the wooden palisades formed by the serried ranks of school-boys and shopmen, and so get at her friends, but all in vain. As soon, however, as her husband saw her fruitless efforts, he placed himself in front of her, pushed aside sandbag number one, in the person of rich uncle Lewis, and sandbag number two, in that of the wit, cousin Bill; then seizing the longest post of the palisade, Fred Triddelfitz himself, he gently lifted him out of the way and placed his school-boy shadow behind him, and so having made a breech in the fortifications, he brought his new wife safely beyond the battlements to where she received warm congratulations coming from the heart instead of from flower-pots, brilliant waistcoats and heavy gold watch-chains. After Mrs. Nüssler had embraced and blessed her children, Rudolph passed his hand across his eyes, and then said: "Suppose we all go out into the garden for a little."--Schulz, the carpenter, who was standing near, heard what he said, and backed him up by exclaiming: "Quite right! Out! out! Go out all of you. We're going to lay the tables." And beginning with the Nüsslers, he set to work to clear the room.

When our party--I say *our*--were walking past the celebrated arbour, Bräsig pointed to the cherry-tree, and said: "You must always keep this tree, Mina, as a memorandum and a sign, for your future was decided through it and through me, and as we are talking of signs, Mina, just bring me one of those blue flowers, look there's a nice one." When Mina had gone to get it, uncle Bräsig asked: "Have you always remembered what I said to you before, when I sent Mina for one of those flowers?"--Rudolph said that he had, and Bräsig after looking at him scrutinizingly from head to foot, replied: "I believe you."--At this moment Mina returned with the flower, and Bräsig taking it from her, said: "Thank you, Mina. Now I'll give you my wedding present," at the same time pulling a thick old black pocketbook out of his brown coat pocket. He turned over a number of old milk and corn accounts without finding what he wanted, but at length in the last division of the pocket-book he discovered a dried flower which he took out, and said: "Look, my dear little god-daughter, this is the flower you gave me on the day of your engagement, and it is the same as this," comparing the two, "now if after long years of married life, Rudolph can give you this second flower, you will have every right to say: 'I am a happy woman.' I'll say no more, no more. And I have nothing more to give, nothing more," so saying he walked away, and our party heard him muttering: "Nothing but this memorandum. Rudolph's memorandum."--When we next saw him, he was walking about with his sister, and her daughter Lotta, and the two women were thanking and blessing him for all the loving help and brotherly kindness he had shown them for many years.

Mrs. Nüssler now came up to us, and said: "Come away, friends, everything is ready. But don't take it ill of me if I say that Joseph's relations must be treated as our principal guests, and must sit next the bride and bridegroom--for I can't hurt Joseph's feelings you know--of course Kurz and his wife must be up there too, for, as you would say, Mrs. Behrens, they are 'the nearest'. And Godfrey and Lina must be amongst them also, for it's Godfrey's right as parson, and Lina's as Mina's twin sister, and Joseph too, because he belongs to his clan. But we, that's you, Mrs. Behrens, Charles, Louisa, and you, Bräsig, will sit at the other end of the table, and I'm sure that we'll enjoy ourselves."--"*Aller bon hour!*" said Bräsig, "but where's Mr. Süssmann, I must have a little talk with him about our fraternity ball."--"Oh dear! The poor man is sitting in our back room. He and Triddelfitz were trying which could jump best over a heap of thorn branches, when he fell and split part of his clothing, so that Christian had to provide him with an old pair of blue trousers belonging to Joseph. He absolutely refuses to show his face in day light, and is hiding away until the evening, when he hopes that the unsuitableness of his dress will not be noticed."--"And that's the man who thinks he can lead the dances at our ball!" said Bräsig, as he followed the rest of our party into the hall.

The company all sat down to table in the temple of art, and Mrs. Nüssler's neat maid-servants went about in their pointed caps and white aprons--for it was not the custom in those days to hire waiters in shabby black coats, white neckcloths, and white cotton gloves, the thumbs of which somehow always get covered with gravy while the man is bringing in the roast. The fat Nüsslers eat as much as if they were possessed by a party of French commissioners of supply, such as we used to have quartered on us in 1812, and were required to provision an army for the invasion of Russia. As soon as the fricassées and other such dishes were finished, they attacked the puddings gallantly, and after they had done their duty by them, they had roast pigeons and asparagus, at the same time expressing great surprise that the pigeons in Mecklenburg were not as large as geese, and complaining of the asparagus not being as thick as hop-poles. When the roast was brought in, cousin Bill, the wit of the Nüssler clan, rose, struck his glass to enforce silence, shouted, "Hush!" three times, took up his wine glass, and said: "Let us drink to the health of old General Knoosymong (que nous aimons) who used to be a very celebrated personage, and whose fame is still great amongst, &c.," as he said this he looked at the young couple, and winked his left eye at Mina, and his right eye at Rudolph. Then uncle Lewis--don't misunderstand me; it was *rich* uncle Lewis--stood up, and said: "What a wag you are, William!" and Bräsig whispered to Mrs. Behrens, "I know that you dislike the Reform-club, but I assure you that our wit, the journeyman shoemaker, can make much better jokes than that."--Poor Mrs. Nüssler was sitting on thorns, for she was afraid lest Joseph should now begin to make a speech; but Joseph refrained from doing so; he intended to keep his speech for the benefit of the neighbourhood, and not to throw it away on the world at large, so he only said: "Give Lewis another glass of wine, Bill. Lewis, give Bill another glass of wine."--When the Bowl[5] was brought in, and the champagne, the fat old Nüsslers wishing to be polite said that they had some of the same quality in their own cellars at home, and Freddy Triddelfitz, the shopmen and school-boys drank one glass after another to pass the time. The left wing of the army of wedding guests which was composed of the dancers who had come from Rahnstädt in the waggons now became so excited that the little member of the women's council, told their commander, Fred Triddelfitz, that if he went against the enemy after that fashion he would soon have to beat a retreat, and just as he was making arrangements to prevent the necessity of such a retreat, he, and all present were startled by an unexpected disturbance.--Nay, only think how often an unconscious animal is inspired with a happy thought!--Bolster--Joseph's Bolster--our old friend Bolster, who had been adorned for the occasion by Christian with a green wreath round his neck, and another round his tail, jumped upon the white and green altar which was standing immediately behind the bride and bridegroom, and at which Godfrey and Lina had performed the ceremony. He looked at the newly married couple with his honest old autocratic face, licked Mina with his tongue and slapped Rudolph on the cheek with his tail, and then turning round licked Rudolph and slapped Mina. When he had done this, the old dog sat down on the altar with quiet dignity, and looked round the room with a satisfied air as much as to say that he was pleased with everybody, and intended to remain where he was till the end of the feast.--Suddenly Joseph sprang to his feet, exclaiming: "For shame. Bolster! Down! down!"--Uncle Bräsig jumped up, and cried: "Joseph, how dare you treat your best friend so ill on this solemn occasion!" then turning to Godfrey, he added: "Reverend Sir, let Bolster remain where he is. The dog is showing his love on a Christian altar, and he knows it, although you don't. Bolster is a wise dog. I know it as a fact, for when I was showing my love up in a cherry-tree, he showed his by lying under the bench in the arbour. Reverend Sir, Bolster may be cited as a witness to the marriage, because he was present when they engaged themselves to each other."--Godfrey grew pale with indignation when he heard such horrible sentiments, but he did not succeed in expressing his opinion, for the humming and buzzing around him had now grown deafening, as everyone had seized the opportunity of rising from table and pushing back their chairs, amid shouts of "out! out!" from Schulz, the carpenter. In the confusion that ensued the rector's youngest pupil tripped over a heap of Mrs. Nüssler's best porcelain plates, which were immediately scattered in fragments throughout the room. He stood looking at the work of destruction, and groping in his waistcoat pocket for some treasure the presence of which was unknown to himself as to others; when Mrs. Nüssler passed by and saw the broken plates, he blushed and said that he would gladly pay for the damage he had done, but he didn't happen to have enough money with him. Mrs. Nüssler smiled, patted him kindly on the shoulder, and said: "That's a good joke! But I must punish you," and taking him by the hand she led him to Bräsig's niece, Lotta, saying: "You must dance a great deal to-night to make up for my broken plates."--He paid his debt honourably by dancing his best.

    Then the ball began. First of all there was the polonaise--Fred Triddelfitz led, for Mr. Süssmann had not yet made his appearance. And where did he lead the dancers. Through the hall, through the garden, the kitchen, the entrance hall, the parlour, Mrs. Nüssler's bedroom, and back again through part of the garden to the hall, so that Joseph's fat relatives were puffing and blowing for want of breath, and Bräsig called out to ask why they had not gone through the farm-yard when Mr. Triddelfitz seemed so anxious to take them a long round. Even Joseph took part in this dance, and the only difference between him and the other men was that he had two partners instead of one, for he had aunt Sophie on one side and Bolster on the other, and he looked, when seen between aunt Sophie's flower-pot and Bolster's garlands, either like a pearl set in gold, or an ass between two bundles of hay. When the polonaise had come to an end, David Berger played a slow waltz to the tune of: "Du, du liegst mir am Herzen, Du, du liegst mir im Sinn," and in the distance another band was heard playing: "Nuse Katt hett negen Jung'n." Then, when he went on to the lines: "Du, du machst mir viel Schmerzen, Weisst ja wie gut ich dir bin," there came from the distance: "Mina den Kater, smit'n in't water," and so on, for Mrs. Nüssler had arranged that the servants and villagers should dance in the dairy. The musicians there were old Hartloff, who had only one eye, Wichmann, a carpenter, Rührdanz, the weaver, and several others. Hartloff had given each of his followers a large tumbler of beer, at the same time entreating them to do their best, and not to allow themselves to be beaten by these town musicians, who if the truth were known could not hold a candle to them, so they played their best, and Christian the coachman kept them well supplied with beer. Sometime afterwards Rudolph and Mina came into the dairy and danced, Mina with Christian, and Rudolph with the cook. The overseer cheered the bride and bridegroom, and Hartloff fiddled away so vehemently that Rührdanz and his clarionette could not possibly keep up with him, and were at last obliged to give up the attempt. When Rudolph and Mina had left them. Christian and the cook went behind the door and talked. "Well, Dolly," said Christian, "what must be, must be!"--"Why, Christian, whatever's the matter with you?"--"Ah, Dolly, you and I are engaged, and what's right for one, can't be wrong for another; we must go to them, they can't take it ill of us if we do." Then Dolly said: she felt a little shy, but if she went, she would dance with Mr. Bräsig, for she knew him. And Christian answered that he would dance with the mistress. No one thought it in the least strange, when a few minutes later, Christian took his place in the temple of art with Mrs. Nüssler as his partner, while Bräsig danced with Dolly. Such things could be done in those days, and it is a great pity that they cannot be done now--in many places, at least. Joy and sorrow ought both to bring rich and poor together. Why does the master, who on his death-bed wishes to be followed to the grave by his sorrowing dependents, not also desire to share his joy with them.

    Mina's wedding day was one of great happiness to all at Rexow, but it would be quite impossible to enter into a detailed account of everything that was done. This at least I can testify that Fred Triddelfitz remained leader of all the dances; and that Anna often blushed when she was his partner, and he generally was able to persuade her to dance with him. Between the dances Anna used to take refuge with Louisa as though she felt more comfortable when under her protection. I know that the little schoolboy missed two dances because he had involved himself in an arithmetical puzzle, as to how much his predecessor got as schoolmaster and whether he was sacristan as well. Whether he was very poor, whether he had taken a lease of the shoemaker's potato plot, which cost so much the square pole, and lastly, whether if he himself attained to such a position, rich uncle Bräsig would help him a little, so that he might marry Lotta, whose beautiful blue eyes and golden hair had captivated him. He cast one or two hasty glances at his new black dress coat for which he had already paid Kurz one third of the price on account. I know that the only unhappy man in the whole company was Mr. Süssmann, and he was only unhappy when he happened to look down and see Joseph's old worn out blue trousers.

Yes, that was a happy day, but everything comes to an end. The little fairies, shopmen, schoolboys, and dancers drove home with David Berger and the dance music. The old people had gone earlier. Then Joseph took all the men of his clan and showed them their rooms, while Mrs. Nüssler did the same for the women. Every married woman was given a comfortable bed, but the unmarried ones, with Aunt Sophie at their head, were put into the large blue room which they had to share with each other.

CHAPTER XII

On the Sunday morning after Mina's marriage, young Mrs. von Rambow went through all her housekeeping duties, saw that everything was rightly done in house and dairy, and entered various items on the debtor and the creditor sides of her account book. Having done this, she sat still, trying to master the feeling of undefined anxiety about the state of Alick's affairs that had been worrying her all morning. But she had no notion how very far on the road to ruin her husband's bad management had brought them, for even her fears did not nearly reach the point of reality. She only guessed that Alick was in great want of money from his irritability of temper, and from the restlessness which possessed him, and prevented him from sitting still for long at a time. She had no idea that this embarrassment might be the last, that the knife was already at his throat, and that an accident, or the malice of an enemy might in one moment give him the coup de grace. He had told her nothing; he had only ordered his carriage, and had gone away three days ago. Where had he gone? And to whom? These were questions she had long ceased to ask, for why should she knock at a door behind which she only found dissimulation and lies. She closed her account book with a sigh, and said to herself: "What good does it do? No woman's hand is able to avert ruin from a house." Looking out at the window she saw Fred Triddelfitz sauntering sleepily across the yard, and letting her hands fall into her lap, she murmured: "The responsibility of everything rests on that man's shoulders. It's a blessing that he's honest, and that he was taught by Hawermann.--Oh Hawermann, Hawermann!" she cried aloud, her heart full of sad regretful thoughts. Who has not, at some time in his life, spent an hour such as this, when his thoughts seem to take shape and stand round him like the ghosts of by-gone days, each pointing with a spectral finger to what has become the weak place in his heart? They neither quail nor relent, but stand before him as immovably as a rock pointing at the aching place and shouting in his ears: "You brought all this misery upon yourself by your conduct at such and such a time." But what she had done, she had done from love. That did not make the ghosts draw back--what does a ghost know of love?

While she sat there a prey to sad thoughts, Daniel Sadenwater came in, and said that Mr. Pomuchelskopp had called. "Tell him that your master isn't at home," said Frida. Daniel replied that he had already told him so, but that Mr. Pomuchelskopp had expressly begged to see Mrs. von Rambow. "Very well, I'll go and see him in a few minutes," said Frida. She would not have said that if she had not wanted to escape for the moment from the torment her thoughts caused her, for Pomuchelskopp was hateful to her, but still he was a human being, and not a grizzly phantom.

She would never have sent that message at all if she had known what she would have to endure in that interview. Pomuchelskopp had for some time past, and on that morning also, taken council with David and Slus'uhr, and they had all three at last come to the conclusion, that his best plan would be to buy the estate from Alick as soon as possible, "for," as Pomuchelskopp himself said, "if the estate comes to the hammer I shall most likely have to pay more for it, or it may slip out of my hands altogether. These aristocrats stick to one another through thick and thin, and many of them are very rich men; they'll perhaps pay his debts beforehand, or if it comes to the hammer they'll buy it back for him."--"Catch them!" said Slus'uhr. "Ah but," cried Muchel, "the best plan would be to get hold of the place at once. He's ready for plucking, I know he is. He'll never get over this scrape, for he only thinks of tiding over the unpleasantness of the moment. If I were to offer him enough money to free himself from his most pressing liabilities and leave a small sum over, he would snatch at it eagerly although he knows that it would only increase the burden of his debts in the long run."--"You forget one thing," said the attorney, "his wife is there too."--"Ah, but she knows nothing about it," answered Muchel. "And that's just as well for you. If she had known you'd never have got him so much in your power. Once--when the mystery of the stolen money was talked about--she looked at me in such a way that I shall never forget it as long as I live."--"Well," said David, "what of that? She's a woman--not a woman like Mrs. Pomuchelskopp, who's a horribly clever woman--she's a noble lady, she knows a great many things, but she knows nothing, absolutely nothing of this. If he's ready for plucking, she must be made the same." David succeeded in convincing the others that if Mrs. von Rambow were told everything, the suddenness of the blow would paralyze her and make her consent to an immediate sale of the estate, and it was settled that Pomuchelskopp should begin the attack that very morning, and that his visit should be followed by that of the two other plotters. They all knew that Alick was away from home.

When Mrs. von Rambow joined Pomuchelskopp in the drawing room, the squire of Gürlitz looked as sad and compassionate as if he had been a parson and had come to condole with her after the death of her mother.

He stretched out both hands to her as though he wanted to press her hand sympathetically between his. But as she only bowed, he contented himself with clasping his hands and gazing at her as paternally as a crocodile that is on the point of bursting into tears. He said that he had come to speak to her husband as an old friend and true-hearted neighbour. The matter was pressing, very pressing, and as the squire was not at home, he had asked to see her. It made him miserable to think that he had not been asked to help them before they determined on selling Pümpelhagen by auction. Frida started back, exclaiming: "Sell Pümpelhagen?" And now Pomuchelskopp's expression could be compared to nothing but that of a wretched mother who had accidentally overlain her child in her sleep: "God help me!" he cried. "What have I done! I thought you must have known ...."--"I know nothing," said Frida firmly, though she had turned deadly pale, and as she spoke, she gazed at the old sinner, as though she wanted to look him through and through: "I know nothing, but I wish to know all. Why is Pümpelhagen to be sold?"--"Madam," replied Muchel, speaking as though with a great effort, "the numerous debts ...."--"To whom does my husband owe money?"--"To a good many people, I believe."--"And you are one of the many, are you not?" At these words it seemed as if Pomuchelskopp raised the sluice which for years and years had dammed up all his human sympathies, that he might the more fully pour them out over Pümpelhagen. Yes, he said, he was one of the creditors; but the money he had lent, he had lent from friendly motives, and he could do without it for the present. He had only come that morning to give Mr. von Rambow the benefit of his advice as to how he could best turn and twist the matter so as to get out of his difficulties. From what he had heard, he believed it was Moses who insisted on the sale of the estate, and he thought that if the Jew's mouth could be shut for a short time, Pümpelhagen might yet be saved. When taking leave, he said with fervour, and at the same time winking hard as though to hide the tears that would come into his eyes, that if he had had any notion that Mrs. von Rambow was ignorant of what was going on, he would rather have torn out his tongue than have spoken to her about it.

If the matter had not touched her so nearly, she would have seen Pomuchelskopp's hypocrisy much more clearly, but as it was she had an instinctive distrust of the man. Her head was confused with the suddenness of the shock, and she felt as though the house which had so long sheltered her were shaking with an earthquake, and threatened to fall at any moment and bury her, her child and any happiness she had looked forward to in the future, under its ruins. She must go out, out into the fresh air. She went to the garden, and there she walked up and down in the sun, till at last she seated herself in the cool arbour and thought over what she had heard. She felt as if the trees which overshadowed her, were hers no more, and as if the very flowers which she had planted with her own hands had also passed away from her care. She was sitting on the selfsame bench on which her father-in-law had sat, when he confided his pressing difficulties to Hawermann. Hawermann had helped him then--where was Hawermann now? The same trees were now shading her, which she had first seen when Alick showed her his home so proudly. Where was that pride now? What of the home? To whom did these trees belong? She thought that she had only been sitting there for a few minutes, but she had been there for two hours. She heard footsteps on the path leading to Gürlitz Church, and was rising to go; but before she had time to move, Slus'uhr and David were standing before her.

Slus'uhr was rather taken aback when he saw himself so unexpectedly in Mrs. von Rambow's presence. He thought of how he was about to hurt and pain her. David chuckled like a monkey when an apple has suddenly fallen into its hands. Slus'uhr went up to Mrs. von Rambow respectfully, bowed low, and asked whether he could see the squire. Frida answered, that he was from home. "But we must see him," said David. Slus'uhr looked over his shoulder at David, as much as to say, how I wish you'd hold your stupid tongue; but still he repeated: "Yes, Madam, we must see him."-- "Come back on Wednesday then; Mr. von Rambow returns on Tuesday," and she began to walk away. The attorney stepped forward as if to prevent her going, and said: "It isn't so much our business as Mr. von Rambow's that brings us here to-day. Perhaps a messenger might be sent after him. It's a matter of great importance. We've heard of a purchaser for Pümpelhagen. A very safe man too, but he insists on having an answer in three days, as to whether Mr. von Rambow intends to sell by private bargain, or whether he is going to wait and let it come to the hammer at the time the mortgage is due. This gentleman is the son of Moses, the Jew whose mortgage must be paid at midsummer, and who earnestly advises the sale of the estate through me, his man of business." It is needless to say that this was a lie. The beautiful young woman stood still looking the two rogues full in the face. As soon as she had conquered her first terror, her whole soul rose in arms against her unmerited misfortunes. "Madam," said David, who had felt uncomfortably awkward when he first met her eye, and who had therefore been reduced to pull his gold watch-chain for inspiration, "consider: My father has a mortgage on the estate amounting to one thousand and fifty pound sterling--or counting the interest to twelve hundred pounds--, then there's Mr. Pomuffelskopp's twelve hundred, then the bills owing to various tradesmen in Rahnstädt, which come to four hundred and fifty pounds-- we have brought the accounts with us--besides these debts there are bills amounting to fifteen hundred pounds--or more, for all that I know--given to

Israel in Schwerin. If you were to sell now to a safe man, to sell everything, including furniture, bedding and household linen, you might have a surplus of fifteen hundred, or sixteen hundred and fifty, or even eighteen hundred pounds after paying all the liabilities. And then, you know, you might rent a house in Rahnstädt, have nothing to do, and live like a countess."

Frida made no answer, bowed coldly to the confederates, and went into the house. Nothing makes a brave strong heart arm itself with cold dignity so much as discovering the pitiful meanness of its opponents. The foot that was at first raised to crush the adder, is then drawn back, and pride, honour, and a good conscience unite in thrusting all that had roused its indignation and misery out of the heart; when that is done there is no more inward strife; peace has come instead; but it is the peace of the grave.

"There she goes looking as haughty as a princess!" said David.--"What a fool you are!" said Slus'uhr. "I'll never do business with such an idiot again."--"What's the matter now?" asked David. "Didn't we do the same when we went to dun that yeoman at Kanin, and didn't he give in soon?"-- "Yes, but he was a peasant! Are you a baby that you don't know the difference between a noble and a peasant? We wanted to tire her out and make her ready to fall into our hands at once, and instead of that, we've only made her more obstinately prejudiced against us than before. If we had treated him like that, he'd have said 'yes' to everything, but," he added more to himself than to David, "there are people--and truly--there are women even, who are only made the more firm and decided by misfortune."

When they arrived at Gürlitz and told their accomplice how Mrs. von Rambow had received them, Pomuchelskopp got into a great state of mind: "Bless me! How *could* you!" he said to David. "Whoever heard of anyone coming plump out with a thing like that? You ought to have told her the truth in such a round about way that she'd have been made wretched and anxious, instead of telling her everything plainly at once. Hang it! I'd got the affair into such good train, and now you'll see that she'll make him as obstinate as herself, and so the estate won't be sold till the term when Moses' money is due."--"And then of course you'll buy it," said Slus'uhr.--"No, no, it'll cost too much then, and yet it lies into my place so nicely!"--The worthy gentleman having made his moan, now proceeded to hold council with the two others, and they gave him very good advice as to how he should act so as to make sure of winning the game.

There was another meeting of council on the Gürlitz estate, and this time it was in the house of Rührdanz, the weaver. That morning a number of labourers and labourers' wives assembled in Rührdanz's kitchen where they talked neither passionately nor foolhardily, but thoughtfully and with deliberation, but at the same time with dangerous determination.--"What do you say, brother?" asked one.--"Nay, what can be said, but that he must go, he's a monster in human form. Well, Rührdanz, and you?"--"You're right, I quite agree with you. But, lads, you'll see that they'll bring him back to us. If we could only get papers from the government forbidding his return ...."--"Bother you and your stupid papers," cried a tall masculine looking woman who was sitting near the stove. "When you come home from Rahnstädt in the evening with your heads full of brandy, you think you'll get everything your own way, but very soon your courage melts away like the starch out of a bit of linen when you put it in the wash tub. What, I've got to send my little girls through the country side begging for food! I can tell you this, I've had no bread in the house for the last three days that hasn't been given the children out of charity."--"Things have grown a little better lately," remarked old father Brinkmann.--"Yes," answered Willgans, "but from fear, not from good will. Let's go up to the house each armed with a stout cudgel, and teach him the will of God in this matter, then let's lead him quietly over to the other side of the Gürlitz boundary, go a good bit along the road with him, and then tell him to be off."--"What?" cried Mrs. Kapphingst, "do you intend to let off that demon of a woman, his wife, who nearly beat my daughter to death because of the chicken that the hawk carried off?"--"And the two eldest daughters," said a young woman, "who plagued us out of our lives when we worked at the manor house; those girls looked like angels of mercy when they were in the parlour talking to their guests, but outside amongst us they were perfect devils, and yet you'd allow them to remain here?"--"The whole set must go," said Willgans.--"No, friends, no," remonstrated old father Brinkmann, "don't hurt the innocent little children."--"Yes," said Rührdanz's old wife, who was sitting apart from the rest peeling potatoes, "you're quite right, Brinkmann, and Gustavus must stay too, I saw him taking a quarter of potatoes to old Mrs. Schult. In measuring out the potato and flax land, he always gave a little extra, and then Willgans, he gave your eldest boy one of his old jackets. He can't do all that he would, his father looks after him too sharply for that. No, don't lift your hands against Gustavus or the little ones."--"That's just what I say, mother," answered Rührdanz. "And now, friends," he continued, "I've got something to say to you. Do everything decently and in order. The others ar'n't here just now, let us meet again this evening and talk it over. Mr. Pomuchelskopp won't be at home; John Joseph has had orders to get ready the glass coach to take them to a ball in the town, so we can meet quite easily and talk it over."--"Yes," cried the tall masculine looking woman who was sitting near the stove, "talk, talk! You all muddle your heads with brandy while we are starving. If you don't free us from those people, we'll take the matter into our own hands, and do as other women in the country have done already, a thorn bush and a bed of nettles ar'n't far off."--She then left the cottage, and the rest of the conspirators separated immediately afterwards. "Bernard," said Mrs. Rührdanz, "this may turn out an ugly business"--"That's just what I say, mother; but if we only do everything decently and in order the Grand Duke can't say anything against it. The only pity is that we have no papers to show for our actions, still, if he shows his papers, they'll see from them how the matter stands."

Rührdanz was right--I don't mean about the Grand Duke, for I don't understand such matters--but he was right in saying that Pomuchelskopp had ordered the glass coach to go to a ball, for towards evening the squire of Gürlitz might be seen seated in his carriage, dressed in his blue coat and brass buttons. By his side was his brave old wife in her yellow-brown silk gown, which reminded one both in colour and its pointed trimming of one of her own short-bread cakes, except that she was as dry and withered as a leather strap, and when she walked even on a level road, her joints rattled as much as if she had hidden a small bag of hazelnuts under her skirt. Exactly opposite were her two eldest daughters who were splendidly, very splendidly dressed, but who were also in a very bad humour because their father had insisted on their going to this ball, which was to be attended by tradesmen and their families; they had therefore determined to revenge themselves on their father by not amusing themselves, and by treating everyone as an inferior. Meanwhile they vented their wrath upon him by knocking the heavy hoops in their crinolines against his shins, and that was very cruel of them, for the wheelwright had made them new hoops that very morning of strong hazel wands.--Gustavus was seated on the box beside John Joseph the coachman.

I really cannot dance with my fair readers at another ball, I am too old for that sort of thing, and besides that Rudolph's marriage only took place three days before the fraternity ball, and I did my best on that occasion. It will be sufficient this time to peep into the ball room now and then and see how everything is going on. And now imagine me seated on the bench in front of Grammelin's house on that lovely summer evening, watching the people arrive, and going after a time into the house to have a glass of punch and thus show myself to be a friend and a brother.

There were a great many people at Grammelin's that evening. All the dignitaries in the town were there with their hats and caps and all their belongings; several landowners with Pomuchelskopp at their head; several noblemen with their sons--their wives were unfortunately prevented from coming at the last moment by bad toothache or headache, and their daughters were from home--a number of tenant farmers and small landed gentlemen came, but of our friends there were very few to be seen. There was a party at Joseph Nüssler's to accompany the bride and bridegroom to church, and Mrs. Behrens, Hawermann and Louisa had remained at Rexow, while rector Baldrian and Kurz with their wives and Bräsig had returned to Rahnstädt after dinner in order to go to the ball. Kurz, however, had to give up all thought of going to it in the end, for he had grown so cross with Joseph's relations that his beloved wife found it necessary to send him to bed, which was not only a blessing for himself, but also for Mr. Süssmann, who could now lead the dances without fear of interruption. Mr. Süssmann had had a new pair of trousers made for the occasion, and had deluged his hair with pomade.--Little Anna went with her parents and Fred Triddelfitz, who had got himself up like a country gentleman of the first rank.--The little school-boy, who was in fear and trembling lest Bräsig's niece should not come, seated himself at a rickety old piano and played and sang mournfully: "My happiness is dying, &c. &c.", and then to comfort himself: "I joy to see you little flies."--Mr. and Mrs. Baldrian arrived; then came Bräsig with Schulz, the carpenter; and Slus'uhr and David arrived together. David had put on two more gold rings than usual; he held the rings in pawn and thought there was no harm in giving them an airing, and he amused himself with chewing cinnamon which was always his favourite spice and perfume.--Everyone had now arrived and dancing might begin, so David Berger struck up the Marseillaise--or Mamsellyaise as dyer "For my part" called it--and Mr. Süssmann sang these words aloud to the music: "Allons, enfants de la partie!"

All went well at first; but there was very little brotherly feeling shown taking it as a whole. Still, it must be confessed that the young gentlemen of the town and the young gentlemen from the country joined in fraternizing with the pretty little daughters of the tradespeople, but that was nothing new, while the sisters of these same young gentlemen refused absolutely to dance with the tradesmen's sons. The first disagreement between the two parties arose from the conduct of Mally Pomuchelskopp. The journeyman shoemaker and wit of the Reform-club, who was the son of a respectable tradesman in Rahnstädt, asked Mally to dance with him, and she refused, alleging that she was already engaged. She then sat waiting till Fred Triddelfitz, Mr. Süssmann, or some other equally eligible partner should come and ask her to dance the next waltz with him. But as no one came she had to remain sitting.--The shoemaker saw this and began to laugh and joke about it, at last saying loud out, that if the young ladies would not dance with them, their daughters and sisters must not dance with the young gentlemen, adding that they had not come to the ball only to look on at the dancing. And now the storm broke on the heads of the innocent little burgher girls, who had been enjoying themselves so much. Their brothers and lovers came to them, and said: "You're not to dance with that apothecary fellow again, Sophie!" and, "You'd better look out, Dolly, or I'll tell mother!" and, "If you dance with that barrister again, Stina, I'll never speak to you any more!" This sort of thing was repeated throughout the room, and so of course it reached the ears of father Pomuchelskopp, who was not long in discovering the reason of the new tactics. He became very uneasy, and going to Mally explained to her what she had done. He said that the shoemaker was a person of great consequence, and was looked upon as worth any ten ordinary men in the Reform-club because of his sharp tongue, so she must soothe him down again. And in spite of all her repugnance, father Pomuchelskopp made her take his arm and walk down the room to where the shoemaker was standing. He then said that there must have been some great misunderstanding, for his daughter would only be too happy to dance with such a well known member of the Reform-club. And a few minutes later Mally and the shoemaker were whirling round the room together.

Father Pomuchelskopp had now--so to speak--sacrificed his first-born on the altar of fraternity, but without much effect, the two parties did not amalgamate well. Uncle Bräsig did his best to bring people together, he rushed about in his brown coat, here, there and everywhere, for he was determined that brotherly kindness should prevail. He introduced Mr. von so and so to Mrs. Thiel, the cabinet-maker's wife; he forced himself to walk up and down the dancing-room arm in arm with his greatest enemy in the Reform-club, Wimmersdorf, the tailor, and in the presence of the whole company he gave the red-faced wife of John "For my part" a brotherly kiss on the cheek; but it was all of no use; what influence has one man on a number. "Mr. Schulz," he said at last, quite worn out with his labours, "if the supper doesn't bring them nearer each other, I don't know what to do, for the dancing seems to separate them more and more."

But the supper also failed to arouse a feeling of fraternity in the company. The gentlemen and ladies sat at one end of the table, and the tradespeople at the other. Champagne was drunk at the higher end of the table, and at the other end there was a horrible concoction which Grammelin had the impudence to call good red wine, and to sell at a shilling a bottle.--It is true that the shoemaker sat next Mally and her father, and that Pomuchelskopp took care to keep his glass continually full; it is true that the dyer, John "For my part" and his wife placed themselves between two country gentlemen, and that when they wanted to pay for what they had ordered, John put his hand in his pocket and drew out a handful of dyer's tickets instead of the paper money with which he thought he had filled it.--Bräsig seated himself between two pretty little girls, tradesmen's daughters, and treated them with paternal kindness, feeling all the time that Mrs. Nüssler would be angry with him for at least a week, for having gone to the ball instead of remaining with her at Rexow, and that parson Godfrey would lecture him about worldliness. It was of no use his having come, he felt that bitterly. Grammelin's sour red wine looked badly beside the champagne, and the higher and lower classes were even more separate at supper than in the ball-room.--"Mr. Schulz," said Bräsig to his old friend, who was sitting opposite him, "now's the time to play our last trump, do you speak to Mr. Süssmann, and I'll tell Mr. Berger."--So Mr. Schulz asked Mr. Süssmann whether he had the song-books ready.--"Yes," was the answer.--"Very well, deal them out, now's the time."--While Mr. Süssmann distributed the books, Bräsig went to David Berger, and asked: "Do you know that song of Schiller's, Mr. Berger: 'Sister with the linen kirtle. Brother with the order grand'?"--"Most certainly," replied David.--"Strike up then, the sooner the better."--And suddenly: "Happiness, that spark divine", resounded through the room, but with every line the voices grew fewer and fewer, so that at last my dear old uncle Bräsig was the only one who still held up his book and sang, the tears rolling down his cheeks the while; but when he reached the line in which liars were denounced, he could go on no longer.--"Liars?"--Ah they were all liars, false to their convictions.--Everyone rose from table feeling rather uncomfortable, and Bräsig crept away into a corner to hide his vexation. The young people began to dance again, and David and Slus'uhr retired to an anteroom where they drank champagne and laughed at uncle Bräsig.

After a time Schulz the carpenter came to Bräsig, and said: "Do you know, sir, that Attorney Slus'uhr and David are sitting with some other men in 'number 3' making game of you, and dragging in all sorts of political allusions. The attorney said just now that if the French found it difficult to get a king to rule over them, now that they've got rid of Louis Philippe, they couldn't do better than choose you, for you had nothing to do, and so had plenty of time to devote to the business of governing them."--"Did he really say that?" asked uncle Bräsig rising indignantly. "Yes he did," replied Schulz. "And he is in 'number 3,' here at Grammelin's?"--"Yes."--"Come away with me, Mr. Schulz."

Bräsig was hurt and angry that the fraternity ball from which he had hoped so much for humanity had come to nothing. He felt like the patriarch Abraham when he was about to offer his darling son as a sacrifice. He was going to have slipped away home quietly, when he beheld a scapegoat on which he might pour forth his wrath, the very one he would have chosen next to his old enemy Pomuchelskopp. "Come away with me, Mr. Schulz," he said walking energetically across the room to the cloak room where he had left his hat and black thorn walking-stick. He left the hat where it was, and picking up the stick, went to "number 3."

Several men were sitting over their wine in "number 3," laughing at some new witticism of their friend Mr. Slus'uhr. All at once there was dead silence in the room, for another man had joined them whose face scared away their merriment. Bräsig looked with strange significance now at his black-thorn stick, and now at the attorney, and the men guessing what was likely to happen, drew their chairs back from the table rather hastily. "Which rascal was it who wanted to make me king of France?" cried Bräsig, knocking some of the plaster off the wall, from the vehement way in which he flourished his stick: "I *won't* be king of France!"--whack!--and the stick came down on the attorney's shoulders, who shrieked out: "Oh!"--"I *won't* be king of France!" and again the stick did its duty. Bräsig and his stick repeated the assurance again and again that he would not be king of France, until candles, lamps and bottles lost their lives in this battle about the French throne, and David crept under the table to avoid the storm of blows. The attorney shouted for help; but no one stood by him, and only when the onslaught was over did David venture to put his head out from under the table and ask meekly: "Pardon me, Mr. Bräsig, but pray tell me is this part of the ceremony of brotherhood?"--"Out! out!" cried Mr. Schulz, dragging David from under the table. "Gentlemen!" exclaimed Slus'uhr, "I call you all to bear witness as to how I have just been treated."--"I didn't notice anything," said one. "And I wasn't looking," said another. "I was looking out of the window," said the third, although it was pitch dark. "Mr. Schulz," said Bräsig, "you're my witness, and you'll remember how thoroughly I've thrashed Mr. Attorney Slus'uhr." He then left the room, got his hat and went home.

The blows Slus'uhr got in "number 3," were distinctly heard in the dancing room, and did not tend to make matters better. The two noblemen and their sons had left long before, and the few town dignitaries who still remained now slipped away as quietly as possible; little Anna listened unmoved to Fred Triddelfitz's entreaties that she would dance once more with him, and hastened to wrap herself up in her shawl and go with her parents. Pomuchelskopp also prepared to go as fast as he could, for he had an undefined but strong impression that, otherwise, something unpleasant might happen to him, he therefore entreated his wife and daughters to come away, saying it was high time to go home. His family party was difficult to collect. Gustavus was dancing quite happily with Wimmersdorf's youngest daughter. Sally was listening attentively to what Mr. Süssmann was telling her, he said that he had only taken the low place he held in Kurz's shop for fun and added that as he could not remain where he was any longer, he was considering whether it would be better for him to accept one of the situations offered him in Hamburg, Lübeck and Stettin, or to set up for himself in Rostock where he had a rich old uncle, who advised him in every letter he wrote to set up in business for himself and marry, so that he, the old uncle, might wind up his affairs and go and live with him. Mally was sitting in a corner of the sofa crying over her ill-luck in having had to dance with a shoemaker. Henny looked like a stake that had been driven into its place, for in spite of all that had happened that evening, she had never moved once since she had seated herself on entering the room; the uncomfortable little episode with the journeyman shoemaker even, had failed to affect her serenity, and now when Muchel came and told her they must go, she answered affectionately: "Very well. Pöking; but won't you invite your friend the shoemaker to come with us. You might also bring one of your titled acquaintances if you like, and then, if you add Rührdanz the weaver, Willgans and some of your other brethren of the Reform club the party will be complete."

So our poor friend Pomuchelskopp had to drive home with this conjugal shaft rankling in his large brotherly heart.

CHAPTER XIII

Let no man be too certain of anything; above all, let him not paint the devil on the wall, for he often comes when no man calls, and seldom waits for an invitation; some of the guests Henny had proposed that her husband should invite were already awaiting the arrival of their host and hostess at Gürlitz manor. All the inhabitants of Gürlitz village assembled in the courtyard of the manor as the dawn began to break on that summer morning and stood at the door ready to receive their master. "Lads," said Rührdanz, "what must be, must be; but do everything decently and in order!"--"Bother you and your order!" cried Willgans. "Has he ever treated us so?"--"That doesn't matter," said Rührdanz, "we must act so as to have the right on our side. See how foolish you are. When we go to our Grand Duke, as we ought to do, and tell him all about it, he may ask: 'How did you set about it, Willgans?' and if you have to answer: 'Oh, your Highness, we first thrashed the man and his wife and then turned them out of the place,' how do you think it would sound? And what tales do you think Mr. Pomuchelskopp would have to tell against you."--"Yes," replied old father Brinckmann, "Rührdanz is right. If we content ourselves with turning them out of the place, we shall be quit of them, and needn't mind what anyone may say afterwards." It was settled that this should be done. Behind the men were the women and girls, and the tall masculine looking woman who had attended the meeting on the previous morning was standing amongst them. She said: "They've gone as far as they will. If they don't chase that man and his wife out of the place I'll thrash the fellow as long as he can stand."--"Yes, father," cried another woman, "we must get rid of them, we *must* indeed! I went to the parsonage yesterday and Mrs. Baldrian gave me some food, and the parson begged me to be patient.--*Patient!* Can starving folk be patient?"--"Joseph Smidt," said a tall slender young girl, "just run over to the Seeberg, will you, and look if they're coming. How our two young ladies will open their eyes, Sophie, when they find themselves sent off on such an unexpected journey!"--"Father," said Zorndt, a labourer, to Brinkmann, "oughtn't we to tell the parson what we're doing? Perhaps it might be well for us that he should know."--"No, father Zorndt, there's no need to tell him, he couldn't help us, and I don't think he would understand our motives. If our old parson were still alive it would be different!"--"They're coming now," cried Joseph Smidt running up. "Who'll speak?" asked Willgans, "I'll catch the leaders by the head."--"Rührdanz," was echoed from mouth to mouth. "Well if you like, why shouldn't I do it?" answered Rührdanz--not another word was said.

John Joseph, the coachman, drove up and was about to turn into the yard, when Willgans caught the leaders by the head, made them stand a little side ways so as to stop the other two horses, and said: "Wait a moment, John Joseph." Pomuchelskopp looked out of the window of the glass coach, and seeing all the villagers standing about the carriage, asked: "What's the meaning of all this?" Rührdanz, followed by all the others, came close to the carriage door, and said: "Sir, we've determined that you shall no longer be our master, for you've never treated us as a master should treat his servants, and you were every bit as cruel to other people before you came here, for you've got an iron ring round your neck, and we won't have a master with a ring round his neck."--"You rascals! You scoundrels!" cried Pomuchelskopp, who had now discovered what the villagers meant. "So you would seize upon me and mine, would you?"--"No, that's not what we want," answered old father Brinkmann, "we're only going to see you safely out of the place."--"Drive on, John Joseph," cried Pomuchelskopp. "Slash at them with your whip."--"John Joseph," said Willgans, "if you move your whip, we'll knock you down. Now turn the carriage!--So--ho--That's right!" The carriage and horses were now turned towards Rahnstädt. Sally and Mally screamed out with terror; Gustavus jumped down from the box and stood between the labourers and his father; everyone was in a great state of excitement, except Henny, who remained stiff straight and unbending as ever, without uttering a single word. "You band of robbers you! What do you want?" cried Pomuchelskopp. "We ar'n't robbers," answered Smidt, "none of us will steal even a pin from you, and Gustavus here may remain and manage the estate and tell us what we are to do."--"But your wife and two eldest daughters must go with you," interrupted Mrs. Kapphingst, "we can bear their tyranny no longer."--"Gently, friends, gently," said Rührdanz, "let us do everything decently and in order. It won't be enough to take them away over the Gürlitz march as we intended, we must hand them over to our chief magistrate, the mayor of Rahnstädt. I'm sure that that's the proper thing to do."--"Rührdanz is right," said the others, "and you may go home quietly Gustavus, no body will touch you. Now John Joseph, drive on slowly." Then some of the villagers went on one side of the carriage and some on the other, thus forming a guard. They went at a quick march like a regiment of soldiers. Pomuchelskopp had given way to the inevitable, but his misery was great. He wrung his hands and groaned: "Oh me! oh me! What shall I do? What shall I do?" and putting his head out at the window, he said: "I've always been a kind master to you all."--"You mean a cruel monster!" cried a voice out of the crowd. Sally and Mally were crying bitterly, but Henny sat as stiff as a tin thermometer; if the labourers had known what a thermometer was, and that I had likened her to one they would have said that she was marking a point far above boiling. Willgans who had at first been near the door on her side of the carriage, drew back a little, because she once, without uttering a sound or bending forward, stretched out her hand and seizing his curly red hair nearly pulled out a handful, her eyes shining and glaring in the dusk of the early morning like those of a beagle when chasing a hare. "Mercy! I say look at her!" cried Willgans. "Father Düsing! help!--Mercy! Look at the wretch! Do give her a knock over the knuckles." But before father Düsing could free him from her clutches, brave old Henny had thrust his nose down on the carriage door two or three times, so that the blood trickled down his face. "Mercy! Help I say! This is not to be borne; wait a bit and I'll ...."--"Stop!" cried Rührdanz, "you can't blame her, lad, for revenging herself according to the malice of her nature, so take no notice this time, but you can tell the Grand Duke all about it, and can show him your nose, which will bear witness to the way she has treated you." Henny said nothing, and the procession moved on again. When they reached the border of the estate the labourers sent their wives and children home, and about seven o'clock the prisoners and their guard entered Rahnstädt slowly and solemnly.

Uncle Bräsig was stretched out on the window seat in his room smoking, and meditating on the heroic deeds he had done on the previous evening.--Kurz was in a very bad humour although he had not been at the fraternity ball, and was going about his shop grumbling and scolding: "The stupid ass! The idiot! Wait till I catch him!" After a time he came, I mean Mr. Süssmann by "he." He danced over the threshold, and Kurz laying both hands on the counter looked as if he were preparing to jump over it and spring upon his assistant before he was well in the shop, but he thought better of it and waited. "Good morning, chief, chiefer, chiefest!" cried Mr. Süssmann, coming in with a clatter and rattle of everything in the shop that could make a noise, and seating himself on the edge of a herring barrel with his hat cocked very much on one side, went on: "Good morning, Kurzie, woortsie, poortsie!"--Before he had time to make any more rhymes on his master's name, Kurz sprang upon him, pulled his hair with both hands, flung his hat into the herring barrel, and then dragged him further into the shop by the whiskers. Mr. Süssmann clutched blindly behind him for something to hold on by, and chanced to seize the spigot of a barrel of oil, his struggles were so great that the spigot came out, and the oil began to run out of the hole.--"Hang it!" cried Kurz. "My oil, my oil!" and letting Mr.

Süssmann go, he stuck the forefinger of his right hand into the hole in the barrel, Mr. Süssmann who still had the spigot in his hand, waived it round his head in triumph, and as mad or intoxicated people are always fertile in expedients, he determined to clinch the matter and so pulled the spigot out of the vinegar barrel. "Preserve us all! My vinegar!" cried Kurz, at the same time sticking the forefinger of his left hand into the hole in the vinegar barrel. In order to keep a finger in each of the barrels Kurz had to bend forward and to stretch out both arms to their utmost extent, and this Mr. Süssmann deemed too good an opportunity to be lost. "My chiefie!--Kurzie!"--slap!--"Good-bye grocerie-pocerie!"--slap! slap!--"Joanna goes, ne'er to come back again!"--slap, slap, slap!--Having done this, Mr. Süssmann picked his hat out of the herring barrel, set it on one side of his head, laid both the spigots on the counter about twenty feet away from Kurz, and then left the shop laughing and dancing.

"*Help!*" cried Kurz. "He-lp!--He--lp!" but not one of the servants was in the house, and his wife was out in the back garden planting asparagus. The only person who heard him was uncle Bräsig. "Charles," he said, "I think I hear Kurz bellowing. I'll go and see if anything has happened."--"He-lp!" shouted Kurz.--"Bless me!" said Bräsig. "Whatever are you making such a noise for at seven o'clock in the morning?"--"Infamous rascal!" growled Kurz.--"What? Is that the way to treat me?" remonstrated Bräsig.--"Meanspirited hound!"--"You're a rude barbarian!"--"Give me the spigots that are lying on the counter over there."--"You may get your nasty greasy spigots yourself, you ass you!"--"I can't, or else all the oil and vinegar will run out of these casks, and I wasn't talking to you, I was speaking to Süssmann."--"Ah, then it doesn't matter," said Bräsig, seating himself on the counter with a flop, and swinging his legs about, "what's the matter?"--Kurz explained how he had come to be imprisoned at the barrels.--"Well, Kurz, you're a joke, but take warning by what has happened, a man always suffers in the very things which he has used sinfully."--"I entreat ...."--"Hush, Kurz! You have always sinned in your sales of oil and vinegar, for you used to pour out of your measuring tins into your customer's basins with a swoop so as to leave two or three desert spoonfuls in the measure without anyone noticing it. Will you give good measure for the future, and will you never peep into the cards again when you're playing at Boston."--"Yes, yes," cried Kurz.--"Very well then, I'll set you free," said Bräsig, bringing him the spigots.

Scarcely was Kurz free than he rushed out into the street as though he expected to find Mr. Süssmann waiting for him behind the door. Bräsig followed him, and just as they reached the street Pomuchelskopp arrived on the scene escorted by his labourers.--"Preserve us! What's this? Rührdanz, what's the meaning of all this?"--"Don't be angry, Mr. Bräsig, we've turned off our squire."--Bräsig shook his head as he answered: "Then you've done a very foolish thing." He followed the procession and many people they met in the street did the same. When they got to the mayor's house, the labourers unharnessed the horses, while Rührdanz, Willgans, Brinkmann and several others went into the house.--"Well, Sir," said Rührdanz, "we've brought him here."--"Who?"--"Oh, our Mr. Pomuchelskopp."--"Why, what do you mean?"--"Oh, nothing, except that we won't have him to rule over us any longer."--"Good Heavens! What have you been about?"--"We've done everything legally, your worship."--"Have you laid violent hands on him?"--"No, we didn't touch him, but as for his wife, she seized father Willgans by the ...."--But the mayor had left the room, and was already at the carriage door asking the Pomuchelskopps to come in. They accepted his invitation and the mayor took them into the drawing-room.--"Why have we been treated so badly? Why have we been treated so badly?" whimpered Pomuchelskopp. "Oh, Mr. Mayor, you know that I've always been a good master to my people."--"For shame, Kopp," interposed Henny.--"No," said the mayor without attending to Henny and looking Pomuchelskopp full in the face, "you have *not* been a good master. You know that I have often been obliged to remonstrate with you about your conduct, you know that I refused to have anything to do with your law affairs because of the injustice of your cause. I'll have nothing to do with this except as a private individual, and what I do will be for the sake of those poor mistaken peasants. Pray, excuse me ...."--"Oh, please advise me. What shall I do?"--"You can't go back to Gürlitz for a short time; if you did it would only rouse the people to violence, so you'd better wait here in Rahnstädt till you see your way clear. Excuse my leaving you for a few minutes, I am going to speak to the labourers."

What good could talking do? The people had made up their minds, and the bad characters amongst them had been obliged to consent to let their quieter, honester neighbours have their own way, and they were so sure their way was the right one that they refused to give it up.--"No, Sir," said Rührdanz, "we can't take him back whatever happens."--"You have been guilty of a great crime this morning, and it'll go hard with you if you stick to it."--"That may be; but if you speak of crime, Mr. Pomuchelskopp has treated us much worse than we've treated him."--"You've allowed your heads to be stuffed with nonsense by some foolish people in the Reform-club."--"Don't be angry, your worship, people say that of us, but it isn't true. Why? Mr. Pomuchelskopp himself is a member of the Reform-club, and he made a speech too, but he told a string of lies in his speech, no one knows that better than we do."--"But what do you intend to do?"--"Mr. Gustavus is at

Gürlitz and when he tells us to do this or that, we'll obey him; but Willgans and I want to go to the Grand Duke and tell him all about it, so we would like you to give us the proper papers."--"What sort of papers?"--"Ah, your worship, don't be angry with me, it doesn't matter what they are. You see I was once sent to the old station without papers--and of course they turned me out--our Grand Duke isn't a station, and he'd never be so rude, so if we go without papers you can show him your nose, father Willgans, and tell him how that woman treated you, and I'll show my honest hands that have never taken what didn't belong to them."--The old man then left the room, and joined the other labourers outside. They all felt their pockets and drew out what pence and halfpence they possessed. They gave them to Rührdanz and said: "Now go! go straight to Schwerin!" and: "Don't forget to tell about Kapphingst's daughter!" and: "If he asks you how we have lived, tell him honestly that we never stole from our master, but that we sometimes took a few of Mrs. Nüssler's potatoes, and she never blamed us."

The two labourers then set out for Schwerin, and the other villagers returned home, while John Joseph drove the empty carriage after them. The crowd that had collected round the mayor's door to see what was to be seen, for the news of Pomuchelskopp's arrest had spread like wild-fire, now separated, and uncle Bräsig said to Hawermann as soon as he got back: "Well, Charles, he hasn't escaped his judge. I joined the crowd for a little, not for his sake, but because of those poor ignorant labourers. As soon as I saw him safe in the mayor's house I came away for I didn't care to see his humiliation."

Pomuchelskopp, his wife and daughters took up their abode at Grammelin's and the former, when he saw his family settled down, went to Slus'uhr's bedroom and bemoaned his hard fate. Slus'uhr had been obliged to remain at Grammelin's in consequence of the thrashing he had had on the previous evening, as otherwise he could not have made out such a good case of assault against Bräsig. "I have sent for the doctor and am going to make him examine me that I may have a better case against Mr. Bräsig. Strump isn't at home, but the other doctor will be here very soon."--"How lucky you are!" said Muchel. "Well," answered the attorney, twisting round on his other side, "I didn't quite look upon it in that light. I don't see any great piece of luck in getting a sound thrashing with a black thorn stick at least an inch in thickness."--"You can have your revenge, while I--wretched man that I am, can do nothing."--"You should send for a guard of soldiers and that'll frighten your fellows out of their lives, and if you don't like to go home at once, send your wife on before, she'll have everything in order by the time you're ready to follow, I'll answer for that."--"Mercy, what do you propose? No, no! I've had enough of it. Pümpelhagen has escaped me, and I'll never go back to Gürlitz; they'll set fire to the house when I'm in it, I know they will. No, no! I'll sell, I'll sell!"--"Have you heard the news," asked David coming into the room, and hearing the last words he added, "yes, you're right. If you sell the place I'll manage everything for you, I know ...."--"Infamous Jewish rascal!" groaned Slus'uhr, getting into a new position, "Ugh! mercy!--Don't you think we can manage it between us? Yes, Mr. Pomuchelskopp, you must sell, for even if they spare the dwelling house, they're sure to burn the stacks and barns, for you've got into a regular scrape."--"Now, Mr. Slus'uhr," said David, "you've made a little money I know, and you can conduct the sale of a farm, or a mill; but this is a large estate, and my father must manage the arrangements for Mr. Pomuchelskopp."--"Your father! When he hears that it's for Pomuchelskopp, he'll refuse to act. We three are in very bad odour with him."--"If I tell him," began David, but at this moment the doctor came in, and he was Anna's father. "Good morning, you sent for me," he said turning to Slus'uhr, "what can I do for you?"--"Ah doctor, you were at the ball yesterday too. Oh I'm in such pain! You must have heard ...."--"He has had a good thrashing," said David, "and I was a witness. He was very severely beaten."--"Hold your confounded tongue," shouted Slus'uhr. "Doctor, I want you to examine me carefully, I'm afraid that I shall never regain the use of my limbs." The doctor made no reply, but went to his patient, and pulling his shirt off his back, saw some very distinct lines scored in red, such as are not to be seen on every human back. Pomuchelskopp sat still, and folded his hands in deep commiseration, but a flash of pleasure lighted up his face when he saw the red weals. David sprang to his feet: "Merciful Jehovah! What a sight!" he exclaimed. "You must examine me too, doctor, for Schulz the carpenter dragged me out from under the table and tore my new coat right down the middle."--"You'd better send for the tailor then," answered the doctor quietly, and turning again to the attorney, he said: "I'll go down to Grammelin's coffee-room and write you a certificate. Good morning, gentlemen." He then left the room, and soon afterwards the housemaid brought in a paper, which she said the doctor had desired her to take to Mr. Slus'uhr. The attorney opened it and read:

"This is to certify, that Mr. attorney Slus'uhr has had a thorough good thrashing as the marks on his back show beyond dispute, but it has done him no real harm.

N. N. M. D."

"Does the fellow write that about me?" stormed the attorney, "'it has done me no harm' for sooth!--Just wait and I'll have something to say to you elsewhere!"--"But," cried David, "surely it's much better that the beating shouldn't have done you harm, than that you should have been maimed."-

-"You're an idiot! What's the good of lying here any longer though?" said Slus'uhr. "Pardon me, but I must get up, and repay Mr. Bräsig for his blows by sending him--a letter demanding damages."--"Don't forget, my friend, that you've to write to Pümpelhagen for me to day," said Pomuchelskopp. "Trust me to remember. I feel so savage, I'd like to write a good many more such letters. Hav'n't you anything for me to do in that line, David?"--"Whenever I have anything to write I do it myself, and when I have nothing to write, I leave it alone," said David, leaving the room with Pomuchelskopp.

CHAPTER XIV

The hours that had elapsed since Pomuchelskopp's visit had seemed to Mrs. von Rambow the slowest and dreariest she had ever known. Wearily had they passed over her, every new minute revealing new cares and anxieties. She had tried to tear out the weeds that threatened to choke the wheat in her field, but alas the busiest hand grows tired in time, and the bravest heart craves rest, the rest that comes when the day of toil is past. Her husband had not come home on the day he had promised; instead of his arrival, a letter came from Slus'uhr brought by a special messenger, who said that he had orders to wait until he could deliver it into Mr. von Rambow's own hands. She had a very good idea of what that meant. As it grew dusk that evening she seated herself in her room beside her child, folded her hands in her lap, and gazed out of the window at the sky over which heavy clouds were rising.

The day had been close and muggy, a day in which the blood courses slowly through the veins, instead of circulating rapidly, and giving the body a sense of lightness and vitality it cannot otherwise enjoy. On such an enervating day as this the blood flows languidly, like the black, almost stagnant water in a moorland ditch, and even as all nature groans and sighs for a storm to clear the air, the heart longs for the whirlwind of action, or the shock of fate to drive away "this stifled, drowsy, unimpassioned grief," wishes at any cost to shake off the deadly lethargy! Frida's feeling was much what I have described, she longed for anything that would clear the air around her, and make it possible for her to breathe once more; and she did not long in vain.

Caroline Kegel brought in the post-bag, and stood about as if she wanted to find something to do in the room. At last she opened the bag, and taking out a letter, laid it on the table beside her mistress. Then she hung about again, and asked: "If you please ma'am, shall I light the candles?"--"No, never mind." Still Caroline did not go, she said: "If you please, ma'am, you told us we wer'n't to repeat any gossip to you, but ...."--"What is it?" asked Frida, startled out of her reverie. "The Gürlitz labourers have chased away Mr. Pomuchelskopp, his wife and two daughters."--"You don't mean to say so!" cried Frida. "Yes, and all of our labourers are down stairs in the yard, and wish to speak to you."--"Do they want to chase us away too?" asked Frida, drawing herself up proudly. "No, no! my dear, dear lady," cried Caroline, throwing herself on her knees and bursting into tears; "there's no talk of anything so dreadful, and my old father says that he'll be the death of the first who dares to speak of such a thing. They only say that Mr. von Rambow won't listen to them, and so they want to speak to you, for they have great confidence in you."--"Where is Triddelfitz?"--"Lor, ma'am, he's going about amongst them talking to them, but they won't hear a word he says, they say they have nothing to do with him, and must speak to you."--"Come," said Frida, and she went down stairs.

"What do you want with me?" she asked as she stepped out at the door, before which the labourers were all collected. Fred Flegel, the carpenter, came forward, and said: "Madam, we have come to you, for we're all of one mind. We told the master about it some time ago, but he wouldn't attend to us. The squire was affronted with us for saying it; but you see we have no confidence in Mr. Triddelfitz, he is too young and doesn't know enough, and we thought perhaps you could help us if you would be so very kind. We are not so impertinent as to ask for more than we have, indeed we're quite satisfied with what we've got, and we get all we ought, though never at the right time so that our wives sometimes find it difficult to manage."--"Yes," interrupted Päsel, "and last year, which was a year of famine, the rye was all sold, and, Madam, you see I always have my wages paid in kind, so when I couldn't get the rye, how could I live; and when I didn't get it, I was told to be patient. Yes, to be patient! Then there was the potato disease! So how could one live?"--"Madam," said a white-haired old man, "I won't speak of food, for we never really starved; but I am an old man and I was sometimes kept standing so long in the marl pit pouring water over the marl, that I couldn't straighten myself in the evening, nor sleep at night from pain, and it might have been so easily managed better. We were used to other ways when Mr. Hawermann was here, but now we're ordered about by folk that don't know what work is."--"Yes, Madam," resumed the carpenter, "that's why we've come to ask you to let us have a bailiff put over us who knows what ought to be done, either Mr. Hawermann or another as good; one who will listen to us quietly when we've got anything to say, who will not abuse us when we don't deserve it, and who will not use his stick to our children when they are doing their work, as Mr. Triddelfitz was in the habit of doing."--"That must never happen again," cried Frida.--"Well, Madam, he has given up doing that now. It must be six months ago that I made bold to speak to him seriously about it one day when I was alone with him, and he has never done it since. I wish that the squire would only see that it would be for his own advantage if he got a good bailiff, for he understands nothing about farming himself, and then the wind wouldn't blow all the grain out of a field of wheat from leaving it standing too long, as was the case last year, nor would the people talk of him as they do now. And, Madam, there's a great deal of talk just now. It's said that he's going to sell the estate to Mr. Pomuchelskopp, but we won't have him for our master."--"No," they all exclaimed, "we won't have him."--"A fellow whom his own labourers have turned out."--"We needn't have him."

The labourers' words had fallen like heavy blows on Frida's heart. She felt how little love and respect they had for her husband, and the knowledge of the difficulty of her position made it hard for her to speak. After a sharp inward struggle for composure, she said: "Hush, my men! When the squire comes home he must decide whether he will grant your request. Go home quietly and don't come back to the house in such numbers again. I will tell the squire what you want, and I believe I can promise you that there will be a change in the farming arrangements at midsummer--one way or another," she added with a sigh. Then she was silent for an instant, as though to swallow a lump in her throat. "Yes," she continued, "wait patiently till midsummer, and then there shall be a change."--"That's all right!"--"That's all we want!"--"And we're very grateful to you."--"Good-night, Madam."-- And they all went away.

Frida returned to her room. It had begun to thunder and lighten, and the wind which was blustering through the yard drove sand and straw pattering against the window. "Yes," she said to herself, "midsummer will decide it. I hav'n't promised too much, for there must be a change then. But what will it be?" and involuntarily she thought of the picture David had so mercilessly drawn of her future life. She saw herself condemned to spend the rest of her days in a hired house in a small country town with her husband and child, leading an idle useless life without hope of remedy, and hearing people whisper that their fate might have been so different. She saw her husband get up in the morning and go out into the town, come home to dinner, spend the afternoon lounging on the sofa, then go out again, and come home to bed. He had always hitherto frittered away the time God had given him to work, and he would continue to waste his days in idleness. She saw herself worn out and wearied with household cares, comfortless and friendless, fighting the battle of life alone; she saw herself dying and her child standing by her bed. Her child! Her poor child! The penniless daughter of a nobleman! There are few things that are a greater curse than the possession of rank without the means of keeping it up.--A man can get on pretty well, for he can go into the army; but a girl? Even if God has endowed her with the loveliness of an angel, and her parents have done the best they can for their darling, a gentleman says: "She is poor, so I cannot marry her," and a man of the middle-class says: "She has grand notions, so I cannot marry her."--Frida looked sadly at her child, who was sleeping calmly through the storm that was raging out of doors, and that which was raging in her mother's breast.

Caroline Kegel brought in candles, and Mrs. von Rambow hastily took up the letter that was lying on the table, like one who did not wish it to be perceived that she had been engaged in deep and painful thought. She looked at the direction and saw it was from her sister-in-law, Albertine. She opened the envelope, and another letter fell out addressed to her husband.--"Put this letter on your master's writing table," she said to the maid.--Caroline took it and left the room.

Her husband's sisters had often written to her before, such letters as women write to while away their time.--Frida unfolded the letter, but--oh!--this was no commonplace chatty note such as she was accustomed to receive,--Albertine wrote:

"Dear Sister,

"I don't know whether I am doing right. Bertha advises me to write to you, and Fidelia has twice torn the paper from under my pen, for she thinks it will make our dear brother Alick unhappy if I do. But however that may be, I can't help it. Sheer necessity forces me to write. We have already written to Alick twice, but he has never answered our letters. I have no doubt that he has to travel about a good deal in these bad times, and that besides that, he must have much to occupy his attention at home--for we hear rumours of things going on about you, of the probable truth of which we have only too many proofs here in Schwerin--and so I think that I cannot be doing wrong in writing to you. You will answer me soon, won't you?--You know that Alick has taken the small capital our father left us as a mortgage on Pümpelhagen, and that he has promised to give us 5 per cent on the money instead of the 4½ per cent we had formerly received. It was not necessary for him to have done that, for we could live within our income before. But he promised to send us the money punctually every quarter, and we have not received a penny in the last nine months. Dear Frida, you may be sure that we should never have complained if we had not been in very great need. Our brother-in-law Breitenburg was here lately; he had never heard of our having lent Alick the money, and as soon as he found it out, he--you know how rough he is--swore at Alick, and told us we were three geese to have given him the money. He asked to see our bond, and when we could not show it to him, for Alick has always forgotten to send it to us, he said outright, that our money was gone beyond recall, as it was well known that Alick had ruined himself with his bad farming, and that Pümpelhagen would have to be sold to pay his debts.--We know how to treat our brother in-law's talk, for he has always disliked our dear Alick; and as for selling Pümpelhagen, I don't believe it. It has been in our family for centuries! The Grand Duke would never allow it!--We told him that and a great deal more. Fidelia, especially, gave him a piece of her mind very energetically. So he took up his hat and stick, and said in his rude way: 'Your brother Alick has always been a fool, and now he has capped all his former misdeeds by behaving like a scoundrel.' Fidelia rose and showed him the door at once.--It was a dreadful scene, and I should not have told you about it, if I did not feel rather frightened lest Alick and Breitenburg should meet, and act like those two brothers-in-law, Dannenberg and Malzahn, who in order to avenge their injured sense of honour shot each other dead across a pocket-handkerchief. Please warn Alick to avoid any meeting with him, and if it is possible ask him to send us the interest on our money.--We think of going to see you in autumn, and are looking forward like children to the pleasure of seeing you, and of revisiting the home where we played as children, dreamt our day-dreams as young women, and where, alas, we saw our dear father die. Yes, Frida; Bertha, Fidelia and I rejoice at the thought of seeing Pümpelhagen again, for we live in the past, our present is so dull and empty of interest. Only now and then, and at very long intervals do we see the face of some old friend of our dear father, who comes to tell us what is going on in the world, and Bertha and I think there is something very pathetic in the way our little Fidelia throws down her work on such occasions, and listens eagerly to the news our old friend brings us.--She is especially interested in all that concerns the court.--Good-bye for the present, dear Frida. Forgive me for having troubled you with this letter, and give Alick the enclosed note. I have entreated him earnestly to help us, but have spared him all the disagreeables of our position as much as I could.--We shall meet in August.

"Yours affectionately,
"Albertine von Rambow."
"Schwerin, June 11th, 1848."

Frida began the letter, but did not read to the end. When she got to the place where Albertine has repeated Breitenburg's words: "Your brother Alick has always been a fool and now he has capped all his former misdeeds by behaving like a scoundrel," she threw the letter on the floor, started up from her chair wringing her hands, and began to walk rapidly up and down the room. "It's true," she moaned, "quite true!" Her little girl was sleeping calmly near her. She threw herself into the chair again, picked up the letter, and once more read the dreadful words. As she did so the terrible picture her imagination had before drawn of her child's future faded before the actual horror that confronted her. The new picture she saw was burnt into her brain. She saw in it the faces of the three sisters, and underneath it was written in letters of fire: "Swindled! Swindled by their own brother!" Beyond them she saw her husband, but his features were blurred and indistinct so that she could hardly trace them, and underneath this figure the single word "scoundrel" was written. Horrible, most horrible!--She had lost her all!--And it was a double loss!--She had only herself to trust to now on earth, for she had lost him she had loved as her own soul. That was the terrible part of her grief! Oh for help to wash away the brand of dishonour from the forehead she had so often kissed lovingly. But how? Who would help her? Alas, the people whose names occurred to her were all far away and she could go to none of them in her distress. She wrung her hand in agony. It seemed as though she were being more and more hemmed in every moment. Pomuchelskopp's name flashed into her mind, and Slus'uhr's and David's. She sprang to her feet and moved her hands about as if to waive off once more the ghosts of the past. She could think of very few names now, when suddenly in the midst of her anguish she remembered a kind, womanly old face, Mrs. Nüssler's face, and it looked as it had done when it bent over her child to kiss it.

Mrs. von Rambow immediately exclaimed aloud: "That woman has a heart, a large heart that can feel the sorrows of others!" Out of doors the thunder was still rolling, the lightning flashing and the rain coming down in torrents. Mrs. von Rambow snatched up a warm shawl and rushed out into the rain. "For God's sake, ma'am, tell me what's the matter," cried Caroline Kegel, "see how it's raining and how dark it is!"--"Leave me alone!"--"Nay, I won't do that," said the maid going after her. "A kind heart, a kind heart!" murmured the poor thing as she hastened on, the rain beating ever more violently in her face. She still held the shawl in her hand without knowing it, and her feet slipped often in the deep cut limestone road without her knowing it; her whole soul was bent on getting on quickly. "If you *must* go, Madam, we'll go together," said Caroline, taking the shawl out of her hand and wrapping it round her head and shoulders, then throwing her strong arm round her waist, she asked: "Where do you want to go?"--"To Mrs. Nüssler's," answered her mistress, and then murmured: "a kind heart." A kind heart was beating close to her own and yet she never thought of it; nothing separates two human beings so much as the words: "Command and obedience." She had always been kind to her dependents, and had met her servant's good feeling towards her half way; but at this moment she did not think of Caroline Kegel, her heart was filled with the thought of how Alick was to be saved from shame and dishonour, and Mrs. Nüssler's honest face drew her on through the rain and darkness as the only star of hope that shone on her path. "To Rexow, to Rexow!"

"Goodness gracious me, Joseph!" said Mrs. Nüssler, going to the window, "what a storm it is!"--"Yes, mother, but what can anyone do?"--"Oh dear!" said Mrs. Nüssler, reseating herself. "I hope that no one's out on the high road to-night. I feel very anxious." Mrs. Nüssler went on knitting, Joseph went on smoking, and the parlour was as quiet and cosy as heart could wish. Suddenly Bolster, who was lying under Joseph's chair, gave a short sharp bark which was dog language for: "what's that?" As he got no answer he lay still, but next moment he started up and crept to the door on his stiff old legs. When he got there, he began to snarl after the manner of his kind. "Bolster!" cried Mrs. Nüssler. "What's the matter with the old dog?--What is it Bolster?"--"Mother," said Joseph, who knew Bolster as well as Bolster knew him, "somebody's coming." At the same moment the door opened and a pale woman staggered into the room supported by a strong country girl, who placed her on the sofa. "Good God!" cried Mrs. Nüssler jumping up and taking her visitor by both hands, "what's the matter? What is it? Oh dear, how wet you are."--"Yes, indeed she is," answered Caroline. "Good gracious Joseph, why don't you get up from your chair? Go and fetch Mina. Tell her to come here at once, and tell Dolly she must make some camomile tea." Joseph hastened from the room, and Mrs. Nüssler taking off Mrs. von Rambow's shawl, dried the rain off her face and beautiful hair with her pocket-handkerchief. Mina ran into the parlour and was about to ask a number of questions, but her mother stopped her by saying: "Mina, this isn't the time to trouble Mrs. von Rambow with questions, go and bring one of your dresses and some of your underclothing to my bedroom." But as soon as Mina had run away to do as she desired, she herself asked: "What's the matter, Caroline Kegel?"--"I don't know, but she certainly got a letter this evening." As soon as Mina said that she was ready Mrs. Nüssler and Caroline helped Mrs. von Rambow into the bedroom and undressed her, laid her on the top of the bed and gave her the hot tea Dolly had prepared. She soon recovered her full consciousness and remembered why she had come, for it was only the sense of her utter loneliness that had overcome her and had made her feel so faint and weak, and now that she saw the kind motherly face bending over her, she felt strong and brave once more. She sat up in bed, looked at Mrs. Nüssler trustfully, and said: "You once told me that you would help me if ever I was in need."--"And I will do so," said Mrs. Nüssler with tears in her eyes, and stroking her visitor's hands softly, "tell me what it is.--"It's a dreadful state of things," cried Frida, "our labourers are discontented, we're in debt, deeply in debt, and our creditors want to sell the estate ...."--"Good gracious!" interrupted Mrs. Nüssler, "surely it's early days to talk of that!"--"I can't see my way at all," continued Mrs. von Rambow, "but it was for something else I came to you, and I can't, I dar'n't tell you what it is."--"Don't tell me, Madam. But what you have already told me is not a case in which a woman's advice is worth anything, we must consult some man, and if you like, we can drive over to Rahnstädt and speak to my brother Charles."--"Ah, if I could! But how could I ever expect the man, whom I ...."--"That's a mistake on your part, Madam, and shows that you don't know my brother. Joseph," she called putting her head out at the door of her room, "tell Christian to get the carriage ready and to make haste, and do you make haste also. Mina, quick, bring me your new Sunday hat and cloak, we are going out." Everything was done as she desired, and as soon as they were seated in the carriage, Mrs. Nüssler said to Christian: "You know that I don't like going too fast, Christian, but you can't drive too quickly to-day; we must be in Rahnstädt in half an hour. If we don't make haste they'll all be in bed," she added, addressing Mrs. von Rambow.

Anna had just gone home after spending the evening at Mrs. Behrens' house; Hawermann and Bräsig had said good-night, and Bräsig had just opened the window, and looking out at the weather had said: "What a sweet smell the air always has after a storm, it's quite full of atmosphere!" when a carriage drove up to the door, and the light from Mrs. Behrens' bedroom streamed into it. "Bless me, Charles," cried Bräsig, "there's your dear sister and Mina, and every one ought to be making ready to go to bed just now."--"There must be something wrong," said Hawermann taking his candle and leaving the room. "Why have you come so late, Dorothea," asked Hawermann, meeting his sister on the stairs, "Mina ...." then interrupting himself, "and you too, Madam, at this hour?"--"Quick, Charles," said Mrs. Nüssler, "Mrs. von Rambow wants to speak to you alone, so make haste before anyone comes." Hawermann opened the door of Mrs. Behrens' best parlour and showed Mrs. von Rambow in; as he followed her and closed the door he heard the beginning of what Bräsig said to Mrs. Nüssler. "As sure as your nose is in the middle of your face, tell me what's brought you here? Excuse me for having come down in my shirt sleeves, but you see Charles is a thoughtless fellow and he took away the candle so that I couldn't find my coat in the dark. But where is he, and where's Mina?" Mrs. Nüssler did not need to answer the question, for at this moment Louisa came out of Mrs. Behrens' ordinary sitting-room with a candle. "Why, you here. Aunt?" she said. "Come back with me to the parlour, Louie; and you Bräsig, go and put on your coat again and then you can join us." This was done, and Mrs. Behrens came too. All was silent and still in the passage, and anyone who had chosen to listen at the keyhole of the best parlour might have heard Mrs. von Rambow telling Hawermann her story. She began shyly and tearfully, but gained courage as she went on, and felt her hope and confidence in the old bailiff grow stronger every moment. Anyone who had chosen to listen at the door of Mrs. Behrens' sitting-room, which was to the left of the passage, might have heard the horrible fibs that Mrs. Nüssler was telling, for it had suddenly occurred to the good woman that she could not do better than allow everyone to imagine that Mrs. von Rambow was Mina until she had had time to tell all her tale to Hawermann, and that she might not be troubled with questions. So she said that Mina was suffering from dreadful toothache, and that she knew her brother Charles had a wonderful remedy for it which could only be used with effect between twelve and one at night, and in complete silence. Mrs. Behrens said she was sure it could be no Christian work if that was the way of it, and Bräsig remarked: "I never knew that Charles had any knowledge of medicine or doctoring."

Soon afterwards Hawermann put his head into the room and said: "Will you leave the house door ajar, Mrs. Behrens, I have to go out, but will soon return," and before Mrs. Behrens could answer he was half way down the street leading to Moses' house.

CHAPTER XV

Moses was now a very old man, but he was strong and healthy though he found it difficult to walk even a short distance, and did not sleep well at night. He had grown into the habit of sitting up till long after his old wife Flora was asleep. He used at such times to sit in a large arm chair with a pillow under his head thinking over old stories. He would have nothing to do with new things. David generally stretched himself on the sofa as he used to do, and told him anything he thought would interest him, and sometimes enjoyed a little nap between whiles. I must say in David's honour that he was no exception to the rest of his people, and that he was gentle with and careful of his father in his old age, indeed he showed an example in that respect that it would be well if many Christians were to follow. On this particular evening they were chatting together. "David," said his father, "have I not often told you that you ought not to have anything to do with Pömüffelskopp?"--"But, father, have I ever been taken in by him? Hav'n't I always made money by my transactions with him?"--"You have strewed ashes on your head, you have eaten dirt."--"Are Louis d'ors dirt?"--"There's always dirt sticking to Pömüffelskopp's money."--"If you like father, we can do a good stroke of business, Pömüffelskopp wants to sell Gürlitz."--"Why?"--"Because he wants to get rid of it."--"I'll tell you why, David. It's because he doesn't feel safe amongst his labourers, and fears lest they should burn his barns, or knock him on the head. I'll tell you even more than that. I shan't do the business, nor will you do it; but still it will be done, and by attorney Slus'uhr too, whom you account your friend; but he's too clever for you, David, and you're too young."--"Father, I ..."--"Hush, David, I've got something more to say to you. You want to get rich, and to get rich all at once. Now listen to me; a jar with a narrow neck half full of gold is before you. You put in your hand and try to bring it out again full, but you can't do it, if, however, you're content to take one coin at a time, you get as many as you need in the end."--"Did I fill my hand too full?"--"Hush, David, I hav'n't done yet. You see two people, one throws a Louis d'or into a clear brook, while the other throws a handful of them into the mire. You go into the cold water, and get wet in picking up the Louis d'or, but when you've got it, you find it bright and clean; or you go into the mire and pick up the handful of gold, and all men try to get out of your way because you stink in their nostrils. The money Pömüffelskopp has thrown you in the way of business, you have been obliged to pick out of the mire."--"Nay, father, it doesn't smell a bit worse than other gold."--"If men have not yet perceived its evil odour, its stink yet rises to heaven; but it is not true that men do not smell it, all honourable men know it to be what it is, while to Pömüffelskopp and the attorney it is as the sweet savour of myrrh and frankincense." Just as David was about to answer there came a knock at the front door. "What's that?" asked David. The old man was silent, and the knocking became louder. "Go and open the door, David."--"What, at this time of night?"--"Yes, David, open the door. When I was a lad, and used to go about the country with a pack on my back, I often knocked at the door of some man's house, and he let me in, and now that I am old I shall soon stand before another door, and when I knock at it the God of Abraham will say: let him in, he is a human being. Some human being is now knocking at my door, and shall I not let him in? Open the door, David." David obeyed, and Hawermann came in.

"Bless me!" cried the old man. "It's the bailiff!"--"Yes, Moses. Don't be angry with me, I can't help it, but my business is very important, and I must speak to you alone."--"David, you had better go away."--David made a face, but went,--"That doesn't help us much," said Moses, "for he's listening at the keyhole."--"It doesn't matter, Moses, I can't tell you here what I want you to know. Can't you come home with me?"--"I'm an old man now, Hawermann."--"I know that, but the air out of doors is quite warm, and the moon has risen. You can lean on my arm, and if you can't walk so far, I will carry you if you like."--"Why, what's the matter?"--"I can't tell you now, Moses; you must hear with your own ears, and see with your own eyes. You can do a good work if you come."--"Hawermann, you are an honest man, and have always been a friend to me from your youth up, I know that you will act rightly and justly. Call David."--Hawermann opened the door, and found him standing behind it.--"Mr. Hawermann, surely you won't take my father out tonight, he is an old man."--"Bring me my fur-boots, David," said his father.--"Don't go, father, or I will call my mother."--"Call your mother if you like, I'm going all the same."--"Why are you going?"--"On business, business of importance."--"Then I'll go with you."--"No, David, you're too young. Go and get me my fur-boots."--There was no help for it, David had to go and fetch the boots and put them on his father's feet. Hawermann then supported Moses with his arm, and the latter set off with his friend for Mrs. Behrens' house walking with great difficulty and keeping his hand in his left coat pocket all the time that he might hold up his trousers on that side, for he still continued to do without braces on his left side.

Hawermann did not manage to get old Moses over Mrs. Behrens' threshold noiselessly as he had hoped, for Moses tripped and nearly fell as he was going in. Naturally Mrs. Behrens heard the noise as distinctly as the others did.--"Ah!" she exclaimed, hastening to the door, "there's Hawermann come back with poor Mina," but when she put out her head expecting to see Mina's face, a little swollen it is true, she saw Moses in a flowing dressing gown, and fur-boots, and with his wrinkled old face and large black eyes turned full on her: "Good evening, Mrs. Behrens," he said.-- Little Mrs. Behrens was so startled that she drew back, exclaiming: "Preserve us all! Hawermann is trying all sorts of magic and heathen incantations to-night, and now he has brought an old Jew into the house at midnight; what can Moses do to cure Mina's toothache?"--Mrs. Nüssler felt as if she were in her own kitchen at home frying fish, and had just got a fine large pike in the frying pan, when it caught her by the thumb and pressed its teeth gradually deeper and deeper into her flesh, so that she could not move for fear of losing her whole thumb. What business had Mrs. Nüssler to tell such a fib, and a fib that might be disproved at any moment.--"Why, Mrs. Behrens," said Bräsig, "it can only have been Moses' double that you saw, it can't have been himself, for when I went to see him the day before yesterday he told me that he couldn't walk in the streets any more."--"Oh," interrupted Louisa, "my father must have something very important to say to the old man, and my aunt knows all about it, and has only been trying to put us off with a story about Mina. It would be very unlike my father to play foolish tricks at this time of night."--The pike forced its teeth deeper into Mrs. Nüssler's flesh, but she shut her mouth tight and kept her own counsel a little longer: "Ah see!" she said. "You're frightfully clever, Louie! Clever children are a blessing to their parents; but," she could bear it no more, and pulling her thumb out of the pike's mouth, she went on, "I wish with all my heart that you were stupider. I'll tell you the truth, Mina isn't here at all, it's Mrs. von Rambow of Pümpelhagen who has something to arrange with Charles and Moses."--Little Mrs. Behrens was very angry when she heard this, partly because she had been kept in ignorance of the truth although it was her own house, and so she was most assuredly the nearest, and ought to have been told; and partly because it showed her how horribly and heathenishly her good old friend and neighbour, Mrs. Nüssler, could lie: "You told us such a circumstantial lie," she said.--"Yes, Mrs. Behrens," answered Mrs. Nüssler, trying to look as if she had done nothing wrong, "I did."--"Mrs. Nüssler," remonstrated her friend, looking as if the little black cloak of the late parson Behrens had fallen on her shoulders, "lying is an abominable unchristian sin."--"I know that," answered Mrs. Nüssler, "and I never lie for myself. Whenever I tell a lie it's for the sake of other people. I was so sorry for the poor lady, and feared lest she should be troubled with questions.

As everyone thought it was Mina, I just said 'yes' and then invented a little story." And now it seemed as if an invisible hand had bound the Geneva bands worn by her late husband round the little lady's neck; she said gravely: "My love, I fear that you're in a very bad way, for you're deceiving yourself at this very moment, you look upon what is evil as if it were good, you tell a lie ...."--"Begging your pardon, Mrs. Behrens," interrupted Bräsig, taking his stand by the side of his old sweetheart, "for stopping you in the middle of your sermon; allow me to say that I quite agree with Mrs. Nüssler. Look you, last week the town-clerk's wife called me, and asked me very sweetly: 'Pray tell me, Mr. Bräsig, is it true that Mrs. Behrens once gave some one a randy-voo in a ditch ....'"--"Bräsig!" cried Mrs. Behrens, resuming her natural manner.--"Don't be afraid," said uncle Bräsig glancing at Louisa, "I know the prejudice that exists against such things.--'No, Ma'am,' I said, 'it's a confounded lie.' So you see, Mrs. Behrens, that I told a lie for your sake, and if I'm condemned to roast in hell for it, I hope that you'll take compassion on me in heaven, and bring me a little water to refresh me."--Mrs. Behrens was about to answer, when Hawermann looked in to say: "Will you come and speak to me for a moment, Bräsig?"--"Hawermann ...." began Mrs. Behrens.--"I shall return very soon, Mrs. Behrens."--Bräsig went away.

The conversation in the other parlour had been as eager as the one I have described, though quite different from it in every respect. When Hawermann came in with Moses, Mrs. von Rambow rose from her seat on the sofa with a pain at her heart, and Moses started back.--"Mrs. von Rambow," said Hawermann, and then turning to the lady, he added: "This is my old friend Moses, he is very tired after his walk. You will excuse us, will you not, Madam?" and so saying he led the old man up to the sofa and making him lie down, arranged the pillows under his head. As soon as his friend had recovered a little from his fatigue, Hawermann asked: "Do you know Mrs. von Rambow, Moses?"--"I've seen her driving past my house, and I've seen her walking on the road near Pümpelhagen; I touched my hat to her then and she returned the old Jew's greeting courteously."--"Moses, you know that Mr. von Rambow is in debt, deeply in debt."--"I know."--"You have demanded your money from him, principal and interest."--"I know."--"Moses, you must withdraw your demand; your money is safe."--"What do you call safe? Didn't I tell you my opinion on that head in spring. Just now land isn't good security, it's only on the man one can rely, and Mr. von Rambow is not a man whose security is good. He's a bad farmer, he's a fool about horses, he's a spend ....."--"Hush, remember that his wife is here."--"I will remember."--Frida was in an agony of silent misery. Then was not another word spoken for a few minutes, then Hawermann began again: "Supposing things were differently managed, and the estate were let on a lease of ...."--"Whoever would think of taking a lease of it in such bad times?" interrupted Moses.--"Or supposing that Mr. von Rambow decided on engaging a good, bailiff, and on leaving him alone to do his work in his own way ...."--"Hawermann," Moses once more interrupted, "you're an old man, and you're a wise man; you know the world and you know Mr. von Rambow, now let me ask you, did you ever see a master who could say, 'I won't be master any more, but will let another man be master'?"--Hawermann did not know how to meet this question, and looked enquiringly at Mrs. von Rambow, who cast down her eyes, and said: "I am afraid that Mr. Moses is right, I am afraid that my husband wouldn't do that."--Moses looked at her with a smile of commendation, and muttered: "She's a clever woman, and an honest woman."--Hawermann was in great perplexity, he sat thinking silently for some time; at last he said: "Well, Moses, I want to know whether you will give up your intention of foreclosing the mortgage, if Mrs. von Rambow, or I, or the pressure of circumstances should induce the squire to agree to this proposal, and to sign a legal document to the effect that he will give up farming himself, and will engage a good bailiff to manage the estate for him?"--"If he does that, I'll let him have the money for another year; or even two years, if you like."--"Well, you promise to leave your money as it is; but there are other debts that must be paid. There's Pomuchelskopp's £1200."--"I know," muttered Moses.--"Then there are the shopkeepers' and artisans' bills that have been running on for the last year, and which will come to at least £900."--"I know," said Moses.--"Then there's a debt of nearly two thousand pounds that must be paid in Schwerin."--"Why!" exclaimed Moses starting, "I know nothing of that debt."--"In addition to what I have told you," continued Hawermann without allowing himself to be turned from the main point, "we must have three or four hundred pounds to cover the outlay required to begin farming properly."--"That's enough, it's a bad business, a very bad business," said Moses, making a movement as though to get up from the sofa.--"Stop, Moses, I hav'n't done yet."--"Let me be, let me be! I'm an old man, and can't undertake such an affair as this," and he sat up on the sofa and prepared to go away.--"Listen to me, Moses. You're not expected to give the money which will come to £4650, other people, safe people are going to do that, and you are only required to raise it for them by the midsummer term."--"God of Abraham! And I am to raise four thousand six hundred and fifty pounds in a fortnight! *Four thousand six hundred and fifty pounds!* and that for fools who choose to throw away their money on a bad bit of business like this!"--"Well, Moses, we won't speak of that if you please. Just write down the names and sums of money as I dictate. You know Mrs. Behrens? Write down Mrs. Behrens' name for £750."--"Yes, I know her, she's a good woman and helps the poor; but why am I to write down her name?"--"Do as I have asked you."--Moses took a pocket-book out of the pocket of his dressing gown, wet the end of his pencil in his mouth and wrote: "There now," he said, "I've put her down for £750."--"You know Bräsig?"--"Who doesn't know, Bräsig? He's a good man, and a reliable man. He often came to see me when I was ill. He tried to make me a democrat, and to persuade me to make speeches at the Reform-club, but still he's a good man."--"Put him down for £900. You also know my brother-in-law, farmer Nüssler?"--"Have I not always bought his wool? He's a quiet man, and a good man. He smokes a great deal; but he isn't master, his wife is master."--"Very well, put my sister down for £1950."--"No, I won't do that. She's a woman, and a prudent woman, did she not stand out for two pence a stone more than I offered for the wool."--"You can write her name; my sister will tell you this very evening that it's all right. Now, then put me down for £1050, and that brings up the sum to £4650."--"Good God!" cried Moses. "He's going to give his hard earned money, the money he had saved for his old age, and for his only child. And to whom is he going to give it? To a young man who attacked him with a gun, who stole his honest name and who treated him like a dog."--"You've got nothing to do with that, Moses; it's my affair. We ...."--Mrs. von Rambow had hitherto remained silent, feeling the full bitterness of her misery, but now she could bear it no longer; she sprang to her feet, ran up to Hawermann and laying her hands on his shoulders, said: "No, no! It cannot be! These kind good people and you shall not be drawn into our misfortunes. It is our own fault and so we must bear our fate. I will bear it, and, oh, Alick would a thousand times rather bear it with all its misery and shame than ... but--but," here she wailed out in spite of herself, "those poor sisters of his."--Hawermann put his arm gently round her, led her back to her chair, and whispered: "Try to compose yourself. You promised to leave the affair in my hands, and I will conduct it to the end, the happy end."--The tears streamed from Frida's eyes.--"Good God!" thought Moses, laying his pencil within the pocket-book, "she's beginning to be generous now. This isn't business. This isn't business. But it's honest at any rate, and it's enough to bring tears into the eyes of an old man like me," at the same time wiping his eyes with the sleeve of his dressing gown. "Now, let me see how it stands with the Jew."

Meanwhile Hawermann had left the room to fetch Bräsig, and after telling him in the passage what had happened, came back into the room with him.--When Bräsig came in he looked quite scared and Hawermann could not help feeling impatient with him. He went straight to Moses and said: "Moses, I am ready to sign anything Charles Hawermann wants me to sign, whether it is that I'm to give the money down, or only to put my name to a bill; but I can't pay up till S. Anthony's day."--"Good," answered

Moses, "you're a safe man and I'll get you the money."--Bräsig then went to Mrs. von Rambow, who was leaning her elbow on the table, and covering her eyes with her hand as though to shield them from the light. He made her a low bow and asked her how she was, and when she had murmured some almost inaudible answer, he asked: "And how is young Mr. von Rambow?"--Frida shivered, and Hawermann, who had intended to call in the others one by one, saw that it was time to interrupt his friend, lest Bräsig should ignorantly make the poor lady yet more wretched than she was already. "Zachariah," he said, "will you be so kind as to ask Mrs. Behrens and my sister to come here. Louisa may come with them."--"All right, Charles," he replied. Soon afterwards he returned with the three women.--Mrs. Behrens rushed up to Mrs. von Rambow, pressed her in her arms and then burst into tears, and Louisa stood beside her full of deep but silent sympathy.--"God of Abraham!" muttered Moses, "what a night it is! They say that they want to do business, and yet there they are weeping over each other, pressing each other's hands, embracing and showing themselves generous and loving to each other, while they leave an old man like me to sit here till morning. Miss Hawermann," he said aloud, "when you're quite done showing your kind feeling over there, will you be so good as to bring me a little wine, for I am an old man."--Louisa immediately brought a bottle of wine and a glass, and Bräsig said: "Bring me another glass, Louisa." He no doubt considered that it was an excellent opportunity to get up a little clinking of glasses with Moses, for seating himself opposite the old Jew, he began: "Your good health, Moses."--But he failed in his attempt to induce Moses to join him, for the Jew did not take the hint, and when Hawermann brought up his sister to where they were sitting, Moses wetted his pencil and wrote. After Mrs. Nüssler, Mrs. Behrens came, and Moses wrote down what she told him; Louisa meanwhile was talking to Mrs. von Rambow somewhat apart from the others. When he had finished writing, Moses stood up and said: "I have something to say to you. The four thousand six hundred and fifty pounds wanted are covered by the promises given me to-night; but this isn't business, generosity has run away with you all. Now you know the truth. I am a Jew, and it has also run away with me. I will get the money for you. But I am an old man, and a prudent man. If Mr. von Rambow will not place his affairs in the hands of a good bailiff, and make a legal arrangement that they should be so managed, the contract is broken, and I refuse to provide the money, for it will mean ruin. When they bury me under the fir-trees in the cemetery where I have bought a resting place, they shall never have just cause to say of me: He had a tomb built for himself, of oak wood too. Shortly before his death he brought several honest people to misery, merely that he might not lose any business. Mrs. Nüssler, Mrs. Behrens, Hawermann and Mr. Bräsig are ruined by him. I have been a business man from my youth up; I began with a pack on my back; then I became a wool stapler, and lastly a money lender. I shall die as I have lived a business man, but a prudent one. Come and help me home, Hawermann. Good night, Mrs. Nüssler, remember me to Mr. Joseph, and ask him to come and see me sometimes. Good night, Mr. bailiff Bräsig, come and see me too, but don't preach to me about the Reform-club, for I am an old man. Good night, Miss Hawermann, I hope that when you next pass my house, you'll nod to me as kindly as you did last time. Good night, Mrs. Behrens, when you go to bed, you can say to yourself, I've had a number of honourable people under my roof to-day, and even the old Jew was an honourable man." Then going to Frida, he said: "Good night, Madam, you have shed tears to-night because your heart was sore; but never fear, all will yet be well; you have gained a new friend in an old Jew; but the old Jew has wept for your sorrow and he will never forget that, for his tears do not flow easily now." He turned away, said "Good night" once more, but without looking round, and Hawermann led him out, while Louisa lighted them to the house door. Within the best parlour silence prevailed, each was busy with his or her own thoughts. The first to recover herself was Mrs. Nüssler, who called Christian, who was sound asleep in the front hall, and desired him to get the carriage ready. Christian was much more active than usual on this occasion, so that when Hawermann returned from seeing Moses home, he found Mrs. von Rambow and his sister already seated in the carriage. He had only time to say one or two kind hopeful words to Mrs. von Rambow, before Mrs. Nüssler said: "Good night, Charles, she wants to get home to her little child. To Pümpelhagen, Christian," and then they drove away.

Hawermann remained standing out in the street, lost in thought, and following the receding carriage with his eyes. Just as he was turning to go into the house again another carriage drawn by two horses came slowly down the street, distinctly visible in the bright moonlight. The old man was now standing in the door-way, his whole figure brought out clearly by the background of light from the lamp his daughter had put in the hall to enable him to see his way upstairs. He wanted to see who was driving through their quiet street at such a late, or rather at such an early hour in the morning; the carriage came nearer, and at last stopped. "Take the reins," cried a voice which seemed strangely familiar to him, and a man who was sitting on the front seat, threw the reins to the groom behind him, and then sprang out into the street. "Hawermann, Hawermann! Don't you know me?"--"Frank! Mr. von Rambow!"--"What's the matter?" asked Frank. "Why are you up so late?" pushing him a little away from him, "nothing wrong?"--"No--thank God!--nothing; I'll tell you all about it immediately." Then the young man threw his arms round Hawermann, pressed him to his heart, and kissed him. They were not unhappy, on the contrary, their joy was great, and yet in the sitting-room near them a girl might have been seen with pale cheeks and large distended eyes staring at the door. When she got up the floor seemed to rise to meet her, and she pressed her hands upon her heart to still its wild beating when she heard the voice she loved so well. She did not know it, could not see it at that moment, the shock of surprise had come so suddenly; but the modest flowers she had planted in the garden of her soul, and the shady bower from which she had so often gazed at the evening star of memory and where she had hidden away her inmost thoughts, were now lighted up by the sun of joy, the rays of which were so brilliant that she was fain to turn away her eyes; but she could not, and she saw new and wonderful flowers appearing whose existence she had never dreamt of. She saw rising from a bed of violets the loveliest red roses such as brides wear, and the whole air was full of the songs of nightingales, showing that spring had come, the spring of love. As Frank came in, her hands sank down by her side, and when he clasped her in his arms she no longer felt the ground tremble as it had seemed to do before. The storm had passed away and she was happy. They talked a great deal to each other: "Frank!"--"Louisa!" but none could understand their speech, and stood round them comprehending nothing, for it was long since they had heard such language. At last uncle Bräsig took compassion on the young people who were soaring away over the earth and the clouds, and brought them back to every day life with a little shock: "Mrs. Behrens," he said, "when I had three sweethearts at once, I ...."--"Fie, for shame, Bräsig!" exclaimed Mrs. Behrens in the midst of her tears. "You said the same to me, Mrs. Behrens, that time that I told you I had written to young Mr. von Rambow in Paris, through Dr. Ürtling, but I wasn't ashamed of myself then, and I won't be ashamed of myself now, indeed I have never been ashamed of myself all my life. You see, Mrs. Behrens," and he placed himself in front of the old lady with his feet even more in the first position than usual, and blew his nose to hide that he at the same time wiped his eyes. "You see, Mrs. Behrens, that in the last few years I have had many a randyvoo. The first of them was held in a meadow ditch ...."--"Bräsig!" cried Mrs. Behrens. "Never fear, Mrs. Behrens, I won't tell, and I'll even go so far as to tell a lie for your sake if I find it necessary. The second time was in a cherry tree with Godfrey and Lina; the third, Rudolph and Mina, again in a cherry tree; but you mustn't take it ill of me if I am perhaps a little too proud of having brought about a randyvoo between Paris and Rahnstädt, for in that also I have succeeded."--"Yes," said Frank, suddenly falling to the earth from the clouds at that precise moment, "you have, and I thank you for it with all my heart. Your letter was most delightful to me, and I have it here, I always carry it about with me."--"Hm!" said uncle Bräsig, "he carries it about with him, does he! I'm very much obliged! But now tell me frankly, and honestly: did you admire the letter so much that you keep it by you, because of the style in which it is written--for you know Charles, you can't deny that my style was thought better than yours, when parson Behrens used to teach us long ago--or did you keep it because the paper had belonged to Louisa?"--"For both reasons," answered Frank, with a merry laugh, "and also because of the good news contained in your letter.--Yes," he continued, going to Hawermann and throwing his arm round him, "now that all your troubles, your self-made troubles are over, there's no reason why this separation shouldn't end." Then going to Louisa he gave her a kiss, and this kiss was a very peculiar one, for it might have been divided by twelve and yet it was only one kiss in reality. "Bless me!" cried Mrs. Behrens, "Look, it's actually beginning to get light."--"Yes," answered Bräsig, "and here you are going about still. Remember that you're an old woman now, and go to bed."--"Bräsig is right," said Hawermann, "and you should go too, Louie."--"Come away, dear child," said Mrs. Behrens, putting her arm round Louisa's waist, "tomorrow will be another day, and a happy day too," and so saying she kissed the girl fondly. "Yes," she continued, "a happy life is beginning for you, and for me through you." They went away. "And now Mr. von Rambow," said Hawermann. "Why not Frank?" interrupted the young man. "Well then, Frank, my dear son, you may sleep in my bed in the same room as Bräsig, I ...."--"I can't sleep," interrupted Frank.--"Charles," said Bräsig, "I...."--"I can't sleep," interrupted Frank.--"Charles," said Bräsig, "I don't feel at all sleepy; my usual bed time, and power of lying still are both gone." He opened the window and looked out,--"Charles," he said, "it seems to me as if this was just the right sort of weather for the fish to bite. I must go out, for I don't feel comfortable in the house, so I'll take my rod, and see what I can get. I know a capital place to go to, I mean lake Lauban in the pine wood at Rexow, where I'm sure to catch a good dish of tench. Good morning, young Mr. von Rambow, good morning, Charles, have a good talk about everything with your future son-in-law." He then went away.

"Pray tell me, dear father," asked Frank, "why you're up and stirring at such an unusual hour? I left Paris as soon as I got Bräsig's letter, and have travelled night and day as far as my own home, where I arrived the day before yesterday. I found a good deal to attend to there, for my bailiff is going away to be married, and I couldn't get away again to come on here till yesterday morning. I had ordered horses to be in readiness for me at the various posting houses, and when I got to Rahnstädt--I may as well confess"--and he laughed rather consciously. "I couldn't help wishing to see the house where Louisa lived, and I found you all up."--"Ah," sighed Hawermann, "the cause of our being up was a sad one. It was about the affairs of Mr. von Rambow of Pümpelhagen, and his wife came herself to see me and tell me what was going on. She has had a terrible time of anxiety and sorrow; but no one could have saved her from that, and now everything is in process of being arranged. I wish to God that you--had arrived a little earlier, and then the business would have been done at once." Hawermann then proceeded to relate all that had happened with such feeling and sympathy, and such a visible desire that all should be put right, that Frank also began to wish to help, and the best of it was that he could do it. He had had the good fortune to have had wise guardians and honest bailiffs who understood their work, so that his wealth had increased in their hands, and afterwards in his own, for he had not made a ladder of his inheritance by means of which to descend into the abyss of dissipation and foolish extravagance; and on the other hand his good sense and warm heart had saved him from growing into a hard man. He could therefore act as generously as he wished.

Frank and Hawermann talked long and earnestly together, for both desired to help Alick, and after careful consideration they agreed that Frank should go and see Moses that very day. In spite of their frank open dealing with each other, each of them had a secret from the other. Hawermann did not say a word to the young man of Alick's debt to his sisters, for that was a secret Mrs. von Rambow had confided to him with a breaking heart; he felt that he had no right to tell such a thing as that, it was the property of another and did not belong to him. Frank had his secret also, but it must have been a pleasant one, his face looked so happy, and there was such thorough enjoyment in the way in which he first stretched out one leg on the sofa, and then drew the other after it. When Hawermann went on to tell him other things, he nodded smilingly, and went on nodding until he at last nodded himself to sleep. Youth and nature were no longer to be debarred from their rights. When he was asleep old Hawermann rose softly and gazed into his face on which a smile still lingered, reminding one of the way in which the last rays of the setting sun are sometimes to be seen flickering on the clear, calm, transparent waters of some inland lake. He spread a warm rug over the sleeper and then went out to the arbour in Mrs. Behrens back garden, the arbour he himself had made in the days of his sorrow, and seating himself looked up at the window of the room in which his daughter slept. But was she asleep? Who can sleep when the sun of joy is shining in his heart; who can sleep when every sound has become a song of love and happiness. The garden gate clicked softly, and a lovely girl came in dressed in a white morning gown. She raised her face to the sky and watched the rising sun, with her hands clasped, as though she did not fear to blind herself with its dazzling rays, and as she gazed tears ran down her rosy cheeks. Right, Louisa! The sun is God's sun, and happiness is also God's; when they shine in our eyes and threaten to blind us with their beauty tears are good, for they enable us to bear their brightness. She stooped down over a rose, and drank in its fragrance, but without plucking it. Right Louisa! Roses are earthly flowers, and joys are also earthly; they alike bloom for a time, so leave them to live out their life in peace. If you wish to enjoy them before their time, you will find a withered flower in your bosom, and a withered joy in your heart. She walked on slowly, and when she came to the arbour, she saw her father sitting there, and throwing herself on his breast, she cried: "Father, father!" Right Louisa! You are in your proper place, for God's sun is shining in your father's heart, and the roses of earth are blooming there.

CHAPTER XVI

Mrs. Nüssler took Frida home, and on the way there she dropped many a word of comfort into her sad heart, and her words fell like rain upon a dry and parched field. If hope did not spring up strongly in Frida's heart, she was yet able to wait in patience, and to find rest in Mrs. Nüssler's reiterated words: "Don't fret about it. Trust my brother Charles, I am sure that he'll put it all right for you." When Frida went into her room in the grey of the early morning she felt herself a different creature from what she had been when she rushed out on the previous evening. With the spark of hope that had been kindled in her breast, love and faith had come back to her, and she went up to Sophie Degel, who was seated in a large arm chair watching over her child, and stroking her hair gently, said: "I am so much obliged to you, Sophie, but I'm sure that you're tired; go to bed now."--"Oh, Madam," cried Sophie starting up--no doubt from the midst of a dream about her lover, "she has slept quietly all night; she only wakened once, and I gave her some milk and then she went to sleep again."--"That's right," answered Mrs. von Rambow, "but now go to bed." When the maid had left the room, she bent over her little girl's crib and looked at her: no, no, the baby was far too lovely for the sad fate of a penniless lady of rank; the mother's thoughts this morning were quite changed from her desponding forebodings of the evening. Her soul had been writhing in anguish the night before, and out of that anguish hope had been born anew in her heart. This child of pain now clasped her in its arms kissed her and whispered the heavenly words: Faith--and--victory!

Mrs. von Rambow went to bed, and thought of all the people she had seen that night. Caroline Kegel and Mrs. Nüssler, Mrs. Behrens and Louisa, Hawermann and Bräsig, she could recall their faces clearly, and could understand their kindness and sympathy; but there was another person she could not understand, and that was the old Jew. She remembered his speaking expression, the dark heavy folds of his dressing gown, his shadowy wrinkled face--a face such as she had never seen before--then all seemed to grow more misty--when she thought of the last words the Jew had said to her as he was going away, she seemed to see him growing larger and larger, but more and more indistinct, and folding her hands upon her breast, she fell asleep.

She slept and dreamt of the old Jew, but it was a happy dream; at last she awoke thinking she heard a carriage drive into the yard. She listened attentively, but body and mind longed for rest, her head sank back on the pillow, and her happy dream returned to her and whispered marvellous things in her ears.

She had not been mistaken after all, a carriage had really driven up to the door, and her husband had come in it.--Since he had left home Alick had been driving here, there and everywhere, like a man who goes about the country to buy up eggs and poultry. He had knocked at every door like a rag merchant. He had begged from men of business, he had made his moan to friends with whom he had become acquainted at race meetings, and who had won his money. No one was at home, and the few whom he met accidentally, had forgotten their purses at home. As long as we go about the world spending money, we have many friends, but when we begin to show ourselves a little out at elbows our friends become ashamed of knowing us. Alick was to learn this by bitter, bitter experience. He had gone secretly to Schwerin, without his sisters' knowledge; he had gone to the Jews who had formerly done business with him with so much pleasure, but what could he mortgage in these bad times?--He could see Frank's estates in the distance from the window of his inn; but where was Frank?--He had done what he could, he had even gone to his brother-in-law, Mr. von Breitenburg, with whom he had always been on bad terms, had borne with the cool reception he got, and had explained the difficulties of his position but without mentioning his sisters' money, and his brother-in-law had stared at him and turning his back upon him rudely, had said: "'Tu l'as voulu, George Dandin!' And you really want me to throw my money into the quicksands that have swallowed yours? My money that I have made by self-denial and hard work? For, as you know, your sister didn't bring it to me when I married her."--Alick was about to have reminded him of the money his father had once borrowed from Moses for him, when his brother-in-law, wheeled round suddenly and asked point blank: "Where are the £1950 you swindled your sisters out of?"--That was the last straw--his brother-in-law knew that--he turned deadly pale, staggered out of the room, and got into his carriage.--"Where?" asked the coachman.--"Home."--"Where are we to spend the night?"--"At home."--"The horses will never manage it, Sir."--"They must."--So he went home, and when he had got out of the carriage, John went and stood beside his horses: "Ah," he said, "the two horses next the carriage were knocked up before with the long distances we went, and now the two leaders are done for. None of them will be up to any work again."

Alick went upstairs to his room with a slow heavy step. It was full daylight now, and he saw that his room looked the same as usual. He had always felt so comfortable there before, and all his life he had been so much ruled by custom. But his heart was changed, his mind and heart were changed, so that custom had no longer its old influence over him. He was anxious and restless, and opened the window that the fresh morning air might cool his heated brow. He threw himself in the arm chair before his writing table and pressed his head between his hands. Then his eyes fell upon a letter. The handwriting was well known to him, for he had often seen it before; he tore it open; yes, it was from his sister. What was it his brother-in-law Breitenburg had said to him? Yes, that was it. He looked out of the window, and saw the sun rising behind the pine wood at Rexow. He looked at the letter again, it was full of words of kindness; but what good did that do, he had no money.--He looked out at the window once more, and saw the wheat field lying before him. Ah, if the wheat were only ripe, if it were thrashed out and were found to have borne twentyfold more than usual, ah, then--no, no, even that could not save him.--He looked at the letter again: kind words! Somehow the words looked graver and more earnest now than they had done at first--he could not turn his eyes from them--he read on to the end, and this was the last sentence: "that is the reason why I wrote to Frida too, for my dear, dear brother if you have not put out our money safely we poor women are ruined."--"Yes, ruined," he exclaimed, "ruined!" and he started up and began to pace the room rapidly. He went to the window and the face of nature was turned to him in her full glory. Nature has often a soothing influence on the human heart; but then the heart must be open to receive the message of the sunshine, and the green earth and deep blue sky. Alick's heart was not capable of thus receiving the divine message, his mind and thoughts were too much under the dominion of small, miserably pitiful human action. Gold! Gold! He could not coin the sunshine into Louis d'ors.--He threw himself into his chair again; she, his wife knew all. He had often lied to her, when he knew she could not find him out; but he could not lie to her about this, for she knew the truth. He imagined her coming to him with her child in her arms, and looking at him with her clear grey eyes, as she asked: "How have we deserved this at your hands?" Then he thought that his sisters would come with hollow cheeks and white lips, and say: "Yes, Alick, dear Alick, we are ruined."-- And behind his three sisters, he imagined a grave stern figure appearing--a figure not of this world--and he knew that it was his father, who seemed to say to him: "You should have been a prop and support to my ancient house, and instead of that you have pulled it down from battlement to basement, and have razed it to the ground."--He could bear it no longer, and sprang to his feet--the spirits he had called up were gone--he strode up and down the room, but at length stood still before the cabinet in which he kept his firearms.--He knew a good place to do the deed. Nothing could be better for his purpose than Lake Lauban which lay in the pine wood at Rexow. He had often been there shooting with good old Slang, the forester, in the happy days that were gone, and he could do it there without fear of disturbance. He took the pistol out of the cabinet which Triddelfitz had brought him to shoot at the labourers with. He tried it; yes, it was loaded. He went out of his room, but as he crossed the landing he saw the door of Frida's room, the room in which his wife and child were sleeping, and he started back, staggering as if he had received a blow. The memory of all the happiness his true hearted wife had brought into his home and the thought of the noble woman the gentle girl he had married had become, came over him, and sinking on his knees at her door, he burst into silent weeping. Who knows but what these hot tears and that fervent prayer to God may have saved him--we shall see that they did--for God holds our hearts by a light invisible thread. Alick rose, his prayer had not been for himself, but for others. He went out of doors, and walked straight on towards the still, woodland lake. When he was safely in the pine wood, he threw himself on the grass behind a bush, pulled the pistol out of his pocket and laid it down by his side. He gazed at the scene around him hungrily; he looked up once more at the sun, God's beautiful sun; it was his last look, the thick darkness of night would soon enclose him. The sunlight blinded him, so he took out his pocket-handkerchief and covered his eyes with it, and now the last terrible thoughts came into his mind. He murmured with a deep sigh: "I must!"

"Good morning, Mr. von Rambow," said a kindly human voice beside him.--Alick pulled the handkerchief off his face and threw it over the pistol.--"You're up very early," said Zachariah Bräsig, for it was he, and as he spoke he sat down on the grass beside Alick, "but perhaps you're going to fish too?" Laying his hand on the handkerchief and pistol, he added: "Ah, I see you're going to practise pistol shooting." And rising he asked, "do you see that mark on the pine?--Slang's going to have the tree cut down--Now, I bet four pence that I hit it, and I never bet more than that"--bang! and missed it; bang! missed it again, and so on every time till he had fired off all the six shots the revolver contained. "Who would have thought it? Missed them all! I've lost my bet so, here's the four pence. It's a good-for-nothing thing," he exclaimed, throwing the revolver far into the lake, "and it's better there, for children and young people might get hold of it and imprudently shoot themselves dead with it."--Alick felt his thoughts in a strange whirl. Between him and the firm determination he had come to after much internal conflict and painful thought; between him and the dark portal through which he had made up his mind to pass although unsummoned, stood a common man, a mere clown as he had often called him in his thoughts, and withal a man who was as self-satisfied and impudent as a juggler at a fair. He sprang to his feet, exclaiming: "Sir!"--"And you, Sir!" cried Bräsig.--"What are you doing here?" asked Alick.--"And what are you doing here?" retorted Bräsig.--"You're a meddlesome fool!" cried Alick.--"And you're much the greater fool of the two!" cried uncle Bräsig, "You were about to do the most horrible of all deeds here, in your thoughtlessness. You have forgotten everything: Your wife and your child. H'm! you thought it a small thing to do, and then you'd be free. Am I not right? Who's the fool now?"--Alick was leaning against a pine-tree, one of his hands pressed upon his heart, and the other shading his eyes from the sun, while the "clown" who had prevented him entering the gates of death stood before him, fishing-rod in hand.--"Look you," continued uncle Bräsig, "if you had come here three minutes before I did"--these were the three minutes he spent weeping and praying at his wife's door--"you would now have been lying there with a hole through your head, a horrible example to all, and when you appeared before the throne of God, our Lord God would have said to you: You didn't know, Tom Fool, what your dear good wife did for you to-night, and Mr. bailiff Hawermann, and Mrs. Nüssler, and Mrs. Behrens, and Moses, and--and the others. If our Lord God had enlightened you on this subject, do you know where you would have felt yourself to be? In Hell!"--Alick had taken his hand down from his eyes, and was staring hard at Bräsig: "What? What are you saying?"--"That £4650 have been got for you this very night, that Moses is raising the money for you, and that your cousin Frank has come, and he will probably do more than that for you. But you are a foolish sort of man; you employ the greyhound Triddelfitz to get you a revolver to fire upon your labourers, and after all you are about to use it against yourself."--"Frank here? Frank, did you say?"--"Yes, he is here, but he didn't come for your sake; he has come to turn Louisa Hawermann into Mrs. von Rambow. However if you want to know to whom you owe gratitude just now--Frank will probably do something besides--you must go to your own sweet wife, and to Charles Hawermann; you may also go to Moses, and be sure that you don't forget either Mrs. Nüssler or Mrs. Behrens. They have all united in doing you a good turn this night."

    I never wished to shoot myself and I do not know how a poor fellow feels when he is drawn back from the gates of death by a chance such as this. I think it must be as provoking as for a weary, way-worn traveller to be shown a glass of sour beer--and uncle Bräsig looked uncommonly sour that morning--which he cannot get at. But very soon the love of life returned, the dear love of life, and with it came the thought of his young wife and little child, refreshing him as a glass of cool wine drunk to the last drop: "Do tell me what has happened," he said. Uncle Bräsig then told him of the good things in store for him, and Alick staggered forward from his resting place against the pine and throwing his arms round the old man's neck, exclaimed: "Mr. Bräsig! Dear Mr. Bräsig! Can it be true?"--"What do you mean? Do you think that I would lie to you at such a solemn moment." Alick felt dizzy when he thought of the black abyss which had lain before him, and into which he had dared to gaze. He fell back a few steps. The sweet sounds he heard in the air, and the fair earth around him, all that he had formerly looked at, and listened to with indifference, now filled his heart with a sense of harmonious beauty he had never hitherto imagined. He hid his face in his hands and wept bitterly. Bräsig looked at him compassionately, and going up to him, put his arm round his shoulders and shook him gently, saying: "We all have our times of bitterness while we are in this world, and a great part of your misfortunes arise from your own fault; but the fault doesn't lie entirely on your shoulders, for what induced your lady mother to ride the devil of pride, and make you lieutenant in a cavalry regiment? What use is a lieutenancy to a farmer? It's much the same thing as if David Berger the town musician, having blown away half the breath in his body in playing the trumpet, were to wish to turn preacher and hold forth with only a half allowance of breath; he'd break down to a certainty! But," here he drew the young man's arm within his own, "come away from this place, and then you'll feel better."--"Yes, yes," cried Alick, "you're right. All my misfortunes spring from the time I was in the army. It was then that I first got into debt, and after that things grew worse. But," he added after a short pause and coming to a sudden standstill, "what am I to say to my wife?"--"Nothing at all," answered Bräsig.--"No," said Alick, "I have just sworn a solemn oath to myself to tell her the exact truth from henceforth."--"You're right there," replied Bräsig. "Surely you don't think that Mrs. von Rambow will ask you--plump out--whether you didn't want to shoot yourself this morning? If you should get into any difficulty in conversation with her when we go in, I'll lie for you as much as is needful, and I'm sure that it won't be counted against me, for it would be too horrible if the dear good young lady were to go through life with the knowledge that the husband, who ought to take care of her and her child, was once going to have been cowardly enough to have forsaken them both. No," he said decidedly, "she must never know it, nor must anyone know it except you and me. Now listen, she must be still asleep, for it was very late before she got to bed, and she must have been quite worn out."

When they reached Pümpelhagen, they found Daniel Sadenwater at the door. "Daniel," said Bräsig, "will you go and get us some breakfast, for," he added as soon as Daniel was gone, "you must eat to strengthen yourself, what you have gone through this morning is enough to have made you feel faint and weak." This time it is difficult to decide whether Bräsig was actuated by love of his neighbour, or love of himself, for when the breakfast came Alick could eat nothing, while he had the appetite of a ploughman.

Frida came into the room about ten o'clock: "What, you here, Mr. Bräsig, and you too, Alick."--"Yes, dear Frida, I came home this morning," said the young man in a low weak voice. "And now, you won't go away again, you'll remain here," said Frida determinately. "Ah Alick, I have so much to tell you, and good news too. But how did Mr. Bräsig and you happen to meet." Uncle Bräsig thought that the time had now come for him to keep his promise about telling a lie: "I went out early this morning to fish--I hope, Madam, that you won't mind my having put my fishing tackle in your hall--and I met Mr. von Rambow, who had gone out for a turn; we looked at his wheat field together and he asked me to come to breakfast! Oh, Madam, what a capital sausage your cook makes. You must have got the receipt from Mrs. Nüssler."--"No," answered Frida slowly, and looking first at Bräsig and then at Alick, as though she thought it strange that Alick should have invited the old bailiff to come back with him. "What do you think of the wheat, Mr. bailiff Bräsig?" H'm! thought Bräsig, there'll be no end to the lying if I don't look out, I must change the subject, so he said, "Pardon me, Madam, but you always call me 'bailiff,' I used to be that, but have now got an advancement, and am made assessor. Apopo," turning to Alick, "why have you never come for the money that is waiting for you at the town-hall in Rahnstädt?"--"What money is that?" asked Alick. "Why, the two hundred and twenty five pounds that remain of the three hundred you sent by Regel. The mayor wrote to tell you about it last week."--"Ah," said Alick, "I've had so many letters from the Rahnstädt court of justice lately that I've ceased to open them."--"I know all about it," cried Frida, "Mrs. Nüssler told me. I'll go and fetch the letter."--"Young Mr. von Rambow," said Bräsig drawing himself up, "that was another mistake on your part, for we magistrates are not only the punishers of humanity, but also its ben'factors."--"Do tell me how the money got there."--"Here's the letter," said Frida, giving it to her husband. Alick opened it with feelings that may easily be imagined! His soul had longed for money during the last few weeks, money, more money! And now an unlooked for sum was going to fall into his hands; but what was it? "Oh God! Oh God!" he cried starting up and beginning to pace the room with uneven steps and a troubled mien like that of a sleep walker: "Neither is this true! Nothing true! In what hands have I been? Deceived by all! Deceived by myself--and that was the worst deception!" So saying he rushed out at the door. Frida would have followed him, but Bräsig held her back: "Leave him to me, dear Lady," he entreated, "I know how to calm him."--He followed Alick to the garden where he found him in a half maddened state, and said: "What mischief are you hatching now, Sir?"--"Get out of my way!" cried Alick. "No," answered Bräsig, "there's no need of that. You ought to be ashamed of yourself for distressing your wife so terribly."--"Why didn't you let me put an end to myself?" cried Alick, "this is a thousand times bitterer than death. Benefits and what benefits!--to have to accept benefits at the hands of those one has formerly despised and injured, on whom one has even brought shame and disgrace. Oh that I had not to do it--but--if I am to live at all--I *must*. Oh, oh," he cried, striking his forehead, "why should I live? Why should I live with this arrow in my heart?" So he raged against himself and against the world, and uncle Bräsig stood quietly beside him, watching him. At last he said: "Go on like that a little longer. I'm glad to see you so. You're getting rid of all your old stuck-up folly, and that's good for you. What?--you wouldn't have any friendship with honest middle-class people? Wasn't it so? You were quite happy when any Mr. von something or other came, or you could even put up with Pomuchelskopps, Slus'uhrs and Davids, for you thought you could then keep everything snug and secret. But that sort won't come again. However that's quite a second'ry matter. You ought to be ashamed of yourself for having dared to wish that you had shot yourself before the very face of our Lord God who saved you this morning. What? You are doubly a soo'cide!" Alick was quite quiet now, but as pale as death. His head swam when he thought of the abyss into which he had so nearly thrown himself, and Bräsig catching him in his arms, supported him to the bench on which both his old father and his wife had sat in their hour of sorrow. When he was sufficiently recovered, Zachariah Bräsig took his arm again, and said: "Come away. Come to your wife. That's the proper place for you just now." And Alick followed him like a lamb. When they got back to the morning room, Mrs. von Rambow put her arms round her husband, made him lie down on the sofa and spoke so lovingly to him, that the tears came into his eyes, and then the ice was broken by the warmth of the spring sunshine her love spread around him, and his soul was free from the bondage with which he had bound it--free, though not yet at peace! Meanwhile Zachariah Bräsig had gone to the window, where he amused himself by drumming his favourite 'March of the old Dessauer,' and Fred Triddelfitz, who was passing, came and asked: "Do you want me, Mr. Bräsig?"--"No," growled Bräsig, "attend to your own business, and see to the farming."

Soon afterwards a carriage drove up to the door, and Frank and Hawermann got out of it.

About nine o'clock that morning Frank had gone with Hawermann to see Moses, and had told him that he would pay the £4650 for his cousin instead of the people who had promised to do it on the previous evening. Moses nodded his approval several times, and said: "You are good for the money, and so are the others; but you are rich, and it's better that you should do it." When this matter was satisfactorily arranged and Frank and Hawermann had walked a good way up the street, the former said: "Will you sit down on this bench for a few minutes, father, I forgot that I must settle one little point more particularly with Moses." When he went into the Jew's office, he said: "Moses, my future father-in-law, Mr. Hawermann, tells me that Pomuchelskopp intends to sell Gürlitz ...."--"What do you say?" interrupted Moses. "Hawermann--father-in-law? What's all this?"--"I am going to marry his daughter." The old Jew rose from his chair with pain and difficulty, and laying his withered hand upon the head of the young Christian and nobleman said: "The God of Abraham bless you! You are marrying a good girl." After a short pause Frank went on to say: "I want you to buy Gürlitz for me, and to make all the necessary arrangements without letting my name appear--I don't want anyone--especially Hawermann--to know about it. I can pay up £15,000 at S. John's day."--"How much shall I offer?"--"I leave it entirely in your hands; but send in your offer to-day. I'll come back to-morrow, and then we can talk it over more particularly."--"Very well," said Moses, "this is business, honest business, so why should I not do it for you?" Frank went away.

When Alick saw his cousin and Hawermann getting out of the carriage, he tried to put on a look of indifference, and to make it appear as if nothing had happened, but his attempt was a signal failure. The storm that had been raging in his soul had been too terrible to admit of concealment, and the traces of it were so painfully visible that Frida and Bräsig put themselves forward to try and divert attention from him; but he sprang to his feet and was about to rush up to Hawermann and assure him of his repentance, when Frida putting her arms round him, stopped him, and said: "Alick, dear Alick, not just now. To-morrow, the day after, any day will do. You'll find Mr. Hawermann whenever you want him." Then Hawermann took up his hat, and saying he had a message for Fred Triddelfitz from his father, left the room. Frank went to Alick and laying his hand upon his shoulder, said: "Come to another room, Alick, I have a great deal to tell you." When they had been alone for some time, Frank came back and asked Frida to join them. Shortly afterwards Daniel Sadenwater crossed the yard in search of Hawermann, and when he had gone to the others, passing close to Bräsig on his way there, uncle Bräsig found it unpleasantly lonely in the morning room, so he went into the garden, and seating himself in the arbour looked down in the direction of the Rexow pine wood and lake Lauban. He thought: "Strange!--What is life? What is human life?" after thinking of a dozen or so different things small and great for half an hour, he at last said aloud: "I wish I had something to eat, and that there was a quiet place for me to refresh myself in!"

And his wish was soon afterwards granted, for Daniel Sadenwater came and called him in, and when he was shown into the dining room he saw Hawermann and Alick shaking hands warmly, while Frank came forward rubbing his hands and glancing at the dinner table, said: "Ah Mr. Bräsig, ar'n't you hungry?" Frida, who had been looking at her husband with a sweet smile, and happy face, turned to the old man, and said: "Mr. bailiff--I mean to say Mr. assessor Bräsig, when we first came to Pümpelhagen, you sat beside me at dinner, and now that we are going to leave it, you must sit by me again."--"Going away? Why?"--"Yes, old friend," answered Hawermann, "you generally know everything long before other people, but we've stolen a march on you this time. Mr. von Rambow and Frank have exchanged their properties; it's arranged that Mr. von Rambow's to have Hohen-Selchow, and Frank, Pümpelhagen."--"Nothing could be better Charles, and as for your saying that I knew nothing about it, I assure you that years ago, while he was still a member of your household, I was quite aware how young Mr. von Rambow would turn out." He then went to Frank and shook him heartily by the hand.

When dinner was over, there was much talk of the new arrangements to be made, and everyone saw how much lighter Alick's heart was now that he was no longer under a monetary obligation to anyone but his own cousin. He was satisfied with all that was thought necessary for him to do, and consented willingly to sign a bond that he would engage a thoroughly good bailiff to manage his estate for him, for he knew that his doing so was the best security he could give Frank that the money he had lent him had not been thrown away.

Our story is fast coming to an end now.--In a week's time Moses had completed the purchase of Gürlitz from Pomuchelskopp. It cost £19,300. Frank set to work with a will, and went straight from Moses to Schulz, the carpenter: "Mr. Schulz," he said, "can you keep a secret?"--"That I can."--"Well,--Pümpelhagen belongs to me now, and I want you to send some of your people there to pull down the palings you put up round the paddocks."--"Ah," answered Schulz, "I thought at the time that it couldn't go on long."--"Then you understand," continued Frank, "and there's another thing I had to tell you, I am to be put in possession of Gürlitz at midsummer "--"Oh ho! Then Mr. Pomuchelskopp's going at last."--"Yes. But now listen. I am going to build a house there for the widows of the parish clergymen, and I want it to be exactly the same as the parsonage, and to be as near the church-yard as it is. So make out your plans tomorrow."--"I needn't do that, for I've two plans already, one which I took from my own measurements, and the other from the measurements Miss Hawermann took with her tape measure."--"All right," said Frank with a smile, "build according to the last you mentioned."--"But it wasn't right."--"That doesn't matter! I wish you to follow Miss Hawermann's measurements. Order what wood you need to-morrow, hire carters here in Rahnstädt and engage a good master builder to do the masonry; but above all things, hold your tongue. When you want money you can apply to Moses."--And having said this he went away. Old Schulz stood in the doorway looking after him and muttering: "These nobles, these nobles!--What mad notions they have!--Tape measure!--Apron strings!--But Pomuchelskopp: Out! out!--That's real good news!"

Frank set off for Hohen-Selchow accompanied by Hawermann and Mr. Bremer, the bailiff Alick had engaged. Alick then removed there bag and baggage, and he was followed by the mayor of Rahnstädt, who was to make out the deed of exchange; Bräsig went with him as assessor. It took three weeks to complete the arrangements there and to take over the Pümpelhagen inventory, after that everything was settled satisfactorily.

Meanwhile Mrs. Behrens was making preparations for the marriage. I will say nothing descriptive of this wedding; it was solemnized quietly, and so I will let it pass quietly from my book.

The day after the marriage, Louisa, Frank, Mrs. Behrens and Hawermann got into a large carriage, and Bräsig went on the box beside the coachman, and so they set off for Pümpelhagen. When they went through Gürlitz they saw a house being built and a number of men busily working at boards and planks and oaken posts, to say nothing of one great beam which was lying on the ground ready to be used as a support to the roof. Schulz, the carpenter, was hard at work in his shirt sleeves directing his men, and seeing that they did as he desired. Frank made the coachman stop, and called to the old man: "Is all going on well, Mr. Schulz?"--"All's going on well."--"You may say what you like now, Mr. Schulz."--"Here goes then," said Schulz, "but Miss Haw--, I mean to say, Madam, what trouble you have given me to be sure! When I thought I had it all right I found it would never do. I had to get another of those great beams after all."--"What?" asked Louisa, looking at Frank,--"Nothing, dear child," he answered, putting his arm round her waist, "but that I have bought Gürlitz, and am having a house built for the widows of Gürlitz clergymen, and it's to be as nearly as possible the same as the parsonage."--"For me?" cried little old Mrs. Behrens, and the tears that had been in her eyes, ever since she first caught sight of the churchyard in which her husband was sleeping, now fell down her cheeks, and seizing Frank's hand, she wept tears of joy over it. Her tears of sadness were thus changed to those of heartfelt happiness in like manner as with many another child of man.--"And I thought," continued Frank with quiet kindness, "that my father-in-law and Bräsig would still live with you. I thought, father, that you would perhaps undertake the management of this place for me, and that you and Bräsig would sometimes come and overlook my farming at Pümpelhagen to see that I am getting on all right."--"Whenever you like," cried Bräsig from the box. "Didn't I tell you, Charles, that he would turn out well?"--And Hawermann's eyes sparkled with delight. To be able to farm again! To lead an active, useful life once more! To do, and live!----Louisa laid her head on Frank's shoulder, saying: "How dear and good you are, Frank."--The carriage drove on, and they soon arrived at Pümpelhagen. There was no triumphal arch this time. But in every heart there was an arch of gratitude to the Lord God of Heaven.

I have now come to the end of my story, and might stop here, but I know so well what will happen. Many of my readers will want to know what has become of the people about whom I have been writing since the year 1848, so I will tell them that.

CHAPTER XVII

A year before I left Mecklenburg to go and live in Thuringia, I went to see the old homesteads where I had spent so many happy days when I was young; I went to Rahnstädt, and without stopping there, set out for Gürlitz on a lovely Sunday afternoon in the month of June. I intended to visit Hawermann, Bräsig, and Mrs. Behrens, whom I had known from my boyhood, and whom I had often visited afterwards in Rahnstädt. Godfrey, I had also known in his most methodistical days, and--strangely enough--we were very good friends, although he knew that I had quite a different faith from what he had, perhaps he liked me because I was a very quiet young fellow.

When I got to Gürlitz I went straight to the house that had been built for the widows of the parish clergymen. I took hold of the handle, but the door was locked. "Hm!" said I to myself, "it's Sunday afternoon, and very hot weather; I daresay that they're having a nap." I went to the window, and getting on tip-toe was about to look in, when a voice behind me, said: "You won't see anything there, Sir, for no one lives there now."--"Doesn't Mrs. Behrens live here?"--"She is dead."--"And Hawermann?" I asked. "He has gone to live with his daughter, Mrs. von Rambow, at Pümpelhagen."--"Is the parson at home?"--"Yes, he's at home," said old George, the parson's man, for it was he, "yes he's at home, and so is Mrs. Baldrian, they are at coffee just now."

I went into the parsonage and knocked at the parlour door. "Come in!" cried a fat voice. I entered, and--well I've seen many a strange thing in my life, many a thing that has quite taken my breath away with surprise, but I never was so much astonished, so much taken aback before--there sat Godfrey with his hair cut short like a reasonable mortal, and that part of his body one had formerly thought like the hollow of Mrs. Nüssler's baking trough was now well rounded, and evidently on the increase; his cheeks which were pale and hollow when I first knew him were now sleek and rosy, and his full red lips seemed to say: "We always find our dinner a pleasant thing, and the teeth behind us have done their duty well." The man looked as if he liked good eating, but still one could see that he was one who did his duty to the uttermost. There was nothing untidy about him, everything was as neat and trim as possible, and in short, one saw in Godfrey a specimen of hard work followed by quiet rest and good meals. Well, well. There's very little to be said about Mrs. Lina's personal appearance. She had evidently taken Mrs. Behrens as an example of what a clergyman's wife should be. "Hm!" said I to myself, "there must be something fattening in the air here."

When we had all expressed our pleasure in meeting again, we sat down, and I began to ask questions. It was from Bräsig that I got to know of the story I have been telling, but Hawermann also told me a little, for he was always very kind and affectionate to me, and other things I learnt from different people whom I questioned; I wrote it all down at the time when it was fresh in my memory, and as this happened in my youth or strom, I have called the book: "Ut mine Stromtid."

Godfrey gave me a great deal of information, and his wife Lina every now and then helped him with some little incident he had forgotten; when I rose to go on to Pümpelhagen--for I had also known Frank in the days of my youth--Godfrey said: "Yes, go; you'll find everyone assembled there to-day, and we shall soon follow you with our three girls, the eldest of all, a boy, is at school."

I walked along the path leading from Pümpelhagen to Gürlitz church, thinking of all that I had heard. It was the old old story that has been told ever since the earth was created: Joy and sorrow, birth and death.

The first of our friends who died was Bolster, and he did not die a natural death--I do not mean that he killed himself--no indeed! One day Rührdanz, the weaver, came to Rexow with a loaded gun; he put a string round Bolster's neck, and led him away to the garden. The new "crown prince" followed them unnoticed, and as was afterwards said, behaved very badly, by running about yelping. A shot was fired, and then Rührdanz came back to the house and told his employers that Bolster had had a Christian death, for he had shot him in the shoulder instead of through the head, thinking it would be less of a shock to him. When Mrs. Nüssler had given him a glass of schnaps, the weaver took up the glass slowly and drank the contents sadly; then he said, that he and the other Gürlitz labourers had been before the Rahnstädt court of justice that morning, and that they were all condemned to a year's imprisonment, besides which he was to have six months extra, for he was looked upon as the head or ring-leader of the rebellion. He left the room, but came back again to say: "Ah, Mrs. Nüssler, don't forget my old woman. All the mischief comes from our having had no papers."

The next to die was Joseph himself. Ever since he had given up his farm, he had led a much busier life than before. He spent the whole day walking about the fields, generally going to the places where no work was going on, and there he would stand for a long time shaking his head and saying nothing. One Sunday, between Christmas and new year's day, when the snow was lying a foot deep over the fields, he went out to walk round the farm, and while doing so fell into one of the deep ditches. He came home quite numb with cold. Mrs. Nüssler administered bucketsful of camomile tea, which he drank obediently, but next morning he said: "What can't be, can't be, mother. What must be, must be. It all depends upon circumstances, and no one can do anything in this case," and soon after that he slept away quietly. He had worked himself to death, and Mrs. Nüssler thought the following words the most suitable that could be found for his epitaph: "He died at his post."

Then Moses died. The old man had lived a just and upright life, and he died as he had lived. He died true to his faith, and when he was dead, he was honoured as one of the tribe of Judah, for he was one of that tribe. David went to the funeral with a torn coat and with ashes on his head, and many Christians followed the old Jew to the grave, and saw him laid in the tomb he had made ready for himself. I firmly believe that he is now in Abraham's bosom, even though Christians also go there. Three people visited his grave the day after he was buried, and these were Hawermann and the two Mrs. von Rambow--Frida was paying a visit at Pümpelhagen-- Hawermann dried the tears from his eyes as he looked down at the resting place of the old Jew, and the two ladies each put a garland of fresh flowers on it. When they were walking thoughtfully through the town meadows to Rahnstädt, Hawermann said: "He was a Jew in religion, a Christian in practice."

And now it was Henny's turn--our brave old Henny! Pomuchelskopp had gone to live in Rostock, taking with him his whole family in the blue glass coach with the coat of arms on the panel, and a string of wagons full of furniture. When trade grew better again he gained a nickname for himself. He was called 'much too cheap,' for he never lost an opportunity of telling every one who would listen to him, how sad had been his fate in selling Gürlitz, as he had done, and he always ended his story by heaving a tempestuous sigh and saying: "Much too cheap; very much too cheap!" His brave old Henny looked after the house strictly, and kept up discipline; but the devil seemed to possess all the Rostock maid servants, they would not submit to the treatment, that the Gürlitz maids had had to bear. No servant would remain for more than a week, except the cook, a Päsel, and even she turned restive, and worthless creature that she was, rebelled after being in the house three months. Henny was exasperated with such conduct, and seizing the tongs, knocked her on the head with them. The cook made no answer, for she fell down senseless on the hearth. A doctor came and talked a great deal about suffusion, &c., but the end of it was that the poor woman had to be taken to the hospital. The doctor was an honest man, so he made the case known to the authorities, and Henny had to undergo trial for her misdeeds. She could not have been touched if she had used a stick of the same length and thickness as the tongs she had handled so courageously! But tongs are not mentioned in Mecklenburg law books, so Henny was condemned, besides paying costs, and damages to the injured servant, to six weeks imprisonment. Muchel protested, appealed, supplicated, but it availed him nothing; Henny had to suffer imprisonment because of the great courage she had shown. Pomuchelskopp told everyone he could get to listen to him how unjustly his wife had been treated; he reviled the judges, and unfortunately for him, these great personages heard what he had said and gave him four weeks in jail for his evil speaking. He tried to buy himself off, but in vain; even senator Bank said: no, they would see how the coward liked his quarters. So the husband and wife occupied different parts of the same prison during the Christmas and New Year's holidays of 1852--1853; when they had been there for a fortnight, the jailer went to his wife, and said: "What a difference there is between these two people, Sophie; he walks restlessly up and down his room cursing God, and the whole world, while she sits stiff and straight in the same place and attitude as when she first came here." Meanwhile Mally and Sally gave a large tea-party to their gentlemen and lady friends in honour of their parents' misfortunes, and Mr. Süssmann who had taken another place as shopman somewhere in Mill Street, of course out of compassion for his employer, was one of the guests.

As soon as our two old friends were once more free, Pomuchelskopp went to the parlour and bewailed his fate to his two daughters, and Henny made her way straight to the kitchen where she found a charwoman in command, for while she had been out of the house, a great indignation meeting had been held in Slepegrell's dancing room, when all the Rostock maid servants entered into a solemn covenant with each other, that none of them should take the Pomuchelskopp's place. That was the reason of the charwoman being there. "What do you get a day?" asked Henny. "One and four pence," was the answer. Henny snatched up the tongs, but presently bethought herself of what had happened on the last occasion. The effort of restraining herself was too great; she was taken ill upon the spot; in three days she was dead, and in other three days she was buried. Neither Pomuchelskopp nor his two daughters know where she lies, and whenever they are asked their invariable answer is: "Over there,--she is buried over there." Gustavus, who is now a farm bailiff, and who often goes to town on business, is the only one who knows the place. He sometimes takes one of the little ones with him, and showing him the grave, he says: "Look, Chris; that's where our mother lies."

I have been obliged to relate a great many sad events, and am not nearly done yet; but why should I not tell some of the pleasant things I also heard at the parsonage. For many a long year there was much happiness in the house that had been built for the widows of the clergymen of Gürlitz. Mrs. Behrens would sit at the window in the evenings looking at her husband's grave, and ah, how often she longed to go to him; then, when Dorothy brought in the lamp, she turned away from the window, and seeing the old furniture, the old pictures, and even the duster lying in its old place, she would recall to her memory how she and her pastor used to sit under those pictures and look at the homely objects she saw around her, and she was glad to live. Hawermann worked and laboured diligently; no longer for strangers, but for his children and his children's children, for Louisa had several pretty little girls. Once he had a pleasant surprise. Fred Triddelfitz came to see him--of course he was dressed in a blue surtout--accompanied by the little member of the women's council, and told him that he had a good estate in Pomerania, and that he was engaged to little Anna. He talked a great deal to Hawermann that evening about his arrangements, and when he was gone, Bräsig said: "You were right again, Charles--but who would have thought it? Your grey hound has become a sensible man, but don't you crow over that as your doing, it was Anna not you who reformed him," As for Bräsig himself, he employed himself in going about the country and picking up news. Now he was at Rexow, now at Pümpelhagen, and now at Rahnstädt, but his favourite place of resort was Hohen-Selchow. He went there nearly every three months, and when he came home he said: "All's going on well, Charles, he has quite given up farming, and spends his day in the barn inventing. His inventions are no good of course; but Bremer says that he couldn't wish for a better master, and Mrs. von Rambow's as happy and contented as a blessed angel in Paris. But Charles, Mr. von Rambow's by no means stupid. He has invented something that I mean to adopt. This is it. Take an old hat, cut a good sized hole in the front of it and put a small lantern inside, and then you may ride as safely by night as by day." Bräsig was as good as his word, and really made use of Alick's discovery, the effect of which was to terrify all the people he happened to meet. But once when he was at Hohen-Selchow he had an attack of gout that would have been of little consequence, but which seized both legs and then mounted into his stomach, because of a chill he got on his journey home. And that caused his death.

Mrs. Behrens, Mrs. Nüssler, and his old friend Charles Hawermann came round his bed, and Mrs. Behrens asked: "Dear Bräsig, shall I not send for the young parson."--"No, don't, Mrs. Behrens. You've called me an old heathen all my life long; perhaps I was wrong in acting as I have, but oh, how I always hated methodistical twaddle..... It's better to leave me alone, and I like it better so. Charles, remember that my sister's child, Lotta, is to have £300, and the rest of my money is to go to the Rahnstädt school; for, Charles, Mrs. Behrens has enough to live on, and so have you, but my heart aches for the poor little school-children. Mrs. Nüssler has to live, my god-child Mina has to live, you have to live, Charles, and you all have to live, while I have to die." Soon after that he became delirious, and his mind went back to the time of his boyhood; he thought he was herding his father's sheep, and that an old ram was giving him great trouble, so he called Mrs. Nüssler to help him, and she seated herself on his bed and supported him in her arms. He then began to talk of his three sweethearts, and Mrs. Nüssler, saying over and over again that it was she alone he had really loved, and Mrs. Nüssler, kissed the words away from his mouth: "I know that, Bräsig; my dear old Zachariah, I know that," she said. His delirium grew worse, and he spoke of his having been appointed assessor--of the law of evidence--of young Mr. von Rambow and Lake Lauban, and of his having thrown the pistol into the water, and of having lost four pence on a wager. And then a wonderful light came over his face as he told his dear old love, Mrs. Nüssler, stories about the twins, especially Mina, and of Charles Hawermann and Louisa, but all confusedly and mixed up together. He held Mrs. Nüssler's hand tight all the while. Suddenly he raised himself and said: "Mrs. Nüssler, please put your hand on my head; I have always loved you. Charles Hawermann, will you rub my legs, they're so cold." Hawermann did as he was asked, and Bräsig said very slowly with one of his old smiles: "In style I was always better than you." That was all.

Our dear little Mrs. Behrens was not long in following him.--There are very few people who are happy here on earth, and who are yet quite happy to die. She was one of the few, she was perfectly satisfied with her lot here below, but whenever she thought of the world above, a picture of old times came into her mind, and the happy sound of old days rang in her ears, for she always imagined Heaven to be like a pretty little village church, where the angels sang and her pastor preached. She is now with him once more, and let us think of her as putting on his gown and bands for him and singing with him in the heavenly quire; not "songs for the dying," as of yore, but "songs of the Resurrection."

As I was thinking over all of these events, I turned the corner of the path at the arbour where so many of the Pümpelhagen family had sat in their hour of sorrow, and I saw three little girls of from four to eleven years old playing on the grass. A lady with a kind, gentle, and happy face was seated in the arbour sewing, she let her work fall into her lap, and smiling at the little girls threatened them with her finger, saying: "There can be too much of a good thing." Beside her was a strong active looking man reading a newspaper. He put the paper down and shook his head as much as to say that he could not attend to it just then. A little further off sat an old man with a small maiden of twelve years old leaning against his knee, he interrupted her childish chatter to say to the lady: "Let them make as much noise as they like, Louie, they'll be only too apt to grow steady and wise before their time."--When I got quite round the corner the old man exclaimed: "Bless me! Isn't that?"--And Frank and Louisa came forward to welcome me, and Frank said: "That's right, Fritz, I am glad that you've come to see us."--I said: "My Louisa," for my wife's name is Louisa, "wishes to be very kindly remembered to you, Mrs. von Rambow."--And then there was a great deal of talk amongst us for a little while, but our pleasure did not last long, for suddenly there was noise and rushing in the garden as if the wild huntsman and his pack had broken loose, and I saw running towards us four boys with brown eyes and brown cheeks, grey trousers and grey jackets. A tiny little lad of six rushed up to Frank, threw his arms round his knees, and shouted over his shoulder: "I'm first!"--"Yes," said another, who might perhaps be twelve years old, "I should think so, for you ran through the meadow; but I say what a mess you're in! Won't mother scold you!"--The little fellow looked down at his trousers, and certainly if his mother was satisfied, he might be so too.--"Won't your parents be here soon?"--"Yes," said the eldest, "They're just behind us. Our grandmother's coming too, and Mrs. von Rambow, who arrived at our house yesterday evening."--"What, Frida!" cried Louisa. "I'm so glad!"--A few minutes later, Rudolph and Mina came in sight, and they might be said to resemble the noontide of a beautiful day, when the sunlight is brightening the landscape far and wide, when the shadows are short, and when men pull off their coats that they may work better and more easily. Rudolph is now a man of weight amongst his colleagues, for he has not only given up the old system of farming, which in many respects was a mistaken one, but makes money by the change for himself and teaches others to follow his example, thus benefitting the whole land. Behind them came Mrs. Nüssler and Frida. Mrs. von Rambow looked round her half sadly when she reached the arbour, and after the first words of welcome, Louisa said to her eldest daughter: "Frida, bring your aunt a chair," for she remembered that Mrs. von Rambow had once said that she disliked sitting on the bench where she had been so miserable.--Mrs.

Nüssler went to Hawermann and asked: "How are you, brother Charles?"--"Very well, thank you," shouted Hawermann, for his sister had grown very deaf. "And you?"--"Very well except for my deafness. You say that must have been caused by a chill. But, how did I get a chill without knowing it? I'll tell you, Charles, it comes from Joseph's having talked so much during the last years of his life, that he must have strained my ears. He couldn't help it you know, it was his nature to talk."--Parson Godfrey now arrived with Lina and three children. The children all played together while their parents talked. Towards evening tables were spread in the open air, one for the parents alone, and one for the children. Louisa's eldest daughter managed everything at the children's table, and grandfather Hawermann looked after the other, and they both acted on a different plan from that of our old acquaintance Henny. How kind and gentle they all were that day at Pümpelhagen.--While we were all enjoying ourselves at supper we saw some one coming up the garden path. It was Fred Triddelfitz accompanied by his little wife. Everybody jumped up to welcome them, and for a few minutes there was a regular fire of questions and answers. Suddenly that monster Fred Triddelfitz caught sight of me, and asked: "How did you get here, Fritz?"--"And how did you get here?" I asked in my turn.--"Why, Fritz, I hav'n't seen you for seven cold winters," he said.--"Nor I you, Fred," I replied.--And so we went on Fritzing and Fredding each other till everyone was laughing at us.--"Fritz," he asked, "do you still write books?"--"Yes, Fred, I've got a whole heap of my books now."--"Well then, Fritz, do me a favour; I entreat of you *not* to bring me into one of your books."--"Ah," I said, "I can't gratify you there, Fred, for I've got you in one already."--"What am I doing in it?" he asked quickly.--"You're at the '*randyvoo*' in the great ditch, you know."--"What's that?" asked Louisa, who was sitting opposite me.--Frank laughed heartily and said: "I'll tell you afterwards."--"No, no," cried Fred.--"What's the meaning of all this?" asked Anna, looking first at me, Fritz Reuter, and then at her husband, Fred Triddelfitz.--I was silent, and he said: "I'll tell you another time." Old grandfather Hawermann laughed aloud. When we were alone together after supper, Fred laid his hand on my arm, and asked: "Who told you about the rendez-vous?"--"Bräsig," I answered.--"So I thought," he said, "well, Bräsig was the chief actor in the whole story."--"You're right there," I replied.

Perhaps I may be asked: Where are Pümpelhagen, Gürlitz and Rexow? You will look for them in the map in vain, and yet they are in Germany; indeed I hope that they may be found in more than one district of our fatherland. Pümpelhagen is wherever a nobleman lives who thinks no higher of himself than of his fellowmen, who looks upon the lowest of his labourers as his brethren, and who works with and for them. Gürlitz is wherever a clergyman is to be found who preaches what he believes to be the truth, but who is not self-sufficient enough to expect that his people should hold the faith exactly as he holds it; who makes no difference between rich and poor, and who is not contented with preaching alone, but who works amongst his people, helping and counselling them whenever it is needful. Rexow is wherever a middle-class man labours to increase the knowledge and usefulness of others, as well as his own, and who thinks more of the good of those amongst whom he lives than of heaping up riches. Wherever these three places are bound to each other by the love of sweet tender-hearted women and merry children, the three villages may be found close together.

FOOTNOTES

Footnote 1: *Note.* Muschüken (from monsieur) is the Mecklenburg name for rusks.

Footnote 2: *Note.* One of the Chauffeurs who infested the Rhineland.

Footnote 3: *Note.* A corruption of "injuriarum."

Footnote 4: *Note.* Wer niemals einen Rausch gehabt, das ist kein braver Mann, &c. &c.

Footnote 5: *Note.* Bowl is made of wine, water, herbs and fruit highly iced.